GUNSLICK MOUNTAIN

Against the background of the early, wild days of Tombstone, Arizona, Nelson Nye tells a trigger-paced story of gun-fights, killings and unpredictable double-crossings among men in search of treasure.

BORN TO TROUBLE

Guts weren't enough for a greenhorn Ranger, Jim Trammell discovered when a few hours on the job landed him with a crease on his head and a knife wound in the back. If his luck didn't change, it looked like his first assignment as a Texas Ranger would be his last.

Other Double-Barrel Westerns
by Nelson Nye:

THE SURE-FIRE KID/WILDCATS OF TONTO BASIN

NELSON NYE
DOUBLE-BARREL WESTERN

GUNSLICK MOUNTAIN
and
BORN TO TROUBLE

LEISURE BOOKS   NEW YORK CITY

A LEISURE BOOK

Published by

Dorchester Publishing Co., Inc.
6 East 39th Street
New York, NY 10016

GUNSLICK MOUNTAIN
Copyright©MCMXLIV by Arbor House, Inc.
Copyright Renewed MCMXLV by Nelson Nye

BORN TO TROUBLE
Copyright©MCMLI by Nelson Nye

All rights reserved. No part of this book may be reproduced or transmitted in any form or by any electronic or mechanical means, including photocopying, recording, or by any information storage and retrieval system, without the written permission of the Publisher, except where permitted by law.

Printed in the United States of America

GUNSLICK MOUNTAIN

ONE

Shoulders canted, Guy Antrim stood by the tie rail fronting the Crystal Palace Bar and had his careful look down Allen Street. This was Tombstone—dark and still. So still talk sound and the clink of glasses welled clearly into the street's blurred shadows. With a sudden breath pulled deep into him Antrim shook the cramp from his shoulders and dropped his reins across the scarred rail.

He did not step in at once, even then. He seemed debating something; took another long look up and down the dark way.

He made a lone, still shape limned that way in the lamp glow dimly spread through the dust of the window. There was something odd, at once bleak and forlorn, in the arrested placement of this man's high shape; something suggestive of far, dim trails, of wind in the passes, of star shine and fire smoke—something sad and immutable.

His head tipped gently a little sideward and downward as though he were listening. To the music, perhaps, of forgotten fiddles . . . to the faded sounds of some old carousal. Recalling this place at an earlier date . . . its color and tears, its gusts of loud laughter. Remembering old harridans and reckless young beauties decked out in their paint and flimsy finery . . . the sheen of their slippers seen between bars.

With a kind of sigh he put broad shoulders to the slatted batwings and quietly, leisurely—but with a cold, sure glance, stepped smoothly inside.

The Crystal Palace, his glance seemed to say, had not changed much.

There were three or four shirtsleeved men at the bar, a sleepy-eyed barkeep back of it. The remembered pictures looked down from the walls, cobwebbed now, seeming cheap and tawdry, to his grown-up mind. The whole place looked shabby, the shine long departed from its glass and mahogany.

The apron slowly got off his elbow.

"What'll you hev?" he said through his yawning.

"Bourbon," said Antrim, and sat down at a table.

Behind him were the gambling rigs, dust deep on the cloths concealing them. One faro bank was open but the dealer sat snoring with a hat on his face.

The barman brought over a bottle and glass. Antrim said, "What do you call this town, friend?"

"Tombstone."

"No foolin'? I always 'lowed Tombstone was a hell-roarin' twister—a kinda all-night town on the No-Return Trail."

" 'Was' is right."

"What happened? Mines peter out?"

"Flooded. That'll be six bits to you, Mister."

"For the one glass? Ought to bury the place an' put a marker up if you're goin' to charge museum prices. Ain't this where Curly Bill hung out?"

"We buried *him* a long while back," said the barkeep, sniffing contemptuously. "Look—" he said, "I'm a new man here; don't know much about them hellbendin' days. But if it's all the same to you, Mister, we collect for the drinks when we serve 'em."

Antrim dug up a handful of silver. A reflective

light looked out of his eyes as he fingered the coins and stared at the barkeep. "Old Dick Clark still around these parts?"

The barkeep shrugged, but his cheeks showed interest. "He's round off'n on. When he ain't off sharpin' some cattlemen's convention. Keeps a room at the Cosmopolitan; if he's in town now they'll know about it."

"Still runnin' the old Alhambra, is he?"

The man showed a scowl and picked up his towel. "I don't keep cases on nothing but the drinks." He picked up Antrim's money, and the bottle. "Mebbe," he said, "you better talk to the sheriff—that's him over there. With the gun," he added.

Antrim did not appear much perturbed. He fingered his drink as though entirely at ease. He was a wind-burned man in brush-clawed range clothes; a trail-tired man taking relaxation. He sat there loose and comfortably sprawled. A cow boss, maybe, with his mind on his cattle.

But when the man was gone back of his bar again the stranger inspected the men ranged along it, and a grin suddenly turned his dark face boyish.

"Hi, Tex!" he called, and was coming up out of his chair when the sheriff's round-wheeling, unwinking regard suspended the action and left him staring.

There was an austere look to the sheriff's jowls. He was a short, stocky man with a broad pair of shoulders below a thick, red neck. A mustached man whose each hair and whisker was the same glittering black as the look of his stare. He had a Mex cigar clamped between his teeth and a diamond flashed from his left little finger. The other hand's thumb showed tucked in his belt ostentatiously close to a pearl-butted pistol.

The stranger frowned. "Don't you remember me, Tex? I'm the—"

With the glint of his eyes turned blacker, brighter, the lawman declaimed: "My name is John Slaughter. John Slaughter—and remember it."

"Oh—sorry," Antrim said, and sat down in his chair.

He folded lean arms across his chest and focused his stare on the room's high ceiling, covered these latter years with tin. It was the first time he'd thought of this room as big. But it *was* big, he noticed; big as all hell though there the comparison ended. The place was not warm in the slightest; it did not abound in either cheer or friendship. Its chill got deep down into him—

even into his bones like the breath-smoked air of a Dakota morning.

The things he saw in the ceiling's paint were visions dragged out of his past.

"Halt!"

Brake blocks squealed. The Benson stage swayed with every horse back on its haunches. Dust billowed up in a brick-red fog, and three masked men with leveled Winchesters stepped suddenly out of the surrounding mesquite.

Bob Paul, who was driving, grabbed up his shotgun in one smooth, unexpectedly swift sweep of a flying right hand. As the butt touched his shoulder the nearest robber fired. Splinters flew from the seat. Paul triggered both barrels without apparent effect. Timed with the roar of those shots the robber on the far side opened up on Bud Philpot, described in the Wells-Fargo books as 'driver'. Philpot sprang erect—sprang from his seat like a rattler had struck him. His buckling knees wouldn't hold him. He screamed and choked and fell from his perch, pitching headlong between the squatting wheelers.

The terrified horses lunged into a run. Rattle-ty-bang went the careening stage, up the grade at a headlong gallop. There was eighty thousand cached in the boot and the cursing robbers triggered frantically.

But Bob Paul had the reins again and he popped his blacksnake wickedly. To the scream and thump of whistling lead the riddled stage clattered over the crest, leaving two men sprawled dead and stark in the dust and three highwaymen frothing with rage.

Antrim remembered how the Earps had caught him. At the Redfield ranch. He'd been milking a cow. Twelve full boxes of six-shooter cartridges cached in his pockets and a rifle, strapped loaded, across his shoulders. Two shell belts buckled around his waist. Looked kind of suspicious taking all that artillery to get milk from a cow. And his horse had been found at Wheaton's place, all lathered and blown, ashake like an aspen. They wouldn't believe the horse had been stolen. Wouldn't believe one least word he said.

"Stole, my gran'mother!" Behan had sneered.

And they locked him up in the Tombstone jail.

"I got a right to a lawyer!" declared Antrim hotly; but all they gave him was hoots and jeers.

Town opinion had been freely expressed. The stick-up had added un-needed fuel to the feud in progress between the Earps and the Clanton-

McLowery clan. Said one newspaper with flamboyant authority: *"Positive proof exists four men took part in the attack on the Benson stage. The fourth is in Tombstone . . ."*

Antrim was in Tombstone, prey for a mob. Watching, night after night, the pattern of bars pushed across his cell by a waning moon; hemmed by enemies, scapegoat for plotters. Hardly more than a boy, caged and chained like a wolf. Not yet sixteen, what wonder if his spirit quailed? Life was precious and the noose loomed near.

He called for the sheriff. "Tell Behan I'll talk."

"Well?" Behan said. "What's on your mind?"

He looked at the boy's pale face with a grin. "Figurin' to save your hide, are you? Time to of squealed was when we caught you—"

Antrim's chin came up. He was young, but proud. "I'm not 'squealing', Behan."

The sheriff's grin showed a little parched.

"All right," he grunted. "You're a tough one, ain't you? What do you want to tell me?"

Antrim recalled that moment like it had been only yesterday. Recalled the wild urge he had felt to elaborate— to show his part lighter. He might quite as well have. Johnny Behan was a political sheriff—a past master of expediency, a man distrustful of things not compatible to his own way of thinking. Antrim's tale of how three San Simon friends had got up a bet to be decided by a lion hunt left Behan coldly incredulous. One, Antrim said, had bet another he'd not dare tackle a lion with a pistol; the third of the trio was to have held the stakes.

Antrim had been too busy to go along himself. Been working for Redfield, a San Pedro rancher; but they'd given him a part. He was to have brought them the guns and cartridges, all of which were to have been special.

Johnny Behan sniffed skeptically. "Where was they figgerin' to hunt these lions?"

"Up in the Dragoons. They told me to meet them at a woodchopper's camp—"

"I guess so," Behan scoffed. "If that's the best you can do you might's well stop right now."

"You found the guns and cartridges, didn't you?"

"Yeah. An' found you at Redfield's milkin' a cow. An' your hoss at Wheaton's—plumb wore to a frazzle. It don't wash, button. You held them road runners' hosses for 'em. When you seen Philpot drop, you got cold feet an' rattled your hocks. You had the right idea but you didn't go far enough."

Antrim had shut his mouth then. He could see well enough he'd been picked for the scapegoat; picked alike by the law and those he'd thought were his friends. The moral of that had been ground deep into him. It had never left him in the eight years since. It had put that saturnine look in his eye—had enameled him with that cold distrust that was always so evident in all his dealings. Guy Antrim today was what that lesson and subsequent things had made of him.

He had not been hanged—but through no fault of Behan's.

Antrim wished he might find some cure for memory. If there was one it had eluded him. It was something, he guessed, you just had to put up with, like measles and mumps and the greenapple colic. It had killed all the decent things in him, he thought. A thief in the night that had stolen his youth and mortgaged his soul for eternity.

"That cub's goin' to swing," Behan told his cronies; but the sheriff's opinion had been expressed a bit hastily. The horse they had found at Wheaton's ranch proved not so unlucky as the boy had thought it.

The sheriff had gone larruping off to Helm's ranch to rejoin the scalp hunters when a small-spread rancher chanced to ride into town and take a real fancy to Antrim's horse.

"I dunno," the man said, "I kinda like him someway."

"You might's well sell him," the under-sheriff, Woods, told the prisoner. "You won't be ridin' that plug any more."

And so it had been arranged.

They brought Antrim over to the sheriff's office. They got him a pen to write his signature. While the notary was fixing up the dotted line and the rancher and Woods were swapping small talk, Antrim, rather quietly, had stepped out the door and departed forthwith for new pastures.

TWO

Didn't seem like a handful of years could make such a difference in the life of a town. Roaring Tombstone had gone to seed. Gone were the bleach-eyed tinhorns and gunslicks—departed as the dust of the Benson stage. A different breed ran the old town now. A more leisurely tribe. Ranching men, for the most part, who looked quite content to raise cows for a living and leave hell-raising to the ghosts of the past. Texans from the prickly pear country, bringing their stock and their womenfolks with them; bronzed men these, soft and drawling of speech. Quiet, intent fellows. Men with a purpose.

The red lights were out. The mines were closed and the Poker Flats phase of the town's existence had faded into the gray obscurity of all ephemeral things. Farewell to the boomers, the miners and drifters who had been such a comfort to the old regime. Adios to the quick-drawing, hard-swearing sports of the past. Hail and farewell.

Antrim drained his glass. He reached for the bottle, but it was not there. He remembered the barkeep and his lips showed a faint little quirk at the corners.

He rumpled his thick yellow hair and sighed.

He slacked his lithe body back into the chair. Bone weary he was with the miles behind him; saddle-cramped like he had not been since he quit this town, eight long years before.

Eight years! He sighed again; his gray eyes peering around with a remote sort of smiling, as though at something that amused him with its irony.

Seen thus he was a reticent man with a dark and high-boned cast of feature that appeared long acquainted with the way of the elements. He was lean and tall yet broad of shoulder. His legs, when he stood, showed their bow in the sundry cracks and creases of his brush-clawed leather chaps. The soft-topped boots that cased his feet were powdered thick with the gray of the trail; the long-shanked spurs buckled onto them held no gleam, no show of care, no danglers. They were old, like the cartridge belt strapped about his waist. Like the floppy-brimmed hat that he wore on his head.

His hair looked in need of trimming. It straggled about his temples and curled with neither care nor fashion down over the fold of his gray shirt's collar.

But his jaw was clean and freshly shaved and was, in its way, a reflection of character. Like the cold gray way his eyes looked at you from under their yellow, tufted brows.

Night air, crisp with touch of coming dawn, was moving in off the deserted street, bringing a curious mingling of town smells and fetching sharp flavor from the desert beyond.

Antrim worried his glass with the blunt ends of his fingers and scanned the room with an increased awareness. The sheriff, John Slaughter, was watching him. Trying to fit him, Antrim guessed bitterly, into one of the faded dodgers that would be tacked to the walls of his office.

To hell with him.

Let him try—let him try all he damned well wanted to. There had been no picture taken of the only man ever thrown in a jail for that fizzled stickup of the Benson stage.

Talked droned on. Turned at last from women

and cattle to a race, apparently run last year, between some foreigner and one of Slaughter's deputies. Seemed to have been pulled off in New Mexico near Silver City. The foreigner had ridden a velocipede; Bill King, Slaughter's deputy, had done his riding on "Figure 2"—"the meanest damn' bronc this side of hell's furnace." A fifty-mile stretch, and the horse had won by two minutes and a half, and some kind of a sand storm.

Antrim wasn't much interested.

And then a sharper voice brought him out of his thinking. A newcomer's voice that hadn't got into the talk before. That voice, and the sudden silence after it, pulsed a slogging quiver through Antrim's muscles.

The rasp of spur rowels brought his glance up.

The new arrival was coming toward him. Tall and gangling he was, with a bright, queer attention in his sly little eyes.

He brought up beside Antrim, leaned his hands on the table with his bony thighs pressed hard against it. "Don't I know you, Poker Face?"

"Do you?"

"Seems like I ort to." The gaunt man considered him, head cocked, eyes knowing. "Could swear I seen you before some place . . ."

Antrim shrugged. "Could be, I reckon."

The slat-shaped man continued to stare.

He stared with an uncaring frankness; but he finally shook his head, sort of grunted. He rasped a rope-scarred fist on his chin. "How do they call you where you come from, pardner?"

"It ain't been the custom where I come from—"

"Never mind—I got a reason fer askin'."

"Guy Antrim's the name."

Antrim said it coldly but the man only grinned. "That ain't the handle you packed in the ol' days. Never been no Antrims round yere—but *you* been 'ere, friend. I c'n tell by yer eyes—I never fergit 'em.

"No matter." He gave an impatient twist to his shoulders, waggled a hand and called up the barkeep. "Want a job of work?"

"What kind of work?"

Steps were approaching. The man looked around. "Never mind," he said to the apron. Then he pulled up a chair, put his arms on the table. "I'm Gauze—Jake Gauze," he mentioned casually. His bright little eyes kept searching Antrim. They went curiously over his garb, piece by piece, not omitting his hat, his boots or his spurs. They rested longest on the shape of his hands; on his hands and the holstered gun at his thigh.

"Use that gun?"

"If it's *that* kind of job—"

"Hang hold!" Gauze growled. "I'm a rancher," he said, leaning forward, "savvy? Got a two-bit spread over to Skeleton Canyon; run a few bangtails—forty—fifty cows. Hard country. Wildest part of the Peloncillos; I range from the Animas clear down the valley. Hard t' keep any hands. Lonesome. Ride f' days without clappin' eye to another soul. Used t' be the main trail fer smugglers—back in the Curly Bill days, that is. Some of the breed still usin' it. Pick up a bit of my stuff off'n on. Like t' hire you t' watch it. Howcome I ast can you use that gun."

Antrim said, "I see."

The gaunt man looked at him oddly. "I don't reckon—"

"I see," Antrim said, "plenty good enough. I wouldn't care for that country."

" 'F it's a matter of money—"

"Money ain't worth much after you're buried."

Gauze scowled. "I don't get that, friend."

"Does it matter?"

"Matters t' me. Look here—" Gauze's hair-tufted fingers drummed on the table. He lowered his voice. "Mebbe you don't quite savvy my talk, friend. You kin write yer own ticket—"

Antrim shook his head. "Not interested."

Gauze said, "You better *git* interested then. The's on'y two things brings a feller out this way. Fear an' hate. You don't look like yer huntin' nobody."

THREE

All through the black shank of night they rode, and all through the following morning, with never a stop save to breathe the horses. You'd have thought they were chased, to judge by Gauze's actions. Now that Antrim had consented to go with him, all the gaunt man's interest seemed wrapped in speed. Speed and more speed; every bit they could manage—and even then Gauze cursed the horses for laggards, "Must be scared," Antrim thought, "the ghosts of them smugglers have stole him blind while he's been away."

Antrim's seat in the saddle was numb from the business and his weary bones winced to each hoofbeat as mile after stifling mile unreeled, without talk, without pause, without even a sound save what was flung up by the sand muffled hoofs.

Saddle creak and hoof pound. Mile after mile through the greasewood waste that hemmed them unbroken through the day's early hours. Antrim's brows went up a little, when breakfastless, they skirted Gleeson. But he kept his own counsel, consoled with the knowledge that each bone jolting, dust streaked mile was carrying him nearer to that which had determined his unlikely return. All the way from distant Tubac he'd been trying to figure how to reach this region without exciting suspicion. Not that he feared recognition. It seemed hardly likely after eight long years, any would remember him for Luther King. It was simply that strangers, in this kind of country, weren't wanted; they were eyed with distrust and all their movements scanned closely.

This tie-up with Gauze, though he'd made it seem otherwise, was in the nature of a godsend. That Gauze was a scoundrel seemed entirely likely. It bothered Guy Antrim no more than the heat.

Yet more and more as the sun climbed higher his mind got to probing the rancher's hurry. It was an unhealthy haste; and it turned him broodingly thoughtful when Courtland, too, was passed without stopping. What in Christ's Name was so urgent? he wondered. What need kept them flogging through the white glare of midday?

This was desert country, and the time was April.

"Got a claim, or somethin', you're scared'll be jumped?"

Gauze said nothing; never turned in his saddle.

A wicked flame kindled up in Guy Antrim, but he kept his thoughts muzzled for another half hour. Then temper got the best of him. "You must have Injuns camped on your backtrail. What you done—run off with some squaw?"

Gauze sent a curse back over his shoulder. "When I want any wind I kin hire me a windmill!"

"You better be thinkin' where you can hire some more horses."

Gauze snorted; squinched up his eyes and stared off yonder at the blue, hazed distance. Then he brought his glance back, chewed a moment and spat. "Don't worry about them horses," he said.

They nooned at Pearce.

It was 2:15.

The weatherbitten buildings with their warped

and sand-scoured corners and their dusty, cobwebbed windows were like old friends to Antrim. He had known this region well in the old days—too well, perhaps, for the look of his cheeks turned dark and somber and the light came into his eyes again that had attracted Gauze in the Crystal Palace. The gunslick look there was no mistaking.

As at Tombstone, Jake's knowing scrutiny noticed.

He said, "Wonder the place don't curl up and burn," and led the way into a hash house.

They ate without any attempt at talking, the only two men in sight at this hour. When he was finished Jake reached him a toothpick from a plate of the same on the counter. "We'll put on the nosebag at Dos Cabezas. Come you're needin' ca'tridges or other oddments, right here is the place t' be gettin' 'em. No more towns this side of the ranch."

There was a kind of sly challenge curling around in his stare. But Antrim's quick look found the man's blunt fingers toying his fork.

"No more towns," Antrim said. "What's the matter with Bow—"

The shade of Jake's eyes suddenly stopped him.

"Slick, ain't you?" Antrim murmured dustily.

But Jake only grinned. "No reason fer stoppin' at Bowie," he said. "We're goin' right on around it."

Antrim shrugged. Leisurely fished out the makings and shaped up a smoke. "All right with me. We can amble whenever it suits you."

He dragged a match across his pants and eyed Jake through the flare of it.

"Pretty soon," Jake said. "We're gettin' fresh horses first, though." Still with that pleased, sly look in his eye, "We'll be leavin' ours," he mentioned. "What you want for your bronc? Don't want you t' be doin' no worryin' about 'im. I'll take him off your hands."

Antrim stared with a heightened interest. "Seem like you're settin' a powerful store by me. It don't pay, Gauze, to put all your chips in one basket."

"Man's got to chance somethin' someplace."

"You're puttin' your weight on a mighty weak reed."

"Never mind," Jake grinned. "I'll take care o' that." He brought his solid chin up then and eyed his man with an unwinking hardness. "When I hire a hand I figure t' work him. You'll work just as good on one o' my broncs as you ever will on your own, I reckon. I'll take smart care o' your ridin' needs."

Like that, Jake figured to keep him. Going to fix it so Antrim couldn't slide out on him. If he thought to quit he'd have either to steal a horse or to hoof it. Hoofing it was out of the question.

Hankering to see if his guessing was right, "My bronc," Antrim said, "will cost you a hundred."

Jake counted the bills from a well-heeled purse and pushed them down the counter. "I'll look for you at the livery," he grinned.

They rode all afternoon—rode steady. The sun's brassy rays down on their backs and a gusty wind whipped grit off the desert that whistled and stung as it pattered their faces; even the folds of their pulled-up scarfs were small guarantee against its bite.

They made no stops. Not even short ones to rest the horses. The urge to speed was on Gauze again—indeed, it had never left him; and as the day wore on he pushed the broncs with an unsparing hand.

Antrim noticed that, now and again, he would twist his head for a look at their backtrail. Once, after Gauze had swung front again, Antrim took a look himself. But there was little to see. He cut no sign of anyone following.

The Cherrycows were a dark shape southeastward when they reached Doz Cabezas at something past six.

Gauze pulled his staggering bronc to a walk On his own mount, Antrim's eyes showed in their gun-steel depths a look that could never be taken for pleasure. He felt damned bad about those horses.

Gauze's round-swung stare was red-rimmed and glinting. "We ain't stoppin' here—savvy?"

He looked for argument; was plainly cocked to reach for his gun. You could tell by the cast of his shoulders.

Antrim said nothing.

With a snort Jake climbed out of his saddle; left his foundered horse on braced legs in the road. Cramp was in his stiff-gaited walk as he led the way to a ramshackle enclosure built of termitey poles in a group of salt cedars beyond the last house. A dirty man with a scraggle of beard limped out of the trees and came toward them leading a pair of big geldings, all saddled and ready. A bay and a roan. Jake took the roan.

With a thoughtful frown Antrim mounted the other.

No money changed hands. No words were spoken. They departed at once, striking immediately north by east over a wagon road whose ruts and hoof sign ended, Antrim reckoned, at Duncan on the New Mexican border.

At full dark they forded the San Simon. A silver glint marked a sickle moon. But it afforded no light and the brush reached up from either side to scratch at their thighs and elbows. A nighthawk whistled and a cooler and cooler wind whined down off the Peloncillos. The vague, shapeless blob that was gaunt Jake Gauze settled deeper into its saddle.

The wind plucked forlorn sound out of the trees. Only this, and saddle creak vied with the interminable thud of their hoofs as the rancher led through the night at a lope. Without talk they pressed farther and faster into the dark desolation that hemmed these hills. Gauze had spoke truth when he called this a lonesome country.

The wild, earthy smell of it filled Antrim's breathing. Like an animal newly escaped from its cage he was savoring its rank flavor; and the pungence of it tugged at him, fingered his senses like hands on a keyboard. The call of this land was summoning him and he flung up his head, sniffing hungrily, lips peeled back in a thin, queer smiling, while an excitement and an eagerness he had not known in years rushed tumultuously through him.

A wolf's cry wailed from a ridgetop, one refracted note from the vast immensity of these forgotten wastes. The wind dropped, leaving an encroaching stillness that became uncanny—unbelievable. Antrim saw Jake Gauze peering back again, half twisted in his saddle, his face a shapeless blotch of gray against the black of these brush-clad heights.

Resentment dug its nails in him and all the distrust of his years ripped through him on a tide of rage compounded of this monstrous ride, of the man's incessant demand for speed and those covert, sneaking, backward glances. Irritation snapped his guard and he flung sharp words at Gauze uncaringly. "Never mind twistin' your head around. I'm right behind you, Mister—"

"I know damn well you are," Jake said; and appeared to consider that answer enough.

The night's thick hush closed in again. The hoofs droned their song, clop, clop, clop. Cricket sound came against their ears and creaking leather groaned its plaint to the walking gait of the climbing animals. Except for this the hills were still as though no life were in them.

Why was this Gauze so scared of his backtrail?
Why had he hired the gun packer, Antrim?
Was it fear that spurred his headlong travel?
Antrim began to peer around himself.

Up ahead somewhere, halfway to morning, the rancher stopped. When Antrim came up he'd a leg around the saddle horn, bony shoulders humped over it. "There she is," he said, pointing. "That's Skeleton, yonder."

By the moon's brightening light Antrim made out the gash, an ink black crack in the towering walls. No breath of air was stirring. There was a bodeful look about this dark crevice stealthily threading its tortuous way through the hills. Trouble feel hung strong about it. A queer, sour stench. Like the smell of blood.

As though sensing his thought the gaunt Jake grinned. "Been a mort o' men killed in there, fella. 'F it wa'n't so dark you could see Silver Creek cuttin' through this pocket—off there to the right. Used t' be a Curly Bill trail up t' Galeyville. But the' ain't no Galeyville nowadays; ain't nothin' but crumblin' walls an' some purpled piles of empty bottles. Ain't a stick o' wood left big enough t' make kindlin'—pulled it all out when they built up Paradise. Ain't nothin' left but mesquite brush now."

"What're them peaks off yonder?"

"Peloncillos—main range," Jake muttered. "Curly Bill used t' hev a ranch up there; sometime, mebbe, I'll show you the place. I'm rangin' all them mountains now. Animas Valley is off there beyond. That's another old Curly Bill hangout; Clantons used t' hev a big spread there, too. An' a gent named Lang, an' Dick Gray. Real high rollers, them boys. 'Twas their brashness took 'em off, like as not. An' that's a page f' *your* book, Mister. Leave smartness f' them that's big enough t' tote it."

He strayed his glance over Antrim's shoulder.

"Time t' move," he said, and put his horse in motion.

Antrim paused long enough to look back on his own hook. The gaunt Jake's nerves were catching. But all that showed were the dark blobs of foliage, the hemming brush and the far wink of stars. Just the same, something scratched his mind with its warning. Call it a hunch if you feel like. It was Antrim's notion they were being followed.

All his life he'd been governed by hunches, and frequently one had saved it for him. He had neither seen anything nor heard anything; but he knew, deep down inside him, there was somebody dodging their trail.

He scowled as he watched the black sway of Jake's shoulders.

What was the man letting him in for? What need had sent Gauze to town for a gunslick. "Gunslick" was what Jake took him for—or, was it?

Antrim wondered.

They were traveling the depths of Skeleton Canyon.

Over there was a tree called the Outlaw's Oak, and there were gouges from bullets on many another. The scaley old sycamores were pocked with initials. Guy Antrim had talked with the men who had carved them. The way was paved with the bones of the dead; death and this canyon were hunkered close as ever spilled blood could get them.

This was the trail the Mex smugglers had used in the days of Curly Bill's wild bunch. This was where Curly Bill had butchered them—had killed them like dogs for the sacks bulged with silver that burdened the packs of their mule trains. This was the Trail.

A stream's felted whisper licked soft through

the gloom and Antrim, head cocked, faintly nodded. Skeleton Creek that would be; they would soon reach the place called Devil's Kitchen where the towering walls opened out for a bit.

Antrim knew these things. As he knew many others concerning this region. The lay of this land was grim etched in his mind; he would not have been lost with his eyes shut. Just the same he was glad Gauze had found him. Played shrewdly Jake Gauze could be a godsend to him; Antrim aimed for that to be the way of it.

It was easy to believe old ghosts walked here.

Antrim's head came around once, startled. He had thought to hear a mule's bell tinkle, and was twisting his head for another back stare when he dismissed the impulse with a brief, wry grin. It would need something faster than a mule to trail them. The bell he had heard had probably been in his head—the result of a heap too much thinking. Far too often his errant thoughts probed the past. The past was for history; it was the present that interested Antrim.

Right here was where the massacre had been, where nineteen Mexicans had breathed their last, had shrieked and fallen with the gore spurting out of them. One of Curly Bill's gang, it had been— Zwing Hunt—who had christened the Outlaw's

Oak with his blood. Struck in the shoulder by smuggler lead, he'd been carried to the tree by his pard, Billy Grounds; and there, in its shade, his bushwhacking friends had bathed and tended his hurt.

It had been Antrim's collected knowledge of Hunt that had brought him back to this country.

"Ever hear of a fella called Miguel Garcia? *Don* Miguel, the greasers called him," Jake said, slowing down and breaking his silence. "A gold-plated dude in the ol' days. Used t' ride this trail pretty reg'lar. Had a heap plenty savvy, excep' fer one thing: He forgot," Jake chuckled, "as how the ol' colonel, Colt, had made all gents equal. Curly Bill's crowd got him. Shot him down in his tracks for a mule train of silver."

"Bill clean up much?" Antrim asked him.

"I'd like t' hev it," Jake grunted; and twisted around with a quick, hard look and, thereafter, kept his mouth closed.

Antrim grinned to himself as he eyed Jake's back. He guessed old Gauze knew mighty well how much Bill had took from those Mexes. He had been right on tap when Garcia dropped—no farther away than that rimrock.

They rode with a furtive silence while the stars

turned dim and a gray light grew above the ragged tops of the canyon. The walls shrank farther apart and the sun, Antrim thought, was not far off.

Jake Gauze was a pretty sly article. Been about, Antrim guessed, to boast a little. Back there in the Devil's Kitchen, just barely a month after Bill's own raid, Jim Hughes, one of Bill's lieutenants, had come rushing up from below the Line with news of a vastly richer train already en route across the Animas Valley. But they'd told Hughes at Galeyville Bill was away and there'd been no time to go hunting him. Catching up what men were handiest, Hughes had staged this raid himself; a ruthless coup which had netted the hidden owlhoot cache more than two hundred thousand dollars. Antrim knew of every man who'd been in it. Hughes himself, Ike and Bill Clanton, Jack McKenzie, Zwing Hunt, Milt Hicks, Billy Grounds and Jake Gauze.

Oh, yes, Jake was a cute one and no mistake. A very slick article. Extremely sly.

Around their climbing horses dark shadows swirled, ducking and nodding and writhing till it made Antrim's head ache to watch them. And the night had grown damper with dew blown down from the mountain meadows.

A fitful wind brushed the tops of the trees—a further sign of the dawn's approach. And a nameless something got to tugging at Antrim. An urge and a need that was born of this canyon; that was stealthy sprung from its ghosts and its riddles. It was tramping his nerves and it turned him watchful.

Jake's voice rode back on a gust of the breeze. Pitched low, it was, as though he spoke to himself. "Not far," came his words. "Just a whoop an' a holler ... Up yonder there where the canyon forks—"

Antrim, coming suddenly against him, felt the cocked and startled stiffness of him; saw, as an opaque blob against the thinning murk, Jake's rigid shape, bleak-held in the saddle, forward bent with cocked elbow, tensely staring.

The hemming walls had widened away. There was, up ahead, what looked like a fork.

There was, also, something else.

Gauze breathed an oath; and Antrim, peering at the lamp glow yonder, had his own grim wonder and his own swift thoughts.

They were that way, staring, when they heard it again—a scream, and the racketing bang of a shot.

FOUR

She was backed against an angle of the wall with a set, white face and a gun in her hand when she heard the hard, sledging pound of hoofs.

With a flailing sweep of his outstretched arm the tall man batted the lamp into fragments.

Jake's bellowing voice hit the house like a mallet.

"Strike a light!"

Kerrick drawled from the shadows, "That you, Jake?"

"Light up that lamp!"

"On the shelf by your shoulder," Idy Red said tightly.

A match burst to flame in Kerrick's cupped palm. He found the extra lamp and lit it, giving her a grin across his shoulder as he crossed to the table and carefully placed it where the one he had broken had erstwhile been sitting. In the opposite corner the second man, Cope, was still mouthing curses, blood-stained fingers bitterly clamped to his cheek.

Boots drove sound from the planks of the porch.

Kerrick's dropped voice said, "I'll handle this," and then Jake Gauze was a cocked, hulking shape in the black of the doorway, rage, intolerance and an edgy care all wickedly tugging him their separate ways.

But he was not surprised. Idy Red sensed that instantly. She as instantly guessed he'd been expecting these strangers. Then it was she realized there was someone behind Gauze—another strange rider, inscrutably eying them.

Jake came into the room, jaws corded with muscle, glaring eyes showing the effort he made to control himself.

"Quite a wildcat you got here," Kerrick smiled. "Right han'some too—but you always was a good judge of lookers. How's the world been treatin' you?"

Jake stood like a man in the grip of hard choices, jammed breath making a play with his shirtfront, the black, twisted scowl still tight on his cheekbones. She had never seen Gauze look so fierce mad before. The strange man behind him put his back to the doorpost, lounging there calmly, surveying them all with thumbs hooked in his gun belt.

"Well!" Kerrick said. "You might make us welcome. We've come a long piece to get eyed like the smallpox. Where you hidin' the jug at? Fetch it out an' act human."

"Idy Red," Jake said, blackly watching Kerrick, "hev these dogs mussed you?"

The girl shook her head, eyes dismissing them scornfully.

"Sure?"

The way Jake said it put a fire in her cheeks. "That runt in the co'ner kinda 'lowed he had notions, but I don't look for no more trouble from him." She tossed the hair back out of her eyes and tucked the pistol away in her belt. "Friends o' yourn' are they?"

Kerrick laughed.

He was a confident, wide chested man who could stand there and consider Jake with a comfortable amusement. Even when Gauze blackly said: "Keep your skunk's paws off her—hear me?"

Unruffled, Kerrick shrugged it away with a cool, hard smile.

"Hell," he said, "get the jug an' quit growlin'. Ain't nobody goin' to bother your woman. Who's the gent by the door? Ain't met him, have I?"

But Gauze couldn't take up slack that fast. Crouched seconds longer he stood there glowering, the urge plainly in him to carry this further. Then, reluctantly, he shifted weight and, half turned, said thickly, "You'll wanta know these fellas. The long-geared drink is Bat Kerrick— cowman. That skinner over there hangin' onto his face mostly goes by the handle of Taiban Cope. He's a Tombstone product from away back when. This here," he said, with a hand toward Antrim, "is Poker Face. He's ramrodin' these localities."

Antrim looked them over, tipped a nod at them curtly. He had heard of Cope. A pale little worm. Halfbreed son of a Mormon horse thief. He used to travel with men like Downing, Pete Spence and Burt Alvord. He was a saddle-blanket gambler with a sideline—in the old days anyway—of touting for Crazy Horse Lil and some of the other house madams on Sixth Street.

It was Kerrick whom Antrim eyed longest. He was no more a cowman than the pale little Cope was. The man was a gunslick. Every gesture proclaimed it. The leather of the gun sheath thonged to his leg was dark with much oiling and the cut of his jowls showed a gun fighter's brassiness. The strike of his stare was hard as agate, in no way reflecting the quirk of his lips.

Antrim said "Howdy," and Kerrick's glance took him over from hat crown to boot heel.

He said, "I'll put up the broncs," and, tramping past Antrim, ducked his head through the doorway.

The girl crossed the room and stopped by Jake. She put a hand on his arm but it was Antrim she looked at. "Forgetting somethin', ain't you? Why don't you tell him my name?"

"I'll tell *you* somethin'," Jake snorted. "You git to your room an' stay put there."

With a toss of her head she came over to Antrim. "I'm Idy Red," she smiled, and put out her hand.

Her hair, copper red in the lamp glow, was brushed carelessly back from features piquant and vivid. Her eyes, he thought, held an odd excitement.

"Glad to know you," he said, and dropped her hand, not at all sure he liked her. He did not approve of her certainly. He could admire the nerve she had shown in dealing with the trash Gauze's schemes had brought here; but there was a place in this world for women. Men had made it for them, and those who were proper stayed in it.

Perhaps she read his thought. Her eyes changed a little. Then, peering up into his face, she laughed. "I got to know you better."

"You git to your room!" Jake shouted, and had a bony fist lifted to clout her when something he saw in his hired man's eyes dropped the hand and his voice at the same time, startled.

He wheeled to scowl blackly after her, and when the door banged shut behind her he looked again at Antrim's face.

There was nothing on it but inscrutability.

With a final hard stare Gauze went out of the room.

It was lighter outside and a breeze had sprung up. But stringers of fog still clung to the scrubby box elders and moisture was a beaded shine on the waxed-satin leaves of the cottonwoods.

Antrim picked up the reins of the ground-tied broncs and had his thorough look at the place.

There was a corral off yonder built of aspen poles that the broncs had gnawed clean by way of a pastime. There were eight or ten big geldings inside it; and to the left, hard against the far rock wall, was a weather tight stable also built of poles.

The look of that wood told Antrim within an ace of how long Gauze had been here.

It had not been long.

Still with his schooled face taciturn Antrim's head swung around for a look at the house. It was made of sun-cured adobes. Built in the form of an open square it had four rooms, three of which —confirming his guess—could only be entered from the patio; there were no connecting doors between them and only the main room gave onto the yard. This room was flanked by a broad veranda well riffled with dust by the play of the winds. A tall, narrow window flanked the door on each side like a couple of foot soldiers guarding royalty. Indeed, the whole place had a grim, bastioned look to it—more like a fort than where a man did his living. The hard, mud walls were nearly three feet thick.

There was still enough fog to hide the forks of the canyon, but a cowbird was calling from off in some thicket and high in the top of a gaunt old tree a mockingbird sang the opening bars of its day praise. The sun would soon be over the rim and Antrim was tired with his long hours of riding. Tired, but not sleepy; he had too much to think about to feel at all drowsy. Some place, out back of the stable, Bat Kerrick was whistling.

Antrim moved toward the sound.

He was close to the stable when Kerrick came around it.

Self assurance was a kind of humor in the pale, blue gaze Kerrick turned upon him. "Known Jake long?"

Antrim considered. "Long enough to know better."

Kerrick smiled, thinly sly. Then he chuckled. And, without remark, went off toward the house.

All the time he unsaddled the horses and was rubbing them down with handfuls of straw, Antrim thought about it. The incident still rankled while he shook down hay. After that, with a shrug, he put it away from him and turned his attention to the thing which had brought him all the long miles from Tubac. He was deep in this thinking when a shadow dimmed the doorway and his up-whipped glance found Idy Red watching him.

He said without masking his thoughts: "How'd you get here?"

"Clumb through a winder," she said with a grin.

"Then you better 'clumb' back."

"I ain't in no tearin' rush. Besides..." Her regard held interest. She said, "Sure wisht I had your purty black curls," and showed her teeth in a laugh when he scowled. White teeth. "You're fr'm Texas, ain't you?"

Antrim said, "Your Pap will Tex—"

"Jake Gauze ain't my Pap." She wrinkled her nose at him. "My Pap was kilt by the 'Patches— 'way back. Jake's jest a-takin' keer o' me—in a manner o' speakin'," she added; and said with a lift of her shoulders: "My Pappy was 'Red Dan Harris. No better man ever wore boots—ast Jake; *he'll* tell you! Jake says he was the fightin'- est feller he ever did see . . . I reckon Jake's seen a plenty."

"I expect he has—"

"You bet he has! 'Course he's jest plain lazy barroom trash—"

"If you think that," Antrim said, "why stay here?"

"Well . . ." She shrugged her willowy shoulders again. "Jake does the best he can with me— 'cordin' to *his* lights, anyway. Ain't every feller that would bother around with a damfool girl. We git along pretty toler'ble. Only trouble with Jake, he's so goddam bossy."

Antrim found nothing to say to that. Idy Red declared pridefully, "My Pappy was a Texas man. Come up f'm Eagle Pass, he did, with fourteen hunderd Mex'can cattle." Her smile flashed out, bright, excited again. "You come f'm Texas, didn't you?"

"No."

"Well, you don't hev to take my haid off!"

Idy Red sighed. "I'd shore like t' find me a Texas man. I'm a-gittin' all-fired tired of these damn back-country brush poppers. Just think— Eagle Pass!" She sighed again. "I'd mighty well like t' git a look at that place—ain't it got the fetchin'est sound? Bet you it's big as . . . as . . . Well! Betcha it's bigges' place no'th o' Mexico City!"

"You been to Mexico City?"

"Jake has. Jake's been all over hell an' back. He says—"

"You better be thinkin'," remarked Antrim dryly, "of what he'll be sayin' 'f he catches you out here."

Her hands came expressively up to her hair. She swept its red mass back from her cheeks and looked at him, observing him critically, wonderingly, her scrutiny as frankly personal as the one she'd given him in front of Jake. She said, a little exasperated, "I can't see why you don't like me."

"I like you all right—"

"You don't ack like it."

"What," Antrim frowned, "you wantin' me to do? Spark you or—"

"You better not try it!" she scowled, backing off. "I got a gun an' I can sure as hell use it."

"Humph!" Antrim snorted and went back to his work.

"I can shoot good as you can! You seen what I did t' that tinhorn, didn't you?"

Antrim continued his work like she wasn't around.

Idy Red gave a sign of temper. She kicked a horse chip across the stable. "I c'n see damn well you ain't no Texican! Texas men is polite to women—"

"I've known some that wasn't."

Idy Red stared.

"Trash!" she scoffed, and sent another horse chip bouncing. "You c'n allus tell what kind a man is by the way he acks with a woman."

Antrim twisted his head and looked at her. "That been your experience?"

It brought her up stone still. Her eyes went black. The points of her breasts made two stiff shapes against her shirt and a leaping anger bleached her cheeks to the color of chuck wagon canvas. Then, astonishingly, she laughed—laughed till the tears shone bright on her lashes.

"Oh, lordy me!" she gasped at last; and laughed again at the way Antrim eyed her. "Gosh, but you are a tough one, ain't you? I bet you're one of our toughest sort—live fo'ever an' then turn into a whiteoak post. Scowl the bark plumb off'n a tree!"

Abruptly her mirth fell entirely away. There was a sudden grimness in the set of her shoulders and the glint of her eyes was sharp as a hatchet. "What's Jake up to bringin' you out heah? You ain't no friend o' his—he ain't the kind to hev no friends. He's brung you out heah to ride herd on someone—me, or them owlhooters! Which one cuts it?"

FIVE

Half turned by his horse Antrim stood there while the buzz of a fly droned into the flare and fall of men's distant talking. Then he lowered the gear in his hands and faced her. He made a picture of indolent, careless grace as he stood with broad shoulders brushing the stall. The bronze of his cheeks showed no sign of his thinking, but the gray of his gaze made a cool, searching scrutiny. He quietly drawled, "I'm allowin', ma'am, that ain't rightly your business."

"Never mind the poker face. I'm askin you why you've come out heah."

"And I've told you it ain't your worry."

"A lot you—"

She broke off in mid-sentence; whirled toward the door.

Antrim, looking over her shoulder, saw a man

dismounting in the yard outside .

The man came toward them, peering into the stable.

He saw them and stopped. "Your pardon. Hadn't aimed to intrude."

"Lookin' for someone?"

"Fella named Gauze. I was told—"

"Expect you'll find Gauze up at the house."

The man nodded. He roved a casual glance around the stable. He had a deep-tanned face and the look of intelligence. He had a way that at once showed knowledge and tolerance. Too much tolerance, to Antrim's thinking. The man's look got under his temper.

But the fellow seemed not to have noticed.

"I'm obliged," he said, and blandly smiled at the girl, removing his hat to show black, curling hair that had been recently trimmed and was brushed with care. He bowed with a paraded reverence that made Antrim's fists itch to bat him.

"Your servant, ma'am," he declared, strictly grave, and then gave her the flash of his quick smile again and, wheeling, turned into the yard's flood of sun.

Antrim saw Idy Red's eyes follow him, excited and wondering and filled with interest.

She said, admiring his swing to the saddle, "Bet

you *he* come f'om Texas! Gosh! It plumb sticks out all over 'im—*there's* a *gentleman!* Just like—"

"No one but fools ever gets took in by a easy smile an' a passle of store clothes."

She flung him a scornful glance and said tartly, "Blah!" and thereafter turned to watch the stranger from sight.

Antrim lifted broad shoulders in an uncaring shrug, and without remark turned through the stable's rear door and left her.

He had, then, his watchful look of the region, observing that now, with the fog departed, the trees, gently nodding in a tiny wind, looked born anew, their leaves fresh and clean, asparkle with dew.

He took his look and went into the brush. All his nerves were on edge, pitching his temper with brashness and truculence. There had been no call to antagonize the girl. That was a price of doing without sleep. Boot Hill was filled with gone gents who had tried it.

He crawled into the thorny tangle and the earth felt good to his saddle-tired body. He closed his eyes and forthwith slept.

The sun was ablaze behind the westward crags

when Antrim opened the ranch house door and heard men's talk go abruptly still. They were there, all four of them. Jake's look was black.

"Where hev you been?"

"Sleepin'. Don't you never eat around here?"

"Openin' doors without knockin's got a mort of gents killed," Kerrick mentioned.

"You wouldn't be figurin' to pass any threats, would you?"

"Choke off the blat, you two," Jake grumbled. "Poke, shake hands with—"

"Sundance," smiled the new arrival, but did not offer to extend his hand. "What kind of ante you got in this business?"

"He's roddin' the spread," Jake told him gruffly; and Antrim said: "What's he wantin'—a job?"

"He's a guest," Jake said.

Guy Antrim looked skeptical.

"You ain't got no use for a range boss, Gauze. What you're needin' is a dry nurse around here."

The saturnine Kerrick pulled up his brows. He murmured at Jake, "You ain't loadin' nobody. Any fool could guess what you hired this feller for."

Sundance said, "And we ain't impressed."

"What the hell are you talkin' about?"

Unease crouched plain behind Jake's bluster.

A kind of grin curled Kerrick's mouth corners.

It was Taiban Cope that drove the nail. "When a gent hires a gun fighter he's generally got reason. Either he's scared himself or he's figurin' to scare other folks."

"We don't scare worth a damn," Bat Kerrick grinned.

There was a film of sweat on Jake's bony face.

"How much have you offered him?" Sundance asked.

"I ain't offered him nothin' but the wage he's hired for—"

"An' how much is that?"

"It ain't none of your business," Antrim said.

"Oho!" Kerrick jeered. "So the Sphinx can talk."

There rose in Antrim an urge toward violence. But no change disturbed his dark, baked cheeks. He held himself ready for whatever might come, and his watchful glance absorbed all significance as he said, very soft, "He can do other things, too. They might surprise you more."

"They might, for a fact." Sundance said it coolly, and wheeled his probing look back at Jake. "Get rid of this fellow if you want to stay healthy.

Get rid of him tonight or he'll be got rid of for you."

He got up to go out and the rest of them followed him.

Antrim's arm blocked the door. "Just a minute, mister. Let's get this straight. Is that a promise you made or just conversation?"

Sundance stopped and showed his teeth.

"It's just conversation—so far."

"Which owns the spread? You or Jake?"

"Jake owns the spread—"

"Then I'll be takin' my orders from Jake—not you."

Sundance chuckled with a casual politeness. "Every goose to its gander—"

Antrim's hand on his sleeve pulled the big man around. "What's that?"

"Just an old Sundance saying," answered Sundance coolly. "You're pretty damn touchy for a young fellow, ain't you? That's the trouble with you gunslicks—always on the prod. That's what gets so many of you killed."

Antrim smiled back at him, grin for grin. "We might make a deal."

"Not this time, bucko. There's enough in this now."

"I might be in it whether you like it or not."

"Not long."

"If that's your notion, why not settle it now? Three to one should be odds enough for you."

"When I get the notion I don't wait on odds."

"What's a man need to get you into the notion?"

Sundance smiled, very suave, urbanely. "I came here for a rest—"

"*What* rest?" Antrim jeered. "You mean the rest of that *map* Zwing Hunt passed on?"

Sundance's face didn't change, but his eyes did.

A stillness settled that was tight and brittle. Brittle, almost, as the cant of their postures. In that frozen quiet a door was shut some place, but in this room there was no sound, no movement. The feel of the place turned thick with thinking.

"So the bastard told you!" Kerrick growled at last. He thrust an intolerant hand through his hair and his shoulders lowered . . . like the creep of a shadow. Jake's stertorous breathing was perceptibly noisier and the gambling man, Cope, nervously fingered his collar.

Some reluctant urge got to knotting Jake's muscles and the wish to be elsewhere was bright in Cope's stare when Kerrick, scraping a chair from his path, growled, "I reckon—"

It was then Antrim's laugh crossed his words

with a file. "You ain't got enough savvy to reckon, Kerrick. All we're needin' to make this gatherin' complete is Virgil Boucher—or the ghost of that Mex."

Jake's jaw went slack and dropped wide open. Kerrick stopped in his tracks like a shot had struck him, and the gambler's eyes bugged out like saucers. Only Sundance had the wit to chuckle. The chuckle broke into full-fledged laughter and he clapped Kerrick's shoulder till the tall man, cursing, backed out of his reach.

With the mirth still shaking his voice, Sundance said, "You're a rare one, friend—where the hell did Jake find you?"

"Mebbe," Antrim said, "it was me found Jake. Whichever the way, you better count me in this—"

"You Boucher's pardner?"

"The only pardner I need is packed right here," Antrim touched his holster with dark suggestion. "A reliable one, an' plenty efficient. Just remember that, Sundance, when you start gettin' notions."

Antrim, turning his back on them, left them staring. Left them prey to distrust and suspicion; left each warped soul to its own vile acid.

Lone wolves, each and every one of them, he could guess quite well what had brought this crew to foregather at Jake's—the selfsame lure that had brought himself to return to this country after all the time he had spent away from it.

A cool three million in buried loot.

Hid away in his hatband was the map he had mentioned, the one drawn by Hunt and given to Hunt's uncle. That map had been made by Zwing Hunt on his deathbed; Antrim had all of it but one tiny corner. They could have that, and welcome. He was playing this hand for something else entirely. And the chance seemed good that he would find it here. These others were pinning their hopes on gaunt Jake Gauze; figuring, no doubt, that he had the map. But it seemed certain to Antrim that Gauze, if he'd known where the treasure was hid, would have dug it up long ago.

Perhaps he had.

Antrim did not think so.

Four years, he mused as he strode toward the stable, was a passle of time out of any man's life. But what were four years against three million dollars in owlhoot gold, with a sprinkling of silver thrown in for good measure?

Gold and silver, some currency too, and a box full of baubles.

Well worth the time he had spent chasing clues, the time he had spent gabbing around with old-timers.

He had talked with Hunt's uncle in far-off Santone; with others much closer. He had knocked around for a hand's span of weeks with Virgil Boucher, who was by way of being an older brother of the dead Billy Grounds.

When he'd made his map, Hunt had issued instructions. On a separate paper. Virgil Boucher had had it—but not when with Antrim. Someone else had got it then; had cunningly stole it one dark of the moon. "Stole it, by Gawd," Boucher growled, "from my pocket!"

Antrim lifted his saddle, heaved it onto a horse. While his lean hands were busy making ready to ride, his thoughts harked back to the tale Hunt had told as he lay abed dying.

SIX

The ranch house was still with a tight, bitter silence till the ring of Guy's spurs quit the yonder porch planking. Then Kerrick's lips parted in an explosive curse and three pairs of eyes raked Jake intolerantly.

The smile was gone off Sundance's lips.

It was Kerrick who said with the spleen almost choking him: "You hound-yellow rat!" and came out of the corner like a lunging cat. Jake threw out both hands to ward him off; but his bony shoulders were jammed to the wall and the wall wouldn't give and Kerrick, eyes glinting, came in for the kill.

Jake Gauze showed his age. He was an old man, cringing.

It was Sundance kept Kerrick off him.

"There's a good-sized chance," drawled Sundance softly, "it wasn't old Jake tipped this leather slapper off."

"Wasn't Jake!" Kerrick snarled. "Who you think done it—Santa Claus? Who the hell else would have anything t' tell him?"

"We'll be learning that presently. What all do you know about this pelican, Jake?"

Jake roused himself. "Not a thing," he declared— "not a goddam thing. I picked 'im up over at Tombstone t' he'p me—"

"Help you what?" Cope scoffed. "Help you count yer chickens?"

Some of the gray seeped out of Jake's cheeks and the swerve of his eyes went slyly crafty. "To he'p me around the place," he said. "I been havin' trouble—been losin' stock—a right damn good passle of it. Some o' them oilers f'm below the Line 've taken t' usin' the Trail ag'in. Hosses, I reckon. Way I read the sign, they're bringin' broncs up f'm outa Sonora, palmin' em' off on them ranchers round Tucson; stealin' more there an' driftin' it back—"

"What's all that got t' do with—"

"Tellin' you, ain't I? I took on this fella—"

"When?" Sundance asked.

Jake said glibly: "Four—five weeks ago."

Cope showed a gambler's brow-raised skepticism. "A real hog for work, ain't he?"

"Didn't you know," Kerrick growled sarcastically, "Jake keeps his stock corraled on the porch here?"

Sundance cleared his throat. " 'Poker Face' all the handle he give you?"

"He can eat jest as much by thet name as another. Anyhow," Jake said, attempting virtue, "I ain't the kind t' go diggin' my nose—"

Kerrick's remark was obscene and lively. "To hell with your nose! This goddam gabbin' makes my gut ache. This baloney's too wise—we got to get rid of him. 'F you'd had the wit to keep your trap shut—"

"I kep' it shut!" Jake flared, fiercely glowering.

Sidelong his badgered stare flicked Sundance.

Butter-smooth and bland, big Sundance said, "Bein's I wasn't sent no personal invite to this jamboree, I ain't rightly entitled to do no talking. But it seems to me—"

"What *I* say," Kerrick cut in curtly, "let me get my sights lined up on a sidewinder—"

"After a sidewinder's bitten you," Sundance smiled, "blowin' its head off won't help you any."

"It would make me *feel* a damn sight better! Jake's spilled his guts to him, an' I say, by Gawd—"

"By Gawdin' ain't like to help you much either." Sundance looked at the other man tolerantly. "You birds should be glad I'm willing to help you; left to your own poor wits you'd wizzle. Since this guy knows so much he's probably *got* that map... It could be," he said, and Kerrick's jaw tightened.

"Nobody's asked for your help that *I* know of. You hogged in here just like this other guy—"

"Not *just* like this other guy," Sundance grinned. "You wrote me yourself there was something big cookin' here. If you hadn't said that I'd never thought to of come here—I never would of guessed old Jake had a spread here. I'm obliged to you, Batwick—"

"Don't call me that goddam name!" Kerrick snarled. "An' don't try makin' out *I* ast you into this. I'd of cut off my tongue—"

"I'll bet you would, at that—Jake, too," Sundance chuckled. "Well, its' a damn ugly wind that blows nobody good. I'm satisfied. And you fellows ought to be. It ain't every bunch has a talent like mine. If I hadn't bought in this here Poker Face gent would of had you stole blind in no time. If I had my rights I'd get the biggest share, because without my help you wouldn't get so much as the price of one drink; this Poker Face gent would of glommed the whole of it. Not," he grinned, "that I'm askin' that much. I wouldn't dream of it. I'll take my share and thank you kindly—"

"You'll take what you get an' keep your mouth shut!"

Sundance shook his black curls as though dismayed at Kerrick. "Harsh words," he said, "never buttered no parsnips. Well, Jake," he drawled, "let's have the truth of it. Did you ask this guy in?"

Jake juned around like the seam-squirrels had him. He could not seem to hold his eyes on Sundance; they frittered around like a harried heel fly.

He mopped his face with the back of a sleeve. "You've made up yer mind—the' ain't no use o' *me* talkin. The' wouldn't none o' you believe me—"

"We're willin' to listen."

Jake scowled, swallowed hard, rasped a hand through his bristles. He edged a quick look over Sundance covertly, took a deep breath and plunged in.

"Like I said," he muttered, "I been losin' stock—not no two or three critters like a man might expect to, but great jags of stock—it's fair got me rattled. I seen I had t' hev he'p. So I got up a hoss an' went over t' Tombstone. I was in the Palace chinnin' with Slaughter—"

"The sheriff!" Cope swore. "By—"

"Hang hold," Sundance grunted. "Let's hear the rest of it."

Jake didn't seem to know where he was at, hardly. He was palpably scared of the burly Sundance; you would almost have said he was scared of his shadow. His next words were pitched in a plaintive whine, an incongruous blend of pleading, resentment and surly defiance.

"You mus' think cowpunchers grows aroun' here on trees! I *had* t' ast Slaughter. I'd awready ast all the rest of the men in town. Besides that chisel-faced hyena was standin' right there by the bar when I come in. Y'expeck me t' pass 'im up like a dishrag? Folks don't pass John Slaughter up—*no ways*. He been sniffin' my tracks fer quite a spell an' this looked like a firs' class chanct t' smooth his fur down. So I—"

"Well, *go on*," Kerrick snarled. "What the hell are you waitin' on?"

Jake spat back at him. "Man's got t' ketch 'is

breath *some*time, ain't he? What d'ye take me for —a goddam *phonograph?*"

"Never mind him, Jake," soothed Sundance. "He wouldn't know a gnat's heel from a hole in the ground. How you reckon this guy got onto you?"

Jake looked baffled. "It's got me fightin' my hat," he grunted. "Alls I know is what I done tol' you. I ast him was he huntin' a job—somebody pointed him out when I was jawin' with Slaughter. He sure didn't show much interested. Had t' exercise my talkin' talents fer up'ards of a hour 'fore I finally augured him into takin' my money. How the hell'd *I* know—"

"Sure," Sundance nodded; "how would anyone?" But Cope said darkly:

"Lay you ten to one he's a goddam star packer."

"Who—*me!*" Jake flared; and Kerrick's lip curled.

"Nobody's ever take *you* for a tinbadge!"

"No," Sundance said, "this Poker Face ain't no lawman. There's somethin' else back of him crowdin' this play."

"Don't keep it so secret," Kerrick jeered.

Sundance's black eyes jabbed up a twinkle. "I'm no oracle, but I can tell you this—it ain't nothing that can't be fixed by a forty-five barrel on a forty-four frame."

In his mind he applied the same thought to Kerrick.

There was a pretty good chance Bat Kerrick sensed it. "Better get up goddam early if you try it." His angular eyes jabbed Sundance brashly, then he swung his look on old Jake again. "If you got me an' Cope out here on a goose chase—"

"You don't think," Jake blustered; and Sundance chuckled.

"Called, by grab! An' first pop out of the box, at that!"

Kerrick's cold jaw came around like a yard arm. His squinched-up eyes were bright and ugly. But he made no remark; he didn't say anything till he brought his look back to Jake again. "You said," he told Jake, "if we all joined up and put our cards on the table we'd find that stuff—"

"You ain't put no cards on the table."

"I ain't seen no reason to," Kerrick growled; "an' I sure ain't puttin' down nothin' for *that* guy! You said we was goin' to divvy this equal—"

Jake said, "I'm still willin'."

"You ain't got much choice," allowed Sundance, smiling. "You ain't got no more choice than Batwick here."

GUNSLICK MOUNTAIN 71

Again Kerrick's stare came around at Sundance. His cheeks swelled out like a grassfed bronc, but he kept the hatch on his temper doggedly.

Cope said to Jake, "You was one of the jaspers that helped Curly Bill pile up that plunder—you was one of Curly's right-hand men. Why split with us—why ask us in here?"

"Probably couldn't find it on his own hook," said Sundance.

"But he said—"

"Old Jake's said a lot of things besides his prayers."

Sundance's low, scoffing words wilted Jake like a sunstroke. They drained all the health from his cheeks; left him shaking. It was startling what effect Sundance had on the man. His slightest sarcasm worked on Jake like an acid; yet this time they pulled a protest out of him. He seemed to feel the need of justification. "I never said I knowed where it *was!* Alls I said—"

"You said you knew," Kerrick gritted, "where that 'Davis Mountain' was—"

"I never!" yelled Jake. "I said I knowed where the mountain was—but I never put no name to it! I—"

"You said," Cope snarled, "all you was needin'

was the map or directions—"

"Sure! When I see your directions—"

Sundance drawled, butter smooth: "We'll have us a look at your mountain, first. Come along. Point it out an' we'll get down to cases."

SEVEN

There were many things about these men that Antrim could neither guess nor fathom; but of one thing he felt wickedly certain. Lure of the Curly Bill cache had drawn them over the desert miles to this place; over the trackless sands of time. They were here for a purpose—the same purpose he was. To unearth that bloodstained plunder that was someplace hidden in these roundabout hills. Hard cash and smugglers' gold and silver—God only knew how much of the latter, but in Hughes' haul alone there had been over ninety thousand Mexican dollars, and thirty-nine bars of solid gold. Zwing Hunt and his men had crossed with two four-horse wagons piled high with loot; they had gutted a bank at Monterey of two big gunny sacks crammed with money and a fifty-cigar box stuffed with diamonds. They had sacked Matamoras and raped the cathedral of its golden statues—life-sized figures of the Virgin and Jesus. Besides all this there was the plunder of bullion Curly Bill had taken from the nineteen Mexicans his gang had slaughtered right here in this canyon eight years ago.

In all, three cool million. If you were one to believe rumor.

Guy Antrim wasn't.

But he knew in his bones there was treasure here. Scoff as you would, there was no getting around the bleached bones in this canyon. Everywhere they littered the trail, human bones and the remains of dead mules. Plenty of gents had found hide *aparejos,* twisted and cracked from sun and rain. More than a few had found Mexican dollars. Ranchhands around the San Simon had played all one winter with dinero picked out of the brush of this country; and even so recent as just last year a number of tarnished old coins had been found.

A good many people had prowled through this canyon, covertly searching for Curly Bill's cache. Some had come with divining rods, others had come from bent old dames who bragged of second sight and witchery. Medicine men had garnered fortunes telling damned fools just where they could find it. Several had come sporting wands of willow as though loot would bend them like a source of water. Even the spirits had been consulted; and one old codger had sworn up and down he could have put his finger right smack on it if that "damned quake" hadn't shaken the country. That temblor of '86, he'd meant.

But Antrim was wasting no worry on temblors. In his bones he was sure there'd been little change. This country was pretty much as the outlaws had left it. Sand might have drifted out some of its contours, winds and spring freshets might have cut a few trees out; but in the main, he guessed, if you had the right slant on it, you'd be finding Hunt's markers just about where Hunt said you would. Where Hunt's band had drawn them on that cheap piece of writing paper.

Antrim's desire to uncover this plunder had never been crossed by any question of ethics. Past experience had not been such as to endow his thought with high regard of virtue. Virtue, he'd found, was its own reward, and more often than not proved a mighty lean comfort. Justice was something to be catalogued with luck, too frequently dependent on whim or indebtedness.

This is not to describe him an unprincipled ruffian. He had his ideals but no hope of encountering them. There was a sadness in him— a consuming bitterness, but he'd learned to take the world just as he found it. He was done with illusions; had got his eyes fully open. Men, the best of them, were a despicable breed. A selfish and vain, conniving, treacherous lot. Whatever of good had been born into them was swiftly contaminated, stifled by greed. He would like to have thought much better of them. There had been, indeed, a time when he had—when he'd looked on his fellows with warmth and tolerance, when he'd deliberately sought to find things good in them, blinding himself to their faults and their avarice.

But that had been prior to the Benson stage. Prior to his acquaintance with the Tombstone jail.

Luther King he'd been called in those carefree days.

He was Guy Antrim now, the frozen-faced gun packer. A man without friends, without trust, disillusioned. The change had been slow—near eight years it had taken, but now the metamorphosis was done, was complete. The last of the dross had been burned out of him, purged by experience. He was no longer fooled by men's cunning ways; no longer deceived by their shows and false goodness. Nothing they did could further surprise him. He could see through their righteous parades of virtue—see to the foul, rotten core of them. His first keen glance could observe their guilt and nothing they might thereafter strive could effect his opinion by one iota.

Yet he was not unjust. He took care to be fair. He had reminded himself of this many times, and believed it.

There was nothing wrong in his seeking this treasure. It was there for the finding. Let the smartest man get it.

The smartest man aimed to.

"We come up out of Mexico," Zwing told his uncle, "with two four-horse wagons well loaded with plunder. We'd been down there, raidin', for around three months. There was twenty-nine of us started, swingin' down through the San Luis Pass. But there was on'y eighteen crossed the Border back, an' some of them was bad wounded. Down in Monterey Billy Grounds an' me held a whole mob back while the rest cleaned the bank out. We got two big gunny sacks stuffed with money an' a wood cigar box filled with diamonds. We sacked Matamoras—got two big statues.

"Oh, we had a high time, I can tell you. Grabbed more loot than you c'ld shake a stick at. We hauled the whole works to Davis Mountain."

Zwing had paused a bit then. "Like he was collectin' his thoughts," Zwing's uncle said. "Or mebbe it was pain that stopped him— God knows there was plenty of that to his dyin'."

Zwing hadn't stopped long. He hadn't long to stop.

"One of the boys," he said "who got shot at Monterey, gasped his last when we come to the mountain. We buried him there. By the spring. In the shade of a juniper. We'd give him his share—in gold. He'd earned it. He worked like a nigger for that five hundred, so we let him keep it—buried it with him. It's in a can at the head of his grave.

"We all took a bath in the waterfall then. After a while we played some poker in a cave we found. Mighty slick hideout we had up there. You could hunt forever an' never find it. Less'n you had a map or somethin'. An' hard to get at without bein' spotted. Up there on the mountain, with a pair of glasses, you could look out plumb across to N' Mexico."

There'd been a number of other things Zwing had said, but Zwing Hunt's uncle seemed to have got them all scrambled. "Main thing is I got him

GUNSLICK MOUNTAIN 79

some paper and he wrote down instructions—mighty particular, too. Very definite. So many paces this way and that. Sorry I've lost it—but I've still got the map. There's been some tough gents camped around my place here; I've had to use my wits to get shut of 'em. But I've still got the map—just think of it, boy! Three million dollars!"

Antrim had thought of it.

A lot of others had, too.

In especial these fellows that were bulldozing Jake.

Head bent, Antrim stood in the gloom of the stable, considering ways and means. Probing chances. There was part of a frown across his cheeks; but he straightened finally with a thin little grin.

He readied his horse; led it into the yard.

He was in the saddle, coolly twisting a smoke, when his ears picked up the faint *clop* of hoof sound.

He stayed where he was and continued his thinking.

"First," Zwing had said, "you go to Davis Mountain. Then head west. In a mile or so you'll come to a canyon—pretty fair sized one. The west wall of this gulch is solid rock. You'll hear the creek; it boils down over a ten-foot ledge. You'll likewise see, along this west wall, a good sized juniper; Silver Spring'll be right alongside of it. Be a grave there, too—there's stone slabs markin' the head an' foot of it. From the spring go south about a mile and three tenths. You'll find another—we called it Gum Spring. There'll be a passle of brush on the canyon floor but, somewhere between the two springs, you'll notice the west wall of the canyon sort of gouges out. Makes a kind of cove. At the deepest point of this cove, a pace or two out from the wall, you'll see a straight up-an'-down rock. It's three feet high, shaped square—not over a scant foot thick. We cut a pair of crosses in it, one over the other. When you find this, stand there an' face Davis Mountain. Step east twenty paces. You're bound to see the wreck of that wagon. Be dead ahead. Right there's where you want to start diggin'. There'll be three million dollars right under your feet."

Just as plain as plowed ground.

Zwing had put his instructions just as lucid as that. Billy Grounds, his pardner, had died too sudden to do any talking. But there was Maggie Clinger, Grounds' sister, an emphatic believer in Zwing's famous story. Mrs. Clinger said, "I'm as sure about that treasure as if I'd been right there when they buried it. I can see them two springs, that rock with two crosses and all the rest of it just as plain as if I'd been there helpin'. I could walk straight up to that buried treasure—if," she declared, "somebody would only find me that mountain."

There were a great many other folks felt the same way.

That *if* was the hell of it. It had stumped the whole crowd of them. You could stick a shovel into the cache yourself if only you could sight that gunslick mountain.

According to Zwing's uncle's account of Zwing's story, it was a "rounded, bald, granite sugarloaf" type. But the men elected to map Arizona had left Davis Mountain clean out of the picture. And Zwing, droll fellow, had put down every slightest detail but the all-important mountain's location. Boucher had called him a bloody fool—and worse. "By grab," he'd told Antrim, "it's around yere someplace! There ain't such a hell's smear of mountains around yere you can look clean into New Mexico off'n. 'F I can't do no better I'll comb ever' one of 'em!"

Well, he'd combed them, Antrim sourly reflected, but he hadn't uncovered the Curly Bill hoard.

EIGHT

The shank of evening had blown around with the cool down-draft flowing off the mountains. The distant crags of these tumbled hills showed silver and blue in the moon's pale light as Antrim pinched out his smoke and dropped it.

He did not pick up his reins, or touch them.

He got out of his saddle and stood there, silent.

The horse he had heard was close—arriving. From the San Simon Valley. He made out the animal's shape; its rider. He was mildly astonished by what his eyes told him.

He stepped up into his saddle again. He got out his pipe and filled it, thoughtfully. He flexed his knees and the horse moved forward.

She saw him coming. Where the brush narrowed in, almost choking the trail, she stopped, deliberately, obviously waiting.

Antrim had his moment of wonder then. He stopped beside her and she laughed at him softly.

The thin slice of moon threw its light full across her, bringing out the lush curves, the easy grace of her body.

She was lithe and slim and without a hat. Black hair framed her oval face like a picture. Red lips, parting, disclosed a shine of teeth. There was something quick and alive in her posture, something vibrant, unexplainably provocative that, against his will, came to stir and unsettle him.

She laughed again, a silvern tinkle of sound.

"Hel-lo!" she exclaimed, and leaned closer, studying him, the sound of her breathing excited and quickened.

She was Spanish, he guessed—at least she had Spanish features.

He touched his hat. "You lookin' for somebody?"

The shake of her head set gold earloops dancing.

She appeared to eye him more closely, her interest turned personal, frankly appraising.

Antrim stirred in his saddle.

"You mus' be the one that called John Slaughter 'Tex,' " she smiled. "I 'ave hear of that. Not many make bold to call that one 'Tex.' "

"Kind of off your range, ain't you?"

He saw the flash of her eyes and said grimly: "I called John Slaughter 'Tex' in Tombstone."

Her soft laugh approved him. It was intimate, friendly. "Oh! but you are curious—no? You are wonder who is this—this hussy w'at ride through the night een strange places. Where does she come from—to where does she go—"

"Not at all," Antrim said. "That ain't none of my never-mind."

He touched his hat with a brief civility, and would have picked up his reins but her hand forestalled him. Just the tips of her fingers, barely brushing his arm, yet a gun being cocked would not have stiffened him swifter. "You are the brave one," she said, "to go to work for Jake Gauze."

He did not ask why that made him brave. He was held by the look of her eyes.

Long lashed, black, like her hair they were—black as midnight; intensely expressive. "I mus' tell you . . . I am Lolita . . . Lolita Garcia— That means nothing to you? You do not know me then?"

She seemed a little surprised. Her look changed suddenly.

"No matter. I am a dancer. Used to work for Big Minnie when Joe ran the Bird Cage—you know: the opera at Tombstone."

He listened more to the warm, rich tones of her voice than to those things her words might have conjured for him. He could guess her class; it was there to be read in every bold, reckless line of her. Yet there was a fineness about her, a something beyond and above this mere bait of adventure; something quickly sensed but too vague to pin down.

He eyed her more closely, observing the fit of her divided riding skirt, observing the strain of the silk at her breasts; and grew suddenly conscious of her heightened color. Yet her look did not falter. Neither was it bold.

"This concerns me, Madame?"

She returned his glance with one completely as searching. "Does one ever divine what concerns another? I mean—truly? It *could* concern you. Many have found my words of import."

"Yeah? And what gives you the notion that I—"

"A man like you would not come out here for the sake of the wage Jake Gauze might have promised."

Antrim looked at her carefully.

"For a dancer," he said, "you sure—"

"Don't forget," she reminded, "I used to work for Big Minnie..."

Another second he stared. Something quick and surprised recolored his glance then. "Lizette!"

"Sure—the 'Flying Nymph,'" she laughed softly. "Did you think any woman could ever forget the boy Johnny Behan dragged in to play goat for the Benson Stage robbery? I was there when they locked you up. L—"

"Don't use that name here," Antrim said. "I don't know you. We never laid eyes on each other before. Do you get it?"

Her smile showed excitement. "So it *does* concern you! And I called the turn on Jake and his wages. Don't worry. I'll keep—"

The opening squeak of the house door stopped her.

A man came out, striding off through the shadows, the clank of his spurs setting up little echoes that eddied and died in the brush around the stable. They could hear him swearing off there at the horses.

The girl looked a question.

Antrim said, "Bat Kerrick. One of Jake's little playmates. Makes me feel kinda sorry for that girl of his. There's three of 'em camped here, and—"

He broke off to stare at the shadow blocked doorway. Two more black figures were coming out.

He said, curtly short: "You better be lettin' 'em know you're around here," and without further words put his horse through the chaparral.

Sundance's tone had not admitted of argument when he told Jake Gauze to show them the mountain. But Jake was of that breed of men turned balky and stubborn by the lash of pressure. "Now?" he said. "What do you take me for—a goddam *owl?*"

"An owl," mentioned Sundance, "is supposed to be smart. No . . . I'd never take you for an owl, friend Jake. Your conniving ways more resemble the magpie—"

"He's goin' to be a dead doornail—"

"You can't see no mountains in the middle of the night!"

"You don't know us, Jake. We can see lots of things a man wouldn't think for. We can see plain enough what you got up your sleeve. Better forget it, son, an'—"

"Damned if I know what t' make of you fellas. A guy would think," Jake blustered, "I was tryin' t' *steal* somethin' off you 'stead of workin' my tail off t' do you a favor! 'F you're s' damn' suspicious—"

"Easy, son . . . easy," murmured Sundance quietly. "Don't think too high on the strength of that mountain. It might let you down. If it comes to trusting, I ain't trusting no one. You can have till morning to mull it over—"

It was then Bat Kerrick got up and stamped out.

Sundance's glance never left Jake's face.

The gray look clawed Jake's cheeks again. He had known all along they would get to this finally. It was the most ticklish spot in his well-rehearsed plan—the plan that was back of his hiring Antrim.

The look of Sundance made his scalp crawl. He sat rigidly still in his wall-anchored chair; decided reluctantly to tell the truth. Or such part of it, leastways, as might best serve him.

He said, with as much indignation as he thought he dared show them, "You boys got no call t' be eyin' me that way. You oughta remember I'm a man keeps his promise. Told you I'd he'p you find that cache an' I'm goin' to—if you'll give me a chanct. 'F I'd knowed fer sure where the stuff was hid I'd not be stuck in these hills herdin' cattle. Bat called the turn on that, all right; but I can he'p you—*plenty*. It was Grounds an' Zwing Hunt ackshully done the hidin', but they learned all they knowed of this country from me—"

"Is that your 'help?'" Cope asked sarcastically.

He bent and brought up a knife from his boot. Suggestively tried it on the flat of a thumb.

The wrinkled skin of Jake's hollowed cheeks showed a change of contour and the way of his thought winked out of his stare. He took a nervous swallow and tried again.

"Now wait—don't do nothin' brash. I can savvy things make me look like a liar, but it's Gawd's own truth I'm a-tellin' you—Gawd's own, believe me. All workin' t'gether, we're *bound* t' find it. I got a real lead on it jest this week— I . . . I found that juniper . . . where they buried that fella—'member? His share of the swag come t' five hundred dollars. He'd worked s' hard fer it they let 'im keep it—buried it with him. At the head of 'is grave. In a little tin . . ."

Jake gauged aright the looks they gave him. Saw Cope begin fiddling with his knife again. His neck sank into his bony, hunched shoulders and a wildness boiled up into his eyes.

He raised a shaking, blue-veined hand. "Wait—"

"Just hand me that knife, Cope," Sundance said.

Jake lurched to his feet. "Goddam you—*listen!* I *dug up* that can— I kin show you the *gold!*"

NINE

When Antrim left the girl he had no definite purpose, no mapped-out move in mind. His head was full of questions, not the least of which was puzzlement over what had brought Lizette here. Had she, too, come attracted by the pull of that owlhoot cache? Or was that something beyond her knowledge, something in no way concerned with her motives?

Lizette . . . Been a long time since he'd seen her—eight years ago, come grass. She'd been at the jail when they brought him in for the Benson stage job. This was the extent of their acquaintance.

He recalled the stricken white face of her as she'd shrunk back to let him pass, that day—the wide and startled depth of her glance.

She'd changed; though not so much as you'd

think for. He'd always imagined her kind aged early. But Lizette hadn't aged; leastways her look and the shape of her hadn't. Kind of odd, when you stopped to think of it. Time must have used her kindly. You might sense a harder twist to her lips, a more knowledgeable gleam in the flash of her eyes; but if this were so it was a tempering —not the ravage of disillusion.

Where did she fit into this thing?

Nowhere, probably. At least there didn't seem much chance that she did. Had probably come out to see Jake Gauze about something. He wondered what she was doing now—dressmaking? hatmaking? What did dancers usually do when the call for their talent proved on the wane?

It never occurred to him she might have got married.

He got to wondering instead about Jake's visitors, those hard-faced rannies from hell knew where. The tall and saturnine Kerrick. The pale little tinhorn, Taiban Cope. The coolly casual, smart-eyed Sundance, who'd been so quick to supply a name when Jake had been passing out knockdowns. Who were they? What was the connection between them and Jake?

That they were scoundrels went without saying. It was also a cinch they'd come hunting that treasure. What else were they here for? Was that the sole reason?

He thought again of Sundance, so obviously a leader.

He was a smiling man who dressed like a dude and affected grand manners, looking more like the cowboy of the tobacco ads than . . . Well— than what?"

It had Antrim stumped. He admitted it. There was something about the man that bothered him. But he could not pin it down, could not fasten a name to it. The sum total of his convictions was that Sundance warranted watching.

The man was burly, dark-faced, broad of shoulder, yet with an underlying hint of softness about him which Antrim laid to over-indulgence. He showed no sign of hard work or hard riding. His pinto vest was worth considerable money, as was the watch whose chain sagged across his shirtfront. His doeskin pants were of a frontier type and his boots had been built by a master craftsman, well-chosen to set off his gold inlaid spurs and the pearl-handled sixguns that joggled his thighs. He made a bold impression with his laughing eyes and that thick mane of hair that was black and curling—so lustered with glints you'd have sworn he used bear grease. He was the kind,

Antrim thought with a curl of the lip, to make quite a splash with the ladies.

He had known this debonair kind before. More often than not, behind that smiling plaster of tolerance and banter, you found the soul of a shopkeeper, adamant and grasping, ready to whittle you out of your pants if you gave them so much as a toehold for purchase.

Antrim's horse had not stopped for these jaundiced reflections. When he finally shelved his thinking they were far up the canyon, well away from all sight and hearing of Jake's place. The gorge hereabouts wore a quite different aspect. Its red walls dipped lower, were more open, less rugged. The undulent floor was a carpet of wild flowers through which the trail meandered with an easy pleasantry. For some the place might have held rare beauty, but Antrim's interest lay in hideouts for treasure.

There were a plenty of mountains cutting the skyline; he could see their escarpments, pale and vague in the moon glow. Lofty peaks and crenelated hogbacks, wind-scoured crags and sheer-lipped cliffsides. In all this waste of upthrust stone who could tell where the fools had hidden it? Who could say which of these was the mountain?

Yet this was the canyon that once had echoed to the cries of agony, battle and butchery. This was the gulch where men had died for sake of the silver in Curly Bill's cache. This was the place of the unburied dead, whose bones had been mauled by the wolves and buzzards; whose ghosts, according to local tell, still tramped the dark and brooding hush and sometimes, of a night, could be heard a-screeching. The way they'd screeched when Curly Bill's lead struck them and tumbled them out of their saddles headlong.

This was the place.

But which was the mountain? That gunslick mountain Zwing Hunt had called Davis?

There'd been times when Antrim was mightily tempted to believe the whole thing was a cooked-up myth. But there was no gainsaying the bones men had found here. Folks had died here right enough. Most of the bones were gone now, washed away by the creek's flooding waters; but many a San Simon rancher washed his hands with soap that was kept in a skull—skulls their ranch hands had brought from this canyon.

This was the trail down which eight years ago black-eyed, jovial Don Miguel had led his hard-faced smugglers from out of the Animas Valley with their belled mules daintily picking their way under bulging *aparejos* of Mexican silver bound north through the waving San Simon grasses, around the Cherrycows and through Dragoon Gap, across the San Pedro and up the Santa Cruz Valley to Tucson. There they would buy all manner of things while Tucson merchants praised their ingenuity and winked at their smartness in avoiding the customs. They would have, that is, if the Don had got through.

Which he hadn't.

He had died right here. With his boots on.

Only one of his company had gotten away— a handsome youth, lithe and fleet as an antelope. He had raced away in wild flight up the canyon and later—one month, so they told you—had come back with companions and lifted five hundred head of good cattle from Clanton and other Las Animas ranchers. But Curly Bill caught them in the San Luis Pass, recovered the cattle and killed half their number. He did not, however, get his hands on the leader, this same young buck who had slipped him at Skeleton. Since then many stories had gone the rounds of a solitary horseman who haunted the Border and scanned every wayfarer using the Trail.

Old Man Clanton, freshening up his chew, allowed one day he had beef to be marketed. Experience told him he'd do best at Tombstone where they paid good prices and were not too particular. Harry Earnshaw and Snow, Dick Gray, Billy Lang and Jim Crane saddled up and were with him when he started the drive—Antrim had taken pains to ascertain because this same Jim Crane was one of the men who'd jumped the Benson stage that time.

The Mexicans caught them in Guadalupe Canyon. Of the Clanton boys only Earnshaw escaped and led the Cloverdale boys back to pick up the bodies. This revenge seemed to have satisfied Don Miguel's survivor; the solitary horseman was seen no more.

Just the same, Antrim mused, a lot of queer things had been happening since. Of the men concerned in the Skeleton massacre, few had lived long or pleasureably after. So far as was known Jake Gauze was the last. Hard luck and the devil dogged the rest to the end.

It was no great wonder when you stopped to consider it that old Jake Gauze felt the need of a gun packer.

The nicker of a horse pulled Antrim up. Sharp and sudden it stopped him, tensely cocked in the saddle. A damp, earthy smell came out of the tree line behind which the creek ran with increased loudness.

Antrim's horse blew out a gusty breath; Antrim's hand clamped down before he could answer. The sound of the creek became plainer and plainer and the horse, off yonder, softly nickered again.

An empty camp.

Antrim's shoulders relaxed and his cheeks lost their tautness. He had thought at first this might be some of the horse-running brotherhood. In such case, however, that horse off yonder would not have nickered again. It was not compatible with thieves to advertise.

He started forward then stopped, at a loss for direction. The call seemed to come from beyond the creek; yet this could not be, for the gulch wall here rose directly behind it. He must have been tricked by some distortion of echo.

He let his horse speak and stood by for the answer.

When it came he frowned, eyed the gulch wall intently. It certainly seemed to have come from there—yet, how could it?

Antrim rolled up a smoke and then dropped it, unlighted. There might, of course, be a cave back there. This willow growth flanking the creek might conceal it . . . Hunt had mentioned a cave where the bunch had played poker; but the cave in Hunt's story had been up on the mountain. There was no mountain here. None, that is, in this canyon.

He lifted his pistol out of leather and urged his horse at the dark line of trees. Shadows closed around him, branches brushed him; then his horse skittered down the low bank to the creek bed.

It was blacker than hell on a holiday here. The creek was shallow, firmly floored with rock; it made a great play with his clattering hoof sound. He was cursing himself for a fool, turning back, when the unseen horse abruptly whinnied again—right in his ears it almost seemed, and he stopped, arrested, baffled, uneasy.

He turned narrowed eyes to the far bank, raking it. There was little to see in this moonless murk, just blackness on blackness, and yet—

He urged his horse nearer with flexing knees. The far bank loomed close. Less than three yards away it confirmed his impression there was brush growing along it. Which was odd. Unless there were a ledge or outcrop holding the creek from the canyon wall.

There was, he found. And not of sandstone, either. The bank was heavy loam, and there were hoofmarks in it. By the match he had struck he could see them plainly. They were not very old. There'd been no effort to conceal them. They went directly into the brush before him.

The match flickered out and he struck another, snapping it to flame on the edge of his thumbnail, peering upward above the tops of the brush, endeavoring to locate the gulch wall behind it.

It was there, all right, rough contour showing plainly. He was that way, staring, when the match left his hand.

The sound of that shot ripped the night wide open.

TEN

Antrim stood completely still.

The sound of the shot hit the canyon walls, bounded off and clattered away in the darkness. A risen wind clouted into the willows, and still he remained there, head canted, listening. With a sudden, brash spin of his weight he whirled, took one swift backward step and crouched, the pistol gripped in his fist again, some dark and violent thought in the stare that was wickedly probing the felted gloom.

A dry stick snapped, and near the trail he heard brush break before a traveling body. Flame leapt out of his gun like a snake's head; for a second the runner's pace was blotted—then the crashing growth sent back his stride. Antrim fired again with his glance gone slitted. There was a whistle of air like a quirt descending, a startled grunt, a burst of hoof sound that swiftly faded down the canyon trail.

Antrim's look was grim as he prodded the spent shells out of his pistol. The man had struck, had fled and vanished; but this was far from being the end of it. The man would be trying his luck again.

Reloading he dropped the gun back into its holster, picked up the reins and led Jake's horse to a tree where he carefully tied him. The bushwhacker, leaving, had gone down the trail. It was in that direction that Jake Gauze's ranch lay.

With a match in cupped palm Antrim quartered for sign. The tracks, when he found them, were not easily read. The trail was hard and the would-be assassin had kept his horse carefully on it. The sign was well laced with the track of others, but a cool smile wreathed Antrim's lips as he straightened.

The man had come up the trail just as Antrim had. His horse was shod and its left hind shoe had not been properly set—either that, or the hoof had known more growth than its fellows. It left a mark to remember.

A search disclosed where the man had mounted. There was one fair print at the side of the trail which the man's weight had left as he swung to the saddle. He wore, Antrim thought, a pretty damned small boot.

Going back to the creek Antrim splashed across it. Found the loam shelf and climbed out on it. He came to the growth that fringed its bank and paused there, listening, eyes raking the shadows.

There was nothing to hear save the occasional swish of the wind-waved branches.

Antrim shrugged morosely and picked his way up the gummy bank, still on a hunt for that horse sound, still intrigued by the puzzle of how such sound could appear to come from an unbroken wall of sandstone.

The curdled gloom and the midnight silence picked up the sound of his travel loudly. When he came upon drier footing, small rocks left there by countless freshets rolled and struck the water with miniature splashes that were swiftly lost in the night's black shadows.

It was a lonely spot, well shaped for murder.

Antrim's look was watchful as he moved into the willow brush whose fluttering tops lay against the wall. The creek, he thought, did not sound quite right; did not sound quite so loud as it ought to have; not so loud as refraction from rock should have made it.

And then he was through the wind-trembled growth and night lay pitch black before him, a black unbleached by any paler shade, unleavened by a shape any blacker. His outstretched hands could not find any wall, could not touch anything above him.

It was then that he heard the whisper—the soft exhalation of an outpushed breath . . .

Sundance stared at Jake keenly, an obsidian glint in his angled glance. "So you can show us the gold, eh?"

He appeared to mull something over in his mind for a moment; then he smiled very thinly and looked at Cope. "Did you hear that, Taiban? He can show us the gold."

"Yeah." Cope scowled. "What's holdin' him back? *I* ain't sittin' on his shirttail."

Sundance nodded at Jake. "Seein's believing. Trot it out, if you've got it."

"In the mornin'—" Jake said; but Sundance's glance stopped him.

"There's a lot might happen between now an' morning."

The gambler, Cope, began sharpening his knife

again. There was an evil glint in the man's slatted stare; and Jake's look, brushing the man's bandaged cheek, flinched away as though the knife's cold steel were at his throat already.

He lurched to his feet, both hands spread to the wall.

"I—" Jake's supper turned over inside him. This was not the way he had planned this at all. He'd had no intention of showing that gold—no intention whatever of admitting he had it. He'd been bluffed, browbeaten into that foolish admission. No telling what the sight of that gold would do to these loot hungry wolves he had brashly lured here.

"Well," Sundance said. "If you've got it, let's see it."

Like a man in his sleep Jake Gauze turned and lumbered to the fireplace. He bent and thrust an arm up the chimney. Then he came tramping back to the others again, dropped a sooty poke on the table.

It made a dull, metallic sound as it hit, and Cope shot out a trembling hand; but Sundance said: "Just a minute, Cope," and coolly picked up the poke himself.

He broke the knots with his thick, strong fingers and spilled the sack's content out on the table where it lay, dully gleaming in the lamp's smoky light.

Greed was a shine in Cope's glinting eyes.

Sundance poked the ingot with the end of a finger. "What else you got up that chimney, Jake?"

Jake stood like a man struck across the face.

Sundance smiled at him, thinly, slyly. "It was your idea; you said we'd pool our knowledge— like those Three Guardsmen. Remember? One for all, and all for one."

He chuckled maliciously and Jake Gauze shivered.

"Well," he said then. "What's it goin' to be, pardner? This gold's all right, but it ain't the main thing. You got something else that's a heap more important . . . Ah—you wasn't by no chance thinking to cross us, was you?"

Cope turned and looked at him. Felt of his knife again.

Jake's shoulders drooped like a quirted cur. A groan welled out of him; a sound of anguish. This Sundance knew how to torture a man.

The wish rose in Jake to defy big Sundance. But the wish was as far as his nerve would take him. Sundance's stare seemed to read Jake's thinking.

"What the hell, Jake," he said. "We're your friends. Don't be foolish. Better to split than not to get any. If it comes to a showdown we can find it without you."

"So why the hell should we split with him?" Cope said. He tossed the knife back and forth in his hands and Jake, with a curse, went back to the chimney.

The other two bent to see what he'd brought them.

A soiled scrap of paper, much wrinkled with handling.

"It don't mean much," Jake told them sulkily, "without you know which one's Davis Mountain. It's just them instructions Zwing Hunt wrote out."

Peering over his shoulder they studied Hunt's scrawling. "You're right," Cope scowled. "We knew this much already." And Sundance nodded, glance reflective, considering. "Still and all—"

"Well," Jake glowered, "you was hellbent t' see it. It's your turn now. Let's see—"

"Why, I supposed you knew, Jake," Sundance smiled. "We don't have anything. Not a thing but the rumors which are common property."

He grinned at Jake blandly. "You kind of jumped to conclusions if you figured different.

We been pokin' around—you were right about that part; but we hadn't a blasted thing to go on . . . just a chance word from Grounds it was near this canyon."

ELEVEN

Antrim, crouched on the balls of his feet, tipped his six shooter up and hung there, moveless, while a cricket sound rose two full octaves and nothing else disturbed the night.

Abruptly, then, he laughed, aloud, its curtness flavored with an ironic derision that was geared to the restive stamp of a hoof as a horse, dead ahead, pawed the ground impatiently.

There was nobody here but that nickering bronc. He should have known as much, he told himself, for bushwhackers seldom ran in pairs and only a fool would try again where one ambush had failed already. Excess caution would be the death of him yet.

Holstering his gun he shoved through the brush. The hidden horse softly winnied again as a match burst to flame in the man's cupped palm.

Antrim saw the horse—there were two of them, really. A stud and a filly that was rising four. In height they were little over fourteen hands. But their look, the clean lines of them, more than offset any prejudice this might raise. Antrim loved horses and had no need to be told that here were a pair easily worth a king's ransom.

The stud was a chestnut, the filly a gray. Both had intelligent contemplative eyes that scanned every move of the man before them.

The young stallion's head was short and wide. It's dark, liquid eyes were twin luminous ovals set deep in the middle of its wedge-shaped skull. Its forehead was convex, bulging, shield-like above a nasal profile that was sloping, dish style. There was a diagonal flare to the cut of its nostrils; and in all these things the filly's head was identical save that only, perhaps, its shape was somewhat longer. Both had the same large, disklike jawbones, wide between the jowls; both had the same small, firm lower lip.

They were a picture, those two, that he had long remembered.

He had never forgotten those slim, graceful bodies, those beautifully arched necks or that high tail carriage. It had been a long time, but he had not forgotten.

Thought of where he had seen them turned his gray eyes somber. Never, he decided, would their owner have sold them. There might, after all, be some fire in the smoke of Jake's tales of horse runners plying their trade on this trail again.

Ibn Allah this chestnut stud was called. He was gaunt just now, looking rough and abused. His mane was a snarl and there were burrs in the tail that had once been the pride of all Torreon. Yet Antrim was in no doubt that this was Ibn Allah. Nothing could ever disguise that action, the inherent beauty of iron-hard muscles, the bold, jutting head or the fierce, proud spirit that looked out of his eyes. He was a horse in a thousand—fit mount for a king; and, indeed, in his own unique way Don Lorenzo Enrico Porfiro Fanegas y Lugo was by way of being right considerable of a king: he was Governor of Coahuila.

It was while he'd been checking the Matamoras end of Zwing Hunt's tale that Antrim first had seen these horses. Some kind of Mexican fiesta. There had been a great parade and Don Lorenzo had ridden at its head upon the back of Ibn Allah who had been vastly praised by the multitude. At one point Don Lorenzo had been pleased to exhibit Ibn Allah's intelligence, and had stopped the parade for that purpose. With the rabble cheering lustily Ibn Allah had shaken hands with his master. He had shown comprehension of more than twenty words. Don Lorenzo, with no sign or signal, had abruptly fallen prone on the ground; immediately Ibn Allah had composed himself beside him. After a moment, as though wounded, the old Don had crawled across the animal's legs and draped himself across its back. "Arise!" he said in Spanish, and with extreme care Ibn Allah rose. There were many things Ibn Allah knew and he could run like a very antelope. There was a tale afoot in Torreon that no horse in all Coahuila could pass him at two miles.

Antrim's match burnt out and he struck another seeking to find what means had been used to keep these horses safe here. They had been tied, each by a hind foot, to a stake driven deep in the ground with lengths of horsehair rope. This gave them freedom of movement to browse the grass growing rankly here, stopping them only short of the willow growth that masked their prison from the trail beyond. They got their water from a tiny fissure which had been eroded through the loamy bank.

This hideout was a beauty; it seemed almost built for the purpose. A natural fault in the canyon wall. Not a cave, exactly, but a sort of cove, a forty-foot dent in the sandstone wall . . .

Cove!

Antrim stopped in his thinking and looked about him while a kind of pucker narrowed down his eyes. There had been such a cove in Zwing Hunt's story. In the Davis Mountain Canyon, between Gum Spring and Silver Spring, where the canyon floor was overgrown with brush, the canyon wall curved inward, Hunt had said, to form a shallow cove. It was, of course, quite possible the outlaws, among themselves, had deliberately renamed Skeleton Canyon as an added means of protecting their cache. This *might* be the elusive "Davis" canyon; this *might* be the cove Zwing Hunt had mentioned. If it were, then somewhere close there should be what time and the elements had left of that wagon—the burnt wagon four horses had brought out of Mexico piled high with the plunder of Monterrey and Matamoros.

If it were.

There should also be, within this pocket, the slender stone that was gouged with two crosses. Guy Antrim decided he would have a look.

He was moving forward when a new thought stopped him.

It might be better to do his looking in daylight. No telling how far this matchlight traveled. It mightn't show ten feet beyond the brush. It might, however, show a great deal farther. And who could say who'd be using this trail? There might be others abroad tonight; or the man who had fired and missed and fled might not have fled far, or might return with companions for another installment.

It would be a heap smarter to do his looking in daylight.

Grimly nodding, Antrim turned to retrace his steps; but Ibn Allah nickering reproachfully, stopped the man in mid-stride, and he wheeled, tramping back through the murk to the stallion's side.

There had been many a stud in Antrim's experience that a man would do well to keep plumb away from; but he felt no fear of Ibn Allah. No horse intelligent as this had proved would have any mean or vicious impulse—at least, Antrim felt, Ibn Allah had not.

He approached without hesitancy. He slid a hand up under its mane and spoke to the horse, stroked the arch of its neck, felt the smooth, rippling muscles beneath his fingers.

Ibn Allah whickered with joy—wagged his

flaxen tail like a tickled puppy. He rubbed his head against Antrim's shoulder, buried his muzzle beneath the man's arm while Antrim talked to him. Now and again, as if to show his spirit, he would paw the ground and snort a bit; and twice he reached down to sniff Antrim's boot toes as though he would memorize the scent of this fellow, playfully twiggling the leather with his lips. Then he raised up suddenly and shook his head, exhaled a gusty breath and groaned through his teeth as though fed up with solitude—such a mournful sound it fetched a laugh from Antrim.

"Never mind," he said, slapping the stallion's chest, "you'll be quittin' this place before you're many hours older—that's a promise, horse. Straight from Guy Antrim."

"If we're lucky, that is," he added under his breath.

Lamplight raveled the squares of Jake's windows, split across the broad sills and yellowed the porch planks. Beyond the rocks the gun-gray drab of the eastern sky was brushed with the hint of a coming pink. Dawn was not far off—not much farther than a handful of minutes, yet the lamp still burned and Jake's gruff tones made a steady rumble through the yard's utter quiet.

There was a somber quality to this pre-dawn hush that turned Antrim's thoughts to the creek-bank gunplay, to the man who had opened that treacherous attack. It seemed logical to suspect it was someone from this place. It could have been Sundance, but it was probably Kerrick. Recollection gave Antrim a picture of Kerrick slamming out of the house while he'd been held in talk by that woman from Tombstone. "Lizette" she'd been billed in the old days. A dancer. But now she was calling herself "Lolita"—Lolita Garcia. He wondered which was her real name.

Burying one's past behind a new monicker was quite the fashion—he had done it himself. He'd no wish to be known as Luther King, the ex stage robber. Similar considerations had presumably prompted the girl's shift in names. It was all right with Antrim; but he could not help wondering what had brought her here. He wondered, too, what kind of reception she'd got from a man already overburdened with company.

Not too fulsome a one, he guessed. It might be to her Jake was talking now.

He remembered then how Kerrick, soft swearing, had gone stamping off to the pole corral; and he nodded, grimly. It was Kerrick, like as not, who had fired that shot. Was Kerrick the man

GUNSLICK MOUNTAIN 117

who had stolen those horses?

More like to be Jake, Antrim thought, lips curling. It hardly seemed likely Bat Kerrick would know of that slick little cove so well screened by those willows.

Yet it hadn't been Jake who had taken that shot at him. Jake's feet were too big to have left that sign—those small, dainty tracks Guy Antrim had found.

Jake's talk stopped suddenly. The house door opened and Jake's gaunt shape showed against the lamplight. "That you, Kerrick?" he demanded testily. "By Gawd—"

"No," Antrim said. "It's me—Guy Antrim."

There was a strained, ugly silence. Gauze said queerly: "Oh." Then, belligerently: "So you've come back, hev you? Come up here. I got some things t' say t' you."

"Presently," Antrim drawled, and rode on. He heard Jake curse; heard the door slammed shut again.

So Kerrick was still out. Kerrick hadn't come back yet. Maybe one of those shots Antrim fired had marked him. Or, it might just be, Kerrick thought he'd been recognized and was cutting a shuck for some greener pasture lest return to this place bring retribution.

Antrim turned his horse toward the jaws of the stable.

Then he changed his mind. He might as well look at the hoofs of those horses. You never could tell. It *might* not have been Kerrick; it might be one of the others, Sundance or Cope, who had taken that chancey shot by the creekbank. Better see now if he could match that hoof track. If the horse was here he could forget about Kerrick. Kerrick might have gone off somewhere else entirely.

Kerrick had.

Approaching the corral Antrim's horse shied violently, went back on its haunches snorting with fright.

Keeping hold of the reins Antrim slipped from the saddle.

It was not full light, but he saw the trouble at once. Just before him. In the hoof-tracked dust a sprawled form lay, strangely crumpled and still —very dead.

Bat Kerrick.

TWELVE

Blood was a dark, wet stain twixt his shoulders.

Antrim's widening look did not linger there but raced on to the horse that, quiet, nearby stood saddled, its reins carefully tied to a rail by the gatepost.

Antrim crossed to it quickly, bent and with soft words picked up its feet. It was not the horse with the ill-fitting shoe whose hoof had left the track by the creek bank. This horse had not been lately ridden. It had never gone out of this yard at all. It had gone no farther than it stood right now.

There lay its tracks, plain as paint in the dust.

There were other tracks, too.

Antrim's upwheeling glance, cocked to follow them, went suddenly narrow and extremely still.

The planes of his cheeks, in this brightening light, showed an instant discipline as Sundance drawled, "Some takes a mite longer than others . . ."

He let his words trail off. A lazy smile curled his lips with patronage. "It's all right with me. What happens to these guys ain't no skin off *my* nose."

"If you're tryin'," Antrim said, "to connect this stiff—" but Sundance's shrug disclaimed any effort.

"I never dig my spurs in the other man's business. Kill the whole push if you want to, bucko."

With a smug, hateful smile Sundance turned and tramped off.

Antrim watched him cross the yard toward the house; heard the grumbling drone of Jake's talk quit. Heard the bang of a door.

Then Idy Red's voice, high and angry, said: "Either *she* gits out or *I* do—*one!*"

The porch boards skreaked under Sundance's boots.

With a scowl Antrim turned and bent down over Kerrick. It took all his strength to budge the knife that was buried to the hilt in Kerrick's back. But he got it finally and, straightening grimly, bleak of eye, tight-lipped, he made for the house.

He hit the porch just in time to hear Sundance say, "He's down by the gate—your new ramrod's with him."

Antrim crossed the planks in one bold stride, yanked open the door and stopped by the table. "You forgot your knife," he said to Sundance; and buried the blade's bloody point in the table.

Jake choked on an oath. The girl from Tombstone swayed. But Sundance, coolly smiling, said:

"It ain't *my* knife."

"It's—"

"Nope. I can't claim the corpse for you, either, bucko."

Twin dimples dented the man's round cheeks; he grinned at Antrim, enjoying this hugely. He remarked as though expounding some profound truth, "This is geared to patterns. One thing leads to another. A natural law, just like night following day. When a man hires a gun packer there's bound to be blood spilled."

"If you think that—" Antrim began; but Jake's bugged eyes never left the knife.

The Tombstone girl's dark look stayed expressionless.

Idy Red's glance, from the blade to Antrim, told in its horror of some cherished conviction all too adequately demonstrated.

"That—that Bowie . . ." Jake said.

The lines of his face looked more old, more haggard. The glint of his stare held the glaze of a fever. He half raised a hand but it shook and he dropped it. "That's Cope's knife!" he blurted.

"Sure it's Cope's," Sundance jeered. "Don't tell us you figured he'd be usin' his own!"

"If you'd habla in English—"

The burly Sundance chuckled. "I guess you know what Jake hired you for."

"If you're tryin' to say I killed Bat Kerrick—"

"I didn't see nobody else proppin' up the scenery."

"*You was there!*"

"I sure was, bucko."

"Gawd's sake, you two—quit the wranglin', will you?" Jake mopped his face with the back of a shirtsleeve. "If he's dead, he's dead. Argyin' about it ain't goin' t' he'p him. Poke never killed him; Poke jest rode in—"

"Yeah. From where?" grinned Sundance. "From round the back of the barn, for all *you* know. If this guy didn't kill him what are you paying him for?"

Antrim said through locked teeth: "If you reckon I killed him why not do something—"

"No skin off *my* nose," Sundance smiled. "I told you that, didn't I?"

"Then—"

"I just want to get it straight for the record; I don't want you going around telling *I* killed him."

Sundance turned away like he was done with Antrim. He bowed toward the girls, said apologetically, "I'm sorry you ladies had to be hearing this business. I'll not be keeping you longer. I'll be saying good night to you." He bowed again, turned and left the room. The sound of his spurs jingled off toward the stable.

"Where's Cope?" Antrim said, finally breaking the silence.

Jake shrugged, shoved himself from the chair and crossed to a cupboard, coming back with a bottle. He broke its neck on the edge of the table, sloshed some whisky in a glass and downed it; grimaced. He filled the glass again, then his glance crossed Antrim's. "You—you reckon he done it?"

"I don't know," Antrim said. "First thing I knew my horse was back on his haunches, snortin'. I could see a man's shape in the dust by the gate. I got down an' went over. This Sundance opened his mouth about that time. He was behind Kerrick's bronc in the shadow of them peppers. The bronc's reins was tied to a rail by the gatepost."

Antrim considered. "It don't look like Kerrick—"

"He's been gone half the night—since right after you quit us. Prob'ly jest got back."

"He never left the yard," Antrim said. "I took a look at his tracks. That bronc he saddled never went no farther than where he was tied at. Question is, who tied him? If it was Sundance . . ."

A sweat came out on Jake's cheeks again. He shirtsleeved it off. Then he said, short and grufflike, "Chances are, it was. If he was by them pepper trees when you saw him—"

"You got no proof he was any place around theah!" Idy Red, eyes indignant, broke in on them angrily. "All you got is this devil's word fo' it! The word," she flared scornfully, "of a cheap border gun packer! Anyone c'ld see he's tryin' t' lay it on Sundance. He's layin' it on him because he's scared—"

Antrim said, tight and short: "I ain't laid *nothing* on him—yet."

"Well, it ain't f'om lack of tryin', I swear! Of all the killin', lyin' sidewinders—"

"You shet up," Jake snarled, "an' git t' your

bed! I've took all yo' lip I'm a mind to fer *one* night! G'wan—*git!*"

"An' you, Poke," he said, flinging it over his shoulder, "go take you a look at them tracks ag'in. I'll tend t' these hellcats. Come back in a while an' we'll thresh this over—I got a notion or two thet might work out fer you. Anyway, come back."

There was a wind blowing up the canyon and the sun's red tide was just washing the rim when Antrim breasted the dust of the yard. There was anger in him and a kind of grudging respect for the way that fool girl had stuck up for Sundance. That man was a cool, slick customer; of a kind to fool wiser heads than hers. That she liked him was obvious. She had liked big Sundance the first time she saw him; had been impressed by his manners and the cool, easy grace of him.

For that, Guy Antrim did not blame her. Big, magnetic, vital, Sundance was indeed a fine figure of a man and had probably fooled a right smart of folks with his swaggering ways and his gold-toothed smile. His eyes, when he chose, could look deceptively merry, and the dimples that dented those round, dark cheeks made connivery and Sundance appear total strangers.

But Antrim could see to the black, rotten core of him—could uncover the vileness, the greed and viciousness that would govern this man behind his fine airs and graces. He was like a coral snake, Antrim thought—mighty pretty to look at and mighty deadly.

"Go take you another look at them tracks," Jake had said; and Antrim, shouldering his way through the wind, resolved to. He wanted a look at the horses' hoofs anyway, having still in mind that track by the trailside.

Then a thought came to mind that creased his cheeks in a scowl. He should have taken a look at Sundance's tracks—not because Sundance might have taken that shot at him back by the creek bank, but because Sundance's tracks, in the dust of this yard, might plainly have solved the sudden death of Bat Kerrick.

With all this wind it was probably too late now.

He would have a look, anyhow.

The sun stood free of the canyon rim when he paused by the place he had found Bat Kerrick. The man's dead body had been removed; nor was the saddled horse longer tied to the gate's rail. These matters had been nicely taken care of—by Sundance, probably, with his long foresightedness. And the tracks of the gate-hitched horse and his own had been well intermingled with careful efficiency. The wind had erased all boot tracks completely.

Antrim crossed to the peppers and, lounging against one, eyed the broncs in the pole corral. The one he had ridden was there amongst them, unsaddled, unbridled, gnawing bark from the snubbing post. They were a good bunch of horses, as range horses go; and there was one, of the kind called "claybank," of a solid cream color, that was considerably better than the run of its kind. This was a compact horse, short of back, close coupled, deep-middled and heavily muscled. He had a heavy jaw, quiet eye and small ear. He had a fairly short neck and his chest was wide. He would stand, Antrim gauged, about 15.2 and would weigh pretty close to eleven hundred pounds.

"A lot of horse," Antrim murmured, straightening.

"Sure is," a voice said, "if you mean that claybank. Worth right considerable of any man's money."

Antrim casually turning saw Taiban Cope.

How the man had gotten there was not the point; that he'd managed to do so was definite warning. It was time Guy Antrim called a stop to his musing. This was no kind of crew to get absentminded with. Not unless you were hunting a harp or a halo.

"Yours?" Antrim said, lifting up his eyebrows.

Cope shook his head. "I can't afford such stuff."

"Jake's?" asked Antrim.

Cope permitted a pale smile to brush his lip corners. "Nope. That claybank was Kerrick's— his private horse."

"Kerrick's!" Antrim said. "That ain't the horse he had tied to the gatepost."

"I wouldn't know about that," said the gambler, and got a cigar from a stuffed vest pocket. He bit off an end and held a match to the weed. "It's Kerrick's—you've my word for it, Antrim. I recall very clearly the occasion he acquired it. It was over near Lockhart a couple of years ago; the cards really talked for Bat that night. . . ."

Cope paused reflectively, took the cigar from his mouth and eyed it, turning it over in his long, slim fingers. "What will you take for that map— cash talking?"

"What map?" Antrim said.

His eyes met the eyes of the gambler straightly.

"Zwing Hunt's map to the Curly Bill plunder." And the gambler's eyes, bright and hard, met Antrim's. A crease of amusement quirked his mouth. "Let's spread our cards on the table, shall we? I'm pretty well certain you've got the map. I would like to have it. What will you take for it?"

"I'm not sure," Antrim said, "I'd care to get rid of it. In any event you'd find the price pretty steep."

"I'd expect to," Cope said. "But the word 'steep' is relative—a matter of opinion. Make it steep as you want. Let's hear it."

He could not quite hide the eagerness in him. It showed in the rush of those two last words, in the glint of his eye, in his quickened breathing. "Name it, man—name it."

"You'll not get that map," Antrim said, "till you drop me."

He reached out and caught Taiban Cope by his shirtfront, lifting the pale, gangling man to his boot toes. "Not," he repeated, "till you drop me—*savvy?*"

He stared deep into the man's squirming soul. He dropped him suddenly, stepping back disgusted. "You're a small-bore gun for such a large notion. Better stick to your card games, Cope, and forget it."

THIRTEEN

When the man had gone Antrim scowled a little.

He wheeled abruptly and went into the stable.

It had been less than wise to use the gambler that way. Like most little men Cope would long remember it—would cherish it, even, till, poisoning his every secret thought, it would drive the man berserk, to vengeful action.

Antrim frowned, swore softly. But there were things about Cope which he found more urgent, more puzzling, problematical, than predicting the course of the man's future actions. Certain aspects of his talk invited looking into. In particular, his remarks about that claybank gelding. Kerrick's, Cope had named it. But if the horse were Kerrick's why had Kerrick readied another? Why, also, afterwards, had Kerrick tied that other—or hadn't he? What obscure pattern of thought or impulse had been animating Kerrick when death had come out of the dark and stabbed him?

What had put in Cope's head the notion that Antrim was possessor of the map? How had Taiban Cope come to call him "Antrim?" Jake's introduction had named him "Poker Face." Had Gauze later seen fit to amend this—or had Cope learned from the girl?—from that hussy from Tombstone—that Lolita-nee-Lizette; or was it Lizette-nee-Lolita?

If *she* had told them his name was Antrim, might she not also have disclosed the facts of his background and have told them as well that he was Luther King—the man once jailed for the Benson stage job?

This thing had more angles than a pile of split kindling.

What had brought the girl out here, anyway? Was she catering to the animal instincts of Jake, or was she here for some deeper, some more far-reaching reason? Was she the one who had followed them from town?—the cause of Jake's many backward-flung glances? Or had it been that tall buck, Sundance, who had trailed them?

Antrim leaned against a stall-side, thinking.

Did Cope *know* he had Hunt's map, or was Cope merely guessing? Was it generally supposed, or . . . What had Bat Kerrick been doing with all those hours between leaving the house and being found by Antrim? How much of that time had Bat been lying there dead?

Might be a good idea, Antrim thought, if he lost no more time in examining the cavvy for the drygulcher's horse with that bad hind shoe. It was entirely possible of course the man had no connection with Jake's outfit. Either way, continued health demanded that he find out pronto.

His shape was bent to slide between the bars when Jake's gruff call from the porch brought him upright.

For a moment he hung there, mightily tempted to let Jake stew and go on with this business. But common sense prevailed. It would do him no good to be found with the horses. Better get on up there. Jake was not of the type that waits with patience.

He was starting houseward when his boot jogged a rock. The rock jogged his mind and he stopped, eyes narrowing.

That map!

He had better get rid of it. Packing it around was like packing thawed dynamite. It was worse, now that these rannies suspected him of having it.

His glance, raking around, brought up at the stable. The building was founded on an erection of creek rock, laid without binder, rock atop rock. Be quick and simple to stuff Hunt's map in between a pair of them—and who would think to look for it there?

He took off his hat to get the paper, thankful the stable screened him from Jake. He pulled down the band, shook the hat. He stared blankly. And then, very softly, he swore.

"Women," Jake said, "is hell. Take 'em any way you've a mind to. There ain't nothin', hardly, a man kin do that'll bring 'im more grief than a unwed woman. Why, I've seen . . ."

He left it there. Kind of snorted, scowled, wryly grinned a little. "I don't guess you come here t' hear about women. Haul up thet chair, Poke, an' rest your fanny. Here—hev a smoke? Well, I don't blame you; ain't much kin beat a han'-rolled Durham. Y' ain't never felt quite right in yer mind, hev you?—I mean about me—about this layout I got here. You bin figurin', likely, I never got you out here t' stand off rustlers.

"I didn't, neither."

There was a calculant glint in the glance he gave Antrim, a beady alertness that was urgent and probing, that was watchful, inquiring, that was moved by a need not readily determinable.

"There's rustlers, all right. Horse thiefs, mostly. Every two—three weeks they come up this trail. But that ain't what I got you out here for."

He smoothed the leather of his scuffed black chaps. "I got you out here 'cause I knew damn well I was goin' t' need he'p. . . . Well—whyn't you say somethin'?—ast a few questions?"

Antrim drew up his knees and eyed Jake across them. "I reckon you'll tell me what you want me to know."

Jake, staring, snorted. "You're a cool one, all right. You're colder'n a well chain—an' that's the kind I need. You ain't no everyday fly-by-night gunhawk; you got a head on your shoulders. I need that, too. I'm goin' t' tell you somethin'. I was takin' a chance when I hired you, Antrim. I wasn't noways sure you was the kind t' fit in here.

"I ain't sure now. But I got t' hev backin'. I got t' hev it quick, or them gawddamn wolves is goin' t' lift my scalp. So here's what I'll do, boy. I'll make you a sportin' proposition; I'll lay my cards right out on the table so you'll know where you're at every step of the way. That's fair enough, ain't it?"

"I can tell a heap better after I've seen your cards."

"You'll see 'em all right; Jake Gauze, by Gawd, don't doublecross no one. When I deal a fella in I deal 'im *all the way* in."

"Get at it then. What you waitin' on?"

Jake Gauze threw a look at the doors, at the windows. He tipped his gaunt shoulders forward then. "I'm goin' t' tell you somethin' I wouldn't tell another livin' man. By Gawd, I—"

"Choke off the blat an' get at it then."

Jake's bulbous nose abruptly twitched like a rabbit's. His cheeks creased a scowl; but when he spoke he said reasonably enough, "It's important you savvy I know what I'm talkin' about —an' by Gawd, I ort to! I rode with Curly Bill in the ol' days; next t' Ringo an' Hughes I was the one Bill most counted on. Don't ast me why—I never could figure it; but it's so. I knowed a hell's brew of secrets none of them other boys ever did cotton to."

"You'll be knowin', I guess, where the Curly Bill plunder's hid."

"By Gawd I ort to. But I don't! Curly Bill hisself never knowed where they hid the stuff.

'Course he knowed where some of it was; so did I. But thet fox-sly hound, Zwing Hunt, an' his pardner, dug it up one night an' hauled it off t' thet goddam mountain. Every last peso! Every 'dobe dollar!

" 'Fore we c'ld grab 'em an' git the truth outen 'em, Grounds was killed an' thet smart Zwing Hunt had lammed off t' Texas. Bill sent me an' Jim Hughes after him, but he was dead an' planted time we'd got him tracked down t' his uncle's place. He'd bin in thet fight at the Stockton ranch an' the wound he got there finally done fer 'im. Curly an' the boys was plumb fit t' be tied when they found out how he'd put it over on 'em. But there you are—that's the truth as Gawd hears me."

Against his wish Antrim was inclined to believe him. The ring of truth was in Jake's testy words and the twist of his lips showed the bitterness of them.

"Well," Antrim said, "where do I come in?"

"That's what I'm comin' at," Jake rumbled gruffly. "You claimed las' night you wanted in on it. You showed you knowed right smart about it. So—" Jake's bright little eyes met Antrim's fairly. "Here's what I'll do, boy. I know this country inside out. I know, by Gawd, where thet mountain is. You th'ow in your map of the counts an' paces an' I'll pool my savvy of the country with you; jest you an' me—see? Anythin' we git we'll split fifty-fifty."

Antrim eyed him intently.

"Who said anything about me havin' a map?"

"Not a damn soul. Not a shrinkin' soul, boy— but you got one awright. You got Hunt's map. An' with what I got it's a cinch—be jest like rollin' off a log. Y' ain't doubtin' it, are you?"

"What about those hardcases? Where are they comin' in?"

"They ain't," Jake said, and his look was baleful. "I've had about all I kin take off them guys."

He shaped up a smoke from his sack of Durham, licked the paper, pushed the pouch toward Antrim. "What do you say, boy? We goin' t' show these polecats where t' git off at?"

"You're expectin' me to take a heap on faith, ain't you?"

"How's that?"

"I ain't seen nothin' yet that proves you know anything with regard to that mountain."

Jake's bright little eyes grinned back at him. "I ain't seen nothin' yet that proves you got Hunt's map. But thet's all right; I ain't askin' to. I ain't givin' you the dope on thet mountain, neither—not till I'm sure you're goin' t' play square with me. Way I look at it, thet's all thet's standin' twixt me an' the graveyard. But if you'll stick with me, by Gawd we'll clean up here."

Antrim pushed back in his chair and stared at Jake. He let speculation color his glance. All he had worked for these last long years was here before him, was locked in the conscienceless mind of this fellow—of this scheming Jake who would cross a man up with no more qualms than a centipede. This was the contact toward which he'd been working so persistently and continually ever since the night he had talked with Hunt's uncle.

Yet now that he faced him on the man's own terms Antrim felt no triumph, no sense of satisfaction. He felt a strong unease, an edgy need of caution. He knew he would make this deal with Jake, but he did not trust the man. Jake would do what he had to toward keeping the bargain; he would do that much and not a hair's weight more. Jake had claimed his knowledge of the mountain's location was all that stood between himself and death. Hunt's map was all that stood between Guy Antrim and death. What would happen if they learned he no longer had it was not, Antrim thought, any subject for guesswork. He'd be killed out of hand if this bunch could manage it; and either Jake or Cope might try to kill him for it.

He felt sure enough now who had stolen it from him. While he lay asleep in the brush that first day, fast thinking Sundance must have thoroughly searched him.

But two could play at that kind of a game. And two could play at brother Jake's game, likewise.

"Also," Jake said, "I've got Hunt's written instructions. Howsomever I ain't countin' 'em as a basis fer partnership; these other squirts have seen 'em so I'll th'ow 'em in gratis. They got t' crowdin' me last night—"

"If you've got the instructions," Antrim mentioned coolly, "you won't hardly be needin' the map, nor me."

Jake said, "I thought about that. Look—I'll tell you the truth, boy. Them instructions ain't worth a damn without you've got the map. 'Cause why? Because thet stinker, Hunt, never put nothin' in 'em t' give you direction. They say 'From such-an'-such go three steps to so-an'-so—such tripe as that! No north or south nor anythin' else to 'em. Nope— I'm needin' you boy. Is it a deal or ain't it?"

Jake Gauze peered up into his face .

Antrim wondered how much of Jake's talk was dependable. Precious little, probably. A man would have to watch Jake all of the way.

Strangely enough then, Guy Antrim smiled. The smile toughened his look and leaked the mildness out of him. "What about that cove?" he said.

"Cove?"

Jake looked blank.

"You hear all right."

"I dunno what you're talkin' about. Cove! *What* cove?"

"You wouldn't be knowin' about that cove up the canyon? Or about them horses? You expect me to believe that? Right on your doorstep, an' you not know it? If that's the kind of a pardner you are—"

"Hold on," Jake growled ."When I pardner a man by Gawd I'll skate acrost hell's ice with the man if he can show me any reason I ort to. But when you talk about coves an' horses—"

"Okay," Antrim said. "Mebbe I been havin' a pipe dream. Mebbe I imagined that cove—an' that shot you threw at me—"

"Shot!"

Jake mopped at his cheeks with the back of a sleeve, but the move didn't hide the look of his eyes. He said again, "I—I don't know what you're talkin' about."

"What are you scared of then?" Antrim asked.

Jake backed out of his chair like a spider. Stood with crouched shoulders against the wall. "I ain't," he snarled, "scared of nothin', damn you!"

But the words were a lie. Their tone convicted him. The shake of his hand showed him badly rattled.

Antrim looked at Jake's boots. Too large for the track he had seen by the trailside.

Back of Antrim the door opened.

FOURTEEN

Jake's eyes looked trapped.

"There's somebody coming," Sundance said.

Jake's lips writhed back from his yellow teeth. But he did not speak, nor did Antrim speak; the sound of Sundance's laugh came mockingly. "Don't stand there, Jake, like a bronc with the colic. Go make your friend welcome. What do *I* care who you ask out here? Ask the whole damn country if you think it will help you."

He crossed to the table, coolly rested a hip there. He swung his leg and regarded Antrim. "Jake managed to talk you into this yet?"

"And why," Antrim said, "should that interest you?"

"Anything interests me that touches that treasure."

"That why you killed Kerrick?"

Sundance took his hip off the table. His lips quit smiling. A gusty breath fell out of him and a pale glint cut through the depths of his stare.

"I don't take that talk off no one," he said.

Silence crowded the walls of the room. Then Antrim said: "The road's still open."

"You better get up on a horse then and use it."

He folded his gloves with a meticulous care. He looked at Antrim with his eyes half shut and laid the gloves on the edge of the table.

The silence grew.

Jake's eyes were enormous.

A mockingbird lifted its voice outside and the noontime sun through a tree's still foliage laced a network of shadow across the big man's legs. Antrim looked at his boots.

Sundance's ruddy skin was a parchment tight-spread across the jut of his cheekbones. He said in a tone too calm to be real:

"You goin' or ain't you?"

"Ain't," Antrim said, and Sundance leaped.

The man coming up the canyon reined his black horse around a huge red boulder and beheld Jake's ranch at the forks of the way where a trail turned west toward the smoky haze of the San

Simon Valley. He pulled up the black and got out a cigar while his eyes took in the bright view of Jake's buildings.

He was an average sized man in a stovepipe hat who had once dealt a bank in a Tombstone chance parlor. He had, below his pale hazel eyes, a generously proportioned, slightly updished nose. A heavy mustache hid his mouth from view and a square, cleft chin imparted to him an air of strong resolution quite out of harmony with the facts of his past.

He preferred to be known as a gentleman gambler, but those who knew him declared Pete Spence jumped claims a heap better than he handled the cards. When his luck had been out, in the old days, Pete had not been above restocking his larder by donning a mask and exhibiting his six-shooter.

The payrolls for the Bisbee mines had used to come in on the Benson stage, to be later transferred to the Bisbee conveyance, which was hauled by four horses instead of six and was therefore slower on the uphill grades. Pete and the drivers of the Bisbee stage had grown well acquainted during his operations; but the law had eventually put an end to these. Pete knew all about the heat at Yuma. It was after the governor had pardoned him that Pete took a hand in the miners' problems.

Still regarding Jake's yonder ranch house, Pete took off his hat and dabbed at his forehead with a dainty wisp of blue, laced cambric. After which he sighed, ran a hand around his collar and adjusted the set of his black bow tie. His mining income had about played out and he thought he would look up his old friend Cope, who had left word in town he could be found out at Jake's place.

But, now that he sat with Jake's place in the crotch of his gazing, Pete began to have qualms concerning his brashness in coming here. There were quite a few rumors romping around about Jake; they were mostly unpleasant, like the feel of this canyon with its heritage of violence. It wasn't only Mexicans who had fed their blood to these thirsty sands; many a man who'd come into this place had left his bones for the buzzards and coyotes.

He seemed to hear in the sunny stillness the soft, plodding hoofs of an oncoming mule train. But that was sheer fancy. No mule trains used this canyon now; nothing used it but Jake Gauze and his cattle.

Pete Spence got out his blue cambric again,

the unease that was in him grown stronger than ever. He thrust a hand inside his black coat, a prey to sudden chills though the day was stifling. He brought out his six-gun and stared at it thoughtfully. He broke it open and examined its loads, assuring himself it was entirely in readiness to protect his life should the need arise. A flick of his wrist clacked the weapon shut. He gave it a couple of turns by the trigger guard, restoring it carefully to its spring case again.

After which he felt better.

He cocked his hat at a jaunty angle, picked up his reins and lit his cigar. Urging his horse through the heated sand he bolstered his courage with a bawdy song whose heroine was left in a sad predicament when he suddenly stopped, craned forward, listening.

There was a fight going on inside Jake's house; he'd heard enough of such sounds to know. There wasn't no talk—no shouts, no curses; but the impact of flesh on flesh, the stamp of feet, the grunts, the panting—these were sounds he knew every shade of.

Being a cautious man in his sober moments, Pete Spence considered departing at once. But curiosity got the best of him. He swung from the black and catfooted closer.

It was a fight, all right.

The door was open. The floor boards groaned as Spence crossed the porch. He saw Jake Gauze backed against a wall. The ranchman's eyes were bugged like saucers. Then he saw the fighters. They were both big men, both tough, both range bred with strong, hard faces. The one with two guns was a handsome man with curly black hair. He was dressed very flashy. He was confident looking, very sure of himself; quite certain the other man was just where he wanted him.

The other man was crouched in a corner. He had his chin on his chest and his legs looked wobbly. He was a younger man, more rangy, less heavy; a yellow-haired man with a high-boned face that had taken much punishment. By the look of his eyes he could not last much longer.

Pete's glance sawed back to the burly one again. Every detail of build was in this man's favor. He was bigger all over than the yellow-haired man. He had a solidity, a massiveness, a weight too rugged to feel the hurt of blows. There was something, Pete thought, vaguely familiar about him.

Then he saw the man's muscles bunch—saw his shape hurtling forward.

The yellow-haired man went down on his knees.

He was that way when the burly man struck him; and then he was up on his feet again, whirling, as the big man's shape crashed into the wall.

The big man picked himself off the floor. He shook his head as though to still the ringing of it. The smaller man smashed him full in the mouth. It was a terrific blow and he followed it up with two more to the jaw, then a jab to the ear.

The big man's head rolled. His eyes held the glaze of an axe-struck steer's. A groping hand found the wall and clung to it.

The yellow-haired man was all set to finish him when a girl flung out of a yonder room and jammed the muzzle of a gun in his back. Jake Gauze jumped clear of the wall and grabbed her. He wrested the pistol out of her grasp and sent her, cursing, against the fireplace where she crouched, cheeks white, breathing hard, eyes flashing.

"You keep outa this, damn you!" Jake rasped at her balefully.

The yellow-haired man said, "You got enough, Sundance?"

"Never mind—never mind!" the big man growled at him. He weaved away from the wall, pulled his shoulders together. He shook his head, still stupid from punishment. "My time will come —just remember that, bucko. I take care of my debts and I don't forget them."

He lurched past Spence without seeing him, went across the porch and out into the yard.

FIFTEEN

Antrim, turned to look after him, saw the Tombstone man where he stood by the doorway.

The look of those eyes rocked Spence to his bootheels.

Gauze saw him then. He said without bothering to trim his emotions: "What the hell are *you* doin' here?"

"I . . . ah . . . come out to see Cope—"

"This ain't no gamblin' dive—nor it ain't no goddam health resort, neither. Climb back on your hoss, Spence, an' get t' hell outen here."

Pete Spence looked away from Jake's scowling face.

Antrim said, "Maybe this guy is the one that killed Kerrick," and a barbed kind of humor rolled through Jake's stare. "How about it?"

Spence's cheeks went sallow. He seemed to have been caught with a lump in his throat. The lump, by his look, was about to strangle him. All the lines of his face ran together.

He looked, Antrim thought, like a fish out of water.

"I guess," Jake said, "we better send fer John Slaughter."

He lowered an eyelid in Antrim's direction. "Saddle a hoss, Poke, an' fetch him out, will you?"

"Right away," Antrim said.

The man clutched at his shoulder. "Honest to God—I don't know nothin' about it—I never heard of no Kerrick! I ain't never killed nobody!"

"Truth is man's best defense," Antrim said. "If you're tellin' the truth you got no need to worry. The law don't never hamstring the innocent."

Spence saw the dark glitter of his eyes and shivered. "Christ Almighty, Jake! I thought we was friends! You goin' to stan' by an' never lift your hand?"

"D'you think I want *my* neck in a noose?"

"B-but—"

"Git on with it, Poker Face," Jake said blackly. "There's a law in this land an' a man's got t' heed it. The law says anyone that hides a murderer—"

"I never murdered him!" Pete Spence yelled. "I dunno this Kerrick from a barrel of apples— I ain't even *seen* him!"

"We'll take care of that. Tell you what I'll do," Jake said of a sudden. " 'F you want t' save us some trouble an' sign a confe—"

"You'll let me go? You'll let me ride outa here?"

"Well," Jake said, "I'll consider it, anyway . . ."

Antrim, heading for the stable, had plenty to think about. Things were happening too fast— too fast by far. He knew in his bones he should have killed big Sundance. It was not in the fellow's character to forget the hurt of that beating he'd taken. He would bide his time—probably strike without warning after the way of his kind. The look of a snake had been in Sundance's glare—and that girl! That Idy Red!

He could still feel the jab of her gun in his back. He told himself with a wry kind of grin, "When she likes a man she goes whole hog for him."

It was too damned bad she'd hung her liking on Sundance.

What lay behind Jake's fear of the fellow? Jake seemed to wilt every time big Sundance came around. He appeared to work on Jake like a bad case of sunstroke. It was odd, Antrim thought, because Jake showed tough enough when it came to the others. He'd stood up to Bat Kerrick; had been salty enough in his handling of Spence.

Might be worthwhile to find out what lay back of it. Either Sundance had some hold on him, or Jake . . .

It was right there in his thinking that Jake's growl called him.

Jake came lumbering up. "Saddle two broncs. You got to go to town."

"I thought you was runnin'—"

"I ain't talkin' about Spence. I kin handle that fool. It's that damn Lolita. Idy Red won't stay under the same roof with 'er. I got to git her outen here . . ." Jake said irritably: "Damn a man that'll fool around with a woman. I wisht t' hell I'd never laid eyes on 'er!"

"You let Idy Red run your business for you?"

"I don't let *no*body run my business. But there's a limit to what that girl . . ."

"Well, go on," Antrim said; but Jake was all done with talking.

He stood there and looked at Antrim with his eyes gone a little narrow, with his high, flat face unreadable.

Then he wheeled his bony shoulders.

"That's all," he said, and went tramping off.

Antrim got his rope and entered the corral. The horses were quick to sense work ahead. They moved into a weaving muddle, each trying to put himself back of another, getting as far as they could from him, crowding the poles at the corral's far side. Anrtim suddenly remembered he was looking for something.

He had just discovered it when Sundance said: "Goin' for a ride on the dead man's pony?"

Antrim let down the hoof and straightened. Sundance returned his cold stare amusedly. The bruises he'd gathered were still in evidence, but aside from these he seemed quite his old self. He even chuckled when Antrim ignored him.

Antrim tramped through the dust and got his saddle. He heaved it onto the big bronc's back. It was a three-quarters rig, and the sudden yank he gave to the trunk strap puckered the claybank's hide where the fishcord's constriction squeezed the cinch ring.

He stared across his shoulder at Sundance. "For a big guy, mister, you move mighty quiet."

He slipped on the bridle and took his rope off; caught the girl's horse, neat, by a forefoot. "I s'posed you'd be hittin' the high spots by this time."

Sundance grinned. "No bunch-quitter blood in *my* background, bucko."

Antrim saddled Lolita's horse without reply to him. Slipped on its hackamore and led the pair outside the corral.

"Hmm," Sundance drawled, and ironically misquoted, "A jug of wine, jerked beef, and thou beside me—"

One stride brought Antrim hard against him. "If it's another installment you're honin' for . . ."

The big man's dark, bruised cheeks roaned wickedly. "Never put your hand on me again, King. Never get in my way again—"

"Or what?"

"I'll leave it like that. 'Or what,'" Sundance said, and was abruptly smiling, very cool and assured, very broadly tolerant.

"What the hell," he said with a grin. "We're pawin' dirt like a couple of bulls. Let's call it off and get down to business."

"Business?"

The burly Sundance nodded. "Yeah," he said; raked a quick look around, bent toward Antrim with convincing earnestness. He said quietly, "We can use you, King. Even knowing your record we can damn well make a place for you—"

"That's the second time you've called me 'King.' It happens my name is 'Antrim.' I guess you've got it figured I'm an outlaw, or something. Some cut-an'-run breed of skunk. Like yourself."

Sundance said, showing no offense, "Just wasting breath, King. I know you all right. There's just a chance I can clear the slate for you—wipe 'er off clean an' let you start from scratch. I'll expect whatever help you can give me—"

"Got the same itch that's botherin' Jake an' Cope, have you?"

"How's that?"

"They think," Antrim said, "I've got Hunt's map. You wouldn't of sold 'em that notion, would you? Figurin', mebbe, they'd slit my throat for it?"

Sundance showed him a thoughtful smile; tipped his head in a reluctant fashion. "Afraid I did. I was fixing to get them other gents squabblin'—never thought about you . . .

"But never mind that. Here—wait! Don't go

off half-cocked. That's been your trouble, King—always jumping at conclusions—crowding the fence. Like you forcin' that fight on me. I owe you one for that. It may be the means of fixing things for us; it was damn good medicine."

Antrim stared at him.

Sundance chuckled, his twinkling eyes boyish. "You spun better than you knew when you started that fight. Give me just the chance I been huntin' for. But you'll be wantin' to know about that Benson stage job the Earps run you in for. You'll remember there was three guys stepped out an' stuck up that stage; there was a lot of talk around town about them. Lot of folks figured those three was Bill Leonard, Jim Crane an' Harry Head. Expect you been figuring that way, too. As a matter of fact, two of them *was* Jim Crane an' Bill Leonard. But Harry Head wasn't near the place. The third gent in the deal was Holliday—yeah, the admirable 'Doc'. The T.B. dentist with the sawed-off shotgun.

"That same afternoon Doc hired him a horse from a Tombstone livery. He told the stableman he might be gone a week or ten days, or that he might, just possibly, return that same night. He left town about four o'clock with a Henry rifle tucked under his arm. He was headed towards

Charleston. About a mile out of town he veered towards Contention. He was seen again sometime between ten and one o'clock that night riding back into town with his horse all lather.

"He got off at the stable; had another horse rigged for him. He left this fresh nag hitched at a tie pole for the rest of the night, trying to make it look like he'd never left town. Johnny Behan's bunch held a private session and poured it into him. Doc just gave 'em the horse laugh. Told them to prove it; told them if it *had* been him that eighty thousand wouldn't have gotten away. Behan told him it was known he had made damaging statements. Doc had a real good belly laugh that time. 'So I'm a stage robber, eh? Just like me to go an' talk a rope around my neck. I stick up the stage, kill a couple guys, an' blab it around all over the country. I guess there won't none of the road-agents trust me no more; I'll just have to be a damn outcast, I reckon.'

"That's what he told them," Sundance said. "Nothing ever come of it; no one tried to arrest him. But he was in it all right. I've uncovered some evidence that ain't been brought out. String along with me and I'll see what I can do for you."

Antrim looked at him.

Sundance grinned.

"Go ahead—go on and call me a liar. But if you want a fresh start you better be helping me."

"A story like that . . ." Antrim said, and paused.

Sundance nodded. "You're right, of course. It needs proof. But here—" he drawled, and brought up a hand. "I guess even you will admit seein's believin'."

Antrim stared and swore. Very soft; the sound scarce a breath in the canyon stillness. On the man's cupped palm lay the flash of metal, the sun's hot gleams striking back from it brightly. A badge lay there. An emblem of justice. The badge of a ranger.

Antrim stood, stiffly cocked, with his eyes pale cracks and listened to the roll of the wind through the pine tops. "I didn't know," he said tight-lipped, "they enlisted crooks in the Texas Rangers."

"They don't," Sundance said. "I ain't enlistin' you. All I want from you is a little help. Back my hand and—"

"Back your hand or get arrested, eh? Get put in the Tombstone jail till they hang me—"

"Don't talk like a fool. I told you once your affairs don't concern me. For all I care you ain't never been here. Anyways, a Texas badge—"

"Would work out fine . . . if you had me in Texas. Might even work all right if you could get me in Tombstone. You could easy tip me off to John Slaughter."

Sundance said with a rasp in his tone: "I'm here after horses—if all the crooks in the Territory was here it wouldn't be no skin off *my* nose! I'm here after *A*-rabs; a couple of hot-blooded broncs that was stole off a Mexican—some bean-eatin' Don with a hold on the Government. Lorenzo Enrico Porfiro Fanegas y Lugo—some mouthful!"

"If pipe dreams was dollars—"

"This ain't no dream! The damn fool's offered five hundred dollars to the gent that'll bring 'em back—an' no questions! The request came—"

"Why don't you get old Jake to help you? He knows the country—might even know who stole your horses. He told me quite a spell back there was horse runners working this trail again. He could find his way around here with his eyes shut—"

"The man I need's got to keep his eyes open." Sundance's grinned toughly, persuasively confident. "You've got yours open all the time, bucko." Some deviltry of thought sent its darkening sparkle through the slant of his stare. "Let's cut out the sparrin' and get down to business. I need you, and it looks like you could use me. What the hell are you throwing dust for? You oughta be glad to work with the Rangers. Damn it! One word from me—"

"Exactly," Antrim said. "One word."

Sundance snorted.

Antrim said, "I'll hand it to you for one thing—you're tough, all right. Gritty as fish eggs rolled in sand. 'One word' says you—and to me, at that! If I had good sense I'd put a slug through you."

Sundance chuckled. "You ain't built that way. If you was really guilty of what you're charged with, I might think different. Hell! you got nothing to lose by helping me. If you want to skip out after I've got those horses *I* won't stop you. You'd be a fool to do it; but you won't find *me* campin' on your shirttail. What do you say? Is it a deal?"

"What about this Zwing Hunt business?"

"What about it?"

"You making a try—"

"Hell! you ain't believin' that, are you? You don't really figure there *is* any loot, do you?"

Sundance looked at him, shook his head. "By God! I didn't think nobody but crackpots like

Jake put any real stock in that flight of fancy. All the treasure you find you can pin on your eyebrow. Treasure! My God!"

Antrim scowled but said nothing.

Sundance put a hand on his shoulder. "I've been packing the star for a good many years, King. I've seen a good many tough ones—known a lot of them personally. But I've never seen any that could boast of one dime when the time came around to cash in their chips."

He backed off, shook his head. "Yeah. I can see you've got it about as bad as Jake. This guy Boucher you mentioned the other night— I hate to think of all the time he's spent hunting that rainbow that Zwing Hunt painted. I don't suppose you ever knew Zwing Hunt? As a outlaw he wasn't worth shucks. I knew him when he was hauling lumber for Morse's sawmill. He made a heap of big brags, did a lot of swaggering, but when it come to gunplay or cutting real didoes he wasn't much better than a tinhorn gambler. Billy Grounds hadn't no more weight than Hunt had; he got killed when he wasn't no more than nineteen. They tried to stick up the stamp mill at Charlestown. They stepped into the office just about dusk. There was three men sittin' in the office talkin'—no, four: the mill manager, Peel—

the chief engineer, a fellow named Cheney, and Hunt—the assayer. Zwing Hunt and Billy Grounds stepped in wearing masks. They never said 'Boo!'—just stepped in the door and opened up. Peel dropped, dead. The other three dropped down back of the counter. Hunt and Grounds got spooked and went larruping off without even pausing to do any robbing. They cut their stick for the Stockton ranch. Breakenridge, Young, Gillespie and some other deputies got on the trail and took after them. They caught up with them at the ranch. Hunt killed Gillespie, wounded Young. Grounds shot a fellow named Allen. Breakenridge killed Grounds. Breakenridge put a slug through Hunt's back, knocking him down. But he jumped up again and went crashing through the brush. He didn't get far, though. The posse got him and took him back to Tombstone. He got away later, skipped out with Bill Hughes.

"What I'm trying to point out—does he sound . . . Well, here, let me give you the rest of the story. Hughes and Hunt turned up after a spell at Buckles' Ranch in Pole Bridge Canyon. They stayed three weeks while Hunt's wound healed over. Meantime, his brother, Hugh, came up from Texas and joined Zwing there. Zwing and his brother took out for Mexico. A few days later the brother rode into Camp Price on the southern side of the Cherrycows an' told the lieutenant Zwing had been killed by Indians. A party of scouts was sent back with Hunt to locate Zwing's body. They found the camp—found a dead man and buried him. On a juniper tree they cut Zwing's name and the date."

Sundance grinned. "I'd like to know when he talked to his uncle. I'd like to have a picture of him making that map."

Antrim shrugged. "You can talk till hell freezes—"

"Yeah. I know it. An' you'll still believe in that Curly Bill cache. You an' Jake Gauze and all the rest of 'em. Well, it's no skin off my nose— believe what you want, just so you give me some help locating them horses. How about it?"

"Right now," Antrim said, "I've got to ride to town."

"That's all right with me. I've got a few things that need tending myself. You'll be back all right. Any guy—"

Antrim said, "I'll be back."

SIXTEEN

Antrim had expected to see the girl's shoulders droop—had expected to find her, if not resigned, either outwardly angry or inwardly seething. She was none of these things.

She was a strange, deep woman with dark, somber eyes that showed no resentment at her curt dismissal as she took in the passing sights of the outtrail. Perhaps she had concluded whatever the business that had brought her out there. She might even be pleased to be leaving Jake's place.

Yet most women, he mused, would have worked this trip to their better advantage; would at least have lightened the miles with some tongue oil.

But not Lolita. She answered when spoken to, civilly, pleasantly, but she made no effort to keep the talk going.

She was self-contained.

She wore, in this sweltering heat, a dark riding skirt and light shirtwaist. She wore a broad-brimmed, chin-strapped hat on her hair, a Stet hat garnished with a bright red feather. Her delicate features were clear as a cameo; they could be, he thought, as reserved as one, also. Just the same, he decided, there was spirit to this girl; behind the serenity—the cool composure, she was fire and flame, an emotional volcano that could loose devastation if ever for a moment she let go of herself.

But that was just it—she didn't; or she hadn't, at least not so far as this trip was concerned. She maintained a taciturn aloofness, appearing friendly enough, quite content with the silence, making no attempt either to trade on her sex or on their present relationship.

He found this odd in a woman. The riddle roused his interest. He wondered again what had brought her out here.

The sun was sinking red behind the ragged peaks of the Cherrycows when she said abruptly, "You had better get out of this . . . Antrim."

He looked at her quickly but got no satisfaction .

"Get out . . . ?"

She remained silent a moment. She said with a lift of her shoulders, "You did not go out there because Jake 'ave ask you."

"Why do you think I went out there?"

"I think you went out there to hunt for treasure." She turned then and faced him. "You would not be the first. Many have gone to find that treasure; that buried plunder Zwing 'Unt 'ave tell about. Poor, foolish people that think to find what 'as never been. Gold and silver and jewels and statues—what a craziness must 'ave been in his head. It was the fever, of course."

"Of course," Antrim said; and she smiled at him.

"You do not believe that. You are like those others who 'ave come to Jake's; you 'ave hear that tale and you will not res' till you 'ave looked yourself. But there is no gold, no silver, no statues—nothing is there only greed and hate. And death for those who go on with this madness. Believe me; I know—I can feel it here."

She laid a hand on her heart and looked at him.

She looked at him fully, her lips seeming to hesitate on the edge of speaking. Then she shrugged, looked ahead and said no more to him.

At seven o'clock they camped in a pocket. Antrim hobbled the horses and cooked the few things the girl had brought with her. They ate in silence; afterwards the girl rolled up in her blankets and slept.

Antrim sat by the fire with his pipe and his thinking.

He reviewed the things Sundance had told him, the man's proposition; Jake's proffer of partnership. Jake was after something—Hunt's map, most likely. Cope wanted that map. Perhaps Sundance, too, despite his asserted interest in horses.

One of them had it.

Which one? Jake or Cope? And where did this gambler, Pete Spence fit in? Was he, too, after the Curly Bill cache? Or had he come, as he said, merely hunting Cope?

Who had stolen those horses? Antrim had thought at first it would prove to be Jake; that Jake had been stealing horses and had hired him to ward off revenge from their owners. Now he was not sure. He was beginning to suspect Idy Red of stealing them. Idy Red with her tomboy ways—with nothing to do with her idle time but rove these hills and long for the city. She was not the kind to stay shut in a house; she must know that canyon's every nook and cranny.

Suppose Jake was right in his claim about

horse runners. Idy Red would know if they were using the Trail. She could have seen the two Arabs and fallen in love with them. She might even have gotten them away from the horse thieves; a girl of her temperament and knowledge *could* have. Her prowls through the canyon would have discovered the cove—it might even have been a rendezvous for her, a place of communion, the stage for her dreams. Unless the thieves themselves had hidden the horses there, Antrim thought, it must have been Idy Red who had done it. They would have represented something to bestow her affection on, would give to her lonely rambles new pleasure and purpose; they would give her starved soul a new interest in life.

Having incurred Idy Red's hostility, Antrim, in riding off as he had, might easily have roused her suspicion. She would have experienced no difficulty in following him; perhaps Kerrick's claybank was already saddled. Idy Red wore small boots. She may have taken that shot at him.

She was a willful girl; wild, primitive, impulsive.

She may even have killed Bat Kerrick....

It was time, Antrim thought, to take stock of the chances, to re-scan the issues and the obstacles presented.

The issues, boiled down, appeared amazingly simple. He, and the others, were equally determined to locate and seize the Curly Bill plunder. There were the stolen Arabs to be considered; the law, as represented by Sundance, who, despite his statement of policy, might no longer prove a disinterested spectator in the event the owlhoot cache was uncovered. These were the main things. There were a lot of side angles that would have to be coped with. This was a pattern geared by wheels within wheels. There was gaunt Jake Gauze and his schemes to be reckoned with. Idy Red's antipathy—her predeliction for Sundance. There was Sundance, himself, both as man and lawman. There was Kerrick's killing—a thing all hands appeared disposed to ignore. There was pale, little Taiban Cope; and that other tinhorn, the stage-robbing, claim-jumping gambler, Pete Spence, who might be a deal smarter than Jake gave him credit for. There was that little matter of Zwing Hunt's map. . . .

The crash of the shot gagged the night with its clamor. It pulled Antrim out of his dozing; yanked him onto his knees, gun lifting, eyes raking the roundabout gloom for a target. Habit took hold then and flung him backward, out of the flare of the fire's dying embers. He crouched there, tight-cheeked, hearing the echoes break and run, hearing them die out, faintly, remotely.

The shot had come from beyond the pocket. From beyond that intervening ridge to the left that rose with its brush like a roach-maned scalp against the star-sprinkled pit of the night beyond.

There was no further sound from those stygian shadows. The silence crawled back.

Antrim stayed in his tracks until certain that whatever play he had caught the tag end of, it was over and done with. For this installment, leastways. Nothing was ever done with, really.

A damp ground chill had settled in the pocket.

He looked toward Lolita, and all the muscles of his face pulled tight. The blankets lay where she'd been curled up in them; but she was not in them now. . . . She was not in sight anywhere.

Trap's smell was strong in his mind when Antrim quartered across to the blankets. He stopped a little short of them and skinned his ear for what the night might tell him; but it told him nothing. There was nothing to hear but the pattering sound of a breeze lightly rummaging its way through the greasewood.

He moved in closer. A match snapped to flame on the edge of his thumbnail. It showed Antrim's face in tight planes and dark shadows as he bent and with bleak gaze studied the ground, swiftly reading the tale of bent grass and scuffed humans.

He wondered then why his horse had not snorted.

The horses were gone. He found the cut hobbles.

SEVENTEEN

Antrim spent the rest of that night in the pocket.

At the first gray of dawn he was up, reading sign, crouched thoughtfully scowling above the girl's blanket.

There were tracks aplenty. Some were sharply defined. Boot tracks, all of them; tangled and scuffed tracks, a few overlapping. He backtracked the incoming pair to the trail where they petered out on the shaley hardpan. Till he lost them they had shown pretty plain, as though their wearer had moved with exceeding caution, pausing long moments with each taken step.

He saw where the girl had been dragged from her blankets—saw the long, gouged furrows left by her heels. Found a place where the tracks showed plain signs of struggle. It seemed strange, he thought, he had heard no cry; that there had been no excitement on the part of their horses. There had *been* no excitement of this kind. The horse tracks displayed an unruffled calm.

But a curious light came in Antrim's stare when he found the place where, by the sign, the girl had been swept from her feet and carried. To insure her silence at this point her abductor would either have had to gag her or keep one hand clapped across her mouth. There was no sign that the man had done so. The tracks showed heavier, more plainly indented from the added weight. But they did not wabble. They did not lurch or stagger. Of course the man *might* have gagged her, but Antrim could find no sign suggestive of it and there were only two other alternatives possible which might account for the singular appearance of this solitary set of outgoing tracks.

Another thing was odd about this vanishment.

Lolita's left boot would have matched exactly the print he had found by the trail at the horse cache.

So would the boot of the girl's abductor.

As alike they were as the proverbial peas.

The horses were gone, but the pair had not taken them.

Antrim saw by the sign where the man had come up, cut their hobbles and quietly, leisurely, hazed them off. He followed this sign nearly a quarter of a mile, at which point the man had coolly stampeded them—larruped them off toward the Cherrycow Mountains. "Figurin', I reckon, if I followed sign this far I'd keep right on with the hope of catchin' em."

He smiled at the thought; smiled leanly and nodded.

It was a pretty good bet those horses would circle, would make a big loop and cut back toward the ranch—or would they?

Antrim's scowl heralded sudden remembrance.

They'd have cut back all right if they'd been Jake's horses. But the claybank Antrim had ridden was Kerrick's. The girl's horse was her own— and she lived at Tombstone. It would be pretty certain to return to town. God only knew where Kerrick's would go.

Antrim, scowling, broke out a few cusswords.

He looked at the sky. It was shot with pink above the Peloncillos. He had better be moving. When the sun came up it was going to be hot. Hotter than yesterday for a man caught afoot. There was a good twenty miles between himself and Jake's place.

Walking in high-heeled boots was no sinecure. It was not so bad as he had heard it described, but it was a mighty far thing from being a pleasure. It stimulated bitter thoughts in a man. He wondered now if Jake hadn't had some better reason for sending him off than the one he'd mentioned.

He got to thinking finally about the shot that had wakened him. What part had it played in in last night's didoes? Why was it fired and who had fired it? No slug had struck in his vicinity; he had not even heard the bullet. Just the shot and those raveling, ridge-broken echoes.

Had the girl got a gun—tried to get herself free again?

It did not seem likely the man would have killed her, not after the trouble he'd been to to snare her.

Antrim, swinging along at a ground-eating stride, began to feel warm before he covered two miles. Sweat broke out on his back and forehead. Where pants and shirt met beneath his belt he was wringing wet and the sun hadn't even got above the peaks yet.

It was going to be hot.

It *was* hot. There wasn't any breeze at all this morning. The scrub oak hung limp and lifeless.

What birds he saw stood with open mouths, their songs forgotten in this wilting heat.

He realized he was thirsty, and then, of a sudden, his thirst was forgotten. All his attention was caught, held bleakly. He stopped, eyes wide on the dusty trail, on the hoof sign stamped there. On a horseshoe's imprint... a hind shoe carelessly set.

It was this queer mark he had seen at the horse cache. This was the track Kerrick's claybank left. Kerrick's claybank... the horse he had ridden yesterday from Jake's. Only now it was going in the other direction, going *toward* Jake's...

Going toward Jake's.

Antrim stood and stared in a clammy sweat while confused thoughts pelted his mind with their questions.

Many hoofs had churned the dust of this trail; its adobe surface was like windrowed flour, only gray instead of white, but entirely compatible with flour's consistency. The tracks of Kerrick's big claybank were plain. They were the last to cross this impressionable surface. Antrim traced them back, saw where they'd come onto it out of the brush—saw a great deal more. The tracks of another horse mingled with them, the latter sometimes overlapping them, which suggested the claybank was following this other horse; it was probably the girl's.

It was then he saw the dainty print of boots and had all he needed to uncork his temper.

"Jesus H. Christ," he said, and loosed a laugh from lips sourly twisted. The girl had diddled him —fooled him proper! She had gauged him right and hung it onto him. She'd been no more kidnapped than he had; it had all been a lie, built and played for his benefit. It was the only possible answer. With this supposition all the queer angles fell neatly into place .

God, but that girl was a smart one! Give the hellcat her due and be done with it. She had taken him in like the greenest lout of a brush popper; had built a loop and jumped him through it. While he'd hunched there dozing beside the fire she had staged this show to rid herself of him— and had done it, too!

Damned well she had done it. By the sign he was anyway six hours behind her, and losing more every passing moment.

No wonder he'd thought those tracks a little odd; the same pair of boots had made every one of them. Lord! the work she had gone to to fool him—to make it seem she'd been snatched away from him!—to get herself free, screened from observation.

He marveled at the amount of thought required to conceive and execute the hoax she had played. Out of all proportion to the possible gain —or *was* it? That could not be appraised till one knew what use she had put to these hours; till one knew what was back of the use she put to them. It was apparent she had been of no mind to be watched. . . .

Antrim scowled and grunted, bodefully shook his head. Of even that much he could not be sure. She was up to something. That was all he knew. She did not wish him to think she had left him deliberately, which argued she expected to see him again. Perhaps she aimed to come back, once her purpose was achieved, with some tale of having escaped from the ruffian. Perhaps . . .

There was one thing, though, he could rest assured of: she had needed privacy, and had been of no mind to have anyone know it. Else she'd not have bothered to stage this act; she'd have simply slipped off and let him think what he wanted.

Some private need for privacy was bound to be the motivating force of her actions. The key— every move she made was stamped with it. Jake must have given her the horse she was riding. A turned-loose horse naturally makes for home; she had known that, too, and had counted on it. She'd been trying to sell Antrim a definite impression. Since the impression was false there was no horse for her need but the ones they had come on.

At their first acquaintance she had twice named Tombstone as the place she customarily thought of as home. Antrim doubted, now, they had ever met in Tombstone; he became sourly skeptical of everything about her—particularly of that "Flying Nymph" background. She was no more Lizette than the man in the moon; that was just another slick impression she had sold him.

But she knew this country. Knew its background, its people. She had recognized *him,* though nobody else had. He'd have bet his bottom dollar just then it had been this girl who had tipped off Sundance.

She had expected Antrim to keep on toward Tombstone—a far piece off, while she returned to Jake's.

Oh, she was smart, all right. Uncannily smart. She had shown a real flair in stampeding those horses; had gauged to a turn how far they would bolt before circling. It seemed preposterous to believe this—yet how could you doubt the facts of those tracks? Those tracks said the girl had shortcut to this place and confidently waited for the broncs to come up with her.

Even the shot that had roused him was motivated, intentionally fired to give effect to her acting, to endow it with color—to breathe life into it and make it seem real.

She had done a good job.

She had made one slip, a very little one. This thing by which he had finally caught up with her —this matter of a claybank's left hind shoe. She couldn't have known he would take Kerrick's horse; it wasn't likely she knew about that bad hind shoe. If she *did* know, she'd not have much reason to suspect *him* of knowing.

Looking off across that dun-yellow valley, across the empty, heat-hazed miles between, a cool, thin smile touched Guy Antrim's lips.

She had left him afoot without water or sustenance—afoot in a country where a man's means of travel was traditionally held sacred. She had left him, deliberately, on the lap of the gods, caring little for his fate just so she was rid of him.

She wasn't rid of him—not yet, by God!

It was a notion that would probably come to her. When she saw him again. Tonight. At Jake's.

If it had been her desire to get rid of him she would better have put a bullet through him . . . or that eight-inch blade that had done for Kerrick.

He considered with relish the things he would say to her. To Jake and to Sundance—to the rest of that outfit.

What a pity those Arabs weren't this side of Jake's.

It was history repeating itself, he thought.

It was not so late as it had been that first time —that night he had come up this trail with Jake. Three minutes or so on the near side of dark. But the lamp was there in the ranch house window, a lemon-pale glow, blackly sharpening the lines of the brush before it.

A lifting breeze whimpered through the cottonwoods; the purl of the creek was a low, strangled gurgle.

Odd how often things shaped to a pattern.

He was lifting an arm when he heard the shot —the racketing bang of a pistol's explosion.

EIGHTEEN

The wind of that shot beat against his cheek, threw the drone of its song in his ears like a hornet. Hard on its heels—even as he was whirling, a second gun hammered the night with its death call.

In the felted gloom by the stable's corner something blurred into movement. Something struck the ground heavily and was instantly quiet. Temper sent Antrim unthinkingly toward it, ignoring the lifting clamor of voices.

He lunged for the stable, plunging crazily into the shadows surrounding it. He passed the dark entrance and raced for the corner, rounding it just in time to catch a leaping shape that struck at him, desperately, frantically, trying to break free of him. He could feel the surge of the caught one's muscles; heard the rip of cloth—almost lost his hold of him. He jammed his gun against the fellow's middle. Now—"

"Mother of God!" came the anguished cry, "Do not hold me, King— unloose me! Hurry!"

"Oh! *You* again, is it?" There was a grim satisfaction in Antrim's tone. "What you trying to get shut of *this* time?"

Lolita said swiftly: "You don't understan'—"

"I will. What you got in your fist there?"

He felt her draw back—felt tension grip her. She thrust the hand he was after behind her, away from him. He couldn't quite see what it was she was hiding. She was like an eel. He had to drop his gun even to keep hold of her.

The force of his effort wrung a cry from her. She cursed him bitterly; increased her twisting. The clamoring voices were nearing them rapidly. The sound inflamed her—brought new strength to her frantic struggles.

The rush of her words came up at him fiercely. "Let me go, you fool! Must you spoil everything with your insufferable meddling? Let go, I say—at once! Before that crazy Jake—*here!* take it, then—*take it!*"

Something cold and hard was thrust into his hands; and that way she left him, left him standing there, foolishly, holding it.

A big-barreled pistol.
There was a gunpowder smell to it.

The voices surrounded him.
Someone lifted a lantern; lowered it carefully through an infinite quiet.

A harsh voice said: "Who is this man?" and Antrim suddenly realized the night had turned cold. There was ice in the air and the ice, some way, had gotten into his bones.

He looked at the man who had spoken and remembered again that same voice saying, "My name is Slaughter—John Slaughter." This was the man who had said that to him in the Crystal Palace bar, at Tombstone. He was a man who took a real pride in his boots; he looked strangely out of place here in his expensive, immaculate tailored clothes. But his eyes were the eyes of a range man and must proclaim him such wherever he went.

He seemed always to have a cigar in his mouth; there was one there now, clamped between his white teeth, and a pearl-butted six-shooter tucked in his belt.

Slaughter cleared his throat and said "Well?" impatiently; and Jake Gauze hurriedly told him: "We don't rightly know, Sheriff. He . . . ah . . .

called 'imself 'Cope'—"

"I know all about Cope," Slaughter said through his teeth. "I'm referring—"

"Oh—*him?*" Sundance drawled. "Why that's Jake's range boss—'Antrim.'"

Slaughter's head didn't turn but his eyes did. "I say—I say tell it in your own way, Antrim, but don't give the whole night over to it."

Antrim was caught in the grind of his thinking. It was the smugness of Sundance's grin that roused him. He wheeled his head to meet Slaughter's gaze. "Over to what?"

John Slaughter said carefully, "When one fellow shoots another one he generally has some reason back of it."

Antrim's glance met the sheriff's straightly. "I ain't been shootin' nobody."

"Then what are you doing with that gun in your hand? And how does it happen Cope's lying there dead?"

NINETEEN

The only sound was the rasp of men's breathing.

Antrim's glance, hard as agate, followed the swing of the sheriff's hand—followed the glint of the ring on his finger, and he saw Taiban Cope, that pale worm of a man, sprawled with his face half hid in the dust. Death gave him less of dignity than even his life and profession had managed. One hand, fingers spraddled, lay near his hat. The other hand, and its arm, was doubled under him, naught of it showing but the edge of an elbow. One pants-leg was pulled halfway up his knee. Blue veins patterned the exposed, bony shank and, aside from these, it was bare as a baby's.

Antrim's eyes came inquiringly back to the sheriff.

"Sorry, Slaughter. I don't know anything about it," he said.

Somebody lifted the lantern again. The sheriff's black eyes showed a look of temper. "You heard the shots, didn't you?"

Antrim nodded.

"What were you doing with that gun in your hand?"

"I—" Antrim saw Pete Spence come into the lantern light. There was a gleam of malevolence in Spence's rheumy eyes. "No use tryin' to make us think you jes' picked it up," Spence said. "Taib's been missin' that gun ever since you pulled out."

"Pulled out?" Slaughter said.

Jake cut in before Spence could speak. "I sent Poke into town t' fetch you. I allus try t' he'p the law all I kin. We had a killin' out here thet I figured you'd ort t' know about."

Slaughter's black eyes bored a hole through Jake. "Am I understandin' you to say there's been somebody else killed?"

A slow wind ruffled Jake's lank hair. The flaps of his vest swayed a little and dropped. "Sure has." He spat, flicked a thumb toward where Sundance's shove was propelling Spence forward. "There's your chicken, Sheriff. Jest ast an' ye shall be answered."

Slaughter seemed to see not only the things in front of him, but those on both sides and behind him, too. He was a man you could seldom catch napping; nor did Jake's maneuvers catch him napping now. His black eyes swiveled a look at Spence. He rolled the stump of his smoke between his teeth and returned his attention to Antrim.

"If you're tired of holding that gun I'll take it."

Antrim shrugged and passed over the six-shooter.

Slaughter said to Spence, "Who'd you kill, Pete?"

"I didn't kill nobody."

Slaughter's look flashed from one to the other of them. What he thought was not made apparent. He said to Antrim: "I guess—I guess you better be telling me about *this* killing." He nudged Cope's body with the toe of his boot.

"Sorry," Antrim said. "I didn't even know Cope was dead till you told me."

"Where was you at when you heard the shots?"

"Back there on the trail."

"What'd you do?"

"Well," Antrim said, "I s'posed they were

fired at me. The first one come within a inch of my ear. I saw what I took to be somebody ducking—over here where we're standin'. I come over here hellbent to find out."

"That all?"

"That's about all. There was somebody here. I grabbed for 'em—lost 'em. And then you come up."

John Slaughter considered. "What about this pistol? Pete says it was Cope's. You got anything you want to add to that?"

"Your guess is as good as mine. I got it away from the guy I was fightin' with."

Slaughter tucked the gun in his belt with his own gun. "Pete," he said, "I say—I say—"

"No need to waste time asking *him* questions," Sundance murmured. "He's already confessed to the killing. Jake's got his statement all signed and ready for you."

"And who are you—where do you come into this?"

Sundance laughed it off with an easy politeness. "Just another T.B. come west for my health."

Slaughter's opinion was not revealed in his face. "Come west from where?"

Sundance smiled. "Don't believe I mentioned."

Jake touched the sheriff's arm. "First thing

GUNSLICK MOUNTAIN 191

Spence done when he got here was t' ast had a fella named Kerrick showed up. I told him he had. This Kerrick had come up the day before; tol' me he come fr'm El Paso—was figurin' t' ranch somewheres up aroun' Prescott. I never ast him no questions. Lotsa guys drifts through this canyon. I figure t' mind my own business mostly, but I couldn't he'p noticin' there was somethin' jeunin' around in his head. Said he'd like t' stop a few days. I told him 'Sure—stop as long as you like.' Then Spence come along an' they was thicker'n thieves. All the time gettin' off by themselfs—takin' rides an' all. Didn't take me long t' guess what they was up to. They was huntin' around f' that Curly Bill plunder; this Kerrick fella was all steamed up. I expect Pete sold him a Zwing Hunt map—"

Spence said: "You goddam liar! I never even *seen* this Kerrick! Don't you never believe 'im, Mister Slaughter—I never even got here till after they'd buried him!"

Slaughter looked from one to the other of them.

Jake shook his head, tendered Slaughter a grimy, folded paper. "Would a guy sign that without he ackshully done it?"

Slaughter held the paper so the lantern would

shine on it. After he read it he put it away. "I say—I say how'd you happen to be out here, Pete?"

"Cope left word I should meet him here. I come to see Cope. Not no goddam Kerrick which I hadn't never heard of. As for that Curly Bill plunder—" malevolence flashed in the look he gave Jake, "nobody but a fool would believe that yarn no way. An' Jake knows it well as I do. He bought this ranch with the money he made sellin' Zwing Hunt maps to credulous suckers."

Slaughter waved that aside. "Where's this Kerrick man buried?"

"I dunno," Jake shrugged. "Sundance—"

"Not me," Sundance said. "Cope had the shovel. I guess Cope planted him."

Slaughter turned his lok from Sundance to Antrim.

Antrim shook his head. "I pass," he said.

The sheriff nodded. "And now Mister Cope is very handily dead."

He threw the dead stump of his cigar away. He got out a fresh one and bit off its end. He gave Jake Gauze a very penetrating look.

"Pete," he said to Spence, "I'm goin' to ask you, Pete, to set up with this body; I wouldn't want to find it gone in the morning. The rest of us, I guess, had better turn in. We got a long, tough day ahead of us tomorrow."

There were still a good three hours before dawn when Jake Gauze, barefoot, with his spurless boots tucked under an arm, began very carefully to cross the patio. He took his way through the deepest shadows and there were times when Antrim could hardly see him; but he kept his place, thinly smiling, waiting.

He had thought Slaughter's coming would change the schedule. The sheriff's presence was discomfiting Jake, was forcing him to alter plans he'd probably spent months on.

Anything might happen.

The sheriff's presence was discomfiting all of them. There was no man here but had ample reason to fear the law's proximity. Why had Slaughter come? What had brought him here to discover these killings? What was he thinking? Who was he after?

Antrim recalled the circumstances which had brought John Slaughter into public service. He'd been put into office to clean up the country; the people's elected choice—the choice of a people fed up with banditry. John Slaughter, in a short three years, had made a name you could do conjuring with. These countless exploits—the tales of this man's daring, furnished after-supper yarning for the campfires of the cow camps.

You might think this a little strange, for the epic days were done with, the swashbuckling breed departed. Outlawry was a withered flower—there was no romance left in it. This was an age of pilferers, a cut-and-run breed who had no stomach for the bolder ways of the generation before them. This was a breed of street-corner robbers, of slash-and-snatch burglars, of two-bit, pussyfooting horse and cow stealers. Coyotes snatching crumbs from the camp snack.

So they'd called John Slaughter from his ranching to stop it.

They had picked the right man.

A man of his word, he was a cold, quiet fellow who lived under his hat; a lonely soul with no bread to butter but the crust of the law. Slaughter seldom found it necessary to draw his gun when he talked to a man. Chary of speech, men saved his words and repeated them for him, and a warning was usually found quite sufficient to move a man out or to bring him to jail. Slaughter rode alone. He was unique and deadly.

He wasted scant thought on hairline distinctions. With little trust in courts and juries, he had unbounded confidence in his own views of justice. He frequently ordered men out of the country—never troubling to order them twice. He was "plain blue hell" on horse thieves. When he set out after a stolen horse he always returned with it—no one ever remembered him bringing a thief back.

Antrim was not surprised to see Jake stampeded. The sheriff's coming was a handwriting Jake could read. He was fixing to move and he aimed to move fast—he *had* to, faced with the presence of Slaughter. John Slaughter was the kind who played for keeps.

Jake had not quite half crossed the patio when Antrim saw a second blurred shape detach itself from the gloom and glide after him. Antrim could not tell whose this second shape was, but he rather inclined toward belief it was Sundance. Whoever it was, he stopped when Jake stopped, bent where Jake bent, and in every way moved like he was old Jake's shadow.

Eyes narrowed watchfully, Antrim followed.

Jake reached the living room door. Stepped through it.

Antrim watched the second shape pause by the door, seeming to hesitate, to be cautiously gauging things. Then, abruptly, he too was dissolved into blackness.

Antrim came to the door.

There was a flicker of light in the room beyond. It came from a match in a man's cupped palm. The palm was Jake's—the match was, too. The second still shape belonged to Sundance. Close to Antrim, he was poised by the table, his gleaming eyes following Jake's every move.

Gauze was crouched by the chimney, bent by the mantel that was hood for the fireplace. He had a bony arm thrust far up the chimney.

When he brought it down Antrim coldly said: "I'm obliged to you, Jake—I surely am. I figured that map was plumb lost for good."

Old Jake crouched there, turned still as a statue.

But Sundance chuckled. "I thought you'd be getting your nose into this—I'd of bet my last dollar on it."

"Never mind the gab—an' get your hand away from that pistol. Try that match on a lamp wick, Jake."

Jake lit the lamp on the mantel. The wheel of his head was without expression. His cheeks showed nothing; the flats of his face were blank, inscrutable.

"Well?" Sundance drawled. "We goin' to do us some knittin' or tat awhile?"

"I think," Antrim said, "we'll get down to business. Who killed that gambler?"

"Cock Robin, likely." Sundance sniffed. "What do *you* care?—that's Slaughter's problem."

"It sure is, mister. An' Slaughter'll be quick to see one of us killed him."

"I dunno," Sundance said, "as I agree to that. You admit, yourself, you found someone crouched over Cope when you—"

"I did," Antrim said, "but I didn't *say* so."

Sundance's lids narrowed slightly. Then he laughed in a way that jarred the silence and Jake Gauze shivered, though sweat was a glistening dew on his cheekbones.

"The point, "Antrim said, "is that Slaughter'll keep on till he's got to the bottom of it. You won't find that pleasant or profitable, either—mebbe you figure that *badge* will protect you?"

Sundance smiled thinly. "What do you figure?"

"I figure you got that badge off a dead man. I'm allowin' you ain't got no right to it, mister."

The grin widened out across Sundance's cheeks, widened till it suddenly showed his dimples. "But color don't count if the colt won't trot. If I was in your boots I'd be keepin' my mouth shut. Savvy?"

There was a cool amusement in Sundance's drawl; and a mocking edge of that same wry humor jeered from the twisting curl of his lips. His look was entirely, sarcastically confident. He caught out his pistol. With a jaunty finger carelessly thrust through the trigger guard he gave it a couple of nonchalant twirls; this dexterity in Curly Bill's day having gone by the name of the Road-agent's Spin. It was by this trick Marshal White got killed, Bill pretending to proffer the gun, butt first, then giving it a flip and, pronto, firming the instant the butt touched his palm.

The gun now twirling in Sundance's hand came abruptly to rest against his palm, and the gleam of his eyes laughed across its barrel.

But Antrim was not impressed. He said: "I'll do as I like," and Sundance holstered his gun with a chuckle.

"I figured you would. Some guys has to get hit with a mallet before you can get anything through their heads. Well, Jake, if that's Zwing Hunt's map you've got, bring it over."

Jake's gray cheeks were like pounded putty. He said through his teeth: "I ain't got it—

honest," and his E-string voice jumped into a wail. "I put it there—right in the chimney—but it ain't there now! Some slinkin' polecat's come an' *stole* it!"

TWENTY

The edge of Jake's tongue rasped across dry lips.

The silence piled up. You could almost hear it.

"Hones' t' *Gawd!*" Jake said, and shuddered.

"Oh, well," Sundance smiled. "Poker Face here can remember the details—I'd trust his mem'ry any old day. I'm trustin' yours, too, Jake; ain't you flattered?"

Jake tried to grin but the result was ghastly.

Antrim said to Sundance: "What do *you* care about Zwing Hunt's map?"

"I'm figuring to have me a look at that plunder—"

"Plunder! My God," Antrim quoted, "I didn't think nobody but crackpots put any stock in *that* flight of fancy!"

Sundance chuckled. "I've changed my mind—this treasure colic's catchin'." He looked at Jake. "You was a Curly Bill man, I've heard—pretty close friend of Zwing Hunt's, too, wa'n't you? I expect you know pretty well where it's buried.

"You ain't dug it up because you didn't want to split it; you figured to hog the whole works for yourself—but you can't outlast every guy that's heard of it. It's a cinch you'll have to split it with *somebody*. Might's well be us. I say it *better* be us. You got just two chances, as I see it, Jake. You can keep your mouth shut an' pray like the devil, or you can open your heart an' take a third share healthy."

It was amply plain Jake wasn't much suited. It was also plain he'd reached the end of his rope.

Bitterness twisted the warp of his cheekbones. He toyed with his vest flaps and made up his mind. "What d'ye think I know?"

"I think," Sundance said, "you know where that mountain is. An' I ain't talking about Mount Ararat, neither. Bear it in mind. I've took off you about all I aim to."

Jake's smile was sickly. "I know—I know."

Antrim watched him stoop and pull on his boots. The man had aged since they'd met in Tombstone. He looked more gaunt, more gone-to-seed, someway, as though big Sundance were a blight laid on him. Jake's reaction to Sundance was a phenomenon that, each time he saw it, gave Antrim fresh cause for wonder.

He said: "What's that tinhorn, Spence, hangin' round here for? Thought you'd run him off—"

"He come back." Jake sleeved his face, slewed his glance around nervously. "Right after Slaughter—"

"Yeah. What brought Slaughter out here?"

"Said he come huntin' hosses."

"You mean 'stolen' horses?"

"He had thet look when he tol' me about 'em."

"Does he know who stole them?"

"I guess *you* know," Sundance said with a chuckle.

"I could hit him, I reckon, if I put my hand out."

Sundance laughed. Without sound. Like an Indian. "Always figured you was smart," he said. "Guy *had* to be smart to pull what *you* did. I guess you an' me understand each other. You wouldn't have such luck with John Slaughter, bucko."

Lean of mouth, Antrim smiled.

Jake stared, suspicious, from one to the other of them.

"All right, Jake," Sundance said. "Suppose you start with that gunslick mountain; tell us how come no one's ever found it."

Jake seemed suddenly scared again. It was almighty odd the way Sundance worked on him. It wasn't just talk—no mere threat of words; it wasn't an atitude. There wasn't a bit of suggestion in Sundance's look. There was no menace at all; nothing sinister.

Yet Jake was scared. Fear had frozen the sap in him. He had the look of a frightened bronc about him, nostrils flared, dark eyes wide and glassy.

It puzzled Antrim. Eager as he was to hear what this wizened old man might tell them, he could not but wonder at his strange appearance. There was nothing to scare him in Sundance's posture, nothing at all suggestive of doom. There was a sour amusement, a kind of scornful humor in the cool black eyes Sundance fixed upon him.

It was baffling, incredible, that gaunt Jake Gauze should be afraid of this man.

But he was. You could see him struggling to get hold of himself. It took a visible effort and his success was not notable. He kept fiddling the flap of his cowhide vest, trying to cover, you'd say, the shake of his fingers. He stared at the floor, at his hands, at his boot tops—at anything short of big Sundance's face.

"Well?" Sundance said.

Jake's shoulders jumped, but it got him started.

"Zwing's uncle claimed Hunt called the place Davis Mountain account of a fella named 'Davis' got buried there. It don't make no diff'rence which done the lyin'—the guy's name was 'Harris.' His fam'ly was jumped by the 'Patches, an' the whole bunch was scalped an' killed there. We planted his wife'n kids with 'im. It was in '73. The's a gouged-out cave not a far piece off—y' kin see int' N'Mexico with yer naked eye."

Antrim, watching Sundance, saw the burly man's chubby cheeks faintly tighten; saw him thrust a hand through his curly black hair—saw the added brightness that raveled his stare. But Sundance's voice was entirely skeptical. "Never mind the red herrin's—"

"Y' think I'm lyin'?" Indignation colored Jake's voice. "Jesis H. Christ! You forgot thet gol' I dug up in the can they buried on thet owlhooter's grave? *Thet* ort t' show you I ain't hevin' no pipe dream! Look—by grab, I'll tell you! West o' the foot of Harris Mountain is Turkey Creek Canyon—y' 'member Turkey Creek, don't you?—up by Galeyville? In this windy Zwing spun he called it 'Silver Creek Canyon'; I've checked thet much. It was in Turkey Creek Canyon they buried thet owlhooter—thet's where I dug up thet can o' gold. It was under a rock, like he said, by a juniper tree—the's a handful of bones there yet; you kin see 'em."

Sundance's tongue licked across his lips.

Jake said with an increased assurance. "Thet's as far as I'd got when you fellas come. But the's another canyon—"

He gritted a curse and whirled, hand dropping.

Sundance, too, flung his shoulders around, and an upsweeping pistol gleamed in his fist as the leap of his glance found the open doorway.

A girl stood there, framed against the night.

It was Idy Red, stormy eyes derisive.

"She's gone," she said, and her look found Jake. "Your bird has flit from her gilded cage an' she's taken that claim-jumpin' tinhorn with her. They went off on them broncs you had out in the willow brakes."

She raked her glance around and wheeled and left them.

It looked like the cords in Jake's neck would burst.

He was like a man gone blind; but passion

grabbed big Sundance roughly. Wild anger darkened his chubby cheeks. He drove his voice at Jake like a hatchet. "I *told* you to get rid of that goddam Spence! What in Christ's hell did you tell that slut?"

Jake stood like a witch had hold of him. His shook, but he stood there mute. An old man burning in his private hell.

Cheeks poisonously bloated, Sundance cursed him.

Jake went half a step back, cheeks livid.

The veins stood out like scars on Sundance; the tube of his pistol whipped to focus and Jake fell back like a cornered rat. The hands at his sides were clawlike, spraddled. No breath disturbed his slatlike chest. He crouched on the balls of his feet, eyes glinting.

Sundance, too, was bent, crouched forward. "Answer me, damn you! *What did you tell her?*"

"I . . ." Jake's knees struck together. "I never—"

"Don't lie!" Sundance snapped through his teeth. "Don't lie to me or—" He let the rest go. "You told her something—"

"I never—I *swear* I never! It was Idy Red told her . . . I tol' Idy Red. What I jes' tol' you— 'bout Zwing mixin' up them names an' all. 'Bout that canful of gol' I foun'—"

"Christ Almighty," Sundance said. "You told her that, eh?"

Jake licked at his lips but couldn't wet them. He put a hesitant hand out and touched Sundance's elbow. "I—mebbe I better git outa this country. You don' know thet girl like I do. When she gits riled . . ."

He looked at them vaguely, staring through and beyond them as though at something not of this earth. "She—she's all riled up account of me bringin' thet woman here. She said las' time—but you fellas wouldn't care nothin' 'bout thet." He said desperately, "But it's *her* told 'Lita—can't you *see* it's her?"

"I can't see her wanting to tell *that* woman. You said yourself—"

"I know. I know but—" Jake groaned and wiped his face with his sleeve. "The' ain't nothin' more I kin say t' you. She's done it t' spite me. Way she figgers, it wouldn't spite me much if she tol' someone else; she saw through 'Lita a heap better'n I did. She knew right off 'Lita'd try t' git it. If you can't see that . . ."

"I can see you're up to your tricks again."

"I'm *not!* Hones' t' Gawd—"

Some dark leap of thought sheered Sundance's

glance. He jammed the pistol back in its scabbard. He shoved past Jake, almost walking over him, wheeled around the table plainly headed porchward. He was at the door when Jake cried scared-like: "Where you goin'? Don't—"

"You goddam fool! Do you think I'll let her steal me out of it?"

Sundance yanked the door open wickedly.

The lamplight showed John Slaughter standing there.

TWENTY-ONE

"Out of what?" Slaughter said, and Sundance stopped like a sledge had struck him.

But not for long.

He was a hair-triggered man in his grasp of essentials, a man in whom both mind and muscle had long been wed to lightning action. He was the kind who could make split-second decisions and must have made quite a few since coming here, as Antrim, just now, was beginning to realize.

It seemed essential to Sundance that he get at once on the trail of that conniving pair who'd made off with Hunt's map on Don Lorenzo's Arabs. He was shoving forward with a hand half lifted when he caught the glint of John Slaughter's pistol.

It stopped him short, cheeks roaning wickedly.

They were that way, glaring, when Idy Red, coolly scornful, rejoined the carnival. Antrim saw her, gracefully posed in the patio doorway, her eyes expressing a warm satisfaction with what she interpreted to be in the making.

She was a rare one all right, and no mistake. And a heap more clever than you'd give her credit for. Already she had neatly jammed Jake's game; and by the look of her eyes she had another wrench handy.

"I say—" Slaughter said; "I say 'out of what?'"

But Sundance had himself in hand again. He grinned at Slaughter and shrugged his shoulders. "Your chew's on fire," he smiled. "Here—have another," and passed the sheriff a fresh cigar.

Slaughter's left hand put the weed in his pocket. Slaughter's right hand held the pistol rock-steady. "It ain't my habit," he told Sundance bluntly, "to ask a man anything more than twice."

"Oh, that," Sundance chuckled. "Well, it did kind of rile me, an' that's a fact. I found a claim up in the hills that I reckoned on filing. I set up my markers. I made me a map of it—that was before I dropped in on Jake, you'll gather. To make a long story short—"

"You mean a 'tall' story, don't you?"

Sundance looked at Slaughter. "If you don't want to listen I'll quit right now."

"I'll fill it in for you. You were goin' to say someone stole this map, that they're on their way to jump your claim—weren't you?"

Sundance, again the serenely suave gentleman, nodded. "You've called the turn, Sheriff. I've good reason to think this Mex dame, Lolita, is the one that stole it. Anyway, she an' this Spence have lit out hotfoot."

Slaughter said, "If you're all through lyin', try tellin' the truth now."

"Suppose you tell it, if you think I'm lying."

"I can do that, too," Slaughter mentioned coldly. "As a matter of fact, this map was drawn by Zwing Hunt—not you. It purports to show where Zwing and some other fellows buried a batch of Curly Bill loot. I've never put much stock in that story—"

"Of course not," Sundance grinned at him. "Nobody outside a halfwit would ever swallow a yarn like that."

Slaughter was short, but a powerful man, broad of shoulder, thick of neck; a stocky man—even darker than Sundance. He had thick black hair, black mustache, black beard. His eyes were black as jet, and as hard. He had come from Texas with three herds of cattle and a brand new wife. He owned a big ranch not far from Hereford and was accounted a wealthy man in this country. Most men, in his case, would have taken things easy and let his deputies do the leg work; but if you suppose that was Slaughter's way, you're mistaken. He was the go-gettingest sheriff that ever packed a star in Cochise County.

And he was utterly fearless.

He said, looking straight up into big Sundance's stare: "I'm goin' to let you go after this girl and Spence—as a matter of fact, I propose to go with you. I suggest that we *all* go." Then he said with blunt suddenness: "Did you steal those horses?"

But Sundance had a good grip on himself. He gave Idy Red a broad wink and grinned. "If you mean them horses Miz' Harris mentioned—the ones that dame an' Pete Spence skipped off on, I'd suggest you talk to ol' Jake about 'em—he knows this country a heap better'n I do. *I* didn't even know there was any willow brakes."

You never could tell what John Slaughter was thinking. His bright, black eyes showed no expression.

Old Jake's showed plenty. He'd spent the bulk of his life trailing around with hard customers; knew their ways—had traded on them, matching their slick and baited trickeries, sidestepping their traps and rigging his own. It might seem he'd have had an answer ready, but all he had was a growl in his throat.

If ever a man looked guilty, he did.

Despite this, it was Antrim's belief big Sundance had brought those Arabs out of Mexico—that Sundance, for some purpose undisclosed, had secretly hidden them out in the willow brakes, in that snug little cove so well screened from observance.

"Well," Sundance repeated, "why don't you ask him?"

John Slaughter's look went blackly over him. "Mebbe I will . . . when I get around to it. In the meantime—"

"They're the ones you're after, I think," declared Sundance. Jake's been tellin' me all about 'em, fact is, he's been trying to sell them to me. They're A-rabs, he says—brought 'em up from Torreon. A stud and a filly, chestnut an' gray. Don't that kind of sound to you, Slaughter?"

Slaughter tongued the stump of his smoke around. "You seem powerful anxious to get

Jake hung. You wouldn't be figuring to *use* me, would you?"

Sundance laughed. "No skin off *my* nose if he gets away from you. Suit yourself."

"I aim to," the sheriff said. "You ever been up this way before?"

"I been most places. From the Peace River south to the Rio Grande. A twinkle tweaked through big Sundance's stare. "I been huntin' health—" he coughed robustuously. "While we're standing here gabbin' them horses—"

"Just leave me worry about them horses. I'm gettin' paid for it," Slaughter said. His glance swung to Jake. "You got any talking you want to catch up on?"

Jake licked his lips but he didn't say much. Except with his eyes.

Slaughter said, "You sure?" and Jake nodded.

Idy Red stepped out of her pose in the doorframe. "While you're saddlin' I'll shake up some grub fo' your travels."

The sheriff thanked her and they followed him out and caught up their horses. Kerrick's big claybank was in the bunch and Antrim made a quick throw and snared him. It was in his mind he might be needing that bottom before he got shut of this night's business. He might feel any moment the weight of the sheriff's hand on his shoulder. He was hard put to think why he hadn't felt it already. That he hadn't was almost worse than feeling it—which might be the effect John Slaughter was striving for.

Of one thing Antrim was mighty certain: the sheriff was no man to stamp and yell *boo!* at. He was one to be wary of every instant.

Several times since returning Antrim had been on the point of confiding in Slaughter, of getting the sheriff aside some way and unbosoming himself of his thoughts and fancies; of describing the horse cache—the Arabs he'd found there, the shot and the boot track—the queer print of this claybank. It had even been in his mind to explain, if he had to, his *own* intentions—his reason for coming here; and, of course, that peculiar business of his trip with Lolita. But each time something had held him back—had bid him keep quiet; some hunch or foreboding he could not analyze. There was danger here; it was in the air like a pungent smell; a feel of death that curled with the breeze and could not be shaken.

There was, for instance, Idy Red's odd manner. Not her pleasure at making Jake uncomfortable—the whole push seemed to take pleasure in that; but the curious way she had eyed big

Sundance. Twice tonight he had caught her watching him, without any sign of her former friendliness. Studying him, you might almost say. The look of her eyes had been distinctly probing. A kind of awe had had hold of her cheeks. Fear— perhaps loathing, had a part in shaping them; or it might have been rather a sort of cold scorn which had put that tight, grim crease to her mouth. Whatever it was that had come between them, she no longer looked on Sundance with favor.

Which, some way, kind of pleasured Antrim; though he did not ask why this should be so.

It would not be long before dawn rolled around again; already the eastern rims of the mountains stood sharp and black against the graying sky and Antrim, shaking free of his thoughts, noticed Slaughter and Sundance with their heads together. Sundance appeared to be doing the talking and Antrim wondered what slime he was brewing.

Jake led his saddled horse past Antrim, said gruffly out of one side of this mouth, "Sundance borried thet knife from Cope jest a tail's shake of time b'fore you foun' Kerrick's carcass. Keep 'em out yere a minute. I got a chore thet wants doin'."

He kept on toward the house and Sundance quit talking, chanced to look up and noticed. "You better watch out," his voice carried plainly. "That polecat's figurin' to cut his stick."

Slaughter called: "Antrim will fetch that grub for us, Jake."

Gauze wheeled around with a scowl and mounted. But he made no attempt to put steel to his horse. He sat there, gaunt and slack in the saddle, while Antrim clanked his spurs toward the porch gloom.

Idy Red was at the door when he got there. She gave him the bundle of grub she had fixed. Urged by some unaccountable impulse he dragged off his hat.

The porch, being deep in shadows, he could not tell what might lie on her cheeks. He felt like he ought to say something, ought to offer some sort of apology maybe, but for the life of him he couldn't seem to scare up the words. It had always been his opinion that acts talked loudest. After the guy was planted, saying you were sorry didn't help any.

She seemed to be eying him oddly. He wondered what thoughts might be in her head as she stood there so still staring up at him. It was funny how queer she could make him feel without so much as opening her mouth at him.

Funny, and damn uncomfortable.

It began to get on his nerves. He could feel the squirm of his temper; the prickly feel of his hackles getting up. After all, he hadn't done nothing so terrible; all he had actually done was ignore her. Nothing in that to get looked at so grim like.

"I'm sorry," he growled, and clapped on his hat. But she caught him up like a flash:

"Fo' what?"

"Well . . . for what I said—"

"You don't need t' be sorry fo' me," she said fiercely. "I do' want yo' damn sorrow—I do' want yo' damn charity, neither! I do' want nothin' t' do with you. I kin shift fo' myse'f an' don't you fo'get it!"

Antrim's lip curled. "Like the way you been shiftin' with Sundance, I reckon—" and went back off the porch with the feel of her hand stinging hot on his cheekbones.

"Don't open yo' mouth ag'in—don't you *dast* to! The' ain't no man ever tetched me yet; an' the' ain't no man ever goin' to! Now git!" she cried; and he caught the pale, shining glint of her pistol. "Git 'fore I lose my temper!"

Antrim grabbed up the bundle of food and

left her, the clank of his spurs sounding sharp and angry. He *was* angry, too; though more at himself than he was at her. At himself for being such a rattlebrained fool as to *try* patching up anything with that hellcat. And it riled him bad as her hand had done to think why he ever had wanted to.

He came up with the others and climbed into his saddle. He had an idea Jake peered at him sharply; but it didn't seem likely they'd heard what she said and it was a cinch they couldn't have seen much, either. So it riled him all over when Sundance said:

"Didn't she have no kiss for you, bucko?"

Antrim whirled his horse with a wicked bit. He looked big Sundance hard in the eye. "If it's trouble you're wantin' just say that again."

" 'The Lord is my shepherd,' " quoted Sundance unctuously, and coolly turned his look at John Slaughter. "Ain't it time we was movin'? I'd admire to get me a shot at that tinhorn, if it's all the same to you, Mister Sheriff."

Slaughter said, "If there's any occasion for burning powder *I'll* be the one to burn it. Remember that. It's one of the things I get paid for."

"Well ... no offense," Sundance said. "Won't *no*body be burnin' powder if we don't shake it up an' get started. They got a fast pair of horses if they're the ones Jake says they are. Which way we headin'?"

"Which way would *you* head?"

"They'll get clean away if we wait for daylight. Be over the Border an' out of our reach. Looks to me," Sundance said, "like we better hit straight for the Line. I'd hit for the Line an' chance cuttin' 'em off."

"You won't this trip." Slaughter smiled at him coldly. "We're heading for Turkey Creek Canyon."

TWENTY-TWO

Sundance exhibited a look of surprise. "What do you mean—'Turkey Creek'? I thought you was figurin' to hunt them horse thieves—"

"I am," Slaughter said. "Around Turkey Creek someplace. I've an idea we'll find them in 'that other canyon' Jake spoke about." He smiled at the sullen lump in Jake's saddle. "Once we see Turkey Creek I guess Jake can find them."

It were as though he said, "I guess Jake better."

After that there wasn't much said. There didn't seem very much left *to* say. Jake rode like he was sunk beyond the reach of threats, a man deep buried in the debris of his scheming. Even the impudent wit of Sundance seemed dampened with the knowledge disclosed by those words; but he wasn't quitting. His seat in the saddle showed a mind at work, and Antrim wondered what the man would try next.

There wasn't much doubt in Antrim now that the burly Sundance had done for Kerrick. With what Jake had told him about Cope's knife it seemed pretty certain who the killer was. Of course Cope's death might be another matter, predicated on some different motive; but even here there was a pretty good chance it had been big Sundance that had managed Cope's ticket. Lolita's hand might have squeezed the trigger that had driven that fatal shot into Cope, but Sundance's brain could have contrived the reason. Sundance's brain would *gladly* have contrived it had he sensed any need for being rid of Cope. The mere lessening by one of the number to share any plunder uncovered would have been all the reason Sundance needed.

Though the girl, of course, *might* have killed them both. She was an unknown quantity, this dark Lolita. As the look of things suggested, she might be Jake's mistress; she might also be considerable else besides. She was quick of wit. She knew this country. She knew Guy Antrim was hunting small boots, as disclosed by the hoax she had used to get rid of him. And when he'd found her crouched above the dead Cope's body she'd made another clever play to rid herself of him by thrusting that gun in his hands to be found with.

Perhaps that hadn't worked out quite the way she had figured. In the usual run of events he'd have been arrested for the gambler's murder. But Slaughter was a hard one to reckon with. He was a man who kept his thoughts to himself. He appeared to care little who had killed who, or why, so long as this trail brought him up with those horses. He seemed to feel it incumbent on him to recover stolen stock. Antrim remembered the rumors of many occasions. Stolen stock and John Slaughter were almost synonymous; where the one was taken you would find the other.

Yet it wasn't Lolita who had stolen those horses. It was Sundance. Antrim would have bet his life it was Sundance. The man knew entirely too much about those horses to have got it from Jake, or from any other. Sundance knew because it was Sundance who had stolen them—why he even knew where they'd been stolen from; and he was no more a ranger than Luther King was.

He wondered what Slaughter would say were he to tell the sheriff of that badge Sundance packed. He wondered what Sundance would say if he told him. Some brightness, probably. Some flippant insolence.

Wit and insolence came easy to Sundance. He was quick and deep, a cool, chancy customer, sly and calculating; a man with his eye ever on the main chance.

It was plain to Antrim he had not been invited here. There was no love lost between Sundance and the pair who had come here by Jake's invitation, Kerrick and Cope, both dead now and planted. And plain it was, too, that Jake had known Sundance some place in the past. And the boots Sundance wore might well have left that track he had found by the trail at the creekbank cache of the willow-screened Arabs.

There was method here, and coherence and reason, if a man could only pull the right thread loose. There was a thought slinking around in Antrim's mind, but he couldn't hardly bring credence to it. It seemed too far-fetched, too remotely unlikely.

Yet, it *could* be so. And if it were...

In the dawn's gray light he kept sharp watch on Sundance.

It was no near thing, this Turkey Creek Canyon. From the Skeleton entrance to the San

Simon a man with sharp eyes could see the twistings of Turkey Creek's gorge; but by horse or Shank's Mare it was a long, hot ride. The mesquite leaves drooped in the wilting heat and Jake Gauze, sleeving his bristly face, would frequently curse it and go on muttering under his breath like a man who has lived too long alone, or a man who has reached and passed life's prime and finds little left to look forward to.

As for Jake, Antrim thought, he had cause for groaning. Whatever the schemes he had nursed of late, they were blighted now, jettisoned by things he could not control; by the Cochise sheriff, for one—John Slaughter. For the matter of that, they had all had their schemes—those obscure intentions which had brought them here; and in old Jake's eyes, like as not, they had all conspired to thwart him. Even Kerrick and Cope, who had got themselves killed; for their deaths had helped fashion this trap for him. He was a man without faith or future, a man caught up by his folly and confronted at last with the fruits of it.

They stopped near noon, to sample the food Idy Red had put up, to breathe the horses and take a few lungfuls of smoke while they rested. Antrim, flat on his back in the shade of some ironwood, watched the play of the sun in the clouds and thought, without pleasure, of the girl left behind.

Idy Red. How well he recalled her. The look of her eyes ... of her cheeks ... her slim figure; the quick, birdlike way of her movements. He remembered the soft, drawling sound of her voice, the quick twist of her smile, her freckles. He recalled things about her he'd not even been conscious of noticing. Little things, that now were made precious by memory. He remembered the things which he ought to have said—those things he really had wanted to say, but had stifled because they'd seemed sissy, ill-sounding to come from a grown man's lips. And he cursed himself, recalling the words he had used in their place, the crude ungallantries that had driven her to seek Sundance's company. And the burly man's taunt came back to him. "Didn't she have no kiss for you, bucko?"

Antrim knew that he hated Sundance.

The long afternoon was well advanced and sun's shadows were lengthening, blue on the peaks and deep mauve in the ash and sycamore timber, when their trail crossed the sign of the fugitives. The girl and the gambler had been rid-

'ing hard—were a good four hours ahead of them.

There was no way of telling what Slaughter thought. His black-bearded cheeks were inscrutable.

They pushed on until darkness stopped them.

They camped in a bowl gouged between two peaks, a grassy swale with a cold spring bubbling; and it did a man good to see the horses roll before Jake caught them up and tied them. He was a handy man with horses, and had his own way of hobbling them—a loop of rope passed around a hind foot to a stake that allowed them to graze yet anchored them.

The night was deep with shadow when they dipped again into Idy Red's pack and munched their rations in silence. It was cooler up here in the mountains, cool with a tangy crispness that put new life into saddle-racked muscles; and a new thought came to plague Antrim. He had remembered Idy Red's last name, which was Harris.

"Better not smoke," Slaughter told them gruffly.

Sundance hummed a tune through his teeth and Jake Gauze shoved an oath between his, and Antrim wondered what the idea was. "Are we gettin' that close to that canyon?"

No one had any answer for that, and Slaughter went over and got the rifle from his saddle and came back and sat down with it laid on his knees.

The silence became uneased with men's thoughts, with the wary, covert way of their eyes; and the shadows grew more thick and blackened and night closed in without stars or moon and no man moved for the threat of that rifle.

But it wasn't in Sundance's nature to be held quiet by anything long. "No sense," he said, "sittin' around like corpses. Le's do a little singin'. Let's build us up a fire—"

"There'll be no fire," Slaughter spoke up from the murk. "No fire and no singin'. An' don't be getting no notions. Case you don't know it, I'm a damned good shot."

"I'm a good shot myself," Sudance said irascibly, "but I ain't got no cravin' to root here all night."

"We're leavin', soon as the moon gets up."

"You goin' to track 'em?" Jake blurted. "Hell! No need of us waitin' aroun' fer that. I can take you to Turkey Creek Canyon—"

"I expect you can," Slaughter said. "I can take us myself, if it comes to that. I didn't come here to hunt wild geese. I came here to get them horses."

"What's that got t' do with it?"
"If I track them I know I'll get them."

The night got blacker and blacker. It didn't seem like the moon would *ever* get up. You couldn't see a yard in front of you and Antrim, sitting with his back to a rock, began to think they would never see the fugitives, either. But there wasn't anything to be done about it. The sheriff had made his mind up and all hell couldn't move him.

From time to time Antrim could hear Jake and Sundance fidgeting. Especially Sundance; and it pleased him to think how Sundance would look if this wait let the girl and Spence get away.

Then another thought struck him and he scowled, his mood changing. He'd been figuring there wasn't much danger of the pair getting away with the plunder; and there wasn't, of course. The fruit of the Canyon massacres had been silver bullion and 'dobe dollars. You couldn't take much of that stuff in your pockets; and the stuff Zwing Hunt and Grounds had added had been moved to the cache in wagons. But they could easy ride off with that cigar box of diamonds. In the end, of course, John Slaughter would catch them— he had that reputation. But in the meantime what of the diamonds? And what was to keep them from destroying the landmarks by which the plunder was to be traced to its cache? There was nothing to keep them from *moving* them.

He began to feel as edgy as Sundance.

And then, suddenly, there was the moon come out; come out just as Slaughter had said it would. Shook free of the clouds' damp clutch at last it gilded the hollow with its argent light. Each blade of grass stood blue and clear, and so did the look on Sundance's face.

One horse was gone, and so was Jake.

TWENTY-THREE

There wasn't much said; but the glint of Sundance's eyes turned wicked and Antrim felt like smashing something. He sensed reason now in Jake's care for the horses; sensed reason in a whole lot of things that before hadn't held much meaning. He had known Gauze was slick as greased slobbers; but the man hadn't seemed to have the requisite nerve to try any stunt so foolhardy. Had Slaughter guessed what was up he'd have killed him—but Jake had known that chance, and had taken it. He must have moved with the stealth of a spider.

And now he had stolen a march on them.

There was a while then when Antrim saw nothing but red as he crashed down the corridors of thought opened up. With Jake sped away he could no longer doubt the tale of this treasure had truth in it; Jake had fled through the night to snatch it away, to catch up with those others—to make off with them. Why, damn his soul!—this had probably been his plan from the start! *This* was the way he had schemed to outwit them and now, by God, he had done it, too! They probably had wagons at the cache, ready, waiting—they may even have had the loot dug up and packed!

No wonder, Antrim thought, Spence had still been around when he'd come back from that snipe hunt with 'Lita. The girl had diddled him neatly. Jake had never intended to be rid of Spence; Sundance and Kerrick and Cope and himself were the ones not counted to share in it. They would probably have been off long ago if Slaughter hadn't come riding in like he had.

When the roar had finally passed from his head Antrim saw that John Slaughter had gone for his horse. Sundance, too, had got his horse and was heaving his saddle up onto its back like it was Jake's neck his big hands had hold of.

As he joined them, readying his own horse—or Kerrick's big claybank, to be real precise, Antrim found himself taking stock of Sundance; he had done it so often it was become second nature. But always he found food for thought in the action. He was not yet sure, but was becoming increasingly confident, that somewhere, sometime, he and the burly health seeker had seen each other before. At any rate, one thing was sure: though it might have been Jake who had hidden those Arabs in the willow brakes, Sundance—and Sundance only, had brought them up out of Mexico. It might be his duty to tell Slaughter so—to relate, as well, the tale Jake had told of Cope lending his knife to the burly man just before Bat Kerrick's body was found.

It might be his duty, Antrim thought with a scowl, but some things came *before* duty.

And, besides, who was *he* to be shaping up tunes for a star-packer's ear? Lute King, the only man ever thrown into jail for that ill-timed assault on the Benson stage. Be like the pot scoring off on the kettle!

He was the last man into his saddle but they waited for him; Slaughter's black regard and ready rifle were not to be fooled a second time. "We goin' to trail him?" Antrim asked them.

"What for?" Sundance asked. "You ain't got no doubt where he's gone, have you?"

Antrim shrugged; and they hit a fast lope on the moon-revealed trail of the Mexican girl and the gambler. They had neither the mood nor the time for talk, but Antrim's mind never quit its fretting. He recalled scraps of rumor he'd heard of the gambler. Pete Spence, rumor said, was in his late forties, a tall and gaunt and taciturn man whose right name was held to be Ferguson—"Lark" Ferguson, to give it its handle. He had hailed, folks claimed, from Texas, from somewheres around the Big Bend country where, it was thought, he had killed a round score of Mexicans. Like Buckshot Roberts, of Lincoln County fame, Pete Spence was held to be a walking lead mine, salted with bullets other people had fired at him during the hectic years of his outlaw career. On one occasion, often cited, he'd been nearly killed by a load of buckshot while robbing a store at Corpus Christi; he'd been shot in the head in New Mexico someplace—probably Silver City or Shakespeare, both of which places had been treated to a sample of his skill at faro and monte. He had also dealt cards at Galeyville and Charlestown, where the famous Curly Bill had used to hang up his hat what time he wasn't out augmenting fortune. At the time of the Benson stage robbery he, Pete Spence, had been living in Tombstone with a Mexican woman, Antrim recalled, and had been thought to have directed Frank Stillwell and Florentine Cruz in their assassination of Morgan Earp. He was, intuition told Antrim, entirely capable of showing his teeth should he find himself backed in a corner. Nor was the girl, Lolita, of a sort to be accounted pint size. When it came to a final reckoning, Slaughter had probably gauged events rightly when he'd hinted the possibility of gunplay.

And there was Jake yet to be considered. He had likely joined up with the others by this time. They would probably rig up an ambush. Jake could expect no mercy from Slaughter.

The killings came into Antrim's mind again, the deaths of Cope and Kerrick. He had found Lolita with Cope that night—with the gambler's dead body, to put the thing rightly. Had her's been the hand to fire that shot? Lolita, seeing Antrim and fearing exposure, may have snatched Cope's pistol and fired at him; but who, then, had killed Taiban Cope? And what exposure had the girl been afraid of? Not exposure for the hoax she had played on Antrim—that looked too farfetched to suppose for an instant.

There'd been only one shot fired out of Cope's gun.

It was too mixed up for Antrim. It was easier and much more plausible to believe big Sundance had killed them both, killed Cope and Kerrick, for reasons best known to himself. He had, Jake claimed, borrowed Cope's knife just before Bat Kerrick was killed with it. Not suspecting Jake of knowing this, Sundance might, later, have killed Taiban Cope to keep his mouth shut.

There was something about big Sundance...

He recalled Idy Red's proud words of her father—"But, dammit," he growled, "he was killed at Iron Springs—or supposed to've been, and Earp had plenty witnesses."

It was Sundance—dimple-cheeked Sundance, who brought their travel to a sudden halt with an arm reached out to Slaughter's bridle.

There was excitement and a bitter conviction in the way his stare swept Slaughter's face.

The sheriff's black eyes showed nothing. "Well?"

"That girl! I knew damn' well I'd seen her before!"

"I've seen her before, myself," Slaughter said. "In Tombstone—"

"You don't get it!" Sundance caught the sheriff's arm. "You been tryin' to figure who killed 'em—Cope and Kerrick, I mean. So've I; an' I believe, by God, I've done it. It's *her!*" He said excitedly: "Maybe she's rubbed Jake out, too— if she ain't she will if the chance comes right—it's what she's been anglin' around to! She's been makin' a play for this plunder, but—"

"What do you put in them smokes you twist?"

Sundance stared. "By God," he said, "I can prove it!"

"By Godin' won't help you any," said Antrim; and, for a second, Sundance's eyes went narrow.

But he brushed it away, declared heatedly: "If there's one thing a Mex'can never forgets it's revenge—revenge is all that dame's lived for!—revenge on them that did away with her father!"

"What," Slaughter said, "are you talking about? If you're just throwing dust to give Jake more time—"

"My God!" Sundance said. "Can't you *see* it?"

"I might, if I knew what you was talking about."

"Jake's woman! That Tombstone slut—that *Lolita!*"

"You say someone killed her father?"

"Sure—Curly Bill's bunch killed him—eight years ago; they killed him in Skeleton Canyon—"

"What for?"

Sundance said impatiently: "For that mule train of silver his bunch was smugglin' to Tucson. Look! You got to—"

"You're right," Slaughter said with a cold, thin smile; "I've got to get after them fugitives. Come on. We've wasted time enough—"

"Wait!" growled Sundance; but Slaughter was through with waiting. He appeared suddenly consumed with a lust for speed. Putting spurs to his horse he went hard through the gloom of a scrub oak stand and Sundance, cursing, rode after him.

But the burly man, Antrim decided, was right. Against every inclination he was forced to agree with Sundance's thinking. With this girl as Don Miguel's daughter many things became clear that, before, had been closed and locked doors to him. Lolita would have been that handsome young stripling who had raced in wild flight up the canyon; she would have been that solitary horseman who had kept lone vigil on the San Luis hills. For years it had been common talk in the cow camps that some unknown nemesis was stalking the survivors of the Curly Bill gang. Like a curse, bad luck had tracked them down until at last it seemed there was none but gaunt old Jake Gauze left; and here, crouched sloe-eyed and smiling, was the dusky Lolita, turned up to play Delilah to the old man's Samson.

Antrim, hurrying after the others, hadn't much doubt but that Sundance had called the turn on her. He was still a bit puzzled however as to why she had killed Cope and Kerrick. They had had no part in the canyon massacre; or at least he had never heard that they had. The girl might have had plenty of reason. Perhaps they had known her—guessed her secret. They may have tried to blackmail her. Whatever her reason, it seemed pretty evident she'd killed them. Antrim himself had come upon her attempting to flee from the gambler's dead body—attempting to flee with a gun in her hand. A gun acrid with the fumes of burnt powder.

They were following the course of a shallow wash when the sheriff held up his hand and stopped them. "Creek's just ahead—just beyond that belt of blackjack yonder. Don't let off your guns without I tell you. If I tell you to shoot, don't waste no lead. Lead costs money. So do trials, and they don't get horse thieves hung in this county."

They moved into the canyon at a careful walk. Bear grass muffled the hoofs of their horses. The night had aged and the moon grown dim, and though no moon rays got down this far the air was gray with a pearly mist that glinted and sparkled from the grotesque shapes of the dark growth around them.

They advanced with caution. No shouts, no shots broke the pre-dawn quiet; no racketing crash of rifles challenged them. They appeared unmarked, and marked no others. A sound of fury came out of Sundance. His look, flung at Slaughter, was accusing, intolerant. "If you'd struck for the Border like—"

"Quiet!" Slaughter said, and moved forward without so much as glancing at Sundance.

The big man took it like a slap in the face. Antrim knew by the way he cocked his shoulders the urge was in him to kill John Slaughter.

Very swift and smooth Antrim laid his gun across the pommel. He thumbed back the hammer without caring who heard it.

Both of them heard; and the quick, raking wheel of Sundance's shoulder was perfectly timed with Slaughter's turning. The sheriff's hard stare caught the play at once. "When I need any help I'll ask for it."

"You'll ask, all right."

"I'll never ask help from a jailbird, King."

TWENTY-FOUR

Antrim's eyes turned bright and narrow. The slouch of his shape in the saddle shifted; by just that fraction he stood ready for violence.

"So you know me, eh?"

"Of course I know you! There's not many toughs in this country I *don't* know—none I wouldn't recognize if they set their tracks across my trail. That's one of the things I get paid for."

"And what do you propose to do about it?"

"I propose right now to get after them horse thiefs. Walk your horse ahead—you, too, Sundance."

Antrim lingered a moment while his eyes searched Slaughter's. Then he shrugged, sheathed his pistol and rode ahead. Sundance, too, took the sheriff's suggestion; and once more the three pressed warily on.

Antrim murmured presently, "Looks like we've come to the end of this canyon. There's a bald, round knob stickin' up ahead—"

"Harris Mountain." Slaughter, too, put a curb on his voice. "Keep your eyes skinned now. There's a kind of gulch opens off here somewhere. Expect we'll find our friends—"

"Here it is," Sundance called. "Here's your canyon—"

"*Shh!*" Antrim growled; and they heard a low, far-off mutter of voice sound.

Sundance sucked in his breath; leaned forward. "By God," he said, "we've got 'em!"

They swung off their horses, left them hitched to the ground. "Go on," Slaughter motioned ahead with his rifle and Sundance struck off at once without argument. He moved with the lithe, swinging grace of a cougar, head thrust a little forward as though striving to pierce the gray clutch of the fog which seemed even thicker with the coming of day. Their clothes were damp with the feel of it and moisture beaded the sheriff's rifle.

A sudden, explosive grunt came from Sundance. He had stopped and was bending down over something—it was a spring and, beside it, the wreck of a wagon. Just bits of charred boards, two rusted axles and springs with, yonder, snakelike and black in the soaking grass, the twisted and mangled iron rim of a wheel.

Sundance's eyes, coming up, met Antrim's darkly. "Here's the wagon—what's left of it anyway."

His look, still insistent, grew harsh with impatience. "*You* had the map—don't you *get* it?" Sundance's hand swept around intolerantly. "This goddam wagon's got up an' moved!"

Antrim saw it then. Sundance was right. This wagon was not where the map had shown it. On Hunt's map it had been between two springs.

"Go on," Slaughter prodded. "You boys mightn't recall it, but we come here to grab them horse thiefs. I guess you heard me—get movin'."

Antrim's stare had been fixed on the gulch's west wall, probing to locate the 'cove' Zwing had mentioned. It was a strain on the eyes to cleave such fog and he hadn't been giving much notice to where his steps were taking him. Of a sudden something hard struck his knee—rammed pain through his groin as he stumbled. It was a rock with no least give to it; a rock roughly squared, standing three feet high.

"The polecats!" Sundance snarled at him. "They've moved every mark Zwing left us!"

"Never mind the marks," Slaughter said. "Get movin'."

Antrim was already moving, quartering off toward the wall as though there wasn't any law within miles of him. He made it forty paces by count from the obelisk to the gulch's west wall; and the map had held it to be barely three. He saw no cove, no break in the wall any place in sight. He came back into the trail again. To the rock—ran a hand across its chiseled surface, his fingers tracing the crosses cut in it.

"Well?" Sundance growled.

Antrim nodded. "They been moved all right."

"And now," Slaughter said, "we'll move ourselves." His voice was honed fine as peach fuzz. "We'll be biddin' good-bye to Hunt's fairytale map an' get on with our hunt for them horse thiefs."

They were that way, wills clashing, eyes glowering, when a rifle cracked from the swirls of fog and the screech of the shot banged off the rock into which Zwing Hunt had cut his two crosses. So wickedly swift was Antrim's turn he saw the man's shape diving back of a tree. Three things Antrim caught with his raking stare: the man's blurred shape, a rearing, frantic pair of tied horses, and the startled, rage-filled look of Sundance.

Antrim kept his eyes on the tree; stayed crouched in his tracks, gun lifted and ready. But his mind stayed wickedly fixed on the cause of big Sundance's cursing—that terrified pair of tied horses. They were not the horses they should have been; they bore no least resemblance to the stolen Arabs. They were a pair of forty-dollar cow broncs.

Antrim felt much the way big Sundance must have, reflecting how slickly they had all been diddled; and he saw in that moment where the truth must lie.

Jake Gauze had gotten the best of them. He had beautifully salted this canyon with markers; had gone off with his treasure and left them. It was plain as day in Guy Antrim's mind they would not find Jake within miles of this place. He had not only fooled Antrim, Sundance and Slaughter, but had tricked Lolita and Spence as well. Very cannily he had played each one against the other and was now gone off to laugh with his plunder.

Antrim's glance, brightly fixed, was still on the tree when Spence's voice tore from the fog behind him: "Git out of there, Curly, you damn fool—leave me line my sights on that darned sheriff!" And *crack!* on the heels of his words came the rifle; and Antrim's whirled look saw the sheriff reel, saw his outflung arms lose their hold of the Winchester—saw him stumble and fall on his face in the bear grass. In that selfsame moment Sundance's pistol roared and Lolita's shrill scream pierced the gun-pounded bedlam, and died.

TWENTY-FIVE

The rush of events seemed to have paralyzed Antrim; he stood hung up in the crush of his thinking and let big Sundance get clear away.

To hear a bold, handsome woman sob out her last breath—to see that hound of the law, John Slaughter, toppled, were reason in plenty to stand there rooted. But on top of this there came rememberance. He had had the hunch only yesterday, and had scoffed it away as preposterous. To find that hunch was well-founded—to hear it confirmed by Spence's own words—that here in the warm, quivering flesh was the man Wyatt Earp had claimed to have killed eight years ago in the mesquite brush and greasewood of the Iron Springs water hole—in a word, that Sundance was Curly Bill Brocius come back for his plunder, was a startling enough thing to stagger anyone.

Small wonder Jake Gauze had feared him!

Sudden fear gripped Antrim, pulled him bodily out of his thinking; but too late. Curly Bill was gone. And gone were the broncs he had seen tied yonder. Hid by the swirling mists of the fog he could dimly hear the far pound of their travel. Then a nearer sound drew his eyes, spike sharp, to find Pete Spence still within his reach, a wraithlike shape trampling down the wet growth as he floundered through the clutching brush, panting, snarling, gone hoarse with his cursing of the man who had left him afoot in this waste.

"Spence!" Antrim called, and lifted his gun. It brought Spence around with his insane face all warped and twisted. There was froth on his lips; a blaze in his eyes. A snakehead of flame licked out from his middle and the whine of its bullet jerked Antrim's hatbrim. Antrim held his arm straight out and fired.

Spence dropped. With his mouth stretched wide he came to a knee and steadied his wabbling gun on a branch.

Antrim fired again, and after that Spence did not move any more.

It came to Antrim suddenly that, in Curly

Bill's boots, tricked and cheated twice over, he would be on fire with desire for revenge; that he'd find Jake Gauze if it took him through hell. "An' that, by God," he told himself, "is exactly where that lobo is off to!"

Off to find Jake—off to settle the score.

He remembered the horses they'd left with dropped reins in the salt cedars back by this canyon's entrance. He broke into a run.

The small of his back was wet with sweat when he came to the entrance. There were rivers of sweat streaking down his cheeks; but the horses were there. Sundance had been too much in a swivet to remember these broncs, or to waste time hunting them through this fog just to loose them when, in all probability, by his way of thinking, Pete Spence would account for Antrim.

Antrim was glad now he had taken Kerrick's claybank; that horse had more guts than you could hang on a fence post. If any horse Jake had could make this trek and return without rest, it was Kerrick's. Curly Bill had a pair to depend on.

Antrim stripped off his spurs and threw them away. He would take no chance on temptation's urging. He knew if he had those spurs he might use them. He just couldn't afford to. If this horse played out—

He would not let himself envisage such thought.

The long day crawled.

Fog was a dirty sheet wrapped around him. It was a gray woolen blanket when he circled the mesa. Juniper trees and live oak on the slope made crazy patterns in the steamy vapor. Through the ash and sycamore the going was tough; became tougher still when the claybank pulled out of it. But the horse wasn't lame; Antrim had fixed that mis-set hind shoe long before they'd been ready to leave Jake's ranch.

A pang of remorse briefly touched him presently when he recalled with what haste he'd come tearing off with never a look at the girl or Slaughter. Not that a look would have helped them much. The girl had known what chance she ran. As for Slaughter—dying was one of the things he got paid for.

The Cherrycow Mountains glimmered blue in the west.

In a way it was lucky, what had happened to Slaughter. Antrim couldn't help feeling so. He wouldn't have willed it, or had any hand in it; but Slaughter, alive, would have taken him in. He might not have got out of that jail this time.

Well, the treasure he'd come here seeking was gone. Jake had beat them all out of it. Some way it didn't seem to make much difference. He had spent a lot of time tracking down that plunder and he reckoned he had ought to be feeling like Sundance; but he couldn't seem to get up a sweat about it. Another goal had taken its place, and thinking about Idy Red that way brought his mind squarely back to Sundance.

The man would be in a fine sweat of hate by the time he sighted Jake's buildings. If Sundance caught him he would carve Jake's heart out. But if, instead of Jake, Sundance found Idy Red . . .

It was this drear thought that was cording the muscles on Antrim's jaw—that had caused him to throw his spurs away lest desire for speed should prove his utter undoing. He must nurse this horse, keep it going and able. Time and again he had strained his eyes on the forward distance, but never once had his stare found Sundance.

It was dusk by the time he reached Jake's ranch.

He groaned when he saw it. He had come too late. Sundance had come and wreaked his vengeance. A dark huddle lay sprawled on the ranch house porch; he need go no nearer to know it was Jake. He could see the man's face, upturned, ugly twisted, gone warped with his horror.

Antrim stepped around the body. He peered in through the door, at once fearful of what ghastly sight he might see, yet knowing there could be no peace for him ever—

It was then he heard the creak and jingle that comes from the paraphernalia of horses. And there they came, the two stolen Arabs. Through the long, purple shadows of approaching night they came into the yard from behind the stable. Sundance, leading on the chestnut stud, had his head turned airing his wit, and laughing in his cool, suave fashion at the girl who was tied, hand and foot, on the filly.

Sweat stung Antrim's face like needles.

He moved from the porch, stepping over Jake's body.

"Sundance."

He could see the shoulders of the burly man stiffen. Sundance knew that voice and he knew what it meant. And there he was, coming around in the saddle with both guns lifting, both guns gouting flame. But his fire was hurried; he was on a horse that had gone straight up with that first report. Antrim fired just once. Sundance's shape came out of saddle. On the ground it looked no different than Jake's.

Idy Red said coolly: "Kinda reckoned you'd be showin' up round yere; kinda reckoned you'd figger it out, give you time. I been waitin' fo' you. I was waitin' fo' you when Sundance come. We was on the porch—I had a gun on Jake, an' had just got done layin' the law down to him. I knowed Jake would be comin' back quick's he got shut of the rest o' you. He wasn't scared of you gettin' that treasure. He knowed I'd gone an' shifted them markers—"

"*You* moved them markers?"

Antrim looked incredulous.

Idy Red said, "I sure did—me an' my horse. He's a pow'ful strong critter an' we took plenty of time to it. Had 'em long moved 'fore you ever come around yere."

She brushed the hair back out of her eyes and gave him her slow, wholly pleasant smile. "Jake was wantin' that plunder so bad he could taste it. I knowed that—I ain't kep' his house all this while for nothin'. Hell, I been brung up on that treasure!—yarns of the vanished yesterdays—windies of the things that wild bunch done. To hear Jake tell it he was a real hell-tearer. Mebbe he was—I dunno; but I've allus figgered like a heap of that treasure was owin' to me—it was my ol' man helped 'em bury that plunder. Yes, sir! Red Dan Harris! They've allus claimed he was kilt by the Injuns, but I know better—it was Zwing Hunt killed him.

"I heard Sundance come into the yard—heard his hoss, I mean. But I never paid no mind. I figgered it was you an' I had all I c'ld do to keep Jake quiet. He was pow'ful anxious to git away. Then, first thing I knowed, there was Jake keelin' over an' the place all fumed up with gun smell an' racket. I reckon you can piece out the rest."

Antrim nodded. "But I thought you was sweet on Sundance?"

"That skunk! Not after I seen him kill Bat Kerrick!—the honey-tongued sidewinder! I sure been fooled about *him* all right."

A breeze seemed to stir the cottonwoods yonder.

"Well . . . I expect you'll be pullin' on out yere now . . . tearin' off t' new pastures . . ." She shook her rebellious red curls again; poked a dried horse chip around with her toe. "Don't guess you'd be findin' nothin' yere to hold you . . . ?"

Antrim took off his hat and looked at it dubiously. It seemed to have been his fortune ever to say the wrong thing to this girl. He looked at her, his eyes narrowing a little as though this were a thing demanding all his courage. "Them horses," he said—"them A-rabs. I reckon it was you moved them out of that cove; guess you was figurin' to use 'em, mebbe. I been thinkin' 'twould be a good idea 'f we was to take 'em back to their owner. He lives down below the Line a piece at a place called Torreon. We could ride 'em down there an' turn 'em over. That way you could see Eagle Pass. We could come back past it—could even stay there, mebbe, if you think you could stand double harness with me—"

"I ain't got no folks to give you no dowry—"

"I ain't honin' to marry no dowry."

"What'll I do with all that plunder then? Won't nobody else ever find it, now I've moved them markers—"

"Leave it there," Antrim said.

"A mighty good idea." John Slaughter moved out of the trees and came toward them. He had bandaged himself with strips torn from his shirt-tail. "I've been listening to you and I'm glad to find I had this gauged correctly. Though it ain't, rightly speaking, one of the things I get paid for, I guess," Slaughter said, and his eyes kind of twinkled, "I'll just bid you good-bye here an' wish you luck."

"Luck," Antrim said, "is a woman."

NELSON NYE
DOUBLE-BARREL WESTERN

GUNSLICK MOUNTAIN
and
BORN TO TROUBLE

BORN TO TROUBLE

ONE

ANOTHER BROILING hot day had practically dragged to its close and I was disgustedly figuring to throw the hull on my pony and head back for town when the rattling stage, northbound from El Paso, pulled up with a screech of brake blocks and stopped just beyond the white picket fence. "Here's the place you was wantin' off at, ma'am," the moustached driver called down from the box.

A woman climbed out. Then Haines cracked his whip and the stage rolled north and was lost in its dust.

I expect I stared like an owl. That was one for the book, him stopping at this place. And for a woman!

I found out I was wrong about that though. With the dust clearing off I could see her better and she wasn't no woman. She was the slickest looking package I had ever clapped eyes on.

Not over sixteen she didn't look in that light, and pretty as a pair of red boots in some kind of blue dress which came snug to her throat. She had a shawl round her head and the hair underneath it in the downslanting sun held the gleam of pure copper.

Hunkered like I was in the shadow of the stable,

I don't reckon she could see me with that sun in her eyes. But I could sure see her and she was something to look at. She was standing right there where the stage had left her, peering across the fence toward Cap Murphey's office. And then she spotted Joe Stebbins, the outfit's hostler, where he was slopping white paint on the flag pole.

"Hello there," she hailed. "Is this the headquarters of Company D?"

Joe tells her that's right. Never missed a stroke with that brush he was using. "But if it's one of the boys you've come here to see you're jest wastin' your time. They're all out on duty. Duty!" he says, like he hated the sound of it.

Some Ranger's wife, I reckoned, and went back to rubbing soap on my saddle. It wasn't my soap, which was why I was so free with it, figuring I'd got something coming for my time. Five days handrunning I'd been soaking up sun here trying to talk the boss Ranger into signing me on.

"Too young," Murphey'd told me the first day, like twenty wasn't more than half out of the cradle.

"But you took on Tap Gainor," I came back at him.

"When you've had as much experience as Tap's had I'll talk to you. You're a good lad, Jimmie, and a fine hand with horses. I know you can bark squirrels with that hogleg you're packin'. But it just don't add up. I'm sorry."

The next day I told him all the outfits I'd worked for—about the time that big Swede and me tangled at Three Bars, how I'd bossed the wagon at Four Peaks last fall, how I'd busted the rough string for the Hanks boys at Ash Fork. Then I told about the time I had gone with Crump's posse and tracked that Mex horse thief across the malpais and caught him.

Cap listened politely but he wasn't impressed.

"I know all that, Jimmie. You've got plenty of

guts. But in our kind of work having guts ain't enough."

"All right," I said. "What else must I have?"

"A Ranger's got to have savvy or he'd damn soon be planted."

"And you figure that's one of the things I ain't got, huh?"

He gave me a slanchways stare and stood frowning. Then his look brightened up. "Let's say you're a Ranger. You're after a hardcase that's just robbed a bank. You've got him tracked to his shack—a place maybe twenty by twelve with four windows. You know he's still got the loot; you know the bank will go broke if you don't fetch it back. You've crept up on the place and now you discover this skunk's not alone; he's got three-four pals inside the shack with him. It's getting dark fast. What are you going to do?"

"These galoots know I'm around?"

"Only thing you're sure of is—if they do—when it's dark they'll make a break for it and scatter. It's your duty to get the robber but you know the bank will fold if you don't fetch back that loot. Quick now—*what are you going to do?*"

"Reckon I'd call on the bunch to surrender. Tell them to pitch down their guns and come out with their hands up."

"They know you're out there now. They tell you to go to hell. Maybe they slam a few slugs in your direction. It's your move, Jimmie."

"All right," I said. "I injun round to the opposite window—"

"It's too late for that now. In about two minutes it's going to be full dark."

"All right. I kick down the door—"

"And probably get killed," Murphey said, and stamped off. He wouldn't talk any more about it and for the next two days I might as well have been in Egypt for all the notice he took of my presence.

And that was the way we started off this morning.

Then, around ten o'clock, he'd come over to the stables and started pawing through the horse gear hung in the harness room. Way he went over them bridles and cinches you'd have thought that stuff was his own private property. He never missed a scratch.

He was in a fine ringey mood when he came over to the bench where I sat whittling. "If you're going to hang around you may as well be of some use," he mouthed gruffly. "Get what you need from Stebbins and see that those leathers are put in first class shape. When you get that done get some soap and start rubbin'."

I never gave him no back talk. I done it.

After that I went to work on my own stuff. I was soaping the skirts of my saddle when that redheaded armful got off at the stage. I couldn't catch all she said to Joe Stebbins but, pretty soon, there she was going on up the path and rapping on the door of Cap's office. It was open, of course, but she rapped on it anyway. And then she went in.

I finished rubbing my saddle and took the soap to the harness room. I'd have caught up my horse and took off right then except I wanted another look at that redhead. I wondered which of the boys she was married to or, if she wasn't hitched yet, which one of them was sparking her. I hadn't never had many dealings with women but I reckoned to know class when I saw it. And what I had seen made me want to see more.

In about ten minutes Cap Murphey poked his head out and bellered for Stebbins to flag down the southbound stage when it came.

I knew right then I wouldn't have long to wait; and I was right. In just a little while there was a racket like hell emigrating on cartwheels and there it came, swooping out of the Empires with the dust boiling up like a lemon fog.

Stebbins put down his bucket and dashed for the

road. I saw the girl come out of Cap's office, pause and turn on the steps for a couple of last words. By this time the southbound's driver had seen Stebbins and had his horses hauled damn near back on their haunches. The girl said, "All right— I'll look for him tomorrow," and came off the steps like a bit of a twister, pantaloons flashing beneath her hoisted-up skirts.

She never looked in my direction but that was all right with me.

I got to look at her anyway. She had the reddest hair I ever saw on a chicken. The reddest hair, the whitest teeth and the—

That was when Cap stuck his head out again, just when she was lifting a leg to climb up into that dadburned stage. *"Trammell!"* he yelled.

I like to dropped the damned saddle. Then his eyes picked me up where I was standing in the shadows. "On the double," he grunted.

He was back at his desk when I came into the office. He was fingering some papers that was covered with doodles and I could tell when he looked up that he was doing some fast thinking. His eyes were bits of shined glass stabbing out of the gloom.

"You still achin' to be a Ranger?"

All I could do was to nod at him dumb like.

"You got any kinfolk around this country?"

"Nossir," I gulped, finally getting my wind back. "Nobody nearer than Flat Rock, Kentucky. My old man had an uncle lived there—or maybe it was a cousin."

"Your father's not living?"

"Redskins got him. Got him and Mom both and pretty near the whole wagon train. That was ten years ago. Soldiers took me back to Fort Apache with them, turned me over to the sutler for raisin'. I stuck it out five years and then I pulled my freight."

"You ever been up in the Cherrycow country?"

"Worked a roundup there two years ago."

"You familiar with Shafts?"

"Never heard of it," I said.

"It's a mining camp. Not far from the ruins of Charleston. Silver, mostly. That girl that was just here came down from there. She wants help. Says she's heir to the Tailholt Mining and Milling Company. Seems to think someone's out to whipsaw her out of it. Father was killed six months ago. Supposed to have been a mining accident— she thinks now he was murdered. Property's being run by the father's brother, man by the name of Shellman Krole, and the mine manager, a fellow named Bender. Lot of funny business going on, mineral concentrates stolen, cave-ins and what not. Girl says they're honest but they can't seem to stop it. Now the uncle's missing. She wants it looked into."

"What's the matter with the local star packer?"

"She thinks he's in with the man that's grabbing the concentrates—"

"And who does she figure is grabbin' them?"

"Local J.P.—some fellow named Frunk. She's guessing, of course, but where there's so much smoke there's bound to be trouble. I've got to send somebody up there."

"You—you mean you'd send *me?*"

Cap frowned. "That girl's got a right to protection. If the local law has broke down it's up to us to step in. I don't like the idea of sending a green kid up there but every one of my boys has got his hands full. If you're bound and determined to be a Ranger—"

I grabbed up his hand and pumped it vigorous. My throat was too full for any words to come. I was remembering the stories of Buckey O'Neill and seeing Jim Trammell, the pride of the Rangers, running the crooks plumb out of Arizona. My heart was pounding my ribs like a single jack.

A grin broke up the harsh lines of Cap's face. Then he let go my hand and said plenty solemn, "I ought to warn you, Jimmie, if this girl's not jumpin' at shadows this is apt to be rough. If I had anyone else—"

"Don't think of it, Captain! You won't never be sorry," I told him earnestly.

"I want you to think a bit, Jimmie. A Ranger never turns back—remember that."

I nodded. "I know the rules, sir. I won't let your boys down."

Murphey eyed me for another long moment. Then he got up with a nod and said, "Raise your right hand."

Shafts was on the San Pedro River. I got my first look at it the following evening about an hour short of sundown. Cap had told me, passing on the girl's description, that when I got in its vicinity I could judge how far off I was from it by the sound of fired pistols—and he wasn't far wrong.

Coming in from the north the first place I saw was the little red schoolhouse hunkered off to itself where the end of Burro Alley fans out in a stretch of bear grass. This had all been open-range cow country before the red shirts moved in with their tunnelings and burrowings and, after them, the Long Tooth Emmas and Faro Charleys that get their knives into every boom.

No one had to tell me that Shafts was booming. I had to duck between buildings three times in five minutes to let shouting riders have enough room to pass. Burro Alley was a red light district with painted faced harridans beckoning and calling from the brothels that lined both flanks of the trail. One canary-haired harlot heaved the bouncers up out of her shift bold as bull spit and ran a wet tongue around the rim of her mouth. When I kept right on going she flung such blasphemies after me it's a wonder my ears didn't break into flame.

Passing Jack Schwartz's saloon I came on to the main drag. It was about as noisy a place as I had ever got into. Horses neighing, cattle bawling, galoots of every description and colour shouting and swearing in forty different lingos and each one trying to outyell all the rest of them.

Through the thick pall of the dust flung up by this traffic I could see the grey shapes of the great rumbling ore wagons grinding their way through the clutter of buckboards. Horsebackers weaved in and out among buggies. One guy with a red dripping Arkansas toothpick made a dive through the crush with three other gents after him. I never did see where he got to but, all of a sudden, some hitched horse gave a screech and went up on his hind legs with five others with him. The tie rail tore loose and came plumb off its uprights and those terrified broncs in the backlash of panic slammed it into a store front whose high wooden awning came down with a crash.

A little of that stuff went a long way with me. There was a bridge to my left and on my right was a hash house. While I was trying to turn my horse in to its rack four whooping cowpunchers in ten-gallon hats tore past on their ponies like hell wouldn't have them, their rocketlike progress punctuated with gunshots. It was every man for himself, let me tell you, with people on foot jumping quick every whichway. I heard more new cuss words in that town in three minutes than a guy could write down in the rest of his lifetime.

I got my gelding wedged in and his reins round the pole, but I still had to buck the mob using the walk. It was a regular millrace. Red shirted Cousins Jacks, cowhands and swampers, mule skinners, desert rats, Mexicans with and without their zarapes, mining men in high-laced boots, poker-faced gamblers in tall beaver hats, promoters and pimps—even a scattering of Indians togged out in the castoffs of renegade whites. An unending procession, but I finally got through it.

The restaurant was packed eight deep round the counters. I had to eat standing but the chuck was good and the java scalding. The place was run by a Chink in a threadbare Prince Albert. Crowded against a back window I watched the San Pedro boiling black and fierce in the stone buttressed current roaring under the bridge.

The crowds had thinned out some by the time I got finished and I was able to reach my horse in one piece. The last of the ore wagons had rolled over the rattling planks of the bridge and were now strung out along the road to the mill which was three miles off along the river's east bank. The throb of its banging was like the rumble of thunder.

I looked down the main drag. In the last of the sun its high false fronts showed a variety of signs: Hogpen Annie's, The Bellyful Bar, Buskirk's Hardware & Notions, Jack McCann's, Gunsmith, Cassie's Casino, Hank's Harness Shop, Frunk's Mercantile, and others, too far off to make out rightly through the still thick haze of the lifted dust.

Untying my horse I climbed into the saddle. A passive cowhand looked up with a grin. "You must be huntin' for bear."

"Not sure yet whether it's bear or plain skunk," I said, kneeing my gelding out into traffic.

But I knew what he meant. The big Sharps cuddled under my left stirrup, heavy calibred though it was, by itself wouldn't have drawn a second look in that country. But taken together with the sawed-off Greener on the other side, I expect it looked like a lot of artillery. I had reckoned that shotgun might invite some attention. I didn't care if it did.

I was to put up at the Eagle Hotel, Cap told me, and I guessed it was time I was hunting the place. It was the only direct order he had given me. "I never tie a man's hands with a bunch of red tape. I'm trustin' you," he said, "to get to the bottom of this thing. How you get the job done is entirely up to you—consistent, of course, with the traditions of the Service."

I knew the traditions. I'd been around enough cow camps to have heard a lot about Rangers. Fact is I'd been raised up with such after-supper yarning round the camp fires. I knew Burt Mossman, now ranching in New Mexico, had started them. With thirteen men he'd practically re-made this country at a time when Arizona was the doorstep to hell. He had fetched the fear of God plumb into the cactus. Had kicked down more doors and gone in through more smoke than any other man in the history of the outfit.

I aimed to be another Burt Mossman.

The first thing, of course, was to find out what I was up against. The quickest place to learn that seemed to be at the mine, but I reckoned first of all I'd better find that hotel.

There was plenty such around. I saw the Antler House and Miners' Rest and, down a little further, was the Cap and Ball. Then I came to Frunk's Mercantile, a great barn of a place that looked to carry everything from wheelbarrows to coffins. I kind of wondered if this Frunk was the one the girl had mentioned; the guy Cap had said she thought was getting the concentrates.

I had a hankering to go in and get the measure of what he looked like, but that was as far as the notion took me. Folks was lighting their lamps now and the golden glow, slanching out of doors and windows, played over the boisterous throngs on the walks and lay in yellow bars across the dust churned up from the potholed road. It was right about then I saw the sign I was looking for.

It was painted in letters two foot high beneath the second story windows of a pine plank building that had its behind to the street like it didn't give a hoot whether school kept or not. And underneath its name it said *Shellman Krole, Prop.* Shellman Krole, I remembered, was the name of the redhead's uncle, the fellow that was running the Tailholt Mining & Milling Company for her—the gent whose disappearance had brought her running to Cap.

It was the very last building at this end of the street. Around its east side, perhaps fifty yards away, the river swung north in a bend that turned the rest of the town up Canada Gulch. Looking that way I could see a livery stable and a bunch of corrals and I judged the stage depot would be somewhere beyond them, though what towns it ran between was more than I could figure. Probably Tombstone and Bisbee—maybe even on south to Douglas. I knew mighty well it never went past the barracks of Company D.

I followed the hotel's east flank around to the entrance and found myself facing a brightly lighted verandah. Ten coal oil lanterns, at two foot intervals, swung shining from hooks along the edge of its roof, their glare intensifying shadows blackly piled beyond the cottonwoods.

There were no horses at the tie rail when I climbed off my own. With all that light in my eyes what I could see of the lobby through the patched and sagging screen looked uncommonly dingy.

I had a feeling right then about this place. I didn't like it.

I was fetching a hand up to hunt for the makings when I looked in again and stopped dead in my tracks.

I couldn't see the whole lobby—couldn't see precious little but the writhing back of a sorrel-topped filly in the grip of some mug who had both arms wrapped around her.

But that was plenty for me. Even before I saw she had both hands wedged pushing against his chest, I was taking those warped steps three to the jump.

As I grabbed for the screen I saw her suddenly tear loose of him.

But he had her again before I could get the door open, and before I could reach the grinning swivel-eyed polecat someone else had got to him. This guy, a burly red-faced six-footer, made a dive from the stairs that would have shamed any hawk.

The girl ducked clear just before Six Foot struck him. The weight of that leap sent them heels over elbows, but Six Foot couldn't hold him. That fancy rigged lady-mauler was wiry as an eel. He was up on his feet before the big guy knew he had got away even. He whirled like a cat and was making for the door when his white ringed eyes abruptly saw me standing there.

He didn't say "Boo!" He just wheeled clear around and made a leap for the window.

That was where Six Foot got him, about a yard this side of it, with a gorgeous left hook fetched clean up from his bootstraps.

That bird hit the wall like he was going plumb through it. He hung there dazed for a moment with his lamps gone off focus. Then he dropped to the floor like an emptied sack.

I threw a look at the girl. She was white cheeked, still panting, her eyes round as marbles, but it was her, all right—the same nifty armful that had called on Cap Murphey.

TWO

"GOSH, MISTER CRAFKIN! I guess I owe you a debt of thanks, but I wish you hadn't done that," she said, like the thought of it really bothered her.

"I ought to've broke his damn neck! Any skunk that would put dirty paws—"

"But you don't understand. He's—"

She let the rest trail off. The big man wasn't paying any attention. He had gone out into another room through an open door beyond the foot of the stairs. While she stood there biting her lip, deep in thought, I heard the clatter of metal, the skreak of a pump that would have probably worked better with a little oil on it. Crafkin came back with a pail of water, his look still riled, and sloshed it over the masher.

It brought him around. He sat up, spluttering.

Crafkin said, "Get up on your feet, you dog, and apologize."

The masher got up. He didn't look to be more than a kid in actual years though his face was rutted with the tracks of vicious thinking. His tobacco stained mouth was malignantly twisted and the expression of his eyes made the girl pull back sharply.

It didn't bother Crafkin. "Come on," he said. "Speak your piece and clear out."

I watched the kid shake his shoulders together and, because I was watching, I caught the bulge of a second gun. He was still pretty groggy and mighty near lost his balance when he bent over for his hat. He jammed it down on his head and cuffed some dust off his clothing.

"Things have come to a hell of a pass around here when a feller can't spark his own girl without—"

"I'm no girl of yours!"

"Ain't you, missy? You was mine right enough until this—"

"Never mind," Crafkin told him. "Speak your piece and get out."

I looked for that kid to snatch for his pistol, but he spoke quick enough when the guy started toward him. "I guess I made a mistake. If that's so I'm sorry. I won't make it again."

That was double talk for my money, coming a whole heap nearer matching the look of his eyes than it did to showing any proper repentance.

But it seemed to suit Crafkin. He said, "Now dust. Haul your freight. And don't let me catch you round here again."

The kid adjusted his hat with his eyes glinting baleful. "I ain't forgettin' this, bucko. An' I ain't forgettin' *you.*"

He gave his hat a final tug and stalked through the door like an outraged cat.

The girl thanked Crafkin. "But I wish," she said, "you hadn't done it. I'm afraid you've piled up trouble for yourself."

"That swallow-forkin' dude?" the big man snorted. "Any time I worry about the likes of him—"

"But you don't understand. He's the one they call 'Short Creek'."

"Him? You mean that rat-faced little sidewinder is the quick draw artist that rubbed out Buckskin Bert the other night?"

She nodded. "He's filed eight notches—"

"He won't file none for me, don't you worry." Crafkin laughed. "If he comes round here botherin' you again let me know."

The girl turned around then and saw me. "Oh— I'm sorry. I didn't realize.... If you're looking for a room I'm afraid I can't help you. Have you tried the Antler? Well, there's the Miner's Rest and the Cap and Ball—"

"They're filled up, too," I told her quickly. "If I could stretch out here in the lobby or—"

The big man said, "He can shack up with me if you've got an extra cot. I'm pullin' out about ten— got a twenty mile ride to the Diamond U. Cattle buyin' sure ain't the job it used to be."

I saw her give him a look. Saw his lips smile down at her. "I'll be back by tomorrow night more than likely."

"Well..." I saw her straighten and square back her shoulders with a deep sighing breath that lifted her breasts against the blue of her dress. "I suppose I could find another cot."

"My name's Jim Trammell," I told her, and took off my hat like I had a few manners.

"I'm Carolina Krole," she nodded. "And this is Joe Crafkin."

Crafkin shook my fist. "Coming up to try your luck at the diggin's?"

"I might prospect around a little," I shrugged. "Cows is more in my line. Been thinking of buying into a partnership. If I could get me a stake..."

Crafkin nodded. "It's a good place to get one."

"I'd better look for your cot," Carolina said, "though what you're going to do about a key I don't know. We don't have any extras."

The big guy seemed to have been sizing me up.

19

"I'll just let him have mine," he said, handing it to me. "Room nine—top the stairs."

He saw the girl's opened mouth. "I'm not forgettin'," he smiled, "but I can't look at cattle poundin' my ear on a pillow. I've got to be at Diamond U. I've got to go to the Y Bench and look over their gather and I promised Ed Gaines I'd be out to the Pot Hook." He patted her shoulder. "Don't you worry, honey. I'll keep an eye on things."

He grabbed up my hand and pumped it with vigour. "Glad to've met you, Trammell. If you're ever up to Tucson I'll stand you a tall one—I'm goin' to hit the hay now. Move in any time you've a mind to."

"If you're pullin' out at ten," I said, "that's good enough for me. I want to look around anyway."

"Sign the book before you go," the girl said, plainly meaning it for me, though she was looking at him. "It's over there on the desk. Put your room number after it."

I took a quick look at Crafkin. He had a good pair of shoulders with plenty of weight behind them, and the style and cut of his garb was what the average cattleman sported. I allowed the guy might be middling handsome if you liked that beefy kind of fried-alive look. I reckoned he wasn't really old—probably not more than forty, but the thing still had me stumped.

I don't know what the guy had but it must have been good. The girl was plenty upset about the thought of him leaving. She couldn't take her eyes off him.

Some guys, I thought, have all the luck.

I picked up her skreaky pen and wrote my name in the book. Thinking she might like to have a few words with him alone, I said I'd go get my roll and leave it there by the desk, that I would put up my horse then and have a look around.

I don't believe that the girl heard a word I said. I couldn't see her face because she had her back to me, having turned plumb around to send a look up at Crafkin where he'd paused on the stairs.

I'd have given a few things to have a chicken like her panting around after me the way she was after that guy. I looked to see a bit of smugness round the corners of his mouth but all I found was tightness—the same peculiar tightness that was mirrored in his eyes.

Why, I thought, *the fool don't like it!*

I pushed the screen door open. The crickets were in full chorus. Nighthawks swooped about the lanterns. I was halfway down the verandah steps, still kicking around the queerness of that cattle buyer's expression, when my eyes suddenly jumped to focus.

Some guy was bent over the back of my horse with his arm to the elbow inside of my bedroll.

I was a little bit riled, but not too riled to see straight.

Nobody had to tell me it was that cross-grained bastard, Short Creek. I crept down off those steps like a moccasined injun, ducked under the tie rail and came up right behind him.

"What the hell do you think you're doin'?" I said.

He spun around like a cat and made a pass for his pistol. I slapped it into the bushes and then I plowed into him. But I was a little too hasty and misjudged my aim. His left rang like an anvil right back of my ear. A wild swing from his right nearly tore my damn jaw off.

One more of that kind would have folded my tent up, but the poor fool got rattled. He dug for the gun strapped beneath his left armpit.

I didn't wait for him to get it. I drove four knuckles up under his chin and his eyes bugged out like they would roll off his cheek-bones. He went back on his haunches wabble-legged and stood gagging. I put my fist in his wind and when he jerked forward I brought my left knee right up into his kisser.

I was just getting set to knock him over the tie rail when the snout of a gun dug me hard in the ribs.

I didn't ask any questions. I didn't wait for no orders. I spun like the kid had, smacking hell west and crooked. I caught him full in the basket.

I watched him go round in a gut-grabbing circle. "Glub glub," he croaked hoarse-like and his knees folded under him. He flopped in the dust like a chicken with its head off.

That was when I first spotted the tin on his shirt-front.

THREE

I watched him roll over and come on to his knees. He swayed there a moment like he wasn't quite sure if he could get up or not. Then his hands grabbed a hold in the hoof tracked dust. I saw a shudder pass over him.

I could easy have matched it.

Thought of the star this gent had pinned to his shirt-front wasn't the kind of mental exercise most calculated to quiet edgy nerves. This feller would probably be peeved when he got up.

I looked around for Short Creek.

The marshal groaned.

I reckoned the easiest way out would be to show him my own tin. But I couldn't well do that knowing the girl had told Cap this guy was in with the *gambosinos*. It looked like the smartest thing to do would be to make myself scarce and light a shuck for the timber before this sport got in any shape to stop me.

But I couldn't do that, either. Not and maintain the traditions of the Service.

Rangers are expected to be brave. Their reputation is based on never backing off from anything.

They are a do-or-die breed that are invariably supposed, no matter what the odds, to pick the nearest crook and charge.

I knew all this. But it was my understanding that Captain John R. Hughes of the Texas contingent frequently used a little guile to strengthen his hand; and the same went for Mossman. I hadn't ever heard anyone question their bravery.

The law of Shafts had quit groaning. He was trying to get up so I went over and helped him. I even brushed off his clothes like I had no hard feelings and handed him his hat. Then I picked up his gun, shook the cartridges out of it, and gave him that, too.

I noticed some other gents had drifted up. They wasn't saying much, but they were doing a lot of looking.

I reckoned Carolina must have got her signals crossed. This guy didn't look like no kind of a crook. A mite taller than me, he had a muscular swell of neck and shoulder that didn't run to burliness, but took away the string-bean look his height might otherwise have given him. Corduroy trousers were stuffed into his range boots. He wore a blue flannel shirt and a grey wipe was knotted tight about his solid neck.

He had corn yellow hair. And a straw coloured moustache crouched above a grim mouth that had a solid chin beneath it. He looked every inch a lawman. The way his glance was combing my map wasn't contributing much to the digestion of my supper.

He never glanced at that bunch gathered around us at all. He dropped the gun in his holster and cuffed his hat. When he'd cuffed it to his liking he re-dented the crown and set it back on his head. He was doing an extra good job of hanging on to his temper.

He had the coldest blue eyes I ever looked into. "If you're ready," he said, "we'll go down to my office."

"All right," I told him, "but I'm taking my bronc along. I'm kind of particular who goes through my belongings."

When we got to his office—a cubbyhole in Canada Gulch catty-cornered across from the stage depot—he dropped into a chair behind his desk, poking out one for me with his foot. "Kind of new around here, ain't you?"

"Just got here tonight."

"Any special reason for picking on Shafts?"

"Just lookin' for a stake."

"Know anyone here?"

"Met a feller named Crafkin a couple of shakes ago, but I can't say as I know him. Look," I said, "I'm sorry about taking that swing at you. Expect I was some excited, havin' just caught a walloper goin' through my bedroll. Nothing personal, you understand. When I felt your gun I thought the guy had a crony."

He considered me awhile without revising his expression. "What kind of looking gent was he? Ever seen him before?"

I said, "He's about my age, take away a year maybe. Duded up like a house afire. Bony face. Lot of fuzz on his cheeks. Lanky."

"You seem to have gotten a pretty good look at him."

"He had a set-to with Crafkin inside the hotel. The girl that runs it told Crafkin this guy was called 'Short Creek'. Seems to be enjoyin' quite a rep in these parts."

"Is there anything in your bedroll likely to invite attention?"

"I think he was just fishing."

"Suppose you fetch your stuff in here."

I got my roll and unravelled it. He looked over my belongings without showing much interest. "Anything missing?"

"I can't think of nothing."

He gave me permission to put the stuff away. When I got my tarp rolled up again I found he was still looking thoughtful. "You haven't any idea what he was after?"

I did kind of have a halfway suspicion that if Short Creek had known about the girl's trip to Cap he might have been hunting something that would hook me up with it. But even to me that seemed pretty unlikely. "Just looking for something he could carry off, I reckon."

"Then why didn't he take your rifle or that sawed-off Greener?"

"Why don't you ask him?" I said.

That made him smile. "There's not more than five hundred people in this camp." The smile went a little twisted. "Ever try to find a needle in a haystack? I've got just one deputy I can put any trust in and I wouldn't trust him much farther than I can throw him. What's this Crafkin look like?"

"Big. Red faced. Black hair and grey eyebrows." I thought back a minute. "Kind of stooped in the shoulders like he's done a pile of ridin'."

"How old would you put him?"

"I'd say around forty."

He considered me awhile like he was turning that over. I couldn't make out if he knew Crafkin or not. Then abruptly he leaned forward.

"What handle do you go by?"

"My own," I said—"Jim Trammell."

"Any kin to those horse raising Trammells around Sweetwater?"

"Don't know them," I said. "I been punchin' cows for Lou Renzer over in Four Peaks country." And I had—about a year ago.

26

"Have you taken up any ground yet?"

"Just got here tonight. Ain't even had time to stable my horse."

He said with his glance coming up from my belt, "You any good with that gun?"

"I reckon I can manage to get a pull on the trigger."

His eyes showed a twinkle. "Would you be interested in a job?"

I done some quick figuring. This fellow, according to what that girl had told Cap, was in with the bunch playing hob with her mine. But women's notions like women's watches is considerably apt to be unreliable. He didn't look like that kind. But on the chance she might have the right of it I said, "I'd be interested in almost anything that would be at all likely to get me a stake."

If he was crooked, I thought, that would give him his cue.

But the look of his face didn't change by a particle. I come near snorting my contempt of that girl. I might have known I was a heap better judge of character than any fool chit of a redheaded filly.

It set me back hard when he said, leaning forward, "You wouldn't mind a little risk?"

"Life's full of risk. What kind of job you got in mind?"

I was proud of the way I flung that right back at him. Tough-hombre style like I was ready for anything. Then he jounced me again.

"I could use another deputy. Town's got too big for any three men to handle. There's a lot of riff-raff come into this camp and somebody's got to put the fear of God in them before they lug off everything that isn't nailed down."

"But why me?"

"Because I think you've got a head on your shoulders that's good for something besides holding your hat. You've proved to me that you can think in a pinch. You've got plenty of guts and I believe you're honest—and that's what I need, one honest man I can trust."

I shook my head. "I came here to get a stake. I'd be trampin' my whiskers before I make a stake at that job."

He considered me awhile like he was chewing it over. "How much money have you got?"

"Not enough to be worth robbin'."

"All right. I'm going to tell you something. You won't make day wages digging round in these hills. All the good ground's grabbed; you'd just be wasting your time. And if by some miracle you happened on to something you'd wind up in some gulch with a hole through your back. I'm not kidding you, Trammell—this camp is plumb rough."

"My feet ain't tender."

"If I thought they were I wouldn't be offering you the job. The point I'm making is that most of what's been found is just float—it's all been gathered. There's maybe twenty or thirty fellows panning day wages out of the creeks. The real money in this camp is coming from the mines—the Lucky Dog, Bell Clapper, Signal Stope and Tailholt. You can't get into those, not even as a mucker. If you had enough jack you could open up a honkeytonk or a saloon and gambling layout. Slough those into the discard and the only way you can make a stake is to take it at gunpoint or get yourself a job."

I said, "To hear you tell it, nine-tenths of this camp is livin' off the other tenth—or trying to."

"That's about the size of it. I think when you've been here a couple of days you'll agree with me. You'll not find many jobs going begging around here. There are too many idle men in this town."

"You won't have no trouble findin' a star packer then."

"Was that locked door a come-on? And that guy in the alley?"

But he waved it away. "I've got a job for you. I didn't want the whole town knowing my business—that's why I had Spence dish up that guff about a lady. I'm Brian Gharst—"

"I don't care," I said, "if you're Theodore Roosevelt! You take a damn funny way to make a man's acquaintance and if I get any more of these tossed in my direction someone's like to wind up in a pine plank box!"

I slammed the point of the knife deep into his desk and the haft of it vibrated like a prodded rattler. It might have been a rattler by the way he stared down at it.

"Where the hell did you get that?"

"Out of that door by the foot of your stairs. And if it had come any closer I'd of been a cooked goose."

He pulled his stare off the knife and rummaged my face. He was not a big man as gents go in this country, but there wasn't nothing puny about him. He had short bowed legs and was so thick through the shoulders it gave him a queer top-lofty look like a farm wagon swaying under a double load of hay. He wore steel-rimmed cheaters over bleached-out blue eyes and his brush of black hair was getting thin on the top and pretty grey around the edges. But he was not an old man and there wasn't any rust got on the wheels in his think-box.

"You trying to tell me someone threw that thing at you?"

I said, very patient, "It wasn't thrown at no chipmunk."

He looked at me, baffled. "But why should I—"

"Look," I said. "What would *you* think if some pasteboard fanner stepped up to *you* in some dive you hadn't ever been in before with a line some warbler was wantin' a talk with you and then, satisfied then I had the place to myself, turned around and took hold of the thing in the door.

It was a bone handled knife with a razor-sharp blade. Its point was driven so deep in the wood I had to holster my pistol and use both hands to budge it. Even then it took all my strength to get it loose.

I could see a lot better now my eyes had got used to the dark, but I had to know something my eyes couldn't tell me. I thrust the knife in my belt and took hold of the doorknob. Very quietly I turned it and cautiously pushed.

The door was locked.

So he was in on it, too. Or wasn't he?

I could probably find out by going up those stairs.

Good judgment told me to let well enough alone and get out of that alley while I still had a chance. Somebody in this camp didn't want me around and had done their best to get me planted. *Why?*

There were only two answers to that one. Settling a grudge or they knew what I was here for. I wasn't too sold on the grudge theory. Nor I didn't see how anyone could know what I was here for unless they also knew the girl had gone to Cap Murphey. I didn't see how they could know that either.

I went up the stairs and pushed open the door. I dived in quick and slammed it shut behind me.

It surprised me a little to see the place was rigged out as an office. "You've changed some," I said, "since I heard you sing."

He wasn't embarrassed. He even showed me a grin. "Put that popgun away and cool off."

"This gun stays right where it's at," I said, "till I find out what kind of game you're dealin'. It'd better be good. You don't look like no red-skirted warbler to me!"

"That was just the come-on—"

FOUR

SWEAT POURED out of me.

My eyes dug into the roundabout shadows and the gun in my fist was ready to cough at the first sign of movement. Only there wasn't any sign. No racket aroused by panicky haste, no stealthy tread of a cautious withdrawal. Not even the rasp of a stifled breath. The loudest thing in that trash strewn alley was the muffled thud of my pounding heart.

By the time it got quiet I had hold of myself, had quit building wild notions and was able to reason. Whoever had tried to stop my clock had not stayed around to find out if he'd done it. That much I was sure of. The passage was empty.

But I'd been foolish enough for one night. I came out of my crouch with a straining care. I kept my gun gripped ready in case I was wrong and, bending again, felt around with my left till I got hold of a rock. I listened one further moment, then tossed the rock out into the murk just beyond where the rickety stairs climbed skyward perhaps twenty paces away to my left.

It struck with a tincanny clatter.

I counted to a hundred and twenty by ones and,

moved to the rail and there was a thunderous quiet. A guitar flung the opening bars of *Jalisco* across it, and she sang.

Her husky voice was enormously stirring. When she quit the crowd went wild with applause. "More!" they cried. "More! More!"

She put both hands to her lips, and was gone.

It was as effective as hell.

My pulse still throbbed with the sound of her voice when someone touched my shoulder. "Lady wants to talk with you."

Tinhorn was written all over him. He had the typical small-time gambler's look—clothes, mannerisms and everything else.

"What lady?" I said.

"The one that just sang. Soledad."

"And what would she be wanting to talk with me for?"

"How should I know?" It was plain he thought I was a fool to stand arguing.

"Where is she?"

He jerked his head and set off toward the bar's far end where, under the balcony's overhang, a heavy door was set into the room's back wall.

I didn't get it. I couldn't see what she would want with me—I wasn't that vain of my looks by a long shot. But I followed him. Stood with churning thoughts while he opened the door.

There was no room beyond it. Nothing but an alley choked black with shadows and the penetrating chill of the river-damped night.

I looked at the guy, the knowing smirk on his face. He stood aside, his eyes shining. "Knock twice on the door at the top of the stairs."

I stepped out, never thinking what a target I made. If I hadn't been turning to ask where the stairs were I'd have caught it dead centre.

I heard the *chunk!* as its blade struck the slammed-shut door.

of the place came against me like the flat of a hand, even before I shoved through the batwings. This was a mining man's hangout and the brogue was so thick you could slice it.

A guitar picker flanked by a couple of fiddlers playing Chicken in the Straw was perched on kegs at the back of the place and a mob of sweating hardrock men were loping their squealing partners round and round a twelve-foot square. Gamblers were doing an efficient business of parting misguided fools from their bankrolls and tobacco smoke swirled round the lamps in blue clouds.

A fat little chick in a one-piece dress that didn't much more than cover her navel got hold of my arm and tried to tow me upstairs. But I had my aim firmly pinned on the bar and after a couple more tries she went after someone else. And that was when I got my first sight of Soledad.

She was up on the balcony, just behind the place where the low spindle rail was hid behind the colours of a Mexican zarape. She was Mexican, too—or maybe half Spanish, blue black hair piled high with a comb. She was supple and tall with the shape of a willow, lips red as cherries and a red dress to match them.

She stood like the daughter of some rich hidalgo, black glance playing scornfully over the crowd.

She was a looker, all right. No mistake about that.

Her eyes caught me watching her. Someone bumped into me. I said "Sorry," without looking away from her, and saw a smile quirk her lips, saw them murmur something. And then a guy in a plug hat stepped up to the rail and raised both hands and the talk fell away.

"Gentlemen," Plug Hat said, "I give you Soledad!"

Hands clapped, feet stomped. The building shook with the roar of raised voices. The girl what about her uncle? True, she said he'd disappeared, but that might mean anything or nothing. And what about this Bender who was supposed to be running the property for her? She'd already told Cap she was sure they were honest. But that didn't make them so in my book. Seemed like I'd get farther quicker if I started from scratch.

And, besides, she was a woman. A damn good looking one, I was ready to admit, but prey just the same to all the fool notions that fill women's heads. And she'd probably talk and let something slip. It was my experience that women usually did. I'd have my work cut out for me if it ever got around this camp that I was a Ranger.

I would be a heap smarter, I thought, to keep away from her. And the farther away the better. There was no place for a woman in a Ranger's life, and I sure didn't want to make no fool of myself.

I went into Jack McCann's, a gambling house and saloon that was just across the road from the Eagle Hotel.

The place was well filled, mostly with cattlemen and cowhands in from the range for a shot at the tiger, but there was a sprinkling of red shirts scattered through the crowd and, like as not, a few rustlers.

The games were going full tilt with a circle of watchers impatiently waiting their turns at each rig. But the bar was the place where the jaws were wagging and a good listener, I thought, should be able to hear plenty. I was right about that, but it was mostly talk about conditions and cattle and the arguments were all over women and horses. It didn't take me more than a quick ten minutes to savvy I'd got into the wrong caboose.

I clanked my spurs outside and up the warped plank walk until I found myself before the Bellyful Bar—Brian Gharst, Prop. This, I saw right away, was more like it. The smells and clatter-bang noise quick as ever he got you out into an alley where light from the door showed you up like a barn afire—"

"Good Lord!" Gharst said. "Is that what happened?"

"I'm tellin' you, ain't I? All I'm askin' you now is what you figured to gain by knockin' off a broke drifter—"

He said with a convincing show of earnestness, "Believe me, Trammell, I had nothing to do with this—"

"You're wantin' me to believe the bird that threw this knife had no connection with you?"

"I can't help what you believe, but it's the truth," Gharst said. "I wanted a talk with you that would be private and not be known about. I didn't figure my name would have any drawing power, so I told Pete Spence to say that Soledad—"

"What did he slam that door for then? Why'd he have to lock it?"

"I don't think he knew there was anyone in the alley—*I* certainly didn't. You have to slam that door to get it properly shut. We always keep it locked."

"It wasn't locked when he opened it."

Thought wrinkled up his cheeks. "It should have been." He sat down behind his desk, stretched out his legs and looked at me. "I don't know what to say to you. I know this business looks suspicious as hell. Nothing I can tell you is going to make it look better. There's a lot of riffraff in this camp. One of them, prowling through that alley just as you stepped out, may have flung that knife for whatever he could get from your pockets."

I gave him a grin.

"Hell's fire!" he said. "What else can I think?"

"Don't ask me to put words in your mouth. I find it damned hard to swallow that some guy happened by just as your understrapper sent me into that alley!"

37

"You find it easier to believe the guy was out there waiting for that door to open? That he was tied in with Spence? That Spence and me and this bird had it figured to plant you? When I'd only just seen you and Spence didn't know—"

"Where?"

"Where what?"

"Where had you seen me?"

"Where you stood looking up at her. Down there in the bar-room. I was out on the balcony when the girl was singing. We both were. It was Spence introduced her—remember?"

That was true. Spence had. But I still didn't like it. I kept remembering the way Spence had slammed that door. The way he had locked it.

"All right," I said, letting him think he had sold me. "So I'm here. What's the rub?"

He got a cigar from his pocket and bit off the end, his eyes checking over me while he got it to going. He said through the smoke, "I'm looking for a fellow I can put some dependence in. I expect you can use a little ready cash, can't you?"

"If it don't involve putting my neck in a sling."

"No danger of that. You haven't a job now, have you?"

"I only pulled in about three hours ago."

"Good," Gharst said, rolling the cigar across his mouth. "You're just what I need for this business. I don't guess you'll mind a little risk if you're well paid for it?"

"Let's get down to brass tacks," I told him. "How much and for what?"

There was something strange in his looks right then and something nervously careful in the way he got up and went over to the door I'd come in by and stood a long moment with his ear up against it. He even toed up a rug against the crack underneath it, and then he catfooted over to the door giving on to the balcony and listened there awhile, suddenly jerking it open and poking his head out before he came back and flopped into his chair.

"I guess you think I've a screw loose, but you don't know this town like I do—even the goddam walls've got ears. This job calls for a man who ain't known around here; above all for a man who can't by any stretch of the imagination be tied up with me. That's why I have to be careful—"

"What about Spence?"

"Spence will keep his mouth shut. I'll see to that. Maybe I'm being unduly cautious—I was a lawyer back East." He put another light to his thin black cigar, puffed it awhile, and then he bent forward. "The big cheese in this camp is a fellow named Frunk. He owns about half of this town right now, including Frunk's Mercantile, the Cap and Ball, the Antler House, three or four of the drink and chip emporiums and the Signal Stope Mine. But that ain't enough for him—he wants the whole works and, as things stand now, he's well on the way toward getting them."

"That don't suit your book?"

"I'm going to bust that woodchuck if it's the last thing I do."

"If he's that big a frog you'll have your work cut out. Does he own this place?"

The light flashed back from his steel-rimmed glasses. "No—nor he ain't about to. Not if he hires every crook in the country, including that stinker that we've got for a marshal. I will burn the place down before I let him get it. Not that he hasn't been trying. He keeps the stage robbed so regular a man can't send a thing out of this camp. Which is how he makes sure we'll have enough cash on hand to make the weekly stick-up worth his crowd's time."

"Plays rough, eh?"

"Hardly a week goes by that my place ain't stuck up. But I can play rough myself, as he is going to find out."

"And that's where I come in?"

Gharst nodded. "You'll be the start. I want you to get a job with him. I want you to work your way into his confidence till you get enough dope to pin the deadwood on him. I'll take it from there.

"And that's all you want me to do?"

"That's all you need worry about now. You come through with enough stuff to fix his clock and I'll see that you're well taken care of."

"I'll see to that part myself," I said. "I'll expect a guarantee of good faith every Saturday. I ain't sticking my neck out for promises."

He knocked the ash off his smoke and nodded. "Two hundred every Saturday—you can get it from Soledad. You're going to have to keep clear away from me or Frunk will get wise. He's no fool, believe me. Two hundred a week and a thousand above when you bring me enough stuff to pin back his ears."

"Any particular kind of evidence you're wantin'?"

"Get anything and everything you can on the bastard. I want his clock stopped. I want enough stuff to do it."

"To convince you, you mean? Or somebody else?"

"You don't have to convince me. What I want is enough to fetch the Rangers in here—and don't write me down as a sucker. I want the deadwood on Frunk inside of a month. If you can't do it in that time I'll get someone else!"

He fetched out his wallet and peeled off fifty bucks. "Here's a little cash to get started. Don't come to me till you've got what I want."

"Suppose I have to have help?"

"If you have to have help you're no good to me."

He turned out the lamp and I went down the back stairs.

FIVE

But not without some disquieting thoughts.

These had nothing to do with the depths of the night, with the creaking of stairs or with the blackness of shadows wedded one to another in the gloom of that alley. The cold glitter of stars, the damp smell of the river were things I noticed no more than I did the rowdy sounds of carousal.

I was being dealt cards from a stacked deck, and knew it.

Everything Gharst had told me about Frunk could be true. He could honestly have been hiring me to do a job for him. But this could well be a trick to throw me off my guard, to shut my mind against the shape of things to come, the easier to steer me up against some blank wall.

I wasn't trusting that fellow no farther than I could heave him.

Trammell he'd called me. And where had he learned that? *I* hadn't told him my name was Trammell. I'd told the marshal, right enough, and I had told Carolina. But not Brian Gharst.

There was a polecat smell in the vicinity of this deal that was beginning to get my hackles up. It was commencing to get inside of my noggin that this fellow Gharst might be a pretty sly article; and for a couple of cents, I told myself, I would go ram that fifty bucks up his adenoids.

Then my mind got to working. There was a number of things about Mr. Gharst that a first class Ranger would want to have answers to, and maybe that job would be a smart way to get them. Since he knew my name there was a whopping good chance he might also know what I was here for. Maybe he didn't but, whether he did or not, I'd be a lot more likely to get my teeth into something I could use if he figured I was stringing along with him.

That was the way it looked to me when I came out of the alley on to the main drag's north walk. The Chinaman's was directly in front of me across the street and the traffic had toned down to where there wasn't but three horsebackers in sight, ranch hands, I reckoned, on their way out of town.

I quartered across the hoof tracked dust and stepped on to the south walk in front of Frunk's Mercantile. It was getting about time I hit the hay, but I thought before I did so I might just as well catch a look at Mr. Frunk. It seemed queer to find a general store keeping open this late, but everything else was open; there wasn't one dark front on the whole main drag.

I went up three steps and into the place. The town's board walks were practically empty now but ten or twelve fellows in various garb were still holding forth inside the store, only one of them actually there on business. The rest were sitting on kegs and boxes whittling and smoking and chewing the fat. Three or four of these birds looked like pretty hard customers, more especially the one in the bullhide chaps. He was a stoop shouldered specimen with rust coloured hair and a hard bitten face bad in need of a shave.

I took a perch on a crate of mining machinery

and couldn't make out if this was Frunk or not. With an idle ear cocked for the gab of the rest of them I watched him limp back of the counter and reach himself down a can of high priced sardines. The clerk never batted an eye as this party scooped a fistful of crackers from a box and, going back to the counter, cleared himself a seat amid the clutter of yard goods by knocking three bolts of printed cotton on the floor.

He got a knife from his boot-top and, cutting open the can, slipped a brace of dead fish between a couple of crackers and sat there swinging his legs while he munched them.

This guy was no puncher. He might be got up like one but he had all the earmarks of a privileged character. He absorbed all the talk but didn't bother to take part in it, not even when the relative merits of two chippies took over the conversational floor. He just chewed his sardines and swung his booted feet, alternating this performance with audible gurgles from a bottle he'd had the clerk fetch him.

Then one of the gabbers twisted his head around to ask, "What's Bucks Younger figurin' to do about Short Creek?"

"Why'n't you ask him?" Rust Hair said, and a fat man next to the asker snickered.

"You mean he ain't takin' you into his confidence?"

"Just on the big things, Roy," Rust Hair said. "How deep have you got that hole down now?"

"Eighty-five more or less."

"Hit anything yet?"

"Not enough to chink the ribs of a sand flea—"

"That why you got four guys with shotguns settin' on it?"

"Well..." The fat man looked sheepish at the laugh the rest gave him. "That's just common sense. I've sunk a pile of good dollars into diggin' that hole. You know how rough things is getting round here. What with all these claimjumpers prowlin' the hills—"

"You're right," a voice said; and Roy broke off, twisting his head. The others twisted theirs, too. Turning my own I caught a look at the fellow.

Coming in from the back room, this jasper was so tall he had to bend his head to keep from smacking his nose on the lintel. With his florid face and yellow goatee, togged out the right way he might have passed for George Custer. On a horse and flourishing a sword he could have made it. He had the same bright yellow hair. The same pair of eagles was looking out of his eyes. Only it was hard to think of Custer in a flat-crowned hat. It was even harder to picture him in string tie Prince Albert. And this guy's size wasn't right.

He was big all over. He had a big voice to match it.

"You're absolutely right!" he boomed, nodding his head vigorously. "It's getting so around here that a man of any substance takes his life in his hands every time he draws a breath. I don't know what's come over this place, or where all these crooked drifters are coming from, but it's time, I say, this camp was cleaned up. You knew Andy Tedron was killed the other night? This morning they found poor old Joe Gantry with his head stove in—killed in his own bed! Murdered, by godfreys! I tell you, if I didn't have so much invested around here I would take the next stage and get clean out of the country."

He gave me a look, swivelled his eyes back to Roy. Seemed like to me Roy was looking a little pale, but maybe it was just the light that made his eyes look so funny. He opened his mouth like a fish but he didn't say anything.

The sardine eater, chewing, grinned from the counter.

Frock Coat said, "The Lord knows I've got all the stuff I can take care of now but as a token of my friendship, Roy, if you're wanting to get out I'll take that claim off your hands. Would three hundred dollars pay for what you've put into it?"

The fat man squirmed.

"The Lord giveth and He taketh away," intoned Frock Coat, in the manner of a man doing his thinking out loud. "A wise man will hear, and will increase learning. But fools despise wisdom and instruction."

Rust Hair said, still chewing with gusto, "Let us wait for blood. Let us lurk privily for the innocent. Let us swallow them alive as the grave; and whole, as those that go down into the pit."

With his piercing gaze on the fat man's face, Frock Coat nodded. "For their feet run to evil and make haste to shed blood. And they lay in wait for their *own* blood; they lurk privily for their *own* lives."

And he nodded again. "Lot of comfort in the Book. You ever felt the power of the Word, Roy?"

The fat man's cheeks were a fish-belly white. I could see sweat gleaming in the creases of his jowls.

"Wisdom crieth without!" thundered Frock Coat. "She uttereth her voice in the streets. She crieth in the chief place of concourse, in the openings of the gates."

From his perch on the counter the sardine eater chuckled. "But ye have set at naught all my counsel. I will laugh at your calamity. I will mock when your fear cometh."

The fat man's tongue crept across dry lips. His glance searched the roundabout faces despairingly.

Frock Coat turned and his lambent eyes, after brushing across, abruptly stopped and came back and looked at me inscrutably.

"Good evening, Brother. I don't recall your features. Are you new to this camp?"

"I ain't been here long."

"Are you looking for lodgings?"

"I got a room at the Eagle."

"Cow puncher, aren't you?"

"Expect I could tell which end takes the grass in."

He considered me a moment, thoughtfully fingering his goatee.

"Mister Frunk—" Roy gulped hoarsely, "could you give me as much as fifteen hundred?"

Frock Coat's stare hung on to mine longer. Then he said to the fat man over his shoulder, "That's a lot of money, Roy, for just a hole in the ground."

"But it's in the right section—Hell, it's smack up against your Signal Stope! The vein is—"

The fat man peered at him and swallowed. "W-Would you give me a thousand?"

Frunk shook his head. "I'm a one price man, Roy. I made the offer as a friendly gesture, not because I've any use for your claim. If you know anyone who'll give you more, you'd better take it."

Rust Hair wiped off his mouth and said, "You hear what happened to that guy the other side of you? That feller Jimson? Fell down into his shaft and broke his neck. Just happened—less than two hours ago."

Frunk smiled at the fat man. "I thought probably you'd heard about it you looked so daunsy. I remember saying to myself, quick as ever I saw you, 'There's a lad that could do with some real help, Gideon. This business of Jimson hath ground his hopes beneath the nether millstone.' I could read your thoughts. I could even understand them, because a thing like that could happen to anyone. So I made you the offer. I figured you wanted to get away from this place."

There wasn't much doubt but what Roy wanted to now. He was a plenty frightened man.

SIX

THE SILENCE STRETCHED like a violin string while his bulging stare went from face to face with the last gleam of hope finally flickering out of it. Fear and shock and desperation levered him on to his shaky legs. Some fatal clarity of insight must have spread that blanched look across his cheeks.

With chin on chest he fumbled the makings but his clumsy hands couldn't build the smoke. The paper wouldn't roll in his fingers. It twisted and tore and fluttered from out of his grasp.

A kind of convulsion writhed through his shoulders and his lifted head showed the face of a corpse. The blind eyes stared unseeingly at Frunk. The stiff lips without inflection, "That's right. That's right. I'm gettin' out."

I got up off the packing crate. "Don't be in no hurry, Roy. You better go home first and think this over."

The fat man probably never heard me.

But the rest of them did. It got so still in that place I could hear the distant clink of glasses, a woman's high laugh coming out of McCann's.

It was like being faced by a ring of watching vultures. I saw the heads twist around on their scrawny necks. I felt the curse of their stares digging into me. I saw three dropped hands above holstered pistols.

Frunk's mouth softly chuckled.

"Go on, Roy," I said. "You go home and think it over. If you still feel tomorrow like you want to sell out—"

"No."

"No what?"

He never moved his head. "I'm sellin' out now." He kept watching Frunk with eyes that didn't see him. I don't guess they saw any part of the room. I don't guess they could see across the rubble in his mind.

I had to wake the guy up. I took hold of his arm but he shook me off. "I know what I'm doin'."

He didn't sound like it.

But Frunk with a grin moved away behind the counter and got out a printed form, a grubby pen and an ink well. "Here you are, Roy."

Roy moved up to the counter like a guy in his sleep.

"You damn fool!" I said. "Going to let them bluff you?"

He dipped Frunk's pen in the ink and scratched his name on the paper. Then he dropped the pen like it burnt his fingers. But he couldn't get his eyes any higher than Frunk's belt. Sweat made an ashen shine on his cheeks. He licked his lips several times and finally muttered, hardly audible, "If you'll give me my money—"

"Money?" Frunk said. "You forgotten that bill you run up here last winter?"

The fat man gaped like a poleaxed steer. "But—but—it wasn't for no three hundred dollars!"

Frunk got out his ledger, flipped a couple of pages. "That's right. Here it is right here. Two hundred and forty-nine dollars and fifty-three cents exactly."

Roy staggered back.

"You want an itemized statement?"

"No...No," Roy muttered. "Let me have the fifty dollars."

"Come around in the morning. If I—"

"But I want to get on to that southbound stage!"

It was a desolate whine the way Roy said it. Frunk said contemptuously, "The southbound don't pull out till 4 a.m. If I give it to you now you'll have it guzzled away by then and be a charge on the town—"

"I won't—I swear I won't—May God strike me dead if I touch a stinkin' drop!"

"Very well," Frunk said. "You all heard him, gentlemen." He counted fifty silver dollars into a poke and passed it over. Like a hungry cur with a bone, the fat man caught it up and with it hugged to his chest went staggering from the store.

Frunk's eyes looked into mine. "I can see you don't approve of us, Brother. Because you're new to this camp I'm going to venture a little advice. You'll see a lot of things more ugly but if you're smart, my friend, you'll whittle your own stick and let the rest of us whittle ours."

There were a lot of things trembling on the edge of my tongue but I managed to keep them hobbled. It was probably just as well, the way that sardine chewer was eyeing me. What Frunk had said was plumb right. I wasn't the fat man's keeper. I was in this camp for one purpose only, to get to the bottom of what was going on at Tailholt. It was time I was remembering that and playing my cards according.

I put away my scowl and tried to show more friendly. I said, "That's damn good advice and mighty fittin' for a gent that's drifted off his home range. You look like a pretty big mogul to me. How's this town fixed for jobs? Know anythin' I could handle?"

"What sort of a job are you looking for, Brother?"

"Any kind that pays well. I don't aim to work for peanuts." I took a slap at my gun. "I'm pretty handy with this thing. Any chores along that line you want taken care of?"

Frunk sucked in his breath and looked at me distasteful like.

"I'm afraid not, Brother. We'd like to make this camp a quiet and peaceful place to live. We wouldn't care to do anything that might encourage more rowdyism."

"Well," I said, "I reckon I could—"

"If you're handy with that gun," Frunk said, "you'd better get in touch with our marshal."

"How much you payin' this star packer?"

"The marshal of Shafts is paid by our Better Business Bureau—"

"How much?"

"I understand he is paid five hundred a month and allowed a little over for expenses."

I whistled. "Five hundred smackers for—"

"We consider the money well spent," Frunk said smoothly, "when it tends to put a curb on the camp's undesirables."

"This guy gets the job done?"

"There's always room for improvement," he said thoughtfully. "But taking the view of Better Business, the most of us believe he's doing all we can expect of him, shorthanded as he is and with at least half this camp out to do the other half."

"The haves and the have-nots, eh?" I said.

"I suppose that would tend to be the popular inference. As a matter of fact, there are quite a few Haves in the local set-up whom I would not regard as being at all 'solid citizens'. Every town has its balance of power, a kind of status quo maintained to ensure that current events run along more or less in their established pattern."

"And this marshal's chief concern, I reckon, is to see that it continues to operate."

Frunk smiled. "I guess you'll have to ask him about that. You'll find his office in Canada Gulch, just across the street from the stage depot."

"And what if he don't want to hire me?"

"In that case, Brother, I'd suggest you leave town."

According to the sky when I stepped out of Frunk's store I had been in this camp just about five hours and, while I hadn't got much forwarder with the thing Cap Murphey had sent me here to do, I'd gathered plenty of food for reflection.

The marshal had offered me a job as his deputy—as one of them, anyway, at two fifty a month; half of what he was getting, according to Gideon Frunk. Then Gharst had gone to considerable bother to offer me a job spying on Frunk at two hundred a week, with a thousand extra thrown in if I could wangle it so he'd get caught by the law. Frunk, himself, hadn't offered me anything but words.

He was a slick talking article and, from what I had seen of him, I was pretty near ready to accept Gharst's estimate—not that I rated Gharst any higher. They were both crooks for my money, and half the cussedness bothering this camp might well be the result of a struggle for power with Gharst on the one side and Frunk on the other.

A first class feud could throw this camp in a shambles. But my job was Tailholt and, up to right now, I hadn't learned one thing I hadn't known before I started. According to the girl, her father had been killed about six months ago. In a mining accident—apparently. Then she'd started losing concentrates. She'd implied Frunk was getting them, but hadn't any proof. She seemed to think the marshal was covering up for him.

Two guys in this deal I hadn't met up with. One was Tailholt's manager, Bender. The other was her uncle who'd been running the works for her— Shellman Krole, whose sudden disappearance had brought her running to Cap.

I decided in the morning I'd have a talk with this guy, Bender.

What I most wanted now was a place to pound my ear. There were plenty of notions still prowling my mind but none of them appeared to have connection with Tailholt. The marshal was the only guy who'd mentioned the mine, and then only to point out I couldn't get a job there, or at the Signal Stope, Lucky Dog or Bell Clapper either.

I had just reached the end of the walk fronting Frunk's place when a girl's sudden scream pulled me out of my thinking. It had come out of the alley I was just about to cross, the passage stretching riverward between Frunk's Mercantile and the dark west side of the Eagle Hotel. It knifed, thinly frantic, through the sounds of raucous merriment, of fiddle-scrape and stamping boots pouring out of McCann's front doors.

A Ranger with any savvy, I reckon, would have done a heap of thinking before shoving his head in a hole like that. But not me. Not then. I yanked my gun and dived straight for the cry.

It was like jumping into a bottle of ink. I could scarcely see ten steps ahead f me but I could hear better now; I could hear a lot better. And I caught the pant of their ragged breathing, the scuffle and slap of struggling bodies.

I made them out when my eyes got to working. Not too good right at first but as a wild swaying blotch of heavier shadow against the black shapes of the trees beyond. He had her squeezed to him with an arm locked behind her. She wrenched away and broke free. But he had her again before she caught her balance, suddenly cursed, let her go and sprang away from her, wheeling.

I guessed what was coming and flung myself headlong. Even so, his blue whistler came almighty near getting me. It ripped through my hat with the sound of a hornet. I saw his gun flash again but I was already rolling. I came up through the echoes, not daring to fire on account of the girl—but it was all over now. She was running straight toward me and that sidewinding Short Creek was heating his axles, loping for the trees like a dog scairt rabbit.

Then the girl was beside me, pulling her torn blouse around her.

We stared at each other. We both cried *"You!"*

She laughed then, kind of shaky, and flung the tumble of hair back out of her eyes. "I'm sure thanking you," she panted, trying to keep herself covered. "You seem to be on hand every time I need help."

"Why's that whelp houndin' you?"

"Look!" She crouched, frightened. "There's someone else coming!"

That sharp, panicked edge to her words swung my head around. A pair of shapes from the street were moving into the passage.

The girl's hand, cold and trembly, caught a hold on my arm. "Oh, please! Let's don't wait. I—"

One of the advancing pair growled, "What's the trouble back there?"

"No trouble," I said.

"Let's have a look at you."

The girl broke into a run. I ran after her. The other man bellowed, "Haul up or I'll fire!"

He fired; they both did. The whine of that lead was a spur to our efforts. We broke out of the alley, tore into the twice-as-dark gloom of the trees. The girl's hand swung me left. We pulled up and stood listening.

"They've quit," she decided. "Be careful with your feet now." Her hand pulled me toward the dark front of the hotel.

"Just a minute," I growled softly. "You blow out those lanterns?"

She shook her head.

I didn't like it. By the tone of her voice she didn't like it no better. "But we can't stand around out here all night." She said, "It's happened before."

"Were they out when you left the place?"

"I didn't think to notice. I went out the side door."

"To meet Short Creek?"

She didn't answer. She let go of my hand. I heard her move toward the verandah. Still scowling, I followed.

She stopped with a sudden harsh intake of breath.

A black shape had stepped from the gloom of the doorway. The hard bore of a gun dug into my stomach.

"That's fine. Stop right there," his voice told us; and: "Gib—get a lamp lit. I've got him."

SEVEN

I HAD WALTZED right into it like a bull with his eyes shut.

And there wasn't one thing I could do about it, either—not with Carolina standing right at my elbow.

He pulled the gun from my belt and dropped it in his hip pocket. A light sprang up and wavered wild in the lobby, abruptly steadied and turned yellow as the chimney was snugged down into its sprockets. The guy motioned us to walk in.

I followed the girl, marvelling at the way she was keeping her mouth shut. It came over me then I might have made a mistake in not going straight to her and letting her know Cap had sent me.

The lamp lighter, Gib, stood by the desk frowning at me, a cold-jawed bravo with a patch across one eye. I didn't know him from Adam. I knew the other guy, though, the one with the gun. It was the stoop-shouldered man in the bullhide chaps, the sardine chewing redhead who had sat on Frunk's counter.

His grin was not pleasant. There was a hard satisfaction in the twist of his cheeks. "You wasn't lyin'. I'll say that for you."

"Well...thanks."

"When you unloaded that brag about bein' so handy. But you showed damn poor judgment—your name's Trammell, ain't it?"

I said I reckoned it was.

He nodded. "This camp's pretty free but it ain't *that* free, bucko."

A vague disquiet began to pound at my bowels. "I'm slow to catch on," I said. "Chew it a little finer."

"You ready to gabble?"

"Gabble about what?"

"About who give you for instance the word to come down here."

"I didn't wait for no word. I go where there's money."

"You do for a fact," he said, scrinching his lips up. "Who give you the job?"

"What job?"

His narrowed eyes showed a glitter. "Set it up for him, Gib."

Eye Patch came over and dropped a hand on my shoulder. "You see this?" he said, and when I looked down I thought a mule had kicked me.

The next thing I knew I was flopped in a chair. My shirt was wet. Water ran off my chin and the bucket in Gib's hand told me how it had got there.

"Stand up!" Rust Hair said. "Or do you wanta be helped?"

I climbed on to my feet. The room rocked around like a chip in a twister. When the girl and the rest of them quit floating past I reckoned I'd be able to keep down my supper.

"Who give you the job?"

We was back where we'd started. I groaned, put a hand up and gently felt of my jaw.

Rust Hair said, "It ain't busted yet. But it's goin' to be soon if you don't unlatch it."

I found the girl's face. "You know this feller?"

"Red Irick," she said, "one of Bucks Younger's deputies."

"And who is Bucks Younger?"

"The marshal of Shafts," Irick snorted. "Any more bright questons? Because if not, I'd admire to know what you two been doin' lopin' round in the dark."

I couldn't see anything wrong in telling him the truth, but Carolina looked nervous. She tried to send me a message.

Irick caught her at it. "The gent's lost his tongue, Gib. See if you can find it."

Eye Patch grinned. He started rubbing his knuckles.

"Don't get excited," I said. "I'm goin' to tell you."

"Then start tellin'."

I gave it to him straight. The only thing I kept back was my hunch the guy was Short Creek.

"That the way you saw it?" Irick looked at Carolina.

"That's the way it *was*" she said, and looked right back at him.

"Maybe," Irick nodded, "an' then again, maybe not. How come you to be in that alley in the first place?"

"Is there any law against it?"

"Funny place for you to be." He dug a match from his pocket and jabbed a back tooth with it. He went over to the door and pushed it open and spat. Coming back he said abruptly, "Who you think jumped you?"

"It didn't get that far," she said, her cheeks crimson.

"Never mind bein' smart. You know what I mean. I want the guy's name."

The torn blouse, the way she held it, showed her breasts like they were naked.

I knew, all of a sudden, this was the question

she'd been scared of. I could see it in her stare, the marble stiffness of her posture.

She finally made up her mind. "He didn't give me his name."

"Why didn't you stop when I hollered?"

"How was *I* to know it was you that hollered?" She fetched up her chin and her eyes came alive again. "I can't see in the dark any better than you can."

"You'd be surprised to know how good I can see. You're a cute little trick but don't push it too far. You was out in that passage all right, baby, but you wasn't out there with Trammell."

She kept her mouth shut.

I kept my lips buttoned, too. I couldn't figure what he was getting at or why so much seemed to hang on that alley. But I could see plain enough he knew more than he was telling.

And the same went for her.

"You want to tell me why you put them lanterns out?"

When she didn't answer that he took his hip off the desk. "Put your gun on this guy, Gib, while I look at his pistol."

He got it out of his pocket, shook the loads out and counted them. Then he held it to his nose and took a sniff of the barrel, nodding. "Smart," he said, and showed a grudging admiration. "You're a slicker piece of goods than anyone around here figured. So maybe you'll get away with it."

He walked up to me. "You've got a lot of nerve, Trammell. You better make the most of it. You can start by tellin' who you done the job for."

I hadn't done any job so I didn't say anything. He didn't, either.

When I came round again I was soaking. I didn't care about that—it was the blood that really got me. It was in my mouth and all over my shirt and my face felt like the whole front was caved in.

Staring up from the horror of my own spilled gore I could see the lips moving in the girl's stormy face and Irick glaring like a prodded steer and, back of him, Eye Patch with his dripping bucket.

Which was when I caught sight of my gun in Irick's fist. I had to see the light flashing off its seven-inch barrel before I understood why I wasn't up there with them.

I commenced to hear sound, feeble at first but very swiftly growing louder till it hit the full bellow of Irick's shouted roar. "Never mind the goddam bucket! Get him on his feet I said!"

Eye Patch's chest floated over me. I felt his hands go under me. He sucked in a great breath and I came off the floor with the room spinning round my head like a rope. My shoulderblades bumped and with a sickening suddenness the walls latched on to their foundations and froze there. I was propped against one of them, held in position by Eye Patch's strength till some of the sag got out of my knee joints.

Irick shoved him aside with his look dark and ugly.

"I'm all through foolin'," he said, grating each word like it was nuts he was cracking. "You come clean an' come quick or I'll ram that goddamn gun down your throat!"

I opened my mouth but no words came out.

"Your name's Trammell, ain't it?"

I croaked assent.

"You got room Number Nine?"

"I ain't got *any* room yet. I'm—"

"Don't give me that! Your name's in the—"

"But all the rooms was filled up! This guy in Number Nine—"

"What guy?"

"Crafkin."

Irick looked at Gib. Gib trotted to the desk. "No Crafkin in the book—"

"But there *must* be," I said. "I talked to the feller—"

"The point," Irick growled, "is that you've got the room now."

"I ain't been near the damn room!"

"Then what's your gear doin' in it? Your shotgun, rifle an' bedroll," Irick snickered, "an' don't tell me they ain't in it because we've already seen them."

"I can't help that. Crafkin—"

"I've had enough of your run-around!" Irick slammed me against the wall. "Search 'im, Gib."

Eye Patch said, hauling his hand from my pocket, "Is this what we're lookin' for?" and held up a key. The 9 on the tag looked big as a house.

Irick's look turned ugly. "Never been near the room, eh?"

I licked the blood off my lips. "Of course I've got the key. I told you Crafkin—"

"There ain't no Crafkin—"

"Ask the girl," I said. "She'll tell you!"

Carolina looked surprised. "We've had no guests of that name."

"What!" I said, not believing my ears. "That cattle buyer! That feller that piled off the stairs on to—"

"You must be mistaken." She looked completely bewildered. "We haven't had any cattle buyer staying at this hotel. The last guest we had in Number Nine was Krentz, the condiments and spice man. The room wasn't occupied when you signed for it."

I guess I stared like a fool. I got cold all over when Irick touched my shoulder. I said through chattering teeth. "What's the matter with the room?"

"I'm goin' to show you, Handy. An' maybe while you're lookin' you can tell us why you killed him."

"Killed who?" the girl cried.

"Why, your uncle. Shellman Krole."

EIGHT

I HAD PLENTY of time to think things over after Irick locked me up in the one-room abode which served as Shaft's official juzgado. It was not an imposing edifice but its walls were twenty-four inches thick and its single window, covered with half-inch screening, backed up by a row of two-inch pipes. It contained no furnishings save a thin pile of oat straw intended for a bed and, in the opposite corner, a little pile of sand which might serve the needs of nature. There was twelve feet of empty space between roof and floor and the door was made of two-inch planks secured by a massive padlock. Nothing short of an Act of God could get a man loose without outside help.

These things I had seen by the light of his lantern which Irick had thoughtfully taken away with him. My untended face was giving me hell and my thoughts weren't anything to brag about, either. I had sure wound up in one beautiful mess for a guy that was going to be a second Burt Mossman.

I couldn't understand that girl at all. But there were other things, too—like why were they going to so much trouble with me when a slug through the back would have stopped me permanent, not to mention being easier and quicker?

The only reasonable answer was that they knew or suspected I had come from Cap Murphey. But didn't the fools know he'd send another Ranger up here if the first one he sent got put out of business?

The pain in my head wasn't helping me think, but I did pull one notion out of the tangle. What happened to me might not bother them any so long as I was stopped and so long as what happened to me couldn't be laid to the mind that had planned it. This might logically explain the slick way I'd been framed for the killing of a man who must have stood in their way. Shellman Krole, according to the dope Cap had passed along to me, had been undertaking to show a profit from the various holdings of the Tailholt Mining & Milling Company which belonged, I understood, to Carolina Krole. The hotel wasn't hers and the milling end of the business, so far as I knew, was doing all right. It was the mining end of the venture, and Shellman Krole's disappearance, which had brought the girl into Cap Murphey's office.

Krole, according to her tell of it, had disappeared between mine and town two days before she had yelled for a Ranger. And now he was dead with two slugs in his back and killed, to my thinking, not more than half an hour before I'd clapped eyes on him. Where had he been in the meantime, and what in the world had he been doing in Number Nine?

It seemed obvious to me he must have stumbled on something, been discovered in his discovery and taken out of circulation before he could pass word along. He had not been nice to look at when Irick had choused us up there to see him. But the girl hadn't fainted. She hadn't sobbed. She hadn't opened her mouth. For all her expression had revealed to the contrary she might have been looking at a piece of waste paper.

It wasn't natural.

It wasn't natural, either, for the sleeves of Krole's shirt to be wrinkled like they were just above both elbows.

There was a heap of unnatural things in this deal, including those blown-out lanterns. Who'd blown them out? Carolina? Or Irick? And what was the object? To conceal what was going on back in that alley?

No one seemed to know exactly what *had* been going on. Except, of course, the girl; and she wasn't talking. Like Irick, I was curious to know what she'd been doing out there in the first place. A funny place for her to be, Red Irick had said; and I thought so, too. Considering time and location I thought it damned queer.

It was a devil of a lot queerer the way she had cut the ground out from under me by denying the existence of that cattle buyer, Crafkin. What the hell had she thought to gain by that? Did she think I was dumb enough to swallow that garble? Or that I wouldn't remember him? Or, knowing already what was in store for me—But, if she had known that much, she must also have known what had happened to her uncle; and if she had known that...

I shook my head, and wished immediately I hadn't for it started my face to hurting full tilt again. If I ever got the chance, I promised myself, I was going to show Irick what a pistoling felt like. With interest.

I walked up and down the cramped confines of my prison, thoughts whirling. Piece by piece I went over the things I had seen or heard since I'd run into Irick on the hotel verandah. But they didn't add up. There was too much missing. Maybe I was just a handy goat, but I felt in my bones I'd been deliberately framed by someone my presence had embarrassed or frightened.

It had to be someone who was mixed up with

Tailholt, else there'd be no point in killing Shellman Krole. Was it Gharst or the marshal? Was it Frunk or the girl? And what about Short Creek—where did he fit into this?

I was damn near certain it had to be one of them. One of five people. But which one was it?

A stealthy sound spun my face to the window. It was lighter outside, but not very much.

Very carefully and slowly I got down on my knees, never taking my eyes from the glassless window. There was someone out there, someone being mighty cautious.

I didn't think it would be any of the bunch who had framed me. But it might be the one who'd buried that blade in Gharst's door.

I hardly dared breathe lest the sidewinder hear me.

Then a voice crept softly in through the window. "Trammell?"

Ever try to peg the person back of a whisper?

I waited, heart pounding.

The screen might keep a knife from whipping through that opening but it wouldn't stop a bullet.

"Trammell? Are you there? This is Carolina."

Maybe it was. And maybe it wasn't. I didn't say a word.

"Listen—where are you? I'm going to get you out of there. There's an ore wagon up the street— I'm going to drive it down here. I'll slip a chain around those bars and yank out the window. I've tied a horse at the corner. Be ready to run for it."

I didn't know what to think hardly.

It might actually be her. I couldn't tell without moving. The whole thing could be a trick.

A lot of questions plagued my mind but I didn't let them plague me into moving or talking.

One thing I felt reasonably sure of. It was her had got me into this. If I hadn't dashed into that alley to help her I wouldn't have been with her when she reached that dark verandah. If she hadn't lied about Crafkin I probably wouldn't have been in this calaboose. I remembered something Irick had said right after he'd sniffed my gun barrel. "Smart," he had said with a kind of grudging admiration. "You're a slicker piece of goods than anyone around here figured." I had supposed at the time he had intended those words for me. Now I wasn't so sure.

But say the whisperer was Carolina. Was it because she had helped put me into this jail that she had come around now with this stunt to get me out of it? Remorse? A guilty conscience? I didn't think a girl who could lie the way she had could have enough conscience to worry about. But she might have plenty of reasons for wanting me out of this camp, I thought.

And that was another thing. Trap or no trap, if I left by that window I'd be laying myself open to the slug of any guy that wanted to take a shot at me—a fugitive, wanted for the killing of Shellman Krole.

I got to my feet and edged across to the window. I didn't see any lurkers waiting round in the shadows. Across the dark open stretch of the unpaved street I could see a lone light in the stage depot office. It was the only light showing now in Canada Gulch.

I tried to scout out the corner where she'd left the tied horse but there weren't any corners in sight from the window. I didn't see any tied horses, either.

I wondered what Burt Mossman would have done in my place, but that didn't help because I couldn't imagine Mossman being caught in such a trap.

I was sure in one hell of a spot for a Ranger!

I guessed I would just have to take my chances and go through that window no matter what happened afterwards.

I had just reached that conclusion when I heard the crunch of booted feet outside. These weren't stealthy steps; they came straight up to the door. I caught the rattle of the hasp and the sound of someone's key thrusting into the padlock, and I thought: *That goddam Irick again.*

But it wasn't Red Irick. I knew that much before the door opened, when the guy outside said, "Trammell? Stand in front of the window. I'm coming in for a talk."

It was the marshal, Bucks Younger, and he had come without a lantern.

I didn't know what that signified, but he had sure picked a first class time to come calling. With the girl probably driving up the street right now.

I reckoned Murphey was right about me and savvy. If I'd had enough sense to pound sand down a rat hole I would probably have come up with some fine inspiration that would have knocked all my problems into a cocked hat. But if I'd had that much sense I wouldn't have been in this jailhouse.

All I could think of to say was "Okay."

"Get over there then and don't be trying any tricks."

He was too alert to be taken in by anything conjured on the spur of the moment. He remained where he was until I'd crossed the room. He came in then, still holding the padlock, and put his broad back against the closed door.

"It will save time," he said, "if I tell you at once she's not coming with that wagon without it suits my book."

In the gloom of this room I could not see his expression. I was just as well pleased to know he couldn't see mine. "What do you want?"

"I want to know first of all if you killed Shellman Krole."

"How could I kill a man I hadn't ever seen?"

"We haven't time to spar around. I want a

straight answer. Did you or didn't you?"

"No. I did not."

"What do you think of Brian Gharst?"

I stared at him tightly. "Any guy as thorough as you are hadn't ought to have to ask!"

"I regret the necessity. It's unfortunate I can't be two places at once, but there it is. I can't quite make myself invisible, either. What did you think of him?"

"I didn't like him," I said. "Did you throw that knife?"

I caught the faint sound of his insucked breath. "Maybe you had better tell me about that."

I told him.

"Someone," he said, "doesn't want you around."

I said, "I'm beginnin' to be of that opinion myself."

"What did you think of Gideon Frunk?"

"I wouldn't care to eat off the same plate with him."

"There's bad blood shaping up between him and Gharst. They've been sniping at each other for quite a while now. I suppose Gharst wanted you to spy on Frunk."

"That seemed to be the general notion."

Younger nodded. "I've an idea Frunk's getting fed up with Gharst's interference. He's got the upper hand right now and means to keep it." He looked at me earnestly. At least, his voice sounded earnest when he said in that quiet direct way that seemed to characterise all of his more serious remarks. "I'd like to help you, Trammell. You're in a bad spot here. I'm in a bad spot myself and I believe you could help me. I think it would be smart for us to put our heads together."

Riding a hunch, I said: "What do you think of Carolina?"

"She's playing with matches," he said thoughtfully. "I haven't had much chance to know her personally. The disappearance of her uncle, following so closely on the heels of her father's death, has kind of started her running in circles. She's convinced someone's trying to beat her out of her mine, and she has some reason for thinking so. Unfortunately she's stubborn, given to making snap judgments and entirely too brash where she ought to be cautious."

"Just how do you mean?"

"Well, for one thing, she's determined to get to the bottom of the business. But she won't let me help her—she won't let me near the place. She thinks Frunk's grabbing her concentrates and, for some crazy reason, she's got the idea I'm helping him."

"You said she was playing with matches."

Younger said gruffly, "She's playing with something a lot more dangerous than matches. In her desire to get to the bottom of this business, she's made some kind of deal with the wrong kind of people. I assume she has, anyway, because she's smart enough to know she would have to have help. Obviously she wouldn't go to Frunk and she hasn't come to me."

"You think she's gone to Gharst?"

"I don't know. The Tailholt's the richest mine in these diggings—I'm pretty well satisfied of that. Like Carolina, I don't believe her father's death was due to any accident, though it certainly was made to look like one. Just between you and me, I wouldn't be astonished to learn that Carolina's mine is the direct cause of the feud that's sprung up between Gharst and Frunk."

"You think they're both after it?"

"I think it's quite likely."

"You got any reasons?"

"Nothing I could put a finger on."

"Either one offered to buy her out?"

"I don't know about Gharst. Frunk made her an offer."

"How much?"

"He is reported to have offered fifty thousand."

"You think it's worth more?"

"Your guess is as good as mine," Younger said. "I have never known Frunk to offer a quarter of what anything was worth."

I told him about Frunk's purchase of Roy's hole and he sighed. "That's his system, all right. First scare the guy and then buy him out cheap. He's done that before."

"You think he's trying to scare the girl?"

"She's already scared. She's got more backbone than the rest of this bunch Frunk has put the pressure on. She's trying to fight back. I think he's playing a freeze-out game. I don't say he's getting her concentrates, but she can't get the stuff to market. She's having trouble underground. She hasn't got much money. I think whoever is behind what's going on is trying to tie her up so tight she'll simply *have* to sell out."

"You think they could do that?"

"I believe that thought is behind present tactics."

"And there's nothing you can do?"

"That remains to be seen. I think I might be able to do something about it if I could manage to find out what's really going on. I can't do much working solely on rumour. She won't let me near the place. She's got a fence around the diggings patrolled by eight men with rifles."

"What about the help? You can't get out ore without miners."

"They're only working three men. And Jeff Bender, of course, the mine manager."

Still riding my hunch, I told him about Brian Gharst's proposition.

"About what I figured," Younger answered. "You won't get much change out of Gideon Frunk. His organisation's all set, he wouldn't risk taking on new blood now."

"Your deputy, Irick, seems on good terms with him."

Younger laughed shortly. "He ought to be," he said. "It was Frunk that had Red Irick made deputy."

"Frunk told me," I said, "to ask you for a job."

"Knowing of course, that if I gave you one he could knock it on the head by having his Better Business Bureau refuse to vote any pay for you."

I thought that over. I said, "What about the job you offered me yourself?"

"I didn't plan to advertise that you were a deputy. It was an undercover job that I was figuring to give you. I was aiming to pay you out of what I'm paid myself."

He stood quiet a moment, thinking. "That's why I'm over here now. When I found out the girl was going to try to break you out of here I got the driver of that wagon to stick around it for awhile."

"What do you want me to do?" I said.

"I want to get you into that mine, if she pulls you out of this place she's going to figure—"

"It won't work," I said, and told him of the conversations which had led up to my being here; of how Irick had got the drop on me and of how the girl had denied the whole existence of Crafkin. "All she wants," I said, "is to see that last of me. She wants to get me out of the country and figures I'll be glad to get out if she gives me half a chance."

"Thinking, of course, you're the only one who can tie her up with that cattle buyer."

"If he *is* a cattle buyer, which I'm beginning to doubt."

"No cattle buyer of his description has ever been through here before. Something odd, too, about him not being registered. I expect we can pretty safely conclude he's some new man she's got working for her. Some fellow she wants to keep out of sight. She obviously has no reason for believing you connected with her uncle's death or she wouldn't be trying to get you out of here. I think if you'd work at it a little you could get her to hire you."

"You mean you're willing to turn me loose?"

"I'm a pretty good judge of human nature," he said dryly. "You don't look to me like the kind of a gent that would shoot another man through the back. I've got to get somebody into that mine before it's too late to do her any good. This mysterious Crafkin convinces me I was on the right track in thinking she was getting in over her head. If she's hired one tough character, I see no real reason why she wouldn't hire another—meaning you. But it will be damned risky. You'll have to watch your step every minute of the time. In addition to that, if you let her snake you out of here, I can't give you any protection. Red Irick will be howling for your scalp soon's he sees that jerked-out window. Frunk will probably post a reward for you and—"

"I'm willin' to take my chances," I said. "You don't think Carolina killed her uncle herself, do you—or had him killed?"

Younger said sharply, "Where'd you get that notion?"

"Irick seemed to think—"

"Irick," Younger said, "thinks whatever Frunk wants him to."

NINE

"I'm sorry I was so long," she whispered, "but we're all set now. I couldn't find anything to cut that screen; you'll just have to pray that when this chain jerks these bars it will pull the whole works out. Irick went off with your pistol and I couldn't find your rifle. But that sawed-off's on your saddle and your horse is tied just around the corner, between here and the assayer's—next building to your left. Are you ready?"

"Been mighty good of you to go to all—"

"You've got that much coming."

"I hope you won't get in no—"

"Never mind me! Listen to what I'm telling you. When this window comes out you come right out after it—don't stop for anything! Pile right into your saddle and give that pony everything you've got."

I reckoned she wasn't going to like any part of this and, as she slipped off into the roundabout shadows, it came into my mind I might not like it much either when the whole hand was down. If she was tricking me again, or if somebody else was, I might easy wind up a mighty dead duck. Especially if that horse wasn't where she said it was.

All kind of wild thoughts was rushing through my head—not to mention the pain from my face, which was plenty. I was a lone white chip in a no-limit game and I had no guarantee that even Younger was backing me.

But a guy has to put a little faith in something and, like Bucks had said, we had one thing in our favour; nobody'd be looking for me to be on the payroll of a galoot I'd knocked around the way I had Bucks Younger.

I could see the shapes of the waiting horses, three pairs of them, hitched to the front of that wagon. The high bulk of that rig was not ten feet from the window. I hoped nobody wondered what the hell it was doing there. Probably they wouldn't. So far as I could see, this whole street was dark, no saloons or honkeytonks on it except for Jawbone Clark's dance hall, next door to the right, about eighty feet away and not doing no business anyway.

And right then was when that struck me as peculiar, but I didn't get no chance to think about it because just at that moment I saw the girl's shape climb on to the seat and unwrap the lines.

I heard her cluck to the horses, saw them take up the slack and move into their collars. Then the whip popped over their heads and they dug into it, the great wheels turning, the chain clanking tight.

One moment that window was where it had always been; the next it was gone, pipes, screen and all, in a great cloud of dust. I didn't wait around for any probable results. I went out through the dust of that wrecked wall running.

The horse was right where she had said he would be, and right alongside of him a guy with his gun out.

I had to look twice because the shadows were thicker than blue tail flies, but I could see enough of him to make damn sure he wasn't cached out there to give me any hand up.

It was the bony faced kid—that sidewinding Short Creek!

I made a wild dive just ahead of the flash, then a jump to the right and a quick lunge left again, wondering how long I'd keep ahead of his bullets. I'd bid goodbye to the horse fast as ever I'd seen him and was bending all my efforts towards getting around that corner where the whipped pine planking of the assayer's office would be between me and that vinegarroon's pistol.

I was bent nearly double and barely inches from my objective when a rolling bottle flung me off my balance. I went through the air like a bird and lit rolling, expecting any moment I would draw my last breath. But the fool had shot his gun plumb dry and before he could get it to banging again I was up on my feet and round the side of that building.

I didn't stop to write no letters.

The black wall of the gulch was straight before me. I couldn't tell how steep it was or anything else. I just tore into it and went scrambling upward fast as I could catch holds to grab on to.

I was almost to the rim when the first of a bunch of gun-waving jaspers came pounding around the corner of that shack and froze me against the wall like a possum. Long as I wasn't skylined I knew that bunch couldn't see me. But I was in a tough spot with one foot half lifted and about to change hands. I was scared to go on and scared even more to set the foot down again lest it dislodge a rock and draw a bedlam of gunfire. I clung like grim death and prayed that nothing would tear loose.

I couldn't see much but I could hear the low buzz of their excited mutterings. To the south and east I could smell the damp cold of the river, the scorching odour of dust churned up by their boots as they went nosing around like a pack of stumped curs. Then one guy said plainly, "Mebbe he went up the cliff," and I could feel the stab of their searching eyes.

Somebody scoffed. "In this dark? No one but a dimwit like you would—"

Irick's punishing voice lunged through it. "You goin' to stand there all night? Spread out and beat the bushes! Couple of you tackle that cliff! Rest of you split up an' comb both sides of these buildin's—by God, I want that walloper caught!"

I could hear them spreading out, breaking up and moving off, and with an increasing clarity I could hear a pair of them somewhere beneath me moving through the brush around the base of the cliff. "Hell," one of them said, "he never went up there. That's a bad enough place to try to scale in the daytime. With all that loose shale we'd of heard him sure."

"Yeah, but you heard Red. He said to go up."

"That guy says a lot of things besides his prayers."

"He's damn quick on the trigger, too, an' don't you forget it."

"What'd this feller do, anyway?"

"Busted outa the jail—"

"I mean before. What'd they put him in for?"

"How the hell would I know? You think I—"

The blast of a gun cut through their talk, followed almost at once by three further shots.

I knew what it was. They were potshotting shadows.

But the pair down beneath me seemed to have froze in their tracks. You could almost feel their bated breath. "Hell's fire!" one cried, and the other yelled, "C'mon—they've got him!" and went crashing off through the breaking brush.

I couldn't tell if they both went or not. I didn't wait to find out. I went over that cliff like a bat out of Carlsbad.

It wasn't near so dark up here as down yonder where the plain-to-view lights of the camp's main drag made every shadow look twice as black. But it was still too dark to go ramming around at the top of your whistle. Soon as I judged I was away from the rim I stopped to catch breath and get my bearings.

I wasn't out of this yet. All I had done was swap jail for the open. I might, in fact, have swapped the witch for the devil. I didn't have no horse. I was on my own without a gun in country I didn't know anything about, pitting my wits against a bunch of tough rannies who could find their way around with their eyes shut. The same bunch probably which had snuffed Krole's light. And would be glad to snuff mine, given half a chance.

If I went straight ahead I reckoned I'd come out someplace just a little beyond the uninhabited end of Burro Alley, somewhere around that little red schoolhouse I had noticed while riding into this camp. That might make me a hideout for the next two-three hours but, when school took up, I would have to move again.

It looked like being a lot smarter to do my moving now.

I started forward slow, feeling my way and keeping my ears skinned. If anybody and me was going to meet up here it was my intention to be the first one to know it.

This ground up here all lay pretty level in a kind of rolling bench sloping gently as I walked and spotted here and there with occatilla and greasewood and the occasional dark shape of a twisted catclaw. A few trees stood darkly limned against the glow from below, but nothing showed this bench was ever used by anybody. All the digging, it seemed like, was on the far side of town.

I thought the best place to hide would be that

room in the hotel where they had found Shellman Krole. That seemed the one sure place where I would not be looked for.

I even managed to figure out how I could get there. By skirting the west end of Burro Alley and heading straight south beyond the town limits I could reach the river. Its near bank was grown to cottonwoods and willows and, by keeping to the water and using a little care, I figured I could leave it right in front of the hotel. If those lanterns were still out I could go right on up.

The prospects of a bed, even shared with a corpse if they hadn't moved him out yet, looked a heap more inviting to me right now than any other prospect I could think of. I was pretty near ready to drop in my tracks. Nothing but the knowledge of what would happen if they found me was preventing me from dropping down and snoozing right up here.

I wondered how much Irick was offering for my scalp.

I got to thinking then of Crafkin, the elusive tenant of room Number Nine whom that girl had never seen or even so much as heard of—to hear her tell the story. He *had* had that room because it was him that had given me the key to it. Had Krole been in there then? Was Crafkin the guy who had killed him? Why had Carolina denied his existence? What was between Carolina Krole and Crafkin?

There were plenty of questions prowling through my head, and one thing. The thought of Cap Murphey. It was that trouble at Tailholt that had fetched me up here, and Tailholt was where I'd ought to be right now.

I had been in this camp going on nine hours and hadn't even got within gunshot of it. I had lost my horse and all my artillery and was being hunted now for the killing of the man who had been in charge of Tailholt. I could see what Cap had meant about savvy.

What I'd ought to do was get into that mine—but how could I? How was I going to get through that fence? And the nine men with rifles that were being paid to watch it? I could try, of course; but my best bet, it looked like, was to talk that girl into hiring me. And the best place to find her was at the Eagle Hotel.

The ground underfoot was slanting a lot more noticeable and I reckoned I was getting pretty close to where this bench angled down toward the schoolhouse. I'd have to keep my eyes peeled. With those Burro Alley cribs still doing a lively business—

Right then was where I stopped, with the toe of one boot shoved into something that was yielding horribly under my weight. I jumped back away from it, bathed in sweat.

All the sounds of the night stepped up their rustlings and the breeze coming out of the gulch grew colder.

I dropped on to my knees and, knowing the full folly of it, rasped a match on my Levis and watched its cupped flare ravel through the layered gloom to wash its oil-yellow shine across the shape of fat Roy. He lay sprawled on his back and he was as dead as a doornail.

TEN

I PUT OUT the match and rocked back on my bootheels, stomach muscles crawling in the dread expectation of hearing the cry that must tell of my discovery.

But nothing happened. No cry came, no bullet.

The rustling quiet disclosed no change, yet I was not fooled into thinking I was safe. Somewhere in this night men with loaded guns were hunting me, prowling the backs of buildings, overturning packing crates, peering into all the dark and secret hidden places—perhaps, even now, they were beating both banks of the river.

I didn't have to see Roy's face again to know he had not died peacefully. Someone had beaten the back of his head in. There was no sign of a weapon on him.

I was beginning to feel kind of dizzy. I knew I had got to get some rest before the shakes in my legs let me down completely. I didn't like to leave Roy laying there but to be caught near him by Irick would be all those birds were needing to fit a hemp necktie around my neck.

I got on to my feet and started back upslope. I'd give up my notion of trying to get to the river. I was scared to cross that Burro Gulch trail lest I be seen and later accused of Roy's killing. It was in my mind maybe that Irick had done it for those fifty silver dollars. Or on Frunk's instructions. Either way, if he had (or if he knew about it even); there was a mighty good chance he was having the body watched.

My aching face was giving me hell and my thoughts weren't calculated to cheer me up much, neither. Any way I turned I seemed to get in deeper; and right about then I began to wonder if the most of this grief hadn't come right out of my trying to play gumshoe without no experience. It wasn't my style in the first place and I was pretty well convinced by now in my own mind that the only damn polecat I was fooling was me.

They hadn't moved my horse.

That was one blessing, anyway.

He was still standing hipshot right where Carolina had tied him. Where I lay on the rim above that pine plank assayer's shack I had an unbothered view of him and I watched him ten minutes and all those roundabout shadows without seeing anything that looked at all suspicious.

I reckoned Irick's hunt had moved to likelier locations.

I eased myself across the rim and started down the cliff face cautious. I didn't want to bump into trouble before I reached that horse.

I took my time, resting every couple of yards or so, and when I got to the bottom I stood quiet awhile, listening. The only thing I could hear was the fitful soughing of that chilly wind.

I didn't aim to make any more mistakes. I worked my way through the brush with a dogged, watchful patience. Coming out of it I moved into the deeper shadows of the pine plank shack where I stayed a long ten minutes, storing up strength and finding out all the night had to tell me. When I judged there was no cause for any further alarm I got on my feet again and started for my horse.

It would feel powerful good, I thought, to get a saddle under me.

My mind was made up now. I was done with caution. I was all through ducking and dodging. I aimed to learn these dadblamed crooks around here that a Arizona Ranger was no guy to yell *boo!* at.

About twenty feet ahead was the corner around which I had so desperately dashed a half hour ago trying to get out of reach of that Short Creek's pistol. A little way beyond the corner was my waiting horse and there was going to be a new deal quick as I could get my legs around his barrel. It might not be any better deal but it was damn sure going to be a different one.

Rounding that corner I got the surprise of my life. A gun went off practically in my face. Unhit but half blinded I tore into the guy swinging. He never had no chance to squeeze his trigger again. My lifted right knee caught him flush in the groin and as it doubled him forward a gorgeous left hook almost unhinged his jaw.

It spun him half around but I could see a lot better now. I got him by the coat collar, swung him quick and wide and let him go crashing up against that plank wall. The gun fell out of his fist with a clatter. As he sagged I went after it.

I was bent over, trying to reach it, when I saw his boot turn. I got back just in time. The downflashing glint of that murderous blade didn't miss my cheek by the thinnest of whiskers. I struck out at him wildly, tried to whirl but he tripped me. His weight slammed into me.

I ploughed through the dust on a hip and one shoulder. He came down on my legs but I rolled, twisting free before he could skewer me.

He was on to his feet almost quick as I was,

panting and snarling, coming right after me. It was hard to keep track of that hand in these shadows. Always it was there, scarcely inches away, a confused weaving blur of thrusting and slashing in its continual endeavour to sheath that steel in my body.

I had to keep giving ground. I had to keep my arms clear. On this uneven footing, with those spurs on my heels, I was in agony of terror lest I get hung up or stumble. I was scared even more of turning my back on him.

But there's an end—even to nightmares. This one ended with the small of my back jammed into a tie rail. I saw the shine of his teeth, saw his hand go up. Then he gathered himself and came at me full tilt.

At the very last moment I lifted a leg up. My boot caught him flush in the chest, drove him backward. He was still off balance when my left fist buried itself in his belly. But his damned knife got me. It got me high in the back. I could feel it lay open my flesh to the bone. I could feel the hot flow of my cascading blood.

The guy was down but by the sounds he was making he was figuring to get up again. I watched him come over on to hands and knees. I heard him groan. I saw him back around like a beak-pinched grasshopper and, after canting his head a couple times, start moving.

He still had the knife. I could see the dull glint of its blade as he crawled toward me. I didn't wait for him to reach me. He had the knife in his right hand and I kicked that wrist as hard as I could. He screamed like a dying horse. He quit when I kicked him in the face and I thought the sound of those breaking teeth was the sweetest music I had heard in a coon's age.

I had a hard time finding the tie rack. I thought I never would get the knot out of those reins. And when I did the damn horse acted like he didn't know me, snorting and shying round like a bronc with a cockleburr under his blankets. I don't know how I got my foot in the stirrup or how long it took me to get into the saddle or what the hell I planned to do after. I remember breaking my Greener to make sure it was loaded and the night kind of fogging up like smoke.

The next thing I knew I was flat on my back in a bed staring up at a lamp lighted ceiling.

I got to know that ceiling like the palm of my hand before I was able to get out of that bed. I knew every crack in it—every knothole. I didn't know whose drawers I was in but they were too loose to be mine. The guy must have a whole raft of them because I'd been here two weeks and every day they got changed by the girl who sang in the Bellyful Bar.

It had taken me some time to recall who she was but on my fourth awakening to full consciousness I pegged her. There was no forgetting such feline grace, that tremendous vitality so apparent in every gesture—those eyes. Though everything about her was of an amazing loveliness it was her eyes that a man would most certainly remember. Tawny, they were, and indescribably female, at once so wise and yet so childlike, so sad yet so eager—like sunlight rocking across windrowed sand in the first flush of the morning. Purely golden.

Soledad, they called her.

That song I had first heard her singing—*Jalisco*—was as truly her as anything I can think of. Like a drumbeat, like the clickety-clack of castanets; the rattle of musketry before a white wall. What words can reveal her? The total impression was not a thing of the features; like the willowy sight of her breath-taking body these were perfection. Can you describe the essence of wind or flame? Or tie a string to the moon?

No more can I tell you what Soledad looked like.

Her living flesh, yes. I could tell you of that. I could tell you her lips were the colour of crushed berries, her nose without flaw, her skin like old ivory, her eyes deep pools wherein a man could willingly lose even honour—yet you would not know her. Words are too easily mouthed, too flat, too threadbare with use to recapture her image. There is nothing to which I could compare her that would make you see her as I did. You would not guess the knife-twisting tenderness of her. Your skin would not tingle to her smile as mine did nor your heart bound as mine to the touch of her fingers.

She was the plaything of moods, unpredictable, distracting. Caring nothing for convention she had her own code of rules and was, in her way, devoutly religious.

I remember the morning of my fourth awakening. Returning just short of dawn from a night's tour of earning her keep among Gharst's boisterous patrons, she found my eyes sensible of her presence and came to my side, dropping a cool hand to my forehead. "You are better," she smiled. "You will mend now, quickly. Ah, pobrecito—I am glad for you. The Blessed Virgin be praised. It was a near thing, that."

She ran the cool hand over my whiskery cheek. "You are hungry."

She went back of the bed then beyond my view. I heard the rustle and swish of discarded clothing, the clatter of kicked-off spike-heeled shoes. I heard her bare feet cross the pine boards of the flooring, more slithering of cloth and she came into sight in fresh gingham, arms twisted back of her, buttoning it up.

I watched her thrust shapely feet into scuffed

huaraches, get her purse from a battered old chest of drawers.

I dozed off then. When next I opened my eyes she was beside me, on the floor with a bowl of steaming broth. "You must eat," she explained, and proceeded to feed me. It was good—to the very last drop it was good. I could feel strength's return flowing into my arteries.

The next time I woke she was in bed with me, sleeping. And the whiskers, I found, were gone from my face.

She was right. I commenced to mend rapidly. My curiosity grew apace. By the end of my eighth day in that room I was fed to the gills with being so useless and, after she'd left, attempted to get up. I did get up—at least I got my feet on the floor. I was glad enough to lie down again quick. I was not as recovered as I had liked to imagine.

During the next couple of days I did a lot of thinking. I asked Soledad what talk she had heard about my sudden disappearance.

"It is thought you have gone, run away," she smiled. "Already you have been forgotten, *mi alma.* Have no worry, we have been at much trouble that no one should guess where you are."

"We?"

"Certainly. Did you think I could get you up here by myself? The Señor Gharst and Pete Spence brought you here between them."

I had thought it very likely Gharst had known I was here. Remembering his words I was surprised he had bothered.

I wondered what Bucks Younger was thinking. Had he known I was a Ranger when he made me his deputy? Someone had known, of that much I felt certain. Either the girl had been followed when she'd gone to Cap Murphey or she'd made the mistake of confiding in someone. I wondered if Gharst knew.

I thought probably they all did by this time. I'd concealed my badge in the skirt of my saddle, between the leather and the lining. I asked Soledad if she knew what had happened to my horse. She said the marshal had him.

I considered Carolina. I still couldn't figure why she'd denied knowing Crafkin unless Younger had the right of it in thinking the fellow was some gunslinger she had fetched in here to help her unravel what was happening at Tailholt. Perhaps that was where he had gone that night with some kind of password that would get him through the fence.

I recalled Irick's talk again, his veiled suggestion that Carolina might know more about what had happened to her uncle than was apparent. I could not believe she'd had a hand in killing him— it was against all reason. And yet, why had she been out in that alley? And how had Short Creek known he would find her there? Who had put out those lanterns that were hung from the roof of the Eagle's verandah?

I asked Soledad if she knew Short Creek.

She thought it over awhile and then nodded. "He is bad, that one—*hombre malo*."

Pressed for reasons, all she would say was that he was understood to have killed several men. She tossed back her hair and regarded me sullenly. "If we must waste time in talk let us talk of ourselves." Kicking off her huaraches she came and sat on the bed. "I would lay with you if you asked me."

"You lay with me half the day," I said gruffly, but she brushed that aside.

"To sleep!" she said scornfully. "Am I then so ugly?" She held up a leg, letting her skirt fall away. "Is it crooked? Here—feel with your hand. Is it rough?

"It's all right," I said without touching it.

She glared. "What's the matter with you?"

"With that hole in my back I don't—"

"Ah, pobrecito!" She swung up her legs, twisted round and put her lips against mine. I thought she'd never let go. I would lie if I said she did not excite me, but as soon as I could I tore loose and rolled over. She came after me, twisting her mouth into mine, hotly, hungrily, straining against me.

I could feel the pound of her heart against mine. Maybe I was too weak for it. She drew back of a sudden and looked at me angrily. "You're afraid!"

I was. Just a little. I was afraid this might be some trick of Brian Gharst's. After all, he knew where I was, and where she was.

I said, "I think right now we'd be smarter to talk."

"About...us?"

"And other things. How do you come to be working for Gharst?"

She said with her face turned away from me, "Oh, *prala,* there is no denying I am not a chaste woman. I am bad, *mi alma*...no good for you," she whispered, peering up at me anxiously from under one arm. "But even an abandoned one has to eat and here I can eat better with less badness."

"You mean, Gharst—"

"That one cares nothing for women. For dinero only he makes covetous eyes. So long as my songs and my dancing bring patrons he cares not what I do in my room. In all Estados Unidos there is no one can dance," she said proudly, "like Soledad. Shall I show you, *prala?*" She reached round to unbutton the back of her dress, but I said:

"Later. This Gharst...what's he after? I mean, besides money?"

"I cannot tell you."

"He's friendly with Frunk?"

"He has much hatred for that one."

"What of the marshal, Bucks Younger?"

She shook her head.

"Red Irick?"

"He is a thing of this Frunk. Very quick with the pistol."

"Short Creek?"

"How can I say? Sometimes he comes here. They do not speak to each other. I have not much understanding of this; only four weeks I have been here."

"And before?"

She shrugged. "Mexico, Queretaro, Zacatecas, Monterey, Laredo, Nueve Rosita, Juarez—my poor wandering feet must always be moving. Since I left the convent—"

"You received instruction? Then what of your people? Where—"

"I do not know this. I think *los indios* ... I recall wagons, *soldados* ... I have not the clear remembrance of this. The nuns of Panuco only. When perhaps I was eight I ran away with gypsies; it was too sad with the sisters. Too beautiful. Too still. They taught me to sing holy songs but the gypsies taught my feet to move."

She twisted round and sat up, caring nothing how much I saw of her legs. She had an expression of thinking. "Well, then, by myself I found how to fill my belly. A thing of the eyes, a little show of bare skin—men are such fools," she said contemptuously. "They think because of this I will share my bed with them."

She began suddenly to cry. Like a child. "I can tell what you think—a dancer! A frequenter of cantinas—an *orzica! Osté!* This is why you will not have desire of me—Oh, *querido mio*, you have tore up my heart and now—"

"Be still," I said, feeling strangely uncomfortable. "I have much gratitude—"

"Do I care about that? I speak of love and you—"

"Now wait—"

"*Por nada.* Keep your gratitude, gringo!" she cried, whirling up from the bed with her eyes like daggers.

ELEVEN

Two nights later I got out of there.

I was far from well but I was able to navigate and, soon as she'd left to amuse Gharst's customers, I climbed out of that bed and into my clothes. I had no plans, knowing well the futility of trying to lay out any given course of action when I didn't know what I was going to run into. I would have to be guided by circumstance. The first thing of all was to get out of this room.

I had to get hold of a gun. Since it was plenty obvious I would run into trouble and equally certain I was in no shape to put up any fight without weapons, my need of a gun was paramount. I buckled the shell belt around my waist and went over to the battered chest of drawers and went through them.

Luck was with me. Among a bunch of junk in the bottom drawer I found a pearl-handled 41-calibre derringer. Loaded.

I tried the door expecting to find it locked but it wasn't. In suprise and suspicion I stood with the cold knob gripped in my hand and wondered if this were deliberate or carelessness.

It had been her custom to keep the door locked—

"so that no one, *mi alma*, will come in here and shoot you."

I stood crouched there listening while sweat came out across the backs of my hands. This smelled like a trap and the more I considered it the less I liked it.

Had she left it unlocked so that someone could cut my throat while I slept or in the hope that I'd get up and try to get out? I could not believe the door was unlocked through oversight.

Speculation was useless.

If I left the room, and this were part of the plan, all the breaks would be with the guy set to nail me. That was one angle. Then I thought of a better one. With this popgun in hand I could get back in bed and, pretending to be asleep, give whoever came in the surprise of their life.

But supposing no one came? I'd be a sucker for sure, dawdling here wasting the best chance I might get. Luck never liked a piker and it was a tenet of the Rangers that the man who took the initiative had the battle half won.

I opened the door and stepped out.

There was nobody on the balcony. The games down below were going full tilt. There was a fair-sized bunch bellied up to the bar. All the tables were filled and tobacco smoke hung in a haze round the lamps and the babble of voices was like the sound of cicadas. From a room two doors to the left of me I heard the low panting moan of a woman abruptly shut off by the scrape of fiddles as the platform buckaroos struck up a quadrille.

I took a quick look along that line of closed doors, wondering which was Gharst's. If I could get into his office.... There was a word in white paint on the third to the right, the one opening off the top of the stairs. It said PRIVATE.

Just as I got there the door swung inward.

"Ah—Trammell," Gharst said around his thin

black cigar, and stepped away from the door.

I went in, kicked it shut and put my back against it. The light flashed back from his steel-rimmed cheaters. The bony mask of his face gave nothing away.

We stared at each other in silence.

Gharst cleared his throat. "I told you," he said in his dry precise way, "when you had anything to report you were to do it through Soledad. If you can't obey orders—"

"Never mind that. You wanted a Ranger. You've got one."

"Indeed. Where?"

"You're lookin' right at him."

"I'm in no mood for jokes," Gharst said dustily. "When I hire a man—"

"Rangers ain't for hire," I said, and tossed his roll of bills on the desk top. I saw the wriggle of the muscles along his jaw and pointed Soledad's derringer at his middle. "I want a gun," I told him—"one that'll shoot six times."

He eyed me a moment longer then went over and pulled open a drawer of his desk. My nerves went tight as catgut as he lifted out a long-barrelled Colt's .45. But he handed it over, butt foremost.

"My advice to you, Trammell, is to get out of this camp just as quick as you are able."

I said, "Unlock that back door—the one that goes down those outside steps."

He crossed the room, high and square and a little ungainly in his high-heeled boots, and turned the key without comment. But I could tell by his eyes he'd misjudged my intentions.

"Now open it," I said, "and start down the stairs."

His stare held a risen vigilance.

He stood there straight and motionless. "What do you think that will gain you?"

"I'm not thinkin'," I said. "Turn down those

stairs. And don't make no quick moves. I'll be right behind you."

When we reached the street he swung about and faced me. "Just what do you think you're about to do?"

"I'm going to get me a horse and I don't aim to lose sight of you while I'm gettin' it. Strike out for the livery."

"There's horses across the street—"

"Head for the livery."

In the pattern of black and brightness induced by the lamps of the roundabout dives his face showed the bony mask of stubbornness. "To hell with you, Trammell. I've gone far enough. You won't shoot me here—"

"There are smarter ways. Move out," I said, "if you want to stay healthy."

It wasn't so late. There was plenty of traffic on the opposite walk and there were four or five riders coming up from the turn into Canada Gulch. I couldn't afford to stand here long and it was plain that this was what Gharst was counting on, that risk of exposure would force me to leave him.

"If I'm stopped," I said, "you're a gone goose, Gharst."

He didn't believe it but the habit of caution was too strong for him to break. I could see the bitterness warping his cheeks, the pale fury of hatred compressing his mouth's corners.

I flashed a look at the street.

Directly across from us, beyond the jammed walk, loomed the cracked-plaster front of the Chinaman's hash house. East of this, half obscured by a clutter of wagons and hitched horses, was the bright facade of Frunk's Mercantile, its coal-oil flares throwing dancing patterns of yellow radiance across the black drift of the night's cruising shadows. Farther down, perhaps two hundred yards from our placement, where Canada Gulch spilled the rumble of ore wagons into the town's main drag, was the dark huddled hulk of the Eagle's rear end.

Our side of the street, by contrast, was practically deserted. A scattering of cow-ponies dozed at the hitch racks before the dim front of Jack McCann's next door where, sixty feet away, a group of high-heeled shapes stood quietly talking, silhouetted against the distant glare of the lantern-lit front of the Antler House, the last building this side of the gulch's intersection.

I brought my look back and saw the tag end of Gharst's glance coming away from that knot of dark figures before McCann's. I watched him take the cigar from his mouth, stare down at it a moment and then pitch it away. He fetched out another and bit off the end.

"Don't light it," I said. "Shove it in your face and chew it, and if those birds down the street open up as we pass them, just toss their gab back and keep right on going. If you stop it's liable to be the last stop you make." I moved against him. "Get going."

With a frustrated growl Gharst swung into action.

I dropped the gun in my holster and came abreast of him on the side nearest the buildings, making sure in this way he'd be between them and me when we reached the gabbers lounged in front of McCann's. They might still make me out, even with the bar-room's lights in their eyes, but it was the best I could do.

What I wanted, of course, was to get hold of my saddle and dig out that five-pointed star of the Rangers I had gone to such trouble to hide in its skirt. With that badge pinned on me it might be tougher sledding to accomplish my chore here but, at least, its significance might hold back a few wild ones from cutting their wolves loose the moment they lamped me.

There weren't more than ten or twelve gents in this camp that would be like to know me if they got a good look. Gharst and the marshal. Irick, of course, and Gideon Frunk and the birds roosting round his store when I'd been there. It was this last bunch that bothered me for I couldn't remember what a one of them looked like. Too much had happened since then—and there was Short Creek. And the one who had knifed me. And the ranny who'd sunk his blade in Gharst's door.

Too many to keep tabs on and watch Gharst too.

I had to watch Gharst. From the moment we'd come face to face in his doorway I had known he had made up his mind about me. Give the guy half a chance and he would bring this camp down on my head like a twister. He didn't want no Rangers snooping around. Right now every wheel in this think-box was probably flying round like a kite in a headwind trying to figure how to get me safely planted.

I tugged the brim of my hat down over my eyes and felt my shoulder muscles tighten as we stepped on to the walk that fronted McCann's and a couple of the gabbing group twisted their mugs around.

"Careful," I muttered. "Take it easy now."

Gharst said nothing. His eyes turned narrow.

The riders who'd been coming up the street went past and I saw the lone shape of a solitary walker round out of the gulch and head this way on our side. Something about him looked uncommon familiar. He came into the lights of the Antler House and I recognized Bucks Younger, the marshal.

I choked back an oath. This could be the break I was needing but it could just as easily work against me. Bucks had sworn me in as a deputy, but that had been two long weeks ago and I had no proof if he wanted to forget it. Much may have happened while I'd been laid up. If he hailed me by name all hell could bust loose if any of the gents in this bunch standing around happened to be friends of Irick's.

I slanched a quick look at Gharst. His step faltered. I caught hold of his arm. "Later," I growled, trying to hurry him on. But he shook me off. Stopped.

My eyes raked his face. He didn't know I existed—or that other guy, either. He was staring at Younger with an expression that lifted the hair on my neck.

Suddenly abandoning a lifetime of caution he let go with his voice in one high yell, made a grab at his side and whirled half around with his jaws wide open.

I stood stunned as the rest while he took three staggering steps and went down. Only, unlike them, I knew what the score was.

Black rage ripped through me. I'd been tricked like a fool.

I heard Younger running but all I could think of was how Gharst had outslicked me. Not content just to get me recognised, he'd made it seem like I'd killed him right in front of their eyes. And, by God, I was minded to do it!

Then I saw the blood leaking out through his fingers.

I didn't hear the shot. It was probably drowned in the voice yelling *"Grab him!"*

That voice woke me up.

I jerked out my gun and ran.

My only chance was to get across the street and I bowled through that bunch like a ball banging tenpins. I heard Younger shout. I heard yells and cursing. Then the guns started barking.

I kept going. Doubled over, I made for the walk in front of Frunk's—made it, and tore through that crowd like a bull through a mismanaged matador's cape.

I cut left, still running, still hearing that voice from the blackness yell *"Grab him!"* The voice was lost now but I remembered the sound and the vague swirl of shadows by the mouth of the alley that provided the boundary between the Eagle Hotel and Frunk's Mercantile. The same murky path I'd been up once before on the night I'd chased Short Creek away from Carolina.

It was Short Creek's face that I had in my mind, and I'd have bet forty pesos it was him had dropped Gharst. By mistake of course—he'd probably meant to drill me.

The passage mouth was barely ten yards away now. With heart pounding wildly and pain like a ragged blade between my shoulders, I redoubled my efforts. I aimed to nail that damned killer once and for all.

I barged into the alley and saw a running shape almost at the far end, blackly limned against the light from the hotel verandah. I didn't catch but a glimpse before he was out in the open with the full light upon him. I couldn't fire then—I was too surprised to squeeze trigger.

It wasn't Short Creek. It was Crafkin.

TWELVE

It did not take me long to reach the end of that alley but there was nothing to shoot at when I got there; Crafkin had vanished. The cottonwoods masking the bend of the river presented a wall of banked foliage as innocent of guile as a barefooted baby. Yet behind this surface deception, as I very well knew, lay a smuggler's maze of twisted trails down any one of which the man who didn't exist may have fled—or, with rifle butt cuddled to baleful cheek, even now be waiting a second chance.

Lit by its ten flaring coal-oil lanterns the deserted front of the Eagle Hotel looked for all the world like a painted stage set, the kind you could see at the Bird Cage in Tombstone. Set down in the midst of the night's deep blackness that brightly lighted verandah offered no chance of concealment.

I would have bet considerable Crafkin had crossed it and was inside even now, perhaps closeted with Carolina. I itched to make certain but was too well aware of the risk I'd be taking going up those bare steps. Too many bravos in this cut-throat camp would be glad of the chance to put a

97

slug through me, and there was always the very real possibility that Crafkin had ducked into those riverbank trees.

Whether he had or not I couldn't stand here. Already I could hear the racket of pursuit avalanching into that murky passage.

I whirled to the left and trotted into the cottonwoods. The shadows beneath their boughs were like clabber, like a cloying fog that cut off all vision. What light came through their clustered leaves was deceitful, confusing, more a hindrance than help. I pressed deeper, stumbling on blindly till breath was a tearing rasp in my throat and slivers of pain thrust into my lungs from the half-healed hole the knife had left in my back. My foot snagged a root and I fell face first into crackling brush that filled my ears with a million echoes. Too spent to move, I lay there, gasping.

A mutter of voices reached me dimly and boots drummed a hollow pounding from the planks of the hotel verandah. But I knew they wouldn't all go inside; some of those rannies would start beating the labyrinth under these trees.

I was right—too right.

I could hear them now, softly swearing in the shadows, the snap and crackle of brush as they drew steadily nearer.

I got to my feet, trying to still the sound of my laboured breathing. I had the rank, pungent odour of mould in my nostrils and my face began to smart where I had scratched it with thorns. But all thought save flight left my head the next moment when, less than twenty yards away, I heard Irick's voice. "To hell with Bucks' orders! That bird's in here some place—you think I'm a fool? He wouldn't cross that bright porch with all these trees growin' handy! Spread out an' quit jawin'."

They spread out and once more I heard the rustlings of their nearing progress. Alarmed as I was, I could still think sufficiently to realise if they heard me they would start throwing lead. I moved as silently as possible but, barely able to see where I was going and not being able to see at all what I was putting my feet into, I knew mighty well I was making enough noise for them to have no trouble placing me if they should happen to stop together long enough to listen.

But I couldn't play possum. I had to keep going unless I wanted them to find me. It was a nerve-racking business.

It presently crossed my mind to wonder what would happen when I eventually came to where there weren't any further trees and I had to move into the lonely open with Irick and his gun grabbers not more than a handful of yards behind.

It wasn't the kind of prospect to induce a man to tarry. I stepped up my stride as much as I dared. If I could put my hands on a tin can or bottle... But if there were any such laying around in this thicket I wouldn't be likely to see them or have any time for hunting. A plainly heard sound to their rear might turn Irick's gundogs, but I hadn't any means of producing such a miracle.

As a matter of fact, I hadn't had much of anything since first coming into this camp but trouble, and it was bound to get worse before it got any better. I had long ago lost all sense of direction and might easily be going around in a circle. Plenty of lost fools had done that.

Belatedly it crossed my mind if I could only be sure which way was the river—and could reach it—I might yet get away from Irick's pack. If I hadn't turned plumb around in this tangle it ought to be some place off to my right and, on the chance it was, I headed that way. Almost anything, feeling the way I was now, looked better than being caught out in the treeless open.

I slogged along for a while and then pulled up to

listen. The sound of the hunters seemed to have become more distant, though I reckoned that was wishful thinking. I could still hear them plain enough, cursing as they beat their way through the bushes.

My head was spinning, every muscle throbbed. My nerves were pulled tight as fiddle strings. The pain in my back was a dull stabbing ache that was like the twist of a knife each time I drew breath.

Somewhere off to the left I heard the crash of a shot, then a drumming of others in swift succession—a confusion of shouts.

Some fool, I thought likely, had fired at a shadow. Ragged tempers would account for the rest of that racket. Now if only, I wished, they'd take off at some tangent...

They did. They came toward me.

While I paused, scarce breathing, to make sure of this fact, a dry stick snapped not twenty paces ahead of me.

I dropped a hand for my gun. Sweat cracked through the dry cold of my skin when the hand found the top of my holster empty. I couldn't believe it. But the big-barrelled gun Gharst had given me was gone. Gone, too, was the derringer.

Another stick snapped—closer. I heard the scuff of a boot. And then I couldn't hear anything but the nightmare crash of breaking brush as I fled through the night in headlong panic. More than once I fell, but scrambled instantly up, never pausing to take stock of the damage. I find it hard to believe I could have been such a fool, but I'll not offer excuses. I ran till I could not run any farther. The last time I fell I just lay there, retching.

When I began to take stock of my surroundings again the hunt appeared to be over. There was no sound in the brush. No calls, no curses. Never a bird disturbed the deep silence. It was a stillness like death, vast, impenetrable, undisturbed by even the chirk of a cricket.

I got to my feet feeling strangely light headed. I had no idea where I was except I seemed to be standing in some kind of trail. The dark bulk of massed foliage was over my head. On either hand the black tracery of straggling brush rose shoulder high without motion.

I was about to move forward when the uncanny depth of this silence assumed significance. It was too damned still to be natural, I thought. It had the quality of stealth, a stealth crouched and listening.

I tried to shrug the feeling away as absurd, as an aftermath of my crazy panic. But some instinct of caution would not let me move. I could only stand there feeling foolish—and then I heard it again. A vague rustling as though someone, very carefully, had moved aside a leafy branch.

Standing frozen in my tracks a moment later I heard the unmistakable sound of someone moving with the greatest of caution into the trail somewhere behind me.

I was frantic.

It took every vestige of will power I could muster to keep my feet from breaking into a run. Sweat stood out upon my cheeks like rain.

I tried to peer into the black labyrinth beyond. I looked over my shoulder, clamping my teeth shut to keep them from chattering. Nowhere could I untangle the real from the fantastic mirages night erected around me. I saw no one. Nothing moved, yet while I was twisting my face to the front again I caught the dry rattle of dusty leaves somewhere back in the brush that hemmed the trail's right hand. Out of the total quiet to the left someone grunted.

I pulled off my boots and once again stared into the pooled gloom ahead. I might step on a centipede or scorpion or put my foot on a rattlesnake, but dangers of this sort were vastly to be preferred to the volley of lead that would reward discovery.

With an extreme reluctance I crept forward.

I dared not stray from the trail lest I make some sound that would betray my location. Hardly daring to breathe I kept going, more frightened of those bravos closing in behind than of any risk of death I might face up ahead.

I came in time to a place where the path I followed was crossed by another, I hated the task of decision forced on me.

I had only three choices—left, right or straight ahead. I could not go back. I refused even to think of going into the brush. Already I thought to hear the pad of feet behind me.

Afraid to hesitate longer, I plunged left into the curdled gloom of the new trail but when next I paused, hoping against hope the ruse had been successful, the whisper of padding feet still came on.

It was uncanny, unnerving, to be tracked through the murk of this maze in such a fashion. My reason refused to believe anyone could do it, and suddenly I saw what must have been the true answer. There were enough of them after me that they could put a new man to every side trail likely to be encountered, and they were close enough to know if I went into the brush.

I pushed on, turning these thoughts over, trying to find some angle which might lead to a chance of safety or to some margin great enough to allow me to escape. Why, I wondered, were they content to remain behind me instead of closing for the kill? The only plausible answer I could think of was that they wanted me out in the open, that they were afraid in here they might shoot down some of their own crowd.

I began scanning the growth on both sides with more care. If I could find some place to lie doggo, some spot to hide out while they went hurrying past, I could then turn around and hit out on the back trail with a pretty fair chance of getting away. But even as I considered this I knew it wouldn't work. They'd be watching for such a place as closely as I would.

I paused to listen again. Under my breath I cursed bitterly when I heard them still coming. They probably knew these trails. They certainly knew them better than I did. My best bet, I thought, would be to take a different turning every time a trail crossed mine; if I could do this often enough I might lose them. Say there'd been six of them after me to start with. If one had turned right at that last intersection and one had gone straight on, there'd be not over four on my heels right now.

I concentrated all my faculties into trying to make certain now many were back there, but it was useless. For all I could tell there may have been twenty. If one had turned right and one left, and the other four had gone straight ahead on the main trail, there'd be just one behind me.

But I couldn't be sure. I couldn't be sure of anything—not even of how many had originally started. Getting up from the fall that had climaxed my run I'd heard three. If only these had followed me down the first trail it seemed a heap unlikely there was more than one still back of me.

It was at this point I realised I was standing in silence. The furtive footfalls had stopped. The pursuit, like myself, appeared to have paused to listen. I moved on. So did they. When I stopped again they stopped.

I gave up all thought of trying to conceal myself in the hope they'd go by. I went on, determined now to take the next fork right and put all the space that was possible between them and me without running. There was no chance, in my present shape, of outrunning them. I was finding it hard enough just to keep going.

Abruptly, without warning, I reached the end of

the trees. Black open stretched before me in a vast fifty yards to the more intense black oblong of a tall unlighted building.

I gaped at it, stunned, plainly knowing I'd never reach it before pursuit broke cover. If I'd had any kind of weapon... But I hadn't.

Then a second shock froze me. I recognised the building.

Sheer amaze locked all my thoughts while I stood staring at it dully. It just did not seem credible after all I'd been through in that goddam brush; but there it stood in smug grim irony, as inscrutably enigmatic—as balefully dark and silent as ever I had found it.

I had come full circle. I was looking at my nemesis, the Eagle Hotel.

THIRTEEN

Though I heard no sound behind me, I was not fooled into imagining I had lost them. Within easy gunshot at least one of Irick's crew was probably standing much as I was, scarce breathing, rigidly motionless, cocked to catch the ghostly tread of tell-tale footsteps.

A flick of the hand could prove or disprove this. All I needed to do was pitch my boots out into the undergrowth. Fortunately I had enough sense not to try it. The report of a gun would do me no good at all. The last thing I wanted right now was to attract attention.

I peered again toward the shadow shrouded front of the Eagle. Odd, I thought, how every trail led back to it. I had not realised this before but it was true enough.

This was the place Cap Murphey had sent me to. In its cramped and dingy lobby I had first met Crafkin and Short Creek. At its hitchrack I had smacked Bucks Younger, the marshal. In one of its upstairs rooms the body of the redhead's uncle had been found and in its lobby Irick had accused me of killing him. I'd been trying to reach its shelter when I'd stumbled over the corpse of fat Roy, and had again been setting out for it when the loss of blood from that stab wound had dropped me off my horse.

Nor was this the whole score. In the alley separating its wall from Frunk's Mercantile I had rescued Carolina from a second instalment of Short Creek's ardour and had, more recently, down its length chased the guy I thought responsible for what had happened to Gharst. Before its dark verandah I'd walked into Irick's gun and it was just over there I had lost track of Crafkin.

Who was to say he was not inside *now?* And that iron-nerved redhead who had calmly told Younger's deputy no such fellow had ever been in her hotel! I'd long been hankering for a talk with her and it might just as well be now.

If I could get there.

I took a look down my back trail but discovered no more than I had seen before. A lot of black shadows. Any number of which could be concealing a man. Or several men.

If I waited long enough I thought it looked pretty likely that one of Irick's crowd might get careless enough or impatient enough to stir up some sound that would betray his location. But that wouldn't help me and in the meantime Crafkin, if he was still inside the Eagle, might take off for other parts.

I particularly wanted to get hold of that hombre for it was in my mind that this elusive cattle buyer might hold the key to many things. He was the only jasper I had ever caught sight of in proximity to Short Creek. They were both of them a heap too familiar with Carolina not to have any part in what was going on.

I had aimed to pack my badge to any talk I might have with Shellman Krole's niece, but that was out now. That badge was on my saddle which was probably at the livery or in Marshal Younger's office with God only knew how many crawlers and creepers between there and me.

Juning around at the edge of this thicket was only postponing the inevitable. Sooner or later they would jump me regardless. If I took to the open at least I might get a brief run for my money.

I stepped out of the trees.

The night was as still as a strangled rabbit.

With a boot in each hand I moved toward the shrouded shape of the Eagle like I was walking on eggs.

Fifty yards doesn't sound like any great distance but it can be as far as hell and back. I advanced across that windless open with every nerve screwed taut as a drumhead and every muscle cringing from the shock of expected impact.

Nothing happened to disturb my progress. No shout rent the night. No bullet touched me yet I lived and died a thousand deaths before the deep gloom of the verandah received me into its tattered obscurity.

Any instant I expected the alarm to go up, the dread hue and cry of the chase to begin. For aught I knew my approach had been noted by those within and perhaps even now was being prepared for. A step groaned in anguish beneath my weight but the die was cast. I could not turn back now.

Boots still in hand, my socks in shreds, I drove bruised feet across the cold planks of that silent verandah to bring up by the sagging screen of its door in a rash of chill sweat as my ears strained to catch any sound from beyond.

A dim mutter of voices came out of the quiet as water crawls out of a green-scummed seep. I could distinguish nothing but their low drone, their murmur—nothing whatever that would identify the speakers or even their number. The lobby looked black as a stack of shined stove lids.

There was nothing to be gained by waiting

outside, nor did I wish to. From having used it before I knew the screen door would kreak like a stuck pig the moment I touched it, but the window was closed and might wail just as loud if I attempted to raise it. I took hold of the door and yanked it wide in one jerk.

It never let out so much as a whimper.

I closed it after me gently, not liking the thought that was in my mind. If the door had been oiled it had been oiled for a purpose and that purpose might not yet have been served. Irick could slip in just as soundless as I had, and all Irick's bravos if I left it unguarded.

I got the chair by the desk and quietly laid it across the threshold and, with an equal stealth, slowly mounted the stairs with my feet squeezed as close to the wall as I could manage. I by-passed the third step which I remembered was warped but the eighth let out a most dismal groan.

I stopped with caught breath. My heart pounded but the talk overhead went steadily on and, after a moment, so did I. I wondered what I would do if accosted. I might, I supposed, heave my boots at the fellow and perhaps after that put my head down and charge. Unarmed, it was about all I *could* do.

At the top of the stairs the sound of voices was plainer. There were only two—some man's and Carolina's. The man's had a gruff fed-up sound as though he were impatient with whatever the girl was saying.

This hall was not as dark as the stairs, its congregated shadows a little less opaque for the bar of light that came from beneath the left side's third door.

I was about to move forward when something blurred against the dim rectangle of the window at its end.

I might have dismissed it as pure imagination

only something was there, less than twenty steps away, something dangerous and crouching. I was aware of its breathing, a suppressed winded sound that was almost like panting.

I became aware also that the window was open. I could feel the quiet draft from it curl around my ankles.

I drew back my right arm knowing a boot wasn't much but that it was better than nothing. Whatever was over there had come in through the window at about the same time I'd been coming up the stairs.

I was minded to edge nearer but stood where I was lest a floorboard reveal my presence and whereabouts. The unknown even now might have a gun trained upon me.

In the intolerable stillness I heard the girl say plainly, "But you knew all that—you knew we couldn't trust anyone. If you—"

The man's voice broke in, unintelligible but urgent, and Carolina told him, "If you can't do it I'll get someone who can! Or I'll shut the mine down. We're not operating Tailholt for the benefit of Frunk!"

The man said testily, "You've got Frunk on the brain. How could Frunk—"

Sharp through his words flared the rasp of a match. The draught whipped the flame out as quick as it kindled, but not before I had seen what was facing me.

I let drive with the boot and flung myself after it. His goddam gun went off right in my face. Then I was into him, grappling him, slugging him, trying half blinded to get hold of the hand that was wrapped round his pistol. I got it, too, and smashed it into the wall—heard the gun hit the floor with a hell of a clatter. He slammed a knee in my groin and I reeled away from him, gasping, just as a door was torn open behind me. Lamplight, flaring into the shadows, revealed the tag-end of his drop through the window.

I caught the glint of his fallen gun and scooped it up, stumbling forward as his boots plucked wild sound from a shed roof. "Grab him!" I yelled, thrusting my head out of the window.

It was too black to see him. I heard his boots strike the ground. Muzzle lights blossomed, rifles cracked viciously and, farther out, two more joined them. Someone ran through the shadows and Irick's bull roar spewed out baulked fury. "Cut him down! Cut him down!"

Then a hand caught my shoulder, jerked me back from the window.

FOURTEEN

I FOUND MYSELF looking at the biggest hunk of man I had ever clapped eyes on. Broad layers of flesh bulged the grey flannel shirt below the huge bald head and face of a shaved hog. He was like a stuffed pig but there was strength in him, too, and considerable consternation when he found the black bore of Short Creek's gun pointed at him.

He let go and backed off like he'd laid hold of a rattler.

"My God! Who's this?" he wheezed, startled.

Then I saw Carolina. She looked plenty startled, too.

I guess I did look a sight with my clothes all torn from the brush and no boots on.

I saw her tongue cross her lips and she said, "Why did you come back?"

I motioned them toward the room. "Let's get out of this hall before that bunch chasing Short Creek find out they've been played for suckers. Pick up my boots, Fatty, and don't start nothing you ain't able to finish."

He didn't care much for that but he kept his mouth shut. He went and picked up the boots and shuffled back toward the door like the weight of the world was bowing him down. Carolina, with her eyes looking worried as well as frightened, said: "Now, just a minute, Trammell. When I got you out of that gaol—"

"Yes, indeed!" I said. "We'll go into that later. If those rannies come back before I get out of sight someone's liable to get their pipe dreams ruptured. I been pushed around enough in this camp. If there's any more shoving to be done I'll do it. Now get movin'."

I gestured with the gun. They went into the room, me following.

The fat man sagged into a chair that was too small for him and sat with hunched shoulders like he was figuring to be patient even though this didn't concern him. Carolina remained standing, cheeks flushed and chin lifted. I toed the door shut and put my shoulders against it.

They had a heavy wool blanket draped over the window and, to make sure doubly certain, they had the lamp turned down to where it wouldn't hardly have lighted up a half-grown junebug. "Pretty snug," I leered, "pretty cozy," and let my glance wander over to the bed.

The fat man scowled. Carolina's cheeks took fire and the look of her eyes would have made some guys uneasy.

But not me. Mad was the way I wanted her. "We're goin' to get right confidential," I said. "You want this sport to listen in on the pow-wow?"

"We have nothing to get confidential about—"

"Think again," I said. "And I ain't meaning that slick little gaol-break you hatched as a means of getting me shot into doll rags."

"If you think—"

"Next time you figure to get a guy planted give your money to someone who'll go through with the business. Don't waste it on bunglers like Short Creek that ain't got hardly dried off behind the ears."

I gave her that and then I said before she could unfurl any back talk, "You went south a couple of weeks ago an' chinned with Cap Murphey. You gave him a lot of gaff about stuff goin' on at that mine your Dad left you, telling him you reckoned a gent named Frunk was trying his damnedest to whipsaw you out of it, aided and abetted by the local law. You want to hear any more with this bird sittin' in on it?"

She was off her horse now all right. Her eyes looked like a couple of holes in a bed sheet. And a sour grin was twisting the fat man's mouth.

"I don't see how—"

"You will before I'm done with it."

Her head turned then and her glance met the fat man's. "You wantin' him to hear any more of this?" I said.

"He knows about that trip—"

"Does he know you been playin' drop the handkerchief with Short Creek?"

The fat man swore. "I told you—" he began, but she said angrily, defiantly:

"You told me not to go to Cap Murphey. You said getting a Ranger up here wouldn't do us any good—"

"Well, has it?"

"I had to do *something*. I couldn't just sit here and let them steal us blind. *You* couldn't stop it. Uncle Shelly wasn't getting anywhere. The bills were piling up and we hadn't anything to pay them with—"

"Making deals with crooks and killers—"

"I had to trust *some*body."

The fat man sniffed. "You certainly picked a lulu if you made any deal with Short Creek. You might just as well have gone straight to Frunk. Hells bells! If you were going to set a crook to catch a crook why didn't you hatch up something with Gharst. At least—"

"I went to Gharst."

The fat man stared. "Maybe we do need a Ranger at that. Did you hire this gun-hung drifter too?"

"No," I said, "she didn't hire me."

"Then maybe we'd better save the rest of our linen to be washed out after you've hit the breeze."

"It's a little late for that," I told him. "She should have thought of that before she went to Cap Murphey—"

"What's he got to do with the price of onions?"

"If it comes to that, how do you stand in—"

"My name's Jeff Bender," the fat man growled. "I'm manager of the Tailholt Mining—"

"Yeah," I said, "you've done a whale of a job, you and Miss Krole between you."

"By God," Bender said, "I don't have to take that!" He started up from his chair.

I twirled Short Creek's gun by the trigger guard. "You'll take anything I decide to hand you. Includin' the sack if I reckon you need it."

His fists gripped the chair arms but he didn't get up. "Who the hell asked you into this?"

"Your boss," I said. "I'm the Ranger she sent for."

He eyed me through a tightening silence.

The girl broke it up with an odd, nervous laugh. "You expect me to believe that?"

"You had better believe it if you want your mine saved."

"Let's have a look at your identification."

"I haven't got my badge on me."

She let go of a long breath and a deal of the nervousness seemed to go out of her. A smile crossed her lips. "I thought not. It was a good try, Trammell, but we are not complete fools. You may as well put up your gun and get out of here."

I gave her a tough look. "Maybe this will convince you. It was on a Friday you stopped off to chin with Cap Murphey. You arrived on the northbound stage from El Paso. As you were crossin' the yard you happened to notice Joe Stebbins where he was painting the flag-pole. You said, 'Hello, there. Is this the headquarters of Company D?' Joe allowed it was and kept right on paintin'—"

She looked startled. "How could you know that?"

"Because I was there—because I heard you. And I can tell you what Joe said—"

"Don't waste your breath," advised Bender. "You was probably there but that don't make you a Ranger. Only Rangers I've ever run into packed stars—"

"I've got a star all right. But how the hell far would I get in this camp trottin' around with a badge on my shirt front? You ever think about that? What I figured to do was to poke around some before makin' myself known. I thought maybe that way I could get some kind of line—"

"You've got line enough, fellow. What you need is some proof."

"If that badge is what's sticking in your craw," I said hotly, "all you've got to do is to get hold of my saddle."

Bender grinned at me coldly. "*I* haven't got to get hold of anything."

I locked eyes with him. Carolina said worriedly, "What's your saddle got to do with it?"

"That's where my badge is, cached away in the linin'."

Bender looked sceptical. "Seeing's believing."

"Maybe you think I'm scared to go after it?"

He shrugged broad shoulders. "Not my worry." He stretched out his legs and crossed his arms behind his bald head. "If you want the plain truth, I doubt if you know what a Ranger's badge looks like. You come in here with a cock and bull tale—"

"No more cock an' bull than you've been shovin' about that mine!"

Bender jumped to his feet. I aimed the gun at his

belly. "Take it easy," I said "if you don't want to get hurt. Maybe we're both wrong. If you're playing this on the level you've got nothing to lose by taking me down in that mine for a look."

"I can see myself. You're not getting near that mine until it's proved to my satisfaction—"

The girl said, "Just a minute, Jeff. I'm not inclined to believe him either but it will do no harm to look."

Bender threw out his hands. "All right. Go ahead." His eyes swept my face. A faint show of malice broke across his round cheeks. "Where's your saddle at?"

"If it's not at the livery then Bucks Younger's got it."

"What would Younger be doing with it?"

"When I got out of gaol," I told Carolina, "first thing I did was to make a run for my horse. Short Creek was waiting beside him with a gun out." I brushed in the highlights of my flight across the cliff, my subsequent return and desperate tussle with the knifeman, my sojourn at the Bellyful (saying only that I'd convalesced there and nothing at all about Soledad), my departure with Gharst and its sensational conclusion, my futile pursuit of Short Creek, my nightmare experience in the woods with Irick's gundogs and, finally, of how I'd run into Short Creek in the hall outside this room.

They heard me through without interruption, Bender giving me his winkless attention, Carolina's cheeks showing an increasing bewilderment fraught with anxiety that was almost consternation when I came to where Short Creek made his jump from the window.

When I finished she drew a long breath without speaking. She seemed paler than I could find reason for, in the grip of some inner turmoil that was far in excess of the emotion displayed when

Red Irick had confronted us with the corpse of her uncle.

I couldn't tell whether she believed me or not but it was Bender's look that really gave me concern. His moon-round cheeks were inscrutable yet there was something in his manner that blew a cold wind of warning across my neck. There was some secret here, some dark stone being turned or cautiously lifted in the mind behind that unwinking stare.

I watched Carolina's tongue cross dry lips. "It's fantastic."

"A little unusual," Bender amended, "but not too out of line to be true. I particularly liked those references to Short Creek. If Gharst has been gunned I agree with Trammell that Short Creek undoubtedly is the one who did it only, unlike Trammell, I think he did it deliberate. I'm not quite sold on the part, however, about Gharst in the role of Good Samaritan, patiently nursing our ailing Ranger—"

"He didn't know I was a Ranger until I told him so tonight. In fact, the first time I saw Gharst since I woke up in there was when I walked out of the place with him tonight. The only person I saw was Soledad."

"Did you find her very attractive?"

I looked at Carolina uncomfortably. "She was the one who took care of me—"

"Same thing," Bender grunted, still pursuing his thought. "She could hardly have gotten you up there without help, or even into the place without his knowledge. I think there's more to this than you've seen fit to mention."

"There's a little," I said, and told them about Gharst's remarks on conditions and his attempt to hire me to spy on Gid Frunk.

Carolina said nothing. Neither did Bender. He kept watching me with his reticent eyes and seemed still to be turning something over in his mind. "I suppose it has occurred to you that girl was Gharst's wife?"

I must have looked pretty shocked. He grinned anyway and said, "You still haven't told us what Bucks Younger would be doing with your saddle."

"Before Miss Krole here got me out of that gaol I had a visit from Younger. He was wise what she was up to and said he aimed to let her go through with it if I'd agree to work as a kind of undercover deputy ... I suppose this sounds pretty loco to you. But Miss Krole had told Cap she thought Bucks was in whatever Frunk was up to, and that she thought it was Frunk that was getting her concentrates. Playing deputy to Younger looked to me like a chance to find out if she was right—a better chance anyway than I was like to get otherwise. So I took him up." I met his glance and shrugged. "Couple of days ago I asked what had happened to my horse and Soledad told me Bucks Younger had him."

Nothing further was said for several moments. In the glow of the lamp Carolina's eyes looked as coldly disdainful as a pair of eyes could.

"So he made you a deputy," Bender said softly.

I dropped the gun in my holster feeling uncomfortably like a fool.

"Well, it's all of a piece," Bender murmured. "Since Bucks obviously knows Carolina dealt with Short Creek, I suppose he saw no reason why she shouldn't hire you. He probably figured you'd do better, and if he could get you into that mine—"

"All I tried to get Short Creek to do," flared Carolina, "was to keep some kind of watch on Frunk and see if he could find where our stuff was going to."

"And what did he find?" Bender asked, smiling thinly.

"Nothing, of course—I don't suppose he even tried. I was crazy," she said bitterly, "to ever think

I could put any dependence in such a man, but I thought if the bribe were big enough—"

"What did you offer him?"

"The same thing I offered Brian Gharst. A quarter interest in the mine. The last time I met him he said it wasn't enough. He'd find out, he said, if...if..."

Remembering the scene I'd come on to in the lobby and what little I'd observed in the alley that time, I hadn't much doubt about the terms he had offered.

Jeff Bender nodded and scooped up his hat. He clapped it on his bald head. He said, "We'll go take a look at that saddle now."

"Wait," she said. "He's no Ranger, Jeff—"

"We can quick find out."

"But there isn't any need to. I know you've plenty of reason to be disgusted with my meddling, but I'm not meddling now, Jeff. I *know* this man's not a Ranger—"

Bender said thoughtfully, "*How* do you know?"

"Because I've already talked to the man Cap Murphey sent up here."

FIFTEEN

THE SHOCK of her words struck clean down to my boot heels.

Through a magnified stillness Bender stared at her face and then his eyes came around and slammed into me roughly.

I had not realised this room was so large or that, heartbeat by heartbeat, it would continue to grow until it no longer had any walls at all. I had a queer sensation of standing alone at the top of a high place that was about to crash under me.

Bender's voice called me back.

I looked into their watching faces.

"He had nobody else to send."

Eyes blazing, she came a step nearer. "Are you calling me a liar?"

"No. You've been fooled. I'm not doubtin' you talked—"

"Just a minute," Bender growled. He said to the girl in a half strangled voice, "Is that the guy you sent down to the mine?"

She had no need to say anything. The defiance in her look was answer enough. Bender, swearing, shoved me toward the door.

But she got there first, put her back to it.

"Jeff—you've got to listen."

"Stand aside," Bender growled.

"You've got to!" she said fiercely. "You've got to give Joe a chance. After all, the mine's mine and—"

I got it then. I said: "Crafkin!"

Her eyes, wide and stirred, looked almost black in that light. She was like a young lioness in defence of her cubs, only it was love she was defending—or what she thought was love. Whoever this Crafkin was he'd taken her in completely.

Bender said, "Stand aside."

"No. You've got to hear me out. Joe's trying to help us and he will if you'll let him. He's been up against things like this before—in Quartsite, Superior, Globe and Goldfield. He's the man who broke up that gang at Bisbee. He's Captain Murphey's best—"

"Cap Murphey," I said, "never heard of that bird."

She ignored me. "You've got to give Joe a chance, Jeff! I'm not going to let you—"

"Now you listen to me, girl," Bender wheezed. "I've had all of your meddling I intend to put up with. When your father hired me to run that mine—"

"But the mine doesn't belong to my father any more," Carolina cut angrily into his words, "and I've lost all the money from this stealing I intend to. In spite of everything you've done we haven't taken one nickel out of that hole since Dad died. If I'm not to have any say in its—"

A loud crash and a curse from below chopped her words off.

We froze where we were, every one of us, listening. The corners of Bender's mouth pinched in. The girl's eyes looked enormous.

The hush got so thick it seemed like even the planks in the floor must be listening. I leaned nearer to Bender. "Irick and Company. I left the chair to the desk just inside the screen door."

Bender nodded. He said in a whisper. "We've got to get out of here. Douse the lamp, Carolina."

With infinite care and much grimacing I put my feet in my boots. I had had all the barefoot walking I wanted. I heard Bender take down the blanket from the window, heard him whisper to the girl, "Put it up after we leave and get that lamp lit again—"

"I'm going with you—"

I said, "Don't be a fool!" but, like before, she ignored me.

Bender got the window up while the girl made a knotted rope of bed sheets and blanket. Bender fixed an end of it to a leg of the iron bed and tossed the rest out of the window. "Lock the door."

I took care of it.

One of the stairs creaked, and against the window's dim oblong I saw Bender stiffen. I guessed he was thinking what I was, that before we could ever all get to the ground they'd be into this room. It took no great amount of mental effort to picture them emptying their guns out that window.

Bender motioned us back. "Get under the bed."

We did. We got under it just in time.

Something hit the hall door with a hell of a thump. I heard the crack of its panel, another thump and the indescribable sound of splintering wood. Spurred boots made racket across the floor. I caught the rasp of a match and beyond the bed's brace bar I saw three pairs of legs standing rigidly still.

Someone cursed. The match dimmed out. Boots rushed to the window and Irick's voice bellowed: "Crantz, Lefty—Barrigen! Wake up, you dimwits! They went out through this window!"

A fainter answering hail came up from the yard

and Irick snarled. "You'll see something when I get down there!" and again boots hammered across the floor. When I heard them stampeding down the stairs I wriggled out from under the bed and got up. The girl got up too and Bender came out of the closet. "Let's have that lamp."

I handed it to him, saw him slip off the chimney and move it to the window. Drawing back his arm he sent the bowl spiraling into the night and the glass chimney after it. We heard the bowl hit and then the crash of the chimney. Three guns began to beat up the echoes; and then Irick's bellow: "After them, you fools! They've ducked up that alley!"

I went over to the window and stood looking down into the cold pre-dawn shadows. I heard the in-and-out wheeze of Bender's breathing.

"Pretty cute," I said, "but that ain't going to keep 'em occupied long."

"Long enough," Bender grunted. "Come on. Let's get moving."

"Where?" I said.

"To the mine, of course," I saw his head twist around. Carolina's breath made a sharp indrawn sound. Bender's voice said imperturbably, "I want to see a couple faces when these Rangers get together."

Carolina said angrily. "This fellow's no Ranger! I told you—"

"You told me to give Joe Crafkin a chance. With considerable reluctance I've been givng him one. If I've been pampering a crook I aim to find it out pronto. One of 'em's lying and I'm going to find out which."

"You can prove Trammell's lying without taking him into the mine!"

"Very doubtful," Bender grunted. "He may have a badge in his saddle and still not be a Ranger. Also it's entirely possible he may be a Ranger even if the badge isn't where he says it is.

I'll decide which is which when I get them face to face."

She wouldn't leave it there. She kept jawing about it after the way of all women.

At the foot of the stairs Bender said, fed up, "How the hell do you suppose I ran that mine before I had you to give me instructions?"

She shut up then and I said, "Where are we going to get horses?"

"We'll have to go on Shanks' mare. It's not over three miles. I guess you can make it."

SIXTEEN

IT WAS PLAIN Carolina wasn't liking this trip. Nor was she making any effort to conceal her displeasure, walking by herself like there wasn't another soul within a mile and forty rod of her. But I couldn't see how she had much to be riled over. If Crafkin, like she had made out to figure, was plumb on the level and a sure-enough star-packer, she had everything to gain and not a particle to lose. Perhaps it had finally worked into her mind she might have made a mistake about that guy Crafkin. If it had I guessed she would never admit it. She wasn't the kind that likes to be made to look foolish.

I wasn't too crazy about this deal myself. I was anxious to get to the bottom of this business but I wasn't at all anxious to get myself killed. If this Crafkin was the kind of a skunk I figured him to be, he was like to turn right ugly when the pasteboards hit the table. In my present condition, and after this damned hike, I wasn't at all certain I could shade him to the draw.

Neither him nor me would be of much use dead.

From Bender's point of view it was an ideal situation and one that did him credit as a conniver of top strategy. He had nothing to lose one way or the other since he had made it plenty obvious he preferred to take care of the mine's troubles himself and without help or hindrance from anyone. The girl's accusations of incompetence meant nothing and, if he were honest, Bender's intention of facing us with each other offered a good possibility of ridding him of one if not both of us. And, if he were a crook, it offered the same advantage in addition to showing him which of us was the liar.

This dirt road through the woods to the west of the river ran fairly straight and almost due south and after a quarter hour of silent tramping I asked Bender where it was that Shellman Krole had disappeared. "Was it along this road?"

The mine superintendent nodded. "I suppose it must have been along here somewhere. So far as we can learn he never showed up in town; that is to say, before Deputy Irick came across his dead body. I think he may have been dead before he entered the hotel."

"What makes you think that?"

"The fact that no one's ever admitted seeing him. There's not many people that didn't know him by sight."

"How did he happen to be going to town?"

"He was going to pay a bill he owed at the store for groceries and mine supplies. He had thirty-five hundred dollars in his pockets when he said goodbye to me and took off. It was every bit of cash he could scrape up."

"Do you know if it was on him when Irick found his body?"

"If it was," Carolina said, "Irick got it."

"And the bill's not been paid?"

"Gideon Frunk says it hasn't. He's refused to give us any further credit—all part of his plan," she said bitterly, "to bring us to the point where we'll have to sell out to him."

Bender said after a moment, "It's a kind of vicious circle. We haven't milled any ore of our own for six months. The hotel's our last bet for getting further cash. All the concentrates we had on hand have been stolen. Through bribery and threats half our men quit and left us. Of those that remained there were so few we could trust I had to fire all of them but a handful. I thought I could manage to keep an eye on those but..." He shrugged, "The stealing continues. Most of the ore disappears before I can get it to the mill. Whenever I do get a load or two through something happens at the mill and we have to close down. By the time we're ready to run again the damned ore's gone."

"What do you mean," I said, "about a vicious circle?"

"It takes cash to operate the kind of mine we've got. We're strapped for cash unless we can mill sufficient ore to produce the concentrates from which we normally acquire our cash. If we don't produce the ore we can't get the concentrates. If we don't get the concentrates to market we can't get enough cash to keep going. I don't say it's Frunk, though it may be. But somebody's carrying on a campaign that before many more days will shut the mine down."

"Suppose you tell me what's been happening."

Bender's fat made a shapeless shadow but I saw the upward jerk of his chin. "Everything's been happening. Every damned thing that could be calculated to stop us. As I've already told you, our crew's been reduced to where we're not getting out more than two carloads of ore to the day. The men won't work at night. We use tramcars to get the ore from stopes to shaft. From there it goes by hoist to the surface and, from there, in cars drawn by mules to the mill. We've had trouble with the hoist. Wheels have come off the tramcars. Mules have disappeared and other mules have been slaughtered. We've had everything you can think of."

It was rough, all right. I began to see the magnitude of what Bender had been having to cope with. I didn't see any answer. But there had to be one because I had to solve it.

"When does all this stuff happen?"

"Any time. All the time." Bender's voice turned savage. "Up until lately most of the dirty work and all of the pilfering took place after hours. Then I put three men with shotguns in the mine with orders to shoot anyone they caught sight of between dark and dawn. They killed one fellow and that stopped most of the night work but—"

"How'd this guy get in?"

"We don't know. It's what's had me licked—how *any* of 'em get in. Up until just lately I've had eight men with rifles patrolling our fence. It's a hog-tight fence that completely surrounds the property, including the mine entrance. The last couple of weeks I've had three of those men inside the mine armed with shotguns—"

"Can you trust these fellows?"

Bender laughed shortly. "I play it safe as I can by rotating them, not telling them in advance which trick they're going to take. It's helped. It's cut the stealing down to a dribble—and the damage. But it hasn't stopped either."

After a couple of hundred yards I said, "A thing big as this ain't the work of no amateurs. Too much planning—there's a pretty slick thinker back of what you're up against."

"I figured that much out two months ago."

"It's Frunk," the girl said. "He tried to buy the mine from Dad. Dad wouldn't sell. Then, after they'd arranged that 'accident' that killed him Frunk came to me and repeated his offer. He upped the price two thousand, even finally agreeing to cancel our bill at the store in addition."

"What was his best offer?"

"Twenty-three thousand five hundred—including the bill."

"I've heard it was closer to fifty thousand."

She laughed without mirth. "I can see you don't know much about Frunk. What's been happening to the mine won't cost a fourth of that amount by the time it's closed us down. He has never been a man to throw away money."

"What do you figure the mine's worth?" I asked Bender.

"Impossible to tell. I haven't been able to get the vein blocked out with any degree of certainty yet; I've been kept too busy trying to keep in operation."

"Put a rough figure on it."

"I can't even do that."

"You can make a guess, can't you?"

"I don't see the point. It's obviously worth all the trouble these fellows are going to or they wouldn't be doing it. This isn't the work of ordinary *gambosinos;* it's a deliberate attempt to cripple the mine."

"Then whoever is back of it must be pretty well convinced..." I said, "Let's put it this way. Do you consider it to be a more valuable—or potentially valuable—property than Frunk's?"

"Signal Stope?" Bender shook his head. "I don't know anything about the worth of Frunk's mine."

"You know what he's producing, don't you?"

"No. He's working Chinese labour. We don't mill his ore. He sends it to Douglas under a guard of twenty rifles. He's the only one who's been able to send ore out of this camp."

"Well," I said, "what's happening to Tailholt is obviously the work of someone you're depending on to see that nothing happens."

"Some of the guards, you mean?"

"Don't it look that way to you?"

"You'll have a hell of a time pinning it on any of them."

"You've got eight guards. You're keeping three of them in the mine. How do you go about deciding whose turn it is?"

Bender said scornfully, "I've thought of all that. I don't use any system. I pick three at random and they never know which ones it's going to be till I tell 'em to go on duty."

"Then they're all in on it and you'd better get rid of them."

"They probably are," Bender sighed, "but when you've saved a man's life it's pretty hard to suspect him of cutting your throat. I pulled two of those boys out of cave-ins. One of the others pulled me out of one. I try to keep one of those three in the mine with each shift. As for sacking the whole bunch, where am I going to get others that will be any better?"

It was knotty, all right. It was rugged as hell. I saw lights up ahead. "That the mine?"

"Not that first batch—that's Signal Stope. The next ones are ours. They're at the mill. I keep 'em lit so our guards will have something to shoot by. We're not running the mill any more. And don't aim to until we get enough ore to be worth starting up for."

"What about Lucky Dog and Bell Clapper? Weren't they milling with you?"

"They were," Bender said, "I thought maybe if we shut down, one or the other of them might figure it would be worth their while to help us, but I reckon they're too scared of Frunk to risk it."

"What are they doing with their ore?"

"Sending it out with Frunk's wagons on percentage."

"It's getting through?"

"Why not? For half of their profit Frunk would help anybody. But us," he added bitterly.

I thought about that. I said, "How many men are you working?"

"Miners? Just three. And they're okay."

"Where was this guy Roy's mine—the fat guy that got killed?"

Bender pointed. I could see his arm against the near lights of Signal Stope. "Just this side of that first batch of flares. It wasn't a mine—just a hole in the ground. I imagine Frunk bought it just to get rid of Roy."

I studied the pattern of lights and judged the flares from the mill to be roughly five hundred yards from those of Signal Stope. I didn't hear any blasting. "Frunk's not working at night?"

"I don't imagine so. I heard he laid off the night shift some time ago."

"Right after my father was killed," the girl said.

It occurred to me to wonder if they'd run out of ore. But that didn't make sense. They would hardly be sending wagon trains to Douglas if Signal Stope's ore was in short supply.

I switched back to the killing of Shellman Krole. "We don't actually know that he was killed for money."

"Well," Bender grunted, "the bill *may* have been paid. Be a considerable job to prove Frunk's lying."

"Let me get this straight," I said, after a moment. "You've got a hog-tight fence around Tailholt's property which you're keeping patrolled by five men with rifles. Night and day?"

"They naturally have to sleep sometime. I've got eight guards in all. I keep three night and day inside the mine. One, night and day, patrols the fence."

"That makes four men on duty all the time?"

Bender nodded.

"How many gates in that fence?"

"Just one. We keep it padlocked. One key's in my

pocket. Carolina's got the other."

"It would be impossible, then, for anyone to get in or out without your permission? Without your personal attention?"

"Nothing's impossible," Bender snorted. "We've been losing both ore and concentrates. It's going out somewhere without my permission."

"Is the fence being cut?"

"It doesn't show any sign of it."

"Could the stuff be passed up over the fence?"

"I suppose it *could*. There's fifty-eight hundred feet of fence—one guard can't be everywhere or see every point of it every minute."

"Then maybe you'd be smarter to put all your guards on the fence—"

"I had 'em all on until the last couple weeks. We lost more before than we're losing now."

"You had more to lose. You were producing more, weren't you?"

Bender grunted.

"You've looked around in the mine? You don't think the stuff's being hid below, do you?"

"In the mine, you mean? No. I thought of that, too. I haven't found any sign of it."

We were abreast of the lights of Signal Stope now. Two hundred yards up the slope there was plenty of activity where a huddle of weather-greyed buildings showed against the black bulk of the cliffside. A string of ore wagons were being loaded at the mouth of Frunk's tunnel and, off to one side, several men with rifles had their heads together, talking. No one bothered to look round as we went past.

"How close is that shaft to the mouth of Tailholt's?"

"Around a thousand yards," Bender said indifferently.

"How far are they down. Do you have any idea?"

"Around five hundred feet, according to rumour. They opened up that tunnel but, inside a little ways, they found they had to go down the same as we did. They went faster, of course, using bigger crews—"

"How far down are you?"

"Two hundred foot level. Number 3 stope. Why?"

"Just wonderin'," I told him. But something was beginning to click at last and the wheels of my mind were right on the ragged edge of meshing.

"Well," Carolina said. "Here we are."

We followed her off the main road and on to a narrower less-dusty one that led by gouged shelves to the eighty-yards distant Tailholt fence. So far as I could see it was pretty well lit by the tall flares that burned before the mill buildings yonder near the end of the bench. Not a tree or bush obscured the vision and just beyond the gate there was a kind of sentry box overlooking the grounds from the relative advantage of a twenty-foot tower built of four-by-fours.

Bender waved at the man in this cubbyhole, got out his key and unfastened the padlock. After we'd filed through he replaced the chain and snapped the big padlock shut again. I followed them toward the black shape of the head frame. I dropped back a bit and started off at an angle meant to fetch me closer to the collar but Bender, twisting around, called me back. "We'll step into the mine office first, Mister Trammell."

I followed them in.

A burly red-faced man with jet hair and grey eyebrows took his feet off the desk and got up and came forward. It was Crafkin, of course, looking much as he'd looked at the Eagle Hotel. "How are you, Trammell?" he said, and put out his hand.

SEVENTEEN

I watched his eyes and ignored it.

Carolina made a small noise under her breath. Crafkin, looking a little puzzled, finally took back his hand. He put the hand in his pocket and jingled some coins. "How'd you like that bed?"

"Oh, Joe!" wailed Carolina. "Uncle Shellman was in it!"

Crafkin's shape went completely still. In the lamplit silence I could almost hear the leap of his thoughts. A wickedness rolled across his cheeks. "Let me get this straight. You say your uncle was in it? You're talking about the bed I gave Trammell?"

She nodded. She told him of Irick's gruesome discovery, of how I'd been charged with her uncle's killing and of how she had got me out of the jail.

He looked at me oddly. "But didn't you tell him you were here on Murphey's orders?"

"Where'd you get *that* notion?"

"What—"

"That I was here on Murphey's orders."

"Why, Cap told me—when he sent me up here to give you a hand." He considered me a moment. "You look surprised..." And then, "Oh, I see. You couldn't have known that, of course. I'd been over on the Blue tracking down a bunch of rustlers. Cap had written Mehrens he was awful short-handed and Mehrens sent me over. I got in just after you'd left." His eyes twinkled. "But why didn't you tell Irick you were a Ranger? Surely—"

"And tip off all the crooks in this camp? Krole wasn't killed. He was deliberately murdered. Bender here says he was packing thirty-five hundred dollars he was aiming to pay Frunk on their account at the store. Frunk denies getting it or seeing Krole, either."

Crafkin looked thoughtful. "How do you know he was murdered?"

"He'd caught two slugs in the back and, near as I could tell, he hadn't been dead a half hour when I saw him. And there's a time lapse we've got to account for. According to Bender, he left here for town with that money on the morning of the 24th. On the 26th, still no word of him, Miss Krole gets anxious and goes to Cap Murphey. It was late on the night of the 27th that Irick found him dead in that room at the Eagle. Where had he been in the meantime?"

Crafkin nodded. "And how did he get into that room?"

"Someone," I said, "got the jump on him. And not long after he left here. They must have known he had that wad of jack on him, but it's a cinch he was either overpowered or knocked out and thereafter held prisoner until it suited someone's purpose to have him found dead in that room. He was put in that room to frame one of us."

"Or both." Crafkin nodded. "No doubt about that. But they couldn't have known about us when they grabbed him. I don't see yet how they could have known we were Rangers if you didn't tell—"

"I didn't tell anyone *I* was."

Carolina had kept silent as long as she could.

"He doesn't believe you're a Ranger, Joe."

Once again Crafkin's eyes twinkled. "Well, you can hardly blame him." He turned part way around and twisted up the bottom of the lamp gleamed from the five-pointed shine of a silver star. He let the cloth drop. "This is Trammell's first detail. He knows he got the job because Cap had nobody else to give it to. Being merely on loan from Company C, and having pulled in after he'd already gone—"

"Let's get back to Krole," I said, feeling foolish. "How does—"

"I think you've figured it right. There's just one point which you'd probably catch yourself once you've thought of it a bit. Krole was obviously overpowered, but I think that came later. Put yourself in his place. Packing all that money he'd be keeping his eyes peeled. I believe he reached town, or very nearly. I think he fell in with someone he trusted—or, at least, had no reason for particularly suspecting."

"He'd of been suspicious of anyone," Bender said. "Except, maybe, Younger."

I stared, open mouthed. "But Carolina told Cap—"

"Carolina," Crafkin nodded, "suspected Younger of being hand in glove with Gideon Frunk. But Krole didn't. I've discovered that Krole and Younger were on pretty good terms. Krole believed Younger was trying to help him recover the lost concentrates. I think Krole met Younger that morning somewhere between here and town, told him what he proposed to do and asked the marshal to go along with him. They may have gone to Frunk's and paid the bill, some of Frunk's bunch—or Younger—overpowering Krole later."

He took a slow turn around the room. His saturnine eyes met mine, very thoughtful. "Frankly, I'm not too fond of that notion. It's a deal more likely that Younger, on one pretext or another, persuaded Krole to meet him at, or go with him to, the marshal's office. I think he was kept prisoner there, or some place close, until Frunk got the happy inspiration of ridding himself of Ranger interference by framing you with Krole's killing."

"What makes you think it was *me* that trap was set for?"

"Several things. It's pretty obvious now that some way or other Frunk discovered that Carolina had gone to Cap Murphey. Granting that much, it becomes reasonable to suppose I was wrong in assuming they couldn't have known about us. They didn't know about *me* because I didn't sign the register and, at the time Krole was killed, I hadn't started to pry into things. I doubt if they even knew I was in town. They'd certainly no reason for thinking I was a Ranger.

"With you it was different. I think you were followed here by whoever it was they had tailing Carolina. The natural thing for him to do, once he'd learned her destination, was to hang around there until he learned what was brewing. When you left, he followed. I think, when you went into the Eagle, he reported to Frunk. Swift disposal of Krole became of paramount importance. Of almost equal importance, in their eyes, was the necessity of getting you out of the way before your connection with Murphey became public."

"But what if I'd come right out and said I was a Ranger—"

"To Irick? Irick's Frunk's man just as much as Bucks Younger. He'd have refused to believe you. You hadn't any badge. You had gone to see Frunk—perhaps the plan took shape then. He'd no way of guessing Cap had sent *two* Rangers; and you were already down in the book for that room. It must have seemed very providential to Frunk. By knocking off Krole and charging you with the killing he not only shut Krole's mouth but landed you right where a drink-inflamed mob would have had no compunctions about stringing you up."

Carolina's breasts were stirred by the depths of her feelings and she turned to me, impulsively holding out her hand. "It looks as though I've had you all wrong, Trammell. You must think I'm—"

"I think you're mighty dang plucky," I said, taking her hand. "I owe you something for getting me out of that jail when you did. Not many girls would have had the courage—"

"The main thing right now," cut in Bender with some impatience, "is to get to the bottom of what's going on. Holdin' hands and chin waggin' ain't going to put any ore in the crusher."

A more lively colour came into the girl's cheeks. She took back her hand and Crafkin, looking at Bender, said, "Have you posted Trammell on what's been happening?"

"I've told him about it," Bender said. "Only thing I ain't mentioned is the stolen timbering that disappeared out of the south end of No. 14. Carrie," he added, showing the edge of a sour grin, "ain't been too happy with the way I've been handling this business. Now let's see what you two sleuths can do. This ought to be duck soup for a pair of smart Rangers."

"We'll sure do the best we can," Crafkin smiled.

Bender's allusion to Carolina's dissatisfaction reminded me of that fragment of talk I'd overheard at the hotel. *"If you can't do it,"* she'd said, *"I'll get someone who can! Or I'll shut the mine down!"* She'd been dissatisfied all right or she would never have tried to do business with Short Creek. Or with Gharst.

What I hadn't been able to understand was why, if she was dissatisfied, she had not fired Bender. A misplaced sense of loyalty might, of course, have accounted for it; or she might have been afraid she couldn't replace him, or been afraid the replacement could have done no better.

These were thoughts which had crossed my mind. But now another thought came and I said to Bender, "How much longer does your contract run?"

"If it's any of your business it runs another three years."

So that was that. But I didn't leave it there. I said to Carolina, "Was it just his handling of this thing that bothered you?"

Her glance was puzzled. "I'm not sure I understand."

"I mean you hadn't any reason to suspect he wasn't trying? You trusted him, didn't you?"

Her startled face was very lovely. "But of course. I still do. Jeff was one of Dad's closest friends—it was why he hired him."

"Did he share your father's belief in the mine?"

"I'll answer that one myself," Bender growled. "Sam Krole thought he had the world by the tail. He thought he'd found another Comstock. There seems to be plenty of ore but it has to be mined first. You don't pick it up like candy off a counter."

"How big a bunch do you reckon we're up against?"

Bender shrugged. "Not too many, I'd say. For most of what's happened two or three could have done it."

I threw a glance at Crafkin. "You're wrong about Younger. I don't think he had any part in Krole's death."

Crafkin said sceptically, "Who else could have taken him in like that? Certainly not Gharst. Not Frunk himself, nor Irick. Who else does that leave you? Packing all that money, you know mighty well he'd have been watching for trouble—"

"He could have been waylaid."

"He could have been, sure. But why don't you

want to believe it was Younger?"

"He just don't strike me as that kind of a gent."

"Well, it don't make much difference who trapped Krole. You can't get around the fact he was killed, or that the killer did his best to tie the job on to you."

"I'll take that," I said, "and I'll accept it as highly probable that Gideon Frunk is after this mine. Bender says there have been quite a number of cave-ins, that timbering's been stolen and, I suppose, tunnels blocked." I looked at the mine boss.

Bender nodded.

"But none of these things have actually ruined the mine. It would have been just as easy, wouldn't it, for them to have hidden a stick of dynamite in the ore being sent to the crusher?"

"Of course," Bender said, "but—"

"So it's plain as ploughed ground that whoever's behind this has no intention of really ruining Tailholt. That's why I'm willing to believe it might be Frunk. But it doesn't have to be. It could just as well have been Gharst."

Carolina said, "I don't think it was Gharst. I'm pretty sure it wasn't. He wasn't a bit interested in my proposition. He said the Bellyful Bar was all the mine he had time for." She shook her head. "It's Frunk. I *know* it's Frunk. Right from the very beginning—"

I said, "It could be Bender."

Bender's look showed a startled anger. He came half around with his big fists clenched and a baleful scowl on his shaved hog features. Then his great shoulders loosened. "This ain't no time for jokin'—"

"I'm not joking. Nor am I accusing you or anybody else. I'm just pointing out a few possibilities. It could be Bucks Younger as far as that goes. Whoever it is, he very obviously believes this mine is worth plenty. When a man doesn't stop at murder he's not going to balk at anything else."

After a moment Crafkin nodded. "I'll subscribe to that. Have you any idea how we're going to stop him?"

"I've got two or three notions, though I doubt if you'll like them."

"What I like or don't is hardly important. You're in charge of this case. What do you have in mind?"

"For one thing, I'd like to get Bucks Younger down here—"

Bender jerked up his head. "Over my dead body!"

Carolina was plainly against it. "What good will that do?"

"I don't know," I said, "but I'd like to find out."

Crafkin, eyeing me keenly, said, "You want Frunk, too?"

"I don't think we'll need to ask Frunk," I said. "Just let me have Younger here for six to eight hours and I believe I'll get to the bottom of this business."

I saw Carolina toss a quick look at Crafkin.

Bender scowled. "That's a damnfool notion. Where is the sense in hiring all these guards if—"

Crafkin said, "What do you think, Carolina?"

She drew a long breath. "I don't know. I've never trusted him. I can't really put my finger on it but there's something about the man..."

"You think he's two-faced?"

She considered that a moment, lifted her shoulders and let them fall. "I don't actually know one thing against him. Uncle Shellman *did* trust him; he believed Bucks Younger was doing all that he could.... But just the thought of the man—I don't like him."

"Then you'd rather not take the gamble?"

"Let me ask you one thing," she said quietly. "Why do you feel that Younger's presence would help you?"

"Let's call it a hunch. I think your uncle was

smarter than he's being given credit for."

Her face showed surprise. Her eyes revealed interest. "How do you mean?"

Even Bender leaned forward.

"I think," I said, "He'd got hold of the answer. Or he was gettin' damn warm."

I could feel their thoughts taking hold of this. Bender's beefy cheeks were still.

Carolina searched my face. "You really believe that?"

I said, "Consider the facts. Your uncle got his living from the Eagle Hotel."

"Yes, that's true," she admitted. "He hadn't any share in the Tailholt properties. By the terms of Dad's will he was named executor and made my guardian. The trouble at the mine upset him."

I said, "Naturally. He was responsible for seeing that the mine showed a profit. He must have realised someone was attempting to cripple it—"

"He believed it was Frunk. The same as I do," she said.

I merely nodded. "He wasn't the kind to shirk his responsibilities. He was trying to find out what was going on and stop it. If he thought Younger could help him he must have had some reason. I think you've been confusing Irick's action with Younger's. I don't believe Younger is Frunk's man and I've a hunch if we get him down here he will prove it."

"That may all be true enough," Crafkin said. "But the thing we're interested in proving, it seems to me, may not have anything at all to do with Bucks Younger."

"We were sent here," I reminded him, "to locate Shellman Krole, to find out what was happening in this mine and to stop it. If Krole believed Younger could help him get to the bottom of it there's no reason to believe Younger couldn't help us."

Carolina, still watching my face, said, "Then let's try it."

"We don't know," Bender pointed out, "that Shellman actually thought Bucks Younger could help him."

"We know *you* weren't able to give him much help."

Bender's shaved hog face looked at me without expression. "All right," he said, "go ahead and fetch him down here." He stared a moment longer. "Rangers!" he snorted, and rammed his hands in his pockets.

He was half-way to the door when Crafkin spoke. "What are you figuring to do when he gets here?"

"Search the mine," I said, and saw Bender stop.

He took another long look at me over his shoulder. "And what the hell good do you think that will do?"

"I've a hunch it may show us what they've been after."

EIGHTEEN

"AFTER?" Carolina's stare swept from me to Bender. She drew in her breath with an increasing bewilderment. "Am I being awfully dense?"

The mine boss's beefy shape swung round and he wheezingly came a few steps back with his rolled-up sleeves looking baleful as the hackles of an angry dog. "I thought it was your notion they were after this mine."

"It was."

"Then what in Christ's name are you trying to pull now?"

"I'm trying to find an answer that will fit all the facts."

"What facts?" asked Crafkin, pressing the lips of his leather-dry mouth together.

"Some of the mismated facts that right now don't gee."

"Like, for instance?" Bender said dustily.,

"Like why would anyone take such risk and trouble for a mine you claim ain't no better than good."

Bender leaned forward. "How many mines have you bossed in your time?"

"I haven't bossed any."

"You've worked in a lot though?"

"Nope."

"You're an authority on ore?"

"Not an authority—"

"Yet you've got the gall to come rampagin' in here and make it appear I'm either a crook or I don't know my business!"

His shape began to swell like a toad. I could see black rage rousing back of his stare but I shook my head.

"You don't have to put any words in my mouth. If I thought you were a crook—"

"Then maybe you think I don't know my business?"

"I don't believe he means that, Jeff." Carolina soothed. "I think probably he means we may have overlooked something—some kind of thing an outsider might catch on to." Her glance sought my face. "Isn't that what you were thinking.?"

I wasn't paying much attention. Something Bender'd said had set a train of thought to rolling and an entirely new concept of unglimpsed possibilities was opening before me.

"Isn't that what you mean? Jim!"

I stared. I said absently, "Maybe it *is* Frunk. Maybe he's back of this whole crazy business. But if Bender has figured the worth of this mine right..."

"Oh, he has—I'm sure he has," urged Carolina.

I met Bender's black stare. I said, "Joe, go and fetch Younger."

Bender pulled up his chin. "I guess you know what you're doing. I guess you know Younger and Short Creek are brothers."

I hadn't known that but I wasn't much surprised. Quite a few of the pieces were dropping into place. "The best of families have their black sheep," I said. "Go ahead, Joe. Go get him."

Crafkin looked at me carefully. He took in a long

breath. He started to say something, changed his mind and, still looking reluctant, finally moved toward the door.

"And fetch my saddle," I called after him.

"You've played hell with things now," Bender snorted. Then he shrugged. "There'll be java on the back of the stove in the cook shack. I suppose, if you're hungry, I could fry up some beans—if you don't mind trustin' my hand with the skillet."

"I guess I'd trust you that far." Through the windows I could see that it was getting light fast. "What time will your crew be going into the mine?"

"They don't work on Sundays."

It kind of surprised me to realise it was Sunday. Where had time gone? There was concern on Carolina's cheeks. She touched my arm timidly. "You'd ought to get some rest," she said. "You look like you've been through the crusher."

"I'll make out. What about the shotgun shift?" I asked Bender.

He consulted his watch. "They'll be up in five minutes. I better go wake the others—"

"Let them sleep," I said. "We're going to pull the guard off."

"Pull it off?" His jaw sagged. Then he clamped his teeth together. "That the way you want it?" he asked Carolina.

She looked at me uncertainly. "Do you really think we should?"

"If you're satisfied," I said, "why did you go to Cap Murphey?"

She chewed her lip in silence.

"Look," I said, too weary to argue. "This stealing's been going on for a good while now. Your uncle tried to stop it and got killed for his trouble. You've given Bender a chance. You've tried your own hand at it. The mine ain't made a nickel in months. If you want this stuff stopped—"

"Of course I want it stopped." Her voice had an edge to it. "Do you think I enjoy—"

"Then put me in charge."

"But what if you're wrong?"

"Hell's fire!" I snarled. "Can I be any more wrong than you? Or Bender?"

Her cheeks turned white, then red, then white again. "What do you propose to do?"

"Get rid of these rifles. Disarm the whole bunch and put them outside the fence."

Bender's eyes altered. "The shotgun guard, too?"

"The whole damn works!"

Bender shook his bald head. "I'll go and put on the beans—"

"You'll stay right where you're at until we get this thing settled."

His look wasn't any more rabid than mine.

Carolina said, "Well..."

I said: "Make up your mind."

She didn't like it. But she gave in a lot sooner than I'd expected her to.

"All right," I told Bender, "we'll go over to the collar now—"

"The mine guard's come up. They're over in the change house—"

"What have they done with their shot guns?"

"Probably left them in the cage," Bender said "That's what they usually do."

"Call that fellow down out of the monkey box."

Bender stepped to the door. When he came back I said, "What'll these birds in the change house do now?"

"Soon's they get dry clothes on they'll come over here to find out when they're on again."

"How do you get hold of the four that are sleepin'?"

"They'll be over."

I heard footsteps outside and a mumble of talk

sound. The man from the tower came in with three others. I said, "You fellows just stand around for a minute."

Pretty soon the other four came in. "Give Miss Krole the key to that padlock, Bender."

Bender grinned sourly and gave her the key.

"All right, boys," I said. "You're going to have a day off. Miss Krole's going to let you out the gate. This treat's on the mine; you'll be paid same as usual. Be back at the gate at six sharp in the morning."

Several of them turned curious faces toward Bender but he kept his mouth shut and they followed her out. Bender went over and stood by the window. "You can go fix them beans now," I told him.

When Carolina came back she looked worried. "Where's Jeff?"

"He's gone to warm up some grub," I said. "He won't run away."

That fetched her head around sharply. "You don't like him much, do you?" She looked tired and discouraged.

"I suppose you locked the gate up again?"

"Wasn't I supposed to?"

"I don't guess it much matters. You can give the key back to Bender."

"Aren't you afraid he might decide to let the men in again?"

I looked at her then. But I didn't say anything. I went over to the window and peered up the road. The sun's welcome smile was gilding the ridgetops but I couldn't see much. Brush grew too thick between the Signal Stope and town and the twisted excuse that passed for a road was too fogged with dust where it dipped through the hollows.

"How long," I asked finally, "do you reckon it will take them?"

Carolina shrugged. "He had his horse. Not long,

I shouldn't think, if he was able to find Younger. Are you satisfied now?"

"About what?"

"About Joe."

"Crafkin?" This was dangerous ground with her feeling about him the way she did. "Satisfied how?"

"About him being a Ranger."

I wished like hell she hadn't asked that. But she was going to have to know the truth sooner or later. I remembered the blood leaking out through Gharst's fingers and the running shape scuttling through the gloom of that alley.

"Joe Crafkin," I said, "is working for Frunk. At least..."

Her face was like something carved out of ivory. But the eyes were alive. They were coldly despising me.

I let her have it without wrappings or ribbons. I said: "He's no more a Ranger than Cap Murphey's pig!"

Her voice tore into me. "You saw his badge, Trammell!"

"You're damn right I saw it—*and the mark I scratched on it!* That guy's been lying from the minute you laid eyes on him. Even that fight in the lobby was faked—d'you think a bravo like Short Creek would of taken that pounding without he was paid to?"

"Get your eyes open! It was Crafkin followed you down to Cap Murpheys; it had to be him for Frunk to know about *me*. And then he gave me his room with your uncle dead in it and, when that didn't stop me, last night he tried again and dropped Gharst by mistake."

She stood without breathing with her eyes gone as black as holes burned in a blanket. Her voice was a whisper. "I don't believe it."

But her look told me different.

I drove a couple more nails in. "After Gharst went down I chased the killer up that alley. I've already told you I thought it was Short Creek; but when that lantern light hit me I saw his face plain. And now we come to the badge you been settin' so much store by; Short Creek stole it. After I'd signed the book for Joe's room I went back outside to fetch in my bedroll. Short Creek was out there going through my belongings. Joe didn't steal my badge. But he's *wearing* it."

She was convinced. No doubt about that. I could have felt damn sorry for myself about then.

I said, "Don't look so damn sick. I've been a fool, too. Come on." I took her arm. "Bender's callin' us."

She jerked away from me, shivering. I didn't much blame her. In her place I would have hated the sight of me.

"What are you going to do about...him?"

"Nothing, right now. I'm going to give him some more rope."

"Hoping he'll tangle up someone else in it?"

She looked pretty bitter. "That could be a big help," I said.

"Why did you want Bucks Younger?"

"Your uncle trusted him. Besides," I said. "I'm probably going to need some help. These fellows ain't playin' for no marbles, you know."

She tried to pull herself together.

"You better come and put some hot grub under your belt."

She shuddered. "I couldn't."

She came after me though. Maybe she just didn't want to be left alone. You never can tell about a woman. I wondered if she was figuring to tip Crafkin off.

She turned to me again as we stepped into the cook shack. "You will admit, won't you, that I've been right about Frunk?"

"About him tryin' to grab the mine? Sure. He's doin' his level best. He's the one that's got your ore, all right. Probably been back of most of your trouble. But he ain't the only one."

Bender, busily eating his breakfast, stopped with a forkful of egg in the air. Then he shovelled it into his face and kept chewing. It was Carolina who turned clear around and said sharply, "Ain't the only one! You mean someone else is after it, *too*?"

I said, "From where I stand that's the way it ravels out. Why else would Frunk try to put Crafkin in here? Not to speed up his stealin'—he's getting it now fast as Bender can mine it."

The mine boss scowled.

I scooped two fried eggs and some beans on a plate. "You better have something," I told Carolina.

She shook her head, sagged into a chair. I took the plate to the table with a cup of black java. It was the first chance at grubpile I'd had in some while and I went right to work on it.

After a couple of minutes Bender shoved back his chair. He twisted a smoke and said as he licked it, "About that crack you just made. Who do you think in this camp is big enough to fight Frunk? Besides Gharst, I mean?"

"Gharst wasn't after this mine. Like he told Carolina, when she went to him for help, he had all he could take care of."

I took a big gulp of coffee, swashed it round through my teeth. "There's two separate parties trying to get Tailholt—Frunk and some other bird. Frunk set the ball rolling. This other guy, then, caught the drift and shoved his oar in."

"I don't see how you arrive at that notion."

"Considering the state of Tailholt's resources—which are practically non-existent—do you think any fellow with the influence, manpower and cash

Frunk commands would take this long to put a mine out of business if there wasn't someone else cuttin' in on his programme?"

Bender lit his smoke.

"Consider the facts," I suggested. "Krole, the mine's founder and original owner, was made a proposition by Frunk which he turned down. Shortly thereafter, about six months ago, Krole gets killed in some kind of 'accident'. Again Frunk offers to buy the mine, this time from Carolina. But her uncle advises her to hang on to the property and starts digging to find out why Frunk wants it. All sorts of things get to happening. You lose mules and tramcars. In addition to the thieving which was already going on you start having cave-ins. Tunnels get blocked. Your miners get trapped and bought off and scared off. Finally in self-defence you have to let most of the rest go. Then uncle disappears. Carolina goes to Murphey for help and somebody follows her. Krole, two days later, turns up dead in his own hotel, killed in such a manner as to implicate *me*. These things I believe, or the most of them, can be charged against Frunk. He may have killed Krole or had him killed, but he didn't waylay him.

"I knew he'd been tied up when I saw the way his shirt sleeves were wrinkled. For two days somebody had been holding him prisoner. But not Frunk. And it wasn't Joe Crafkin because Joe is Frunk's man just as much as Red Irick is."

Bender's eyes widened. "You mean Crafkin's not a Ranger?"

"Did you ever think he was?" I told him the things I'd told Carolina. "But those aren't all the reasons. Why hadn't he told Carolina about me? Why did he insist on giving me his key before he'd even got out of the room? Why wasn't his name on the book? Obviously because he was busy laying pipe that would give Red Irick an apparent basis for charging me with Krole's killing. This tie-up with Irick proves Joe is Frunk's man."

"But if Frunk's crowd didn't engineer Krole's disappearance," Bender said, "how did his body get into that room?"

"I think Frunk discovered what had become of him. I think one of his men, when the time was ripe, staged a fake rescue and, after selling him the notion that he was in friendly hands, talked Krole into going to the Eagle. Not much risk of anyone seeing them. No moon that night. Carolina wasn't there; she'd gone off to meet Short Creek. They'd already put the verandah lights out. Frunk's agent, probably Crafkin, took Krole into that room and shot him."

Bender sighed, looking immeasurably older. "It has a sound, all right. What about this other bird—the feller you say is bucking Frunk?"

"He'll be around."

Bender lifted his head to scowl at me. "Is that why you sent all the guards off to town."

"It's why I told them to report back tomorrow. Seemed a good idea to let him know the field was open. That news will get around. Shouldn't take him very long to come up with ten if we give him four and he has six already."

"What in the world—?" Carolina stopped.

Bender's glance showed a jerky brightness. "You want him to guess we're searching the mine?"

I grinned at the sweat cracking through his skin. Carolina said tightly, "You mean to use us for *bait?*"

"Not you. You're stayin' out of this."

Our eyes met and locked. Her cheeks were pale but her tone was like granite. "If you're going below I'm going down with you."

Bender scowled. "Do we have to take Crafkin and Younger? If you're right about—"

"We can keep our eyes on him."

Bender said irritably, "We haven't got eyes in the backs of our heads." He ground out his smoke and got up, still frowning. "If this other bird hears we've pulled all the guards off you can bet your bottom dollar Frunk will hear about it, too. You thought about that?"

"I'm counting on that."

Bender stared, and suddenly swore. "You're loco!" He flung a look at Carolina. "It's too risky, I tell you."

I asked if he knew any better way.

He was right about the risk, of course. It would be damned risky. Already the word would have spread through the camp. *No one at Tailholt but the owner, her mine boss and that gunhung drifter that broke out of gaol.*

That would bring them, all right. They couldn't pass up that.

"You want to flush 'em out where your law can get at them, and maybe you'll do it," Bender said grudgingly. "But why go into the mine to do it? Why not just—"

"They'll be watching for tricks. We have to make this look good. We're supposed to be trying to find out what the score is. If we don't go into the mine they won't show—"

"And, if we do," Bender said, "they may damn well try to bring the whole hill down on us. You're offering them the chance and that's all that will fetch them."

"But first," I grinned, "they'll make sure we're down in there. And that's where we'll grab them. They'll have to come down. Neither one of those birds will ever be satisfied unless he can trap the other guy with us."

"What about the marshal and Crafkin? If you're right about Crafkin—"

"That's why I want Younger in on this. He's no

fool. He knows about Joe and that room at the Eagle."

Carolina said tightly, "Does he think Joe killed Gharst and my uncle?"

"I don't know but—" I stopped. I looked at her, careful. "How did Joe get through the fence with the gate locked?"

Carolina flushed. "He had my key—"

"How *long* has he had it?" That was Bender talking and he did not look pleased.

"I gave it to him when I sent him over here to see you."

Bender glared at me, exasperated. "You see how it's been? *I* didn't know he had a key to that gate." He said, looking madder, "I never know anything till after it's done with."

"When'd you send him over?" I asked Carolina.

"Four nights ago—"

"And he never showed up until the day before yesterday!"

Bender swore. Then to me he said, "Will he fit the picture you have of this 'other guy'?"

I turned it over, finally nodding. "He *could* be the guy. He's been working for Frunk. If he's managed to discover why Frunk's after Tailholt, I wouldn't put it past him to try to grab it for himself. He's—".

Bender, stopped before the window, said: "They're out there now. Him and Younger are at the gate."

NINETEEN

He stepped into the yard.

"I can't trust that fellow," Carolina complained. "There's—"

"Bender?"

"Bucks Younger. If you had seen him and Frunk hobnobbing round before you—"

She was hipped on the subject. "How come you to put so much trust in his brother?"

"Short Creek? I didn't."

"You tried to use him—"

"I tried everything. But I didn't trust any of them. Except Crafkin." The bitterness of remembrance chased some colour through her cheeks.

"Smooth customer," I nodded. "He's puttin' on the charm act out there now. When did you first come across your uncle's body?"

"When I was taking fre—" She caught her breath on a gasp, her staring eyes grown enormous. "How did you—"

"When we went up there with Irick you had so much on your mind you forgot to show shock. It gave me the notion you might have killed him yourself, or had him killed. While I was flat on my back over at Gharst's I realised you must have known he was up there. That put sense in a lot of other things that had me fightin' my hat; your insistence on me writing my name in the book, your denyin' there was any such fellow as Crafkin. You were doing everything you could to cover him."

"I couldn't believe he was guilty. I thought Frunk had someway found out and was framing him. Even after I felt sure he must have known uncle was up there I couldn't bring myself to doubt him. But when he came back the other night he said Shellman hadn't been there when he gave up the room. Even then I wouldn't let myself really become suspicious. I was sure that wasn't true but—"

"Had you forgotten how he'd insisted on giving me the key?"

"That was what bothered me, what made me feel certain he had known uncle was up there. I still thought someone had been trying to frame him. I don't see how I could have been such a fool."

"We all make mistakes," I said. "God knows I've made enough of them—"

"This other man," she said. "What did you mean when you said to Jeff just now 'If he's managed to discover why Frunk is after Tailholt'? That sounds as though you believe there might be something more behind this—"

"Wait," I said, and took a look out the door. The others were standing round the collar, talking among themselves while they waited for us to join them. "You may as well get this thing straight in your mind. There's only two reasons why Frunk would be after Tailholt. Either it's richer than Bender makes out to think or it's got Signal Stope apexed."

"Apexed!" She was staring at me thunderstruck, unable or unwilling—as I myself had been at first—to fully realise the implications.

"But... but an 'apex'," she exclaimed breathlessly, "is the end, edge or crest of a vein where that vein lies nearest the surface—"

"Under mining laws, as Bender can tell you, the owner of an apex may follow the vein or lode on its dip to any depth or distance within the prolonged end lines of his claim, *even though it enter adjoining lands.*"

"But Dad would have known!"

"He wasn't given much time. Signal Stope, from what I can find, has been going all out from the very first. Your father wasn't given much time to find anything. What he found originally may have only been float. He was killed before he'd done much development. Would you say Bender's estimate of Tailholt was accurate?"

"You mean the worth of our ore? Yes, I think so. It doesn't compare with the chunk on display at Frunk's Mercantile. If the rest of his mine is as good as that sample—"

"It probably isn't. But comparatively, at least, it may be extremely valuable. Say it is and Frunk discovers your mine has him apexed. His natural reaction is to try to buy Tailholt before you discover the truth of the business. Another natural reaction would be to get all he can *while he can* out of Signal Stope. A third step which might naturally follow would be an all-out effort to retard Tailholt's development. You begin to get the picture now, don't you?"

She said, aghast: "Jeff Bender's a mining engineer! He must have known..."

"He must certainly have suspected."

"You think he's the 'other man'?"

"I don't know," I told her honestly. "I don't know how far down he's put Tailholt or how much the workings show at this point. But I mean to find out. That's one of the reasons—"

"But you told him you weren't an authority—"

"A man doesn't have to be an authority on ore to

know whether or not a mine's being swindled. You tell me Bender's an expert. I'm no expert, but with all this hanky-panky goin' on I've got sense enough to know the mine's worth more than he says it is. If he's right about the ore then you've got Frunk apexed. I'm pretty sure you have, and I'm sure Bender knows it. I think that's why he got rid of your crew; he can't afford to have anyone around he can't trust. The ore thieves are still doing business, so those guards and that fence have only one purpose—they're insurance that you don't find out what's going on."

She looked like hell. I could see that she believed me. "You think he knew about Joe?"

"He must have known Joe was working for Frunk or he wouldn't have let him inside of that fence. He *did* let him in. He even left Joe by himself here—"

"Perhaps he believed Joe was a Ranger. After all, Joe fooled *me*."

"Bender's no fool," I said. "He's in this thing right up to his neck. Either he's the 'other guy' or he has sold out to Frunk and to the other guy also. Frunk couldn't operate without Jeff's connivance. I think your uncle found out and that's why they had to kill him. If this mine has Frunk apexed—"

"But how will you find out?"

"I'll know when I get down there."

"Don't you think Jeff suspects—"

"Of course. He knows I'm forcing his hand."

She looked at me oddly. "And you would still go down?"

"It's the best chance I've got of clearing this mess up—"

"But it's suicide! Don't you see that Jeff will tip Crafkin off?"

"He'll try, all right—"

"He's probably done it already!"

"In front of Bucks Younger? I don't think so. Younger's *my* insurance."

TWENTY

YOUNGER, nodding to Carolina, politely took off his hat. "You've had a rough deal here, ma'am. I hope we can get to the bottom of this business."

He reached out his hand. "How are you," Trammell? Glad to have you with us. They tell me you're a Ranger, that we're going to search the mine."

"I don't know how much searching we'll do but I'm going to have a whack at it."

"I doubt," Crafkin said, "if it will do much good. I went down yesterday. The stopes are a mess. Blocked tunnels everywhere and—I suppose it's your notion the ore is still down there?"

"I'm convinced it never went out by the gate."

Bender grunted. "Where do you imagine it went out?"

"As Joe just said, it may still be down there. Behind those blocked tunnels maybe."

"If it is," Crafkin growled, "it'll be there till hell freezes. Wait'll you see them."

Younger looked thoughtful. "We're to hunt for the stolen ore then—is that it?"

"We're going to look," I said, "for evidence that this mine has Frunk's mine apexed."

There was a moment of intense quiet. Crafkin's head came round very carefully. The marshal's lips scrinched a silent whistle. A derisive amusement gleamed in Bender's stare. "All right, Hawkshaw," he nodded. "I'll help you look for that with real pleasure."

Younger twisted his yellow moustache. "You don't think there's anything to it?"

"On the contrary I find it remarkably intriguing. As a theory," Bender emphasized, "it offers the virtues of being the solution magnificent. It would explain so credibly what's been going on; but—"

"If that was the answer," Crafkin said, "you would have found it."

"Exactly. And I don't mind admitting I considered it myself. The facts, unfortunately, fail to cooperate. I've examined the face of the cuts repeatedly. I have found no evidence in support of the theory." He regarded me blandly. "You will have to assume I've miscalculated the value of our ore, I guess, Trammell."

I looked at him straightly. "I have considerable respect for your professional skill, Bender; a great deal too much to imagine you have made any mistake of that kind."

"What kind of operation do you have in the stopes?" Younger asked. "Cut and fill? Horizontal or incline?"

Bender said, "Cut and fill's much too costly for a mine of this kind. This is open stope mining. We're using the panel method."

"How far are you down?"

"Two hundred foot level—"

"You mean in all this time you've only driven three headings?"

Bender's cheeks went deeply roan. But he got hold of his temper before he opened his mouth. "I think that's pretty good progress, everything considered. Three men can't very well—"

"But Krole was working a big crew—"

"Krole quit work six months ago. When Shellman took over we were working twenty-five men. Within three weeks the crew dwindled to twelve. When I cut it to three for lack of money to pay them we quit going down. We've been working Number 2—"

"We'll go down," I said. "Get those lamps, will you, Bender?"

The mine boss, muttering under his breath, started off. "Get one for me, too," Carolina called after him.

Bender turned, still scowling, and said, "A mine is no place for a woman, Miss Krole." And Younger said, "That's right. You'd better wait up here."

"Your crew wouldn't like it," Crafkin told her. "Miners think it's bad luck to have a woman—"

"A little more bad luck wouldn't even be noticed," Carolina said grimly. "Fetch a lamp for me, Bender."

The mine boss shrugged and went on. I said to Carolina, "Hadn't you better change your clothes?"

"They look as good as yours," she said, and grinned at me tiredly. No one else said anything until the marshal, who'd been regarding my torn clothes curiously, asked, "What happened to you, Trammell?"

I told him about Irick's bunch chasing me through the brush.

He frowned. "You'd better pin your badge on—"

I cut in, asking Crafkin: "Did you fetch my saddle?"

"It was your badge you wanted, wasn't it? The badge wasn't there." He actually looked regretful. "You want to borrow mine?"

"Maybe you'd better," Younger said, "before somebody shoots you."

Crafkin passed it over. It was mine, all right. I pinned it on without remark.

Bender came out of the change house with an armful of miners' hats with carbide lamps attached. We lit the lamps and put the hats on, Carolina stuffing her hair inside hers. Bender led the way to the collar and we all climbed into the cage. I picked up three shotguns, handed one of them to Younger, kept one for myself and tossed the other aside.

Crafkin's eyes narrowed. Bender grinned. He pulled the gate down, gave a yank on the cable and the cage began its creaking descent. Increasing darkness accompanied our clattering slow-motion progress. At the 65-foot level, where the original heading had been widened out to form the first stope, the ring of radiance thrown from our carbide lamps showed nothing but the shapes of ghostly pillars. No sign of a back wall was visible.

"Having any trouble with water?" I asked Bender.

"We're not down far enough to be bothered by water. We've got a little at 200."

We dropped below the second level like a load of lost souls. Conversation lagged as the walls of the shaft closed round us again. Dampness was beginning to spot them in patches that were like running sores where they gleamed in the passing light of our lamps. "I was under the impression," Bucks Younger remarked. "that you were working Number 2."

"That's right." Bender stopped the cage and sent the gate clattering up. "We have been. But any search we're going to make had ought to start at the bottom. This is it," he said. "The 200-foot level."

The quiet was uncanny. The monstrous shadows engulfed the wan glimmer of our lights with the stealth of gloved hands closing round a windpipe. I decided as we climbed out after him it was the weirdest damn place I had ever been in. The blackest, too. And the most oppressive.

The air was heavy with the stench of stale blasts. "What's the width of this cut?" asked the marshal, peering round.

"Roughly thirty-five feet. Those pillars were left at thirty-foot intervals. We—"

"When'd you stop work here?" I asked curiously.

"About ten weeks ago."

"Why?" That was Younger.

"Number of reasons. We lost the vein, for one thing. It was while we were cross-cutting, trying to pick it up again, that the cave-ins I told you about started."

"*Did* you pick it up again?"

The circle of his light bobbed as Bender nodded. The walls it illumined showed stained with damp in gangrenous splotches whose leakage was collected in stagnant pools which levelled the floor's hollows with the green shine of slime.

"Where?" Younger asked.

"In Tunnel 14."

"Why aren't you working there now then?" Carolina asked. And Younger's eyes probed the mine boss's face. "Why'd you quit?"

"It was the crew that quit, not me," Bender grunted. "That's the tunnel we lost all the timbers out of. There's some running ground in it we had to retimber. I shored it up twice and each time they were stole again—"

"Between dark and dawn?" I cried, incredulous.

"That's right," Bender nodded. "After the last time they pulled the sticks out of it I couldn't get posts big enough for the uprights. Not a man of the crew would go in the damn tunnel—"

"I'll go in it," I growled.

Bender's turning head flung his light in my face. "You won't for some while," he said grimly.

164

"The whole ceiling dropped out of it two weeks ago—that's why we moved up into Number 2. That tunnel's nothing but a memory."

In the sepulchral hush I got one of the answers I'd been hunting for. The means by which a smart guy like Bender had figured to get away with the job he was doing. I'd been right as rain. Tailholt *did* have Frunk apexed but, if Bender was slick enough for this kind of dodge, it was a cinch he'd been cute enough to fix up the rest of it. We would find no proof of any apex down here.

The vein, to afford proof, would have had to dip toward Signal Stope, and I believed that it did. But if the vein had been recovered at the south end of 14, as Bender would have us believe, it was inconceivable that Frunk, in his Signal Stope was gouging ore from the extended end lines of Tailholt's claim. Frunk's mine adjoined Tailholt on the north and I was pretty well convinced this stope's north wall would tell us nothing, but I meant to make sure.

I turned my light in that direction. As it crossed Bender's face I saw the corners of his mouth quirk. He knew what I was up to. He was really enjoying this. "Nothing over there," he said. "When I was thinking, like you, that we might have Frunk apexed I had the whole crew working there; we moved tons of waste before I gave up the notion. You can see for yourself. We cleared—"

"Where's your set-up from this level?"

"Down this way," Bender said, heading into the western gloom of the stope. We followed him approximately two hundred feet. Taking the lamp off his hat he directed its light upward. We could see the gaping hole where a raise had been driven to the level above for ventilation.

"All right," I said, "Let's see your blocked tunnel."

Again we followed him through the crouching

shadows between the roof-supporting pillars which divided the silent stope into an appearance of empty rooms. The sound of our boots clattered eerily and when Crafkin cleared his throat the echoes flew down the passages with the rumble of a landslide.

"Here it is," Bender said, "all that's left of it."

It was in the south face of the stope all right. The light of our lamps gave ample evidence there had actually been a tunnel, but it was so crammed with fallen rock and earth it would be a lengthy and costly operation to reopen it. Not, of course, that there would be any reason to.

"How far did you go?" I asked Bender, knowing mighty well the whole damn tunnel was nothing but a hoax.

"One hundred and thirty-eight feet," said Bender smugly.

"You're quite a gambler," I said dryly. "Why didn't you tunnel north?"

"Because, like you, I figured the stope dipped north. Every time we touched off a round I was sure the clean-up would show us in ore again."

"So then you used a crystal ball, drove a tunnel south and hit it, eh?"

"Not exactly," Bender grinned. "Number 14 was the fourth we drove on this level—"

"What happened to the other three?"

"Maybe you better take a look for yourself."

"Maybe I had at that," I said, and set off between the pillars toward the north wall again.

He called, "Not over there," but I ignored him.

The way I had this figured Tailholt *did* have Frunk's mine apexed. It was the only answer that made any sense, the reason I'd insisted on this search in the first place. I wasn't expecting to find any proof. I was going through the motions in the hope that it might drive them into making some fool move that would give me the proof I needed.

I was convinced Frunk's mine was apexed. If Bender's estimate of Tailholt's worth was right, Signal Stope must obviously be worth a considerable plenty or Frunk wouldn't have started all this goddam hanky-panky. And he couldn't have got this far without inside help.

Now who, I asked myself, was the most logical guy to provide that help? All the signs and signal smokes pointed arrow-straight at Bender. As mine boss of Tailholt he had a better than even chance to get away with it. But he wouldn't play catspaw for peanuts. Even if he hadn't uncovered any proof he was bound to suspect this mine had Frunk apexed; he may even have pointed that much out to Frunk. These two had obviously come to some agreement. Bender was quite able to add four and six.

But why should he have told Carolina he didn't believe Tailholt had much of a future? The answer to that was what finally had convinced me there was more than one skunk in this woodpile. By telling the girl the truth about the worth of her ore he probably hoped, when the time came, to buy the property cheap. He could then bid himself in as Frunk's full partner.

I'd got this far in my figuring before I'd sent Crafkin off to hunt Younger. By the time they'd returned I'd been reasonably confident Frunk would have learned the guards were off duty. It should have moved him to action. I didn't consider Frunk any bigger fool than Bender. He'd be forced to move to protect himself and, unless he were an idiot, he'd be bound to realise the menace of Bender.

This was the thing I was building my hopes on, to get him and Bender to try and outfox each other.

Still thinking about this I cut back in the direction of the up-cast, hearing the rest of them slosh along behind me. I flashed my lamp along the roof until I found it, then turned right and reached the stope's north face. I took my time and went over it thoroughly, thinking all the while about Bender's duplicity and trying my damndest to guess what he'd do next.

He was going to have to do something and do it pretty soon. Before he could do anything he would have to slip away from us, and he couldn't slip away from us without some kind of diversion. He would have to manage something that would draw our eyes away from him... or would he? Was there any chance he'd dare to wait for Gid Frunk's move?

He might if he were cool enough. It could give him a considerable advantage, especially if he could get Frunk caught and keep his own hand covered. If he could get Frunk caught by Frunk's own actions, and devise some means for keeping Frunk from talking, it would leave Jeff Bender sitting very neat indeed. For he'd know I wouldn't uncover his hand unless I could make it stick.

Still busily examining the stope's north face I switched my thinking to the stolen ore. How could they have got it out of this mine? Even if all Bender's guards had been in on it the stuff was too bulky to be handled with ease. Crafkin had suggested the ore might still be down here and perhaps he'd told the truth. It might have been loaded into one of these blocked tunnels—into 14, maybe, before they'd blasted it shut.

"Shut..." I muttered, and looked at the wall more carefully.

If Tailholt had Frunk apexed the slope of the vein's dip would have had to go north, as I'd been thinking. Now supposing Bender had never lost the vein at all but had followed it north into Frunk's Signal Stope? Or had come head-on smack into a Frunk tunnel? Tailholt ore, going into such a tunnel, could come out of Frunk's mine as Signal

Stope ore and no one be the wiser.

Was that too far fetched?

To me it didn't seem so. All they actually needed was some kind of concealed door, something that when shut would appear to be solid wall.

I was sure I had the answer.

After sloshing back to the ventilator I went over the stope's north wall again, paying no attention to the remarks of the others, flashing my lamp from various angles across its blast and picked scarred surface. I found no indication of what I was hunting for. I saw a lot of cracked rock but none that looked to have been fitted in place again to mask a hidden opening.

But I still liked my notion.

The others followed me back to the shaft.

"We'll try the next level now," I said, and was making ready to step into the cage when a shout stopped the bunch of us dead in our tracks.

TWENTY-ONE

CRAFKIN'S BREATH made an insucked sound as he swung beefy shoulders half around to peer at Bender. The mine boss's cheeks showed the shine of sweat. The shadows seemed to creep in closer and the marshal, looking hard at Bender, said in a voice turned thin with suspicion, "What the hell are you up to now?"

Bender's eyes stared back unblinking, but there was an accent of nervousness about him now and something aroused was tightening the skin folded over his cheekbones.

His lips rolled and squeezed and then opened but, before he could speak, a frantic scream came churning up out of the stope's crouching shadows. It had the dying-woman sound that is sometimes torn from an injured horse.

I felt my flesh turn cold and crawl as, with the rest, I whirled to stand tumultuously peering into that wavering blackness beyond the reach of our lamps.

Here was the diversion Bender must have been praying for, something to take our minds off him and allow him those precious seconds he must have if my guess concerning his intentions held water. Yet there was no elation in the way he stood staring. Visible strain rode his hunched-forward shoulders and there was an underdone look to the fat of his face that was strangely in contrast to its natural appearance.

There may have been no special significance in the way Younger's shotgun was pointed at his middle but the marshal's distrust was too open to be doubted. He was watching Bender as he would a snake.

"Lead off," he said dustily.

Bender did not move so much as a finger. "You fool!" he cried. "That's Frunk up there—"

"Frunk, eh?" Younger's saturnine look branded Bender a liar. Then, surprisingly, he laughed. "It won't wash, Jeff. I wasn't born yesterday. You'll have to—"

"We've got to get out of here!" Bender yelled. "There's something happening in Number 2—"

"Is it these stinkin' lights that make you look so yellow?" Younger jeered, striding forward.

Bender fell back, his big hands fisted. His veins had swelled with a curious rage and a wildness boiled up out of his stare, yet he flung himself round without opening his mouth, striding into the darkness like a cat through wet grass, the beam of his lamp slashing this way and that without turning up any sign of the screamer.

"Further back," directed Younger as we went scrambling after him. "It wasn't this close was it, Trammell?"

I'd been trying to guess how much of my figuring concerning Jeff Bender the marshal had caught up with and if his suspicions coincided with mine. I wished I could have managed to have talked with him privately before we'd come down here, at least long enough to have told him what bait I was setting out for these coyotes. I was in fact putting his head in a lion's mouth without even warning him the lion might bite.

"I don't think so," I said. "Seemed to be nearer the far end of this wall, though it *could* have come out of that air hole—"

"It could," Younger grinned, "have come straight out of hell. But don't let our fat friend mislead you. That cry—"

"That cry," Bender snarled, sloshing back to us, "came out of Number 2 like I told you—you think I don't know how this mine distorts sound? If we don't get up there pretty goddam quick—"

The marshal's grin seemed about to give Bender apoplexy. He goggled, cheeks bloated, like a fish out of water.

Bucks Younger chuckled. "Careful, Jeff—"

"You crazy fool!" Bender shouted. "You want to be trapped in this goddam stope?"

"You should have stuck with the stage," Younger told him. "If I didn't know you so well you would have me scared stiff. But it's no good, Jeff; you might as well come off it. It was you that suggested we start on this level—"

"We goin' to wrangle all night?" cut in Crafkin. "That scream—"

"Wasn't nothing but stage dressing," the marshal said. "Window trimming. We've seen everything Jeff wanted us to, the rubble-blocked tunnel, the blast-scratched wall. He only fetched us here to convince us this mine couldn't have Frunk apexed. That scream was intended to rush us upstairs—"

"Stay down here then if you want Frunk to bury you!"

Slamming Crafkin out of his way Bender bolted.

Younger, with a startled curse, leapt after him.

I was right at his heels, the others behind me. Even above the clatter of boots I could hear the rumble and whir of machinery. I redoubled my efforts. With the taste of defeat in my mouth I passed Younger, but the cage was already out of its berth and commencing the start of its creaking climb upward.

With a terrible cry Bender flung himself at it, got a foot on its floor edge, an arm through the wooden slats of its gate. Carolina screamed as the top of the cage vanished into the shaft. I tried to shut my eyes against the time when the stones of the stope's rocky ceiling must grind through the flesh and bones of his body.

But the stones never touched him. With the ceiling scant inches above the bulge of his body his fist caught the cable and with a clank the cage stopped. He jammed it into reverse and held it there, ashen, even after its bottom was on the ground.

I let my breath go and rushed forward with Younger.

"Latch ahold of that cable," Bender wheezed, and I grabbed it above the gate until he got his arm out. Then he caught it underneath and Younger shoved the gate up and we all got aboard.

Sweat filmed Crafkin's dough white cheeks and Carolina's eyes looked as big as buckets. We were all pretty shaky I guess but the marshal. He said, tight and angry, "How did you know that was Frunk up there?"

"Know!" Bender snarled. "Who else would it be? Ain't you woke up yet that's what Trammell's been up to?"

Younger's shoulders shifted. He brought his flushed face around savagely. But before he could put what he felt into words, something above us gave a twang and a slither and struck the cage roof with a hell of a clatter.

No one had to be told what the something was. There was enough of its sinuous length still twisting and kinking about the sides of the cage to tell its own story.

Frunk, or one of Frunk's hirelings, had taken the edge of an axe to the cable. My trap had been sprung and we were all caught in it. Two hundred feet below the earth's smiling surface.

TWENTY-TWO

YOUNGER'S BLUE EYES were not twinkling now. Temper showed in his cheeks and a hard-held truculence looked out of the stare that beat at my face.

"I'm listenin'," he said as we got out of the cage.

I took him off to one side and explained this deal as I saw it. "So there's two guys after this mine, both of them bucking the owner and each of 'em trying to outsmart the other. Frunk, after making a rich strike in Signal Stope, discovers Krole's mine has him apexed. It's the only logical answer. Maybe Bender told him—it don't make much difference how the hell he found out. Except if Bender told him he would know right away he would have to deal with Bender. He would pretty near have to anyway. Bender, as Tailholt's manager, was in the key spot to make or break him. So they hatch up a deal."

Younger nodded. "I'll go with you that far."

"Then Bender," I said "decides to grab the whole works. Secretly he helps Frunk put the skids under Tailholt. More secretly he manages to keep Frunk from wrecking it. We know this is true because the quickest and simplest way out for

Frunk would be to blow this damn mine to hell and gone.

"Nothing but Bender has stood in his way. Bender didn't want that. The only real hold he could have on Frunk is proof that this mine had Frunk's mine apexed. That proof still exists or we wouldn't be down here. Obviously, then, Jeff Bender's Frunk's partner *and the man who has kept Frunk from putting this mine where it no longer threatens him.* Isn't that the way this thing looks to you?"

Younger said with a quick unaccustomed bluntness: "You're goddam right!" and his eyes shone like agate.

"So I pulled the guards off, knowing the word would get around. Long as Bender and Frunk sat tight I had no proof. I had to spur them to action. I thought the chance of trapping us down here might do it—and I had one other thought."

Younger nodded. "You thought to sell Frunk the notion Bender'd thrown in with us—"

"That was part of it," I said. "But I also figured Bender'd see that, too, and the good chance it gave him of turning the tables on Frunk. Bender saw it all right, only Frunk got going before he was ready—"

"And now your damn trap has backfired—"

"That's what my other thought was about. I thought if it did Bender'd get us out of it. If he hadn't known a way to get out of it himself he wouldn't have come down here with us in the first place."

Younger looked at me intently. "By God, I believe you're right. Come on. We'll twist the truth out of him. If you've outguessed the bastard we don't want to lose him."

That was my notion too but something subtly different about Buck Younger's appearance dug into my thinking and sharpened my look as I returned his regard. I said, "Your light's going out."

He took off his hat, removed the lamp and shook it. Flaring briefly, the flame turned blue and went out. I watched the steel-spring fingers of Shafts' law take the lamp apart. There was nothing but sludge in its firebox.

Younger suddenly swore, but not at the lamp. He was peering toward where he had left the others. I turned too and something dark and ugly started shinning up my spine.

There were no lights showing.

We broke into a run.

"What the hell?" Crafkin growled, and then my lamp picked them out of the roundabout blackness and I should have felt better.

Carolina's wan smile was a precious thing, but it didn't help Younger. I saw his solid chin jump forward. "Where's Bender?" he snapped.

Eyes bulging, Crafkin fell back a step, his lips going white at their corners. "He was right here with us just a minute ago. Our lamps went out and—"

"You fool!" Younger snarled, and flung a black look at me. "You've fixed things now with your goddam meddling! If your guess was right that sidewindin' polecat—"

I grabbed Joe Crafkin by the front of his shirt but it was Carolina's voice that cut into the marshal's. "He can't have gone far. Our lamps went out about the time yours did. We were—"

"Listen!" I said, and we all held our breaths but we didn't hear any clatter of bootsteps. Younger's cheeks turned livid with the rage that was in him. The skin of the hand that was gripping his shotgun ridged with tension.

And then I remembered. "The up-cast!" I cried, and Crafkin tore away from my grip and dashed off snarling curses.

We were right on his heels when he got there. This gaping black hole was the means by which blast fumes were carried out of this level, and I knew it was the practice in mines to sometimes use such vents for pipelines, though there weren't any pipes coming down out of this one. The stope's ceiling here was hardly more than five feet above the floor and right under the hole was a two-foot block of grey sandstone which had obviously been left there for emergencies.

I caught Crafkin's shoulder before he could mount it. "Wait!" I growled, and again we listened.

There was somebody in that dark tunnel all right; we could hear the distant sounds of his climbing.

Across the bones of his face Crafkin's skin was stretched like parfleche. With a snarl he twisted out of my grasp and would have jumped to the block if the marshal's fist had not knocked him sprawling. Younger said through his teeth: "If anyone's going to get out of this mess it will be Miss Krole and not a dog like you."

Crafkin's look was rank as he picked himself up. I thought for a moment he meant to grab for his gun. In the light of my lamp he looked tough and ugly. He said in a cotton-soft voice, "I'm not forgettin' that. No man lays a hand on a Ranger."

"That's enough," I said. "Unbuckle your gun belt and let it drop, Joe."

He turned his head slowly. "This is no time for horseplay—"

"Drop that belt or *I-ll* drop you."

He took in the levelled glint of my shotgun, considered me briefly and saturninely shrugged. "There's a new fool born every minute, I reckon." He let his gun-weighted belt fall into the muck.

I kicked it aside. "Get moving," I said. "You ain't foolin' nobody."

He stared at us blankly. "I don't get it."

"You will if Bender starts throwing lead—"

"Good Lord," he cried, "you don't think I'm in cahoots with him, do you?" He looked genuinely astonished. "Have you fellows gone loco?" He threw a hard glance at me. "What do you suppose Cap Murphey will say when—"

"Never mind Murphey. Get up on that block and—"

"By God," Crafkin said, "have you thrown in with these crooks?" Disbelief and a half-convinced loathing looked out of the stare he fixed on my face. The whole job was so good I'd half started to wonder if I'd doped this all wrong when Younger's short laugh fetched me up with a jerk.

"Another damn actor," he said with a contempt that conjured up a vision of Gharst wilting into the dust of the street while this slick-talking scorpion scuttled up that black alley. "Get yourself into that hole," Younger growled, "and start climbing!"

Crafkin's glance sought Carolina's. "You can see through this, can't you? You understand what they're up to? Younger, as you've thought all along, is in with Frunk, and now he's talked Trammell into backing their—"

"You're just wastin' your breath," I said. "She knows better than to believe any hogwash like that. You killed Gharst and all the slick yarns you can spin won't change that, and it makes no difference that it was me you were after. Murder is murder and your hands are red with it. You killed Shellman Krole—"

"You must think folks are fools if you think they'll swallow that! You will find," he said with a great show of scorn, "it takes more than words to hang a frame on—"

I rammed the shotgun's muzzle hard against his belly. "Get up into that hole and start crawling, you skunk!"

"Get that thing out of my guts," he said savagely. "You ain't shootin' nobody. I ain't taking that rap for you, either. Carolina—"

"No," she said, drawing away from him. "I trusted you once. Even then I was desperately afraid you had done it. No one else had half the oppor—"

"I can explain about that—"

"You've told enough lies now," Younger growled, seizing hold of him. "You're not keeping us talking till that lamp burns out. Get into that hole before I knock your damn face off!"

Crafkin's eyes turned ugly but he climbed up into the hole.

Thinking Younger may have guessed the truth of the matter I had the lamp off my hat and was about to blow it out when he stopped me. "Leave it lit," he said grimly. "Bad as we may get to need that light I don't fancy crawlin' up that air vent in the dark. I want to be able to see what that vinegarroon's up to. You want Miss Krole to go next?"

"You better go next," I said; "and keep an eye on him. If I keep right behind you I think you'll be able to see enough to drop him if you have to."

I was telling him that mostly for its effect on Crafkin who might very well have been figuring out some more skullduggery to try on us when we were in the darkness of the air vent.

I climbed into the up-cast after the marshal and, wedging myself to get purchase, I hauled Carolina into it after me. It was the blackest hole I had ever been in, with the shadows like ink where my lamp failed to cut them. The way led sharply upward, angling this way and that around great blocky boulders which the diggers of this shaft hadn't bothered to remove. Because of these twisting convolutions more than half the time we couldn't see Crafkin's shape at all and sometimes I could not even see Younger. Bender, I realised, must already have vanished into the black obscurity of the stope above and the thought of what he might be doing was not calculated to make me forget the tons of rock hanging over us. Only a very short length of ignited fuse might very well lie between ourselves and eternity.

Younger wasn't making any study of geology. He was moving just as fast as he was able to, and we were right on his heels but, even where we were able to do more than crawl, our pace was hardly faster than a turtle's. In several places the walls were pressed so close by unremoved boulders we had to wriggle to get past, but if Bender could make it I knew we could.

Then Younger's face came around and eyed me over his shoulder. "Only five feet left." With great care and no sound his lips shaped the words. "Crafkin's not in sight. Better put that lamp out."

There was good sense in the suggestion but it wasn't needed. Even as I took the lamp off my hat its light flared and faded and with a sputter went out. Pitch darkness hemmed us in with our terrifying thoughts.

In that blackness I heard the distant sound of someone walking. Carolina put a hand on my leg; I felt her shudder. Then the sound was lost in the nearer sound of the marshal's resumed progress. Through the absolute blackness I began crawling after him, expecting any moment to hear the shattering explosion that would bury us in this damned place forever.

My mouth was drier than a barnful of cotton.

In sudden desperation I increased my pace but my outstretched hand did not find Bucks Younger. It did not touch any wall nor did my other hand, either. I regrasped my shotgun and got to my feet as quiet as I was able with one hand over my head vainly feeling for a ceiling which was not within reach. I knew in that moment I was out of the upcast with my feet on the floor of the Number 2 stope.

I wanted mightily to re-establish contact with Younger but, with Crafkin and possibly Bender somewhere in the dark about me, I dared not speak lest betrayal of my position loose a blast of hot lead.

With extreme care I felt ahead of me with one exploring foot. It came up against something and I felt the something sway away. I bent carefully downward and my extended left hand found an empty boot and, beside it, a second boot. Also empty.

Whose boots? Bender's? Or were they Crafkin's or Younger's?

I listened for Carolina but there was no sound behind me. I crouched down on one knee and felt around some more and, one by one, I got hold of four more boots.

I didn't like it. I didn't like any of the thoughts those boots conjured. The menace in this blackness was rank enough to taste. I was certain I wasn't alone. I was even more certain that I should get hold of Carolina and make some immediate attempt to get out of this black hole. I was fairly trembling with it yet I was rooted where I crouched by the equally certain conviction that the first sound I made would draw gunfire.

With infinite caution I put down my shotgun and quietly eased the .45 from my holster. With my left hand, then, I picked up a boot and flung it ahead with all the strength I could muster. It struck with a splash and not a damn thing happened.

I don't know how long I stayed motionless. Time stood still in that impenetrable blackness. The silence had begun to churn up my nerves when I gradually became aware that something near me was breathing with a careful stealth that matched my own.

I dared not fire lest it be the marshal.

I dared not speak lest it be someone else.

With jaws clamped together I determined to outwait him, but the recurring vision of all those tons of rock got the best of me. I could not undersand why Frunk hadn't caved this mine in already. He might be lighting a fuse somewhere even now.

The thought brought cold sweat and, reaching down my left hand, I gathered up three more boots and heaved them altogether in the same direction I had thrown the first.

For a couple of heartbeats it was just like before with the sounds dying into a cold breathless silence. Then a lance of flame whitely knifed the murk, three other gouts bursting almost simultaneously. Crafkin's scream was swallowed in the bang-banging echoes.

After that there was no sound beyond the awful whimper of his strangling sobs which grew fainter and fainter and finally ceased entirely.

Still unfired I gripped my own gun and waited. Crafkin's gun was in the stope below, yet three guns had spoken—one of them twice. Had Crafkin had a second gun cached away on him somewhere or had there been four men in this stope besides myself? It was a question that gnawed at me and another kept it company. If there had been a fourth was the fourth man Frunk?

One of those guns had gone off very near me and had probably been fired by the man I'd heard breathing, but the most I had seen was the grey wraith of a shape forward crouched above the flash. No details—nothing at all by which I could fasten a name to him.

I thought it might be the marshal but I couldn't be sure.

Wherever she was, I hoped Carolina would have enough savvy to keep down and keep her mouth shut.

I thought to catch the faint pad of bare feet moving somewhere, but again I couldn't be sure and would not have dared fired if I had been. I was all too aware that Carolina was probably behind me, that any slug meant for me might easily tag her. A faint click seemed to come out of the distance and a draught crossed my face very briefly as though a door had been opened and when, shortly later, a soft thud came out of that yonder blackness I knew that one had, and that the door now was closed.

I heard the faint crush of shale to my right and looked that way and, of course, saw nothing. Every muscle in my body was stretched so taut I could hardly breathe. Both my legs were cramped and one foot was asleep. I had to move soon or I would be unable to. The thought of escape just then seemed very sweet to me—all the sweeter since I knew I'd never leave without the girl. If only I could find that door.

I sat down and with my pistol in my lap very quietly pulled my boots off. I wriggled my toes until feeling returned to the foot that had gone to sleep. Gun in hand again I rose and, keeping well behind the place where I'd heard that fellow breathing, I commenced a cautious travel in the direction from which I'd thought to feel that draught.

I wondered if all this fatigue and excitement were not tending perhaps to unbalance my mind. Mines in this country didn't have doors. If there was one in these dark reaches it could have but one purpose, to conceal a connection between this mine and Frunk's.

Now another queer fancy got to chousing my thoughts. I couldn't see a thing but I began to feel certain that somewhere in this stope someone else was moving towards the same spot I was. I had never felt anything as strongly before.

I tried to guess what the fellow was up to and, by that, determine which one of them it was. Perhaps he'd heard or sensed my movement and was making this trek in an attempt to cut me off. Or was he, unaware of my intention, heading this way on the same purpose I was? Maybe what I needed was a good string of spools. Or a nice quiet place to pick the lint off my clothing.

If there *had* been a fourth man in this stope, if that draught had been the sign of his departure and the man had been Gid Frunk himself, would he have taken such a risk for nothing?

I had no way of gauging how long we'd been underground but it didn't seem possible he'd just now be returning from his trip to axe the cable. He might, however, have been completing his arrangements for setting off a blast. He would not have needed to light any fuse if he had a good battery and a sufficient length of wire.

That thought brought the sweat cracking through my skin again but common sense assured me that a man smart as Frunk would hardly have cut that cable if he'd meant to blow the mine up. What he probably had been doing was caving in the air vent between this level and the stope above. Then, with his trick door shut and himself on the farther side of it—

A fragment of sound, as from a bit of scuffed shale, laid hold of my attention like the crack of a whip. Something had moved just ahead and to the left of me and, even as I dropped to a crouch on my hunkers, I again heard that click lancing out of the darkness. A slight wind came with it, whispering of death as it crossed my ankles, and blinding light as a section of the wall swung at right angles, outward. Caught flat-footed in the glare of three lamps Jeff Bender stood with a gun in each fist.

Younger, three feet away, abruptly jerked both triggers of his double-barrelled shotgun and, when neither barrel spoke, hurled the weapon at Bender. In that moment, when time seemed crazily to stand completely still, I remembered the smugness of the mine boss's grin when I had given that sawn-off to Younger.

He ducked and fired from both fists and his face turned choleric when the marshal wouldn't fall. You could see those big slugs biting into the man, shaking and twisting him, smashing him backward, but he wouldn't go down. With his eyes like obsidian, with a terrible, implacable singleness of purpose, Younger's hand reached his belt and without sign of hurry lifted the sleek double-action from its holster and had almost tipped it level when he went down as though pole-axed in a blast from the tramcar.

Something jerked at my sleeve, something slapped at my vest. As I flung myself prone on the stope's barren floor I saw Bender spin and Irick's face just beyond him suddenly jerk its mouth wide and fade howling from sight into the blackness behind him. I hardly felt the gun bucking against my palm in recoil. From behind me somewhere Carolina's pistol made swift crashes of sound and Short Creek, leaping from the car obviously in wild panic, collapsed in mid-air like a pricked balloon.

The reverberations were deafening. The stope was rank with the stench of burnt powder; stringers of blue smoke hung like clouds across the pitiless glare of the carbine lamps. Bender lay where he had fallen beside the open tunnel door, wheezing his life away beside the still shape of the town's dead marshal.

I retched, looking at them—I just couldn't help it.

Carolina called my name. I heard the crunch of

her boots as she picked her way toward me. But I made no move or answer because something else was moving with an inch by inch stealth just behind the lamps that were affixed to the tramcar. I saw the barrel of a pistol edging out of the blackness and knew its baleful focus was being fixed on Carolina. I drove a slug just behind it and, with a snarling curse, Frunk reeled into view clutching his right shoulder with blood-reddened fingers.

I jumped to my feet and as his gangling shape bent to retrieve the dropped pistol I put five knuckles hard against his bearded jaw.

"That's all there was to it," I told Cap Murphey two days later. "We tied him up and by the time he came to I had found Gharst's wife and got all the dope I needed. It was her scream we'd heard. She was in with him hand in glove until she found out I was in that mine with the rest of them. She knew what his plans were and tried to get me out. He caught her opening that secret door they'd rigged between the two mine tunnels. He hit her with an axe but she lived long enough to testify. Carolina heard her story and took it down and had her sign it.

"I had the most of it figured fairly close to the facts, but that guy Younger had me fooled from the start. It was him that was really playing hell with Frunk's plans but he was so damn slick I never caught on until I saw him throw down on Bender with that shotgun. Bender'd looked pretty smug when I handed Bucks that gun and when I realised he must have pulled the loads from the thing, the whole deal fell into focus. Bender, of course, knew exactly what the score was.

"A dog-eat-dog business," I said with a scowl. "What really threw the wrench in the works was me getting rid of those guards of Bender's. I had him over a barrel on that one—those birds were his personal life insurance; he hired them to keep Frunk and Younger off his neck. He must have hated like hell to see them heading for town but he couldn't protest without exposing his hand."

"Well, you made your mistakes," Cap said, thinking it over, "but you got the job done. I suppose you're figuring to turn in your badge—"

"What give you that notion?"

"Well, that girl's going to need a man to—"

"Do I look that foolish?" I said, shoving my chin out. "That gal was born to trouble. I don't want any part of her. I'm goin' to get me a place in the Oregon Mountains where I can hunker in the shade and watch the horses switch flies. No women for me—an' no more Rangerin'."

BLAZING WESTERN ADVENTURE BY *SPUR* AWARD WINNER NELSON NYE

2108-0	A LOST MINE NAMED SALVATION	$2.25
2150-1	BORN TO TROUBLE	$2.25
2214-1	QUICK-TRIGGER COUNTRY	$2.25
2253-2	CARTRIDGE CASE LAW	$2.25
2295-8	THE OVERLANDERS	$2.25

MORE HARD-RIDING WESTERNS FROM LEISURE BOOKS

2326-1	BEYOND VENGEANCE	$2.25
2317-2	LASSITER: WOLVERINE	$2.25
2316-4	FIVE DEADLY GUNS	$2.25
2306-7	BLOOD RIVER GOLD	$2.25
2295-8	THE OVERLANDERS	$2.25
2284-2	HORSETHIEF TRAIL	$2.25
2274-5	LAST OUTLAW	$2.25
2273-7	SILVERMINE TRAIL	$2.25
2253-2	CARTRIDGE CASE LAW	$2.25

Make the Most of Your Leisure Time with
LEISURE BOOKS

Please send me the following titles:

Quantity	Book Number	Price
_____	_____	_____
_____	_____	_____
_____	_____	_____
_____	_____	_____
_____	_____	_____

If out of stock on any of the above titles, please send me the alternate title(s) listed below:

_____	_____	_____
_____	_____	_____
_____	_____	_____
_____	_____	_____

Postage & Handling _____

Total Enclosed $_____

☐ Please send me a free catalog.

NAME_____
(please print)

ADDRESS_____

CITY _____ STATE _____ ZIP_____

Please include $1.00 shipping and handling for the first book ordered and 25¢ for each book thereafter in the same order. All orders are shipped within approximately 4 weeks via postal service book rate. PAYMENT MUST ACCOMPANY ALL ORDERS.*

*Canadian orders must be paid in US dollars payable through a New York banking facility.

Mail coupon to: **Dorchester Publishing Co., Inc.**
6 East 39 Street, Suite 900
New York, NY 10016
Att: ORDER DEPT.